'I'm sick to death of this ridiculous belief of yours that you're not attractive. You're a beautiful and very desirable woman.'

It frightened her. *He* frightened her because she wanted to believe him. Yet in her heart she knew it was all lies.

Mac eased away and she tossed her head. 'I know my worth, Mac, make no mistake. I'm smart and strong and I'm a good friend. But let's make one thing very clear. Boys like you do *not* kiss girls like me.' Not unless it was for a bet or a dare. 'It's a fact of life.'

And then he moved in.

She raised her hands. 'Don't you—'

His lips claimed hers, swiftly, pushing her back against the house, but he took his time exploring every inch of her mouth. She tried to turn her head to the side but he followed her, his hands cupping her face. He crowded her completely, pressing every inch of his rock-hard self against her.

They both breathed hard, as if they'd run a race.

'I beg to differ.'

She blinked up at him blankly.

'Guys like me most certainly *do* kiss women like you. And what's more, Jo, they enjoy every moment of it.'

THE MILLIONAIRE AND THE MAID

BY
MICHELLE DOUGLAS

Printed and bound in Spain
by CPI, Barcelona

Published in Great Britain 2015
by Mills & Boon, an imprint of Harlequin (UK) Limited,
Eton House, 18-24 Paradise Road, Richmond, Surrey, TW9 1SR

© 2015 Michelle Douglas

ISBN: 978-0-263-25124-1

23-0415

Michelle Douglas has been writing for Mills & Boon since 2007 and believes she has the best job in the world. She lives in a leafy suburb of Newcastle, on Australia's east coast, with her own romantic hero, a house full of dust and books, and an eclectic collection of sixties and seventies vinyl. She loves to hear from readers and can be contacted via her website: michelle-douglas.com.

To Laurie Johnson for her enthusiasm, insight…
and for introducing me to mojitos.
It was a joy to work with you.

CHAPTER ONE

MAC PRESSED THE heels of his hands to his eyes and counted to five before pulling them away and focussing on the computer screen again. He reread what he'd written of the recipe so far and fisted his hands. *What came next?*

This steamed mussels dish was complicated, but he must have made it a hundred times. He ground his teeth together. The words blurred and danced across the screen. Why couldn't he remember what came next?

Was it coconut milk?

He shook his head. That came later.

With a curse, he leapt up, paced across the room and tried to imagine making the dish. He visualised himself in a kitchen, with all the ingredients arrayed around him. He imagined speaking directly to a rolling camera to explain what he was doing—the necessity of each ingredient and the importance of the sequence. His chest swelled and then cramped. He dragged a hand back through his hair. To be cooking…to be back at work… A black well of longing rose through him, drowning him with a need so great he thought the darkness would swallow him whole.

It'd be a blessing if it did.

Except he had work to do.

He kicked out at a pile of dirty washing bunched in the corner of the room before striding back to his desk and reaching for the bottle of bourbon on the floor beside it. It helped to blunt the pain. For a little while. He lifted it to his mouth and then halted. The heavy curtains drawn at the full-length windows blocked the sunlight from the room, and while his body had no idea—it was in a seemingly permanent state of jet lag—his brain told him it was morning.

Grinding his teeth, he screwed the cap back on the bottle.

Finish the damn recipe. Then you can drink yourself into oblivion and sleep.

Finish the recipe? That was what he had to do, but he couldn't seem to turn from where he stood, staring at the closed curtains, picturing the day just beyond them, the sun and the light and the cool of the fresh air…the smell of the sea.

He kept himself shut away from all that temptation.

But it didn't stop him from being able to imagine it.

A ping from his computer broke the spell. Dragging a hand down his face, he turned back to the desk and forced himself into the chair.

A message. From Russ. Of course. It was always Russ. Just for a moment he rested his head in his hands.

Hey Bro, don't forget Jo arrives today.

He swore. He didn't need a housekeeper. He needed peace and quiet so he could finish this damn cookbook.

If the rotten woman hadn't saved his brother's life he'd send her off with a flea in her ear.

Scrubbing a hand through his hair, he shook that thought off. He understood the need to retreat from the world. He wouldn't begrudge that to someone else. He and this housekeeper—they wouldn't have to spend any time in each other's company. In fact they wouldn't even need to come face to face. He'd left her a set of written instructions on the kitchen table. As for the rest she could please herself.

He planted himself more solidly in his chair, switched off

his internet connection, and shut the siren call of sunshine, fresh air and living from his mind. He stared at the screen.

Add the chilli purée and clam broth and reduce by a half. Then add...

What the hell came next?

Jo pushed out of her car and tried to decide what to look at first—the view or the house. She'd had to negotiate for two rather hairy minutes over a deeply rutted driveway. It had made her grateful that her car was a four-wheel drive, equipped to deal with rough terrain, rather than the sports car her soul secretly hungered for. After five hours on the road she was glad to have reached her destination. Still, five hours in a sports car would have been more fun.

She shook out her arms and legs. *'You can't put her in that! She's too big-boned.'* Her great-aunt's voice sounded through her mind. She half laughed. True, she'd probably look ridiculous in a sport car. Besides, what were the odds that she wouldn't even fit into one? As ever, though, her grandmother's voice piped up. *'I think she looks pretty and I don't care what anyone else thinks.'*

With a shake of her head, Jo shut out the duelling voices. She'd work out a plan of attack for Grandma and Great-Aunt Edith later. Instead, she moved out further onto the bluff to stare at the view. In front of her the land descended sharply to a grassy field that levelled out before coming to a halt at low, flower-covered sand dunes. Beyond that stretched a long crescent of deserted beach, glittering white-gold in the mild winter sunlight.

A sigh eased out of her. There must be at least six or seven kilometres of it—two to the left and four or five to the right—and not a soul to be seen. All the way along it perfect blue-green breakers rolled up to the shore in a froth of white.

She sucked a breath of salt-laced air into her lungs and some of the tension slipped out of her. With such a vast expanse of ocean in front of her, her own troubles seemed suddenly less significant. Not that she had troubles as such. Just a few things she needed to sort out.

She dragged in another breath. The rhythmic whooshing of the waves and the cries of two seagulls cruising overhead eased the knots five hours in the car had conspired to create. The green of each wave as it crested made her inhalations come more easily, as if the push and pull of the Pacific Ocean had attuned her breathing to a more natural pattern.

The breeze held a chill she found cleansing. Last week the weather would have been warm enough to swim, and maybe it'd be warm enough for that again next week. Having spent the last eight years working in the Outback, she hadn't realised how much she'd missed the coast and the beach.

She finally turned to survey the house. A two-storey weatherboard with a deep veranda and an upstairs balcony greeted her. A lovely breezy home that—

She frowned at all the closed windows and drawn curtains, the shut front door. Heavens, Mac MacCallum *was* still here, wasn't he? Russ would have told her if his brother had returned to the city.

She sucked her bottom lip into her mouth and then folded her arms. Mac would be in there. Russ had warned her that his brother might prove difficult. He'd also had no doubt in her ability to handle difficult.

'Jeez, you save someone's life and suddenly they think you're Superwoman.'

But she'd smiled as she'd said it—though whether in affection at her dear friend and former boss, or at the thought of wearing a superhero outfit she wasn't sure. Though if she burst in wearing a spangly leotard and cape it might make Mac reconsider the soundness of locking himself away like this.

She planted her hands on her hips.

Painted a sleek grey, each weatherboard sat in perfect alignment with its neighbour—and, considering the battering the place must take from sand, salt, sun and wind, that was a testament to the superior materials used and to whoever had built it. The best that money could buy, no doubt. The galvanised tin roof shone in the sunlight. There was even a chimney, which must mean there was an open fire. *Nice!* Winter might be relatively mild here on the mid-north coast of New South Wales, but she didn't doubt the nights could be chilly.

She pulled her cardigan about her more tightly. Still, shut up as it was, the house looked cold and unwelcoming even in all this glorious sunshine.

There's only one way to change that.

Casting a final longing glance back behind her, she set her shoulders and strode towards the house, mounting the six steps to the veranda two at a time.

A piece of paper, stark white against the grey wood, was taped to the door with *'Ms Anderson'* slashed across it in a dark felt-tipped pen. Jo peeled the note away. Was Mac out? And was he going to insist on the formality of 'Ms Anderson' and 'Mr MacCallum'?

Ms Anderson
   I don't like to be disturbed while I'm working so let yourself in. Your room is on the ground floor beyond the kitchen. There should be absolutely no need for you to venture up onto the first floor.

She let out a low laugh. Oh, so that was what he thought, huh?

He finished with:

*I eat at seven. Please leave a tray on the table at
the bottom of the stairs and I'll collect it when I take
a break from my work.*

She folded the note and shoved it in her pocket. She
opened the front door and propped a cast-iron rooster that
she assumed to be the doorstop against it, and then latched
the screen door back against the house before going to the
car and collecting her cases. And then she strode into the
house as if she owned it—head high, shoulders back, spine
straight.

Malcolm 'Mac' MacCallum had another think coming
if he thought they were going to spend the next two months
or so communicating via notes.

She dropped her suitcases in the hallway, wrinkling her
nose at the musty scent of old air and neglect. A large reception room lay to her right. She strode in and flung open
the curtains at the three large windows to let light spill into
the room. She turned and blew out a breath.

Look at all this gorgeous furniture.

Antiques mingled with newer pieces, creating an elegant warmth that reminded her again of Mac's success. She
glared at a gorgeous leather chair. What use was success if
it made you forget the people who loved you? Mac hadn't
visited Russ once since Russ's heart attack. She transferred
her glare to the ceiling, before shaking herself and glancing around the room again. It was all in serious need of
spit and polish.

She grimaced. Tomorrow.

She turned her back on it to open the windows. The
sound of the sea entered first, and then its scent. She
straightened. That was better.

She found her room at the back of the house. Someone
had made a half-hearted effort at cleaning it. Mac, she supposed. According to Russ, the last cleaning lady had left

over a month ago. It would do for now. She'd tackle that tomorrow as well.

Her window looked out over an unkempt lawn to a garage. She lifted the window higher. She might not have a room with a view, but she could still hear the ocean. She leant against the windowsill, reaching out to touch a banksia flower on the nearby tree.

A moment later she drew her hand back, a breath shuddering out of her as she thought back to that stupid note stuck to the door. Perhaps this wasn't such a good idea. Turning her life upside down like this was probably foolhardy, irresponsible—even insane. After all, geology wasn't so bad and—

It's not so good either.

She bit her lip and then straightened. She'd gone into geology to please her father. For all the good it had done her. She wasn't concerned with pleasing him any longer.

She'd remained in the field to keep the peace. She didn't want just to keep the peace any more—she wanted to create a new world where peace reigned…at least in her little part of it. She'd stayed where she was because she was frightened of change. Well, Russ's heart attack had taught her that there were worse things than fear of change.

Fear of regret and fear of wasting her life were two of those things. She couldn't afford to lose heart now. She wanted a future she could look forward to. She wanted a future that would make her proud. She wanted a future that mattered. That was what she was doing here. That wasn't foolhardy, irresponsible or insane. On the contrary.

But…what about Mac? What was she going to do? Follow instructions today and then try to corner him tomorrow? Or—?

Her phone buzzed in her pocket. She glanced at the caller ID before lifting it to her ear. 'Hey, Russ.'

'Are you there yet?'

'Yep.'

'How's Mac?'

She swallowed. *Or not follow instructions?*

'I've only just this very minute arrived, so I haven't clapped eyes on him yet, but let me tell you the view here is amazing. Your brother has found the perfect place to…'

What? Recuperate? He'd had enough time to recuperate. Work without distractions? Hole up?

'The perfect place to hide away from the world.' Russell sighed.

Russ was fifty-two and recovering from a heart attack. He was scheduled for bypass surgery in a few weeks. She wasn't adding to his stress if she could help it.

'The perfect place for inspiration,' she countered. 'The scenery is gorgeous. Wait until you see it and then you'll know what I mean. I'll send you photos.'

'Does a body need inspiration to write a cookbook?'

She had no idea. 'Cooking and making up recipes are creative endeavours, aren't they? And isn't there some theory that creativity is boosted by the negative ions of moving water? Anyway, there's lots of deserted beach to walk and rolling hills to climb. It's a good place to come and get strong—away from prying eyes.'

'You think so?'

'Absolutely. Give me an hour, Russ, and I'll call you back when I have something concrete to tell you, okay?'

'I can't thank you enough for doing this, Jo.'

'We both know that in this instance it's you who's doing me the favour.'

It wasn't wholly a lie.

She'd known Russ for eight years. They'd hit if off from the first day she'd walked into the mining company's Outback office, with her brand-new soil sample kit and her work boots that still held a shine. Their teasing, easy rapport had developed into a genuine friendship. He'd been her boss, her mentor, and one of the best friends she'd ever had—but in all that time she'd never met his brother.

After his heart attack she'd confided in Russ—told him she wanted out of geology and away from the Outback. She grimaced. She'd also told him she couldn't go back to Sydney until she'd developed a plan. Her jobless situation would only provide Grandma and Great-Aunt Edith with more ammunition to continue their silly feud. Battle lines would be drawn and Jo would find herself smack-bang in the middle of them. She was already smack-bang in the middle of them! No more. She was tired of living her life to meet other people's expectations.

She pulled in a breath. When she was working in a job she loved and doing things that made her happy, the people who loved her—Grandma and Great-Aunt Edith—would be happy for her too. She squinted out of the window. If only she could figure out what it was that would make her happy.

She chafed her arms, suddenly cold. All she knew was that another twenty years down the track she didn't want to look back and feel she'd wasted her life.

When Russ had found all that out he'd laughed and rubbed his hands together. 'Jo,' he'd said, 'I've just the job for you.'

And here she was.

She glanced around, her nose wrinkling.

She loved Russ dearly. She enjoyed his twisted sense of humour, admired the values he upheld, and she respected the man he was. She did not, however, hold out the same hopes for his brother.

She planted her hands on her hips. A brother did not desert his family when they needed him. Russ had been there for Mac every step of the way, but Mac had been nowhere to be found when Russ had needed him. But here she was, all the same. Mac's hired help. She didn't even know what her official job title was—cook, cleaner, housekeeper? Russ had dared her to don a French maid's outfit. Not in this lifetime!

Russ needed someone to make sure Mac was getting three square meals a day and not living in squalor—someone who could be trusted not to go racing to the press. At heart, though, Jo knew Russ just wanted to make sure his little brother was okay.

Cue Jo. Still, this job would provide her with the peace and quiet to work out where she wanted to go from here.

She pulled Mac's note from her pocket and stared at it.

There should be absolutely no reason for you to venture onto the first floor.

Oh, yes, there was.

Without giving herself too much time to think, she headed straight for the stairs.

There were five doors on the first floor, if she didn't count the door to the linen closet. Four of them stood wide open—a bathroom and three bedrooms. Mind you, all the curtains in each of those rooms were drawn, so it was dark as Hades up here. The fourth door stood resolutely closed. *Do Not Disturb* vibes radiated from it in powerful waves.

'Guess which one the prize is behind?' she murmured under her breath, striding up to it.

She lifted her hand and knocked. *Rat-tat-tat!* The noise bounced up and down the hallway. No answer. Nothing.

She knocked again, even louder. 'Mac, are you in there?'

To hell with calling him Mr MacCallum. Every Tuesday night for the last five years she'd sat with Russ, watching Mac on the television. For eight years she'd listened to Russ talk about his brother. He would be Mac to her forever.

She suddenly stiffened. What if he was hurt or sick?

'Go away!'

She rolled her eyes. "'There was movement at the station.'"

'Can't you follow instructions?'

Ooh, that was a veritable growl. 'I'm afraid not. I'm coming in.'

She pushed the door open.

'What the hell?' The single light at the desk was immediately clicked off. 'Get out! I told you I didn't want to be disturbed.'

'Correction. An anonymous note informed me that someone didn't want to be disturbed.' It took a moment for her eyes to adjust to the darkness. She focussed on that rather than the snarl in his voice. 'Anyone could've left that note. For all I knew you could've been slain while you slept.'

He threw his arms out. 'Not slain. See? Now, get out.'

'I'd like nothing better,' she said, strolling across the room.

'What the hell do you think you're—?'

He broke off when she flung the curtains back. She pulled in a breath, staring at the newly revealed balcony and the magnificent view beyond. 'Getting a good look at you,' she said, before turning around.

The sight that met her shocked her to the core. She had no hope of hiding it. She reached out a hand to steady herself against the glass doors.

'Happy?'

His lips twisted in a snarl that made her want to flee. She swallowed and shook her head. 'No.' How could she be happy? He was going to break his brother's heart.

'Shocked?' he mocked with an ugly twist of his lips.

The left side of his face and neck were red, tight and raw with the post-burn scarring from his accident. His too-long blond hair had clumped in greasy unbrushed strands. Dark circles rimmed red eyes. The grey pallor of his skin made her stomach churn.

'To the marrow,' she choked out.

And in her mind the first lines of that Banjo Paterson poem went round and round in her head.

There was movement at the station,
for the word had passed around
That the colt from old Regret had got away

Regret. Got away. She suddenly wished with everything inside her that *she* could get away. Leave.

And go where? What would she tell Russ?

She swallowed and straightened. 'It smells dreadful in here.'

Too close and sour and hot. She slid the door open, letting the sea breeze dance over her. She filled her lungs with it even though his scowl deepened.

'I promised Russ I'd clap eyes on you, as no one else seems to have done so in months.'

'He sent you here as a spy?'

'He sent me here as a favour.'

'I don't need any favours!'

Not a favour for you. But she didn't say that out loud. 'No. I suspect what you really need is a psychiatrist.'

His jaw dropped.

She pulled herself up to her full height of six feet and folded her arms. 'Is that what you *really* want me to report back to Russ? That you're in a deep depression and possibly suicidal?'

His lips drew together tightly over his teeth. 'I am neither suicidal nor depressed.'

'Right.' She drew the word out, injecting as much disbelief into her voice as she could. 'For the last four months you've sat shut up in this dark house, refusing to see a soul. I suspect you barely sleep and barely eat.' She wrinkled her nose. 'And when was the last time you had a shower?'

His head rocked back.

'These are not the actions of a reasonable or rational adult. What interpretation would you put on them if you were coming in from the outside? What conclusion do you think Russ would come to?'

For a moment she thought he might have paled at her words—except he was already so pale it was impossible to tell. She rubbed a hand across her chest. She understood that one had to guard against sunburn on burn scars, but avoiding the light completely was ludicrous.

He said nothing. He just stared at her as if seeing her for the first time. Which just went to show how preoccupied he must have been. When most people saw her for the first time they usually performed a comical kind of double-take at her sheer size. Not that she'd ever found anything remotely humorous about it. So what? She was tall. And, no, she wasn't dainty. It didn't make her a circus freak.

'Damn you, Mac!' She found herself shouting at him, and she didn't know where it came from but it refused to be suppressed. 'How can you be so selfish? Russell is recovering from a heart attack. He needs bypass surgery. He needs calm and peace and...' Her heart dropped with a sickening thud. 'And now I'm going to have to tell him...' She faltered, not wanting to put into words Mac's pitiable condition. She didn't have the heart for it.

Mac still didn't speak, even though the ferocity and outrage had drained from his face. She shook her head and made for the door.

'At least I didn't waste any time unpacking.'

It wasn't until the woman— What was her name again? Jo Anderson? It wasn't until she'd disappeared through his bedroom door that he realised what she meant to do.

She meant to leave.

She meant to leave and tell Russ that Mac needed to be

sectioned or something daft. Hell, the press would have a field-day with *that*! But she was right about one thing—Russ didn't need the added stress of worrying about Mac. Mac had enough guilt on that head as it was, and he wasn't adding to it.

'Wait!' he hollered.

He bolted after her, hurling himself down the stairs, knocking into walls and stumbling, his body heavy and unfamiliar as if it didn't belong to him any more. By the time he reached the bottom he was breathing hard.

He'd used to jog five kilometres without breaking a sweat.

When was the last time he'd jogged?

When was the last time you had a shower?

He dragged a hand down his face. God help him.

He shook himself back into action and surged forward, reaching the front door just as she lugged her cases down the front steps. Sunlight. Sea air. He pulled up as both pounded at him, caressing him, mocking him. He didn't want to notice how good they felt. But they felt better than good.

And they'd both distract him from his work. *Work you won't get a chance to complete if Jo Anderson walks away.*

He forced himself forward, through the door. 'Please, Ms Anderson—wait.'

She didn't stop. The woman was built like an Amazon—tall and regal. It hurt him to witness the fluid grace and elegance of her movements. In the same way the sunlight and the sea breeze hurt him. It hurt him to witness her strength and the tilt of her chin and the dark glossiness of her hair.

Jo Anderson was, quite simply, stunning. Like the sunlight and the sea breeze. There was something just as elemental about her, and it made him not want to mess with her, but he had to get her to stop. And that meant messing with her.

With his heart thumping, he forced himself across the

veranda until he stood fully in the sun. His face started to burn. The burning wasn't real, but being outside made him feel exposed and vulnerable. He forced himself down the steps.

'Jo, please don't leave.'

She stopped at his use of her first name.

Say something that will make her lower her cases to the ground.

His heart hammered and his mouth dried as the breeze seared across his skin. It took all his strength not to flinch as the sun warmed his face. He dragged a breath of air into his lungs—fresh sea air—and it provided him with the answer he needed.

'I'm sorry.'

He sent up a prayer of thanks when she lowered her cases and turned. 'Are you really? I suspect you're merely sorry someone's called you on whatever game it is you've been playing.'

Game? *Game!* He closed his eyes and reined in his temper. He couldn't afford to alienate her further.

'Please don't take tales back to Russ that will cause him worry. He…he needs… He doesn't need the stress.'

She stared at him. She had eyes the colour of sage. He briefly wondered if sage was the elusive ingredient he'd been searching for all morning, before shaking the thought away.

Jo tilted her chin and narrowed her eyes. 'I don't take anyone's wellbeing or health for granted, Mac. Not any more. And—'

'This is *my* life we're talking about,' he cut in. 'Don't I get any say in the matter?'

'I'd treat you like an adult if you'd been acting like one.'

'You can't make that judgement based on five minutes' acquaintance. I've been having a *very* bad day.' He widened his stance. 'What do I need to do to convince you that I am, in fact, neither depressed nor suicidal?'

He would not let her go worrying Russ with this. He would *not* be responsible for physically harming yet another person.

She folded her arms and stuck out a hip—a rather lush, curvaceous hip—and a pulse started up deep inside him.

'What do you need to do to convince me? Oh, Mac, that's going to take some doing.'

Her voice washed over him like warm honey. It was a warmth that didn't sting.

For no reason at all his pulse kicked up a notch. He envied her vigour and conviction. She stalked up to him to peer into his face. To try to read his motives, he suspected. She was only an inch or two shorter than him, and she smelt like freshly baked bread. His mouth watered.

Then he recalled the look in her eyes when she'd recovered from her first sight of him and he angled the left side of his face away from her. Her horror hadn't dissolved into pity—which was something, he supposed. It had been scorn. Her charge of selfishness had cut through to his very marrow, slicing through the hard shell of his guilt and anger.

'Stay for a week,' he found himself pleading.

His mouth twisted. Once upon a time he'd been able to wrap any woman around his little finger. He'd flash a slow smile or a cheeky grin and don the charm. He suspected that wouldn't work on this woman. Not now. And not back then, when he'd still been pretty, either.

Mind you, it seemed he'd lost his charm at about the same time he'd lost his looks. Now he looked like a monster.

It doesn't mean you have to act like one, though.

Her low laugh drizzled over him like the syrup for his Greek lemon cake.

'I believe you're serious...'

Yeah? Well, at the very least it'd buy Russ another week of rest and—

What the hell? This woman didn't know him from Adam. She had no idea what he was capable of. He pulled himself upright—fully upright—and the stretch felt good.

'Name your price.'

He wasn't sure if it was more scorn or humour that flitted through her eyes. She straightened too, but he still had a good two inches on her. She could try and push him around all she wanted. He—

He grimaced. Yeah, well, if he didn't want her worrying Russ she *could* push him around. Whoever happened to be bigger in this particular scenario didn't make a scrap of difference.

He thrust out his chin. Still, he *was* bigger.

'Name my price?'

He swallowed. She had a voice made for radio—a kind of solid-gold croon that would soothe any angry beast.

'Well, for a start I'd want to see you exercising daily.'

It took a moment for the import of her words rather than their sound to reach him.

Risk being seen in public? *No!* He—

'During daylight hours,' she continued remorselessly. 'You need vitamin D and to lose that awful pallor.'

'You do know I've been ill, don't you?' he demanded. 'That I've been in hospital?'

'You haven't been in hospital for months. Do you have *any* idea how much you've let yourself go? You used to have a strong, lean body and lovely broad shoulders.'

Which were still broader than hers. Though he didn't point that out.

'And you used to move with a lanky, easy saunter. Now…? Now you look about fifty.'

He glared. He was only forty.

'And not a good fifty either. You look as if I could snap you in half.'

He narrowed his eyes. 'I wouldn't advise you to try that.'

She blinked and something chased itself across her face, as if she'd suddenly realised he was a man—a living, breathing man—rather than a job or a problem she had to solve.

Not that it meant she fancied him or anything stupid like that. How could anyone fancy him now? But…

For the first time since the fire he suddenly *felt* like a living, breathing man.

'If you want me to change my mind about you, Mac, I want to see you walk down to the beach and back every day. It's all your own property, so you don't need to be worried about bumping into strangers if you're that jealous of your privacy.'

'The beach is public land.' He had neighbours who walked on it every day.

'I didn't say you had to walk *along* it—just down to it.'

'The land that adjoins my property to the north—' he gestured to the left '—is all national park.' There'd be the occasional hiker.

'So walk along that side of your land, then.' She gestured to the right and then folded her arms. 'I'm simply answering your question. If you find daily exercise too difficult, then I've probably made my point.'

He clenched his jaw, breathed in for the count of five and then unclenched it to ask, 'What else?'

'I'd like you to separate your work and sleep areas. A defined routine to your day will help me believe you have a handle on things. Hence a workspace that's separate from your bedroom.'

He glared at her. 'Fine—whatever. And…?'

'I'd also want you to give up alcohol. Or at least drinking bourbon in your room on your own.'

She'd seen the bottle. *Damn!*

'Finally, I'd want you to take your evening meal in the dining room with me.'

So she could keep an eye on him—assess his mental state. He could feel his nostrils flare as he dragged in a breath. He was tempted to tell her to go to hell, except…

Except he might have given up caring about himself, but he hadn't given up caring about Russ. His brother might be eleven and a half years older than Mac, but they'd always been close. Russ had always looked out for him. The least Mac could do now was look out for Russ in whatever limited capacity he could. With Russ's health so tenuous Mac couldn't risk adding to his stress levels.

Jo's phone rang. She pulled it from the back pocket of her jeans. He stared at that hip and something stirred inside him. And then desire hit him—hot and hard. He blinked. He turned away to hide the evidence, adjusting his jeans as he pretended an interest in the horizon.

What on earth…? He liked his women slim and compact, polished and poised. Jo Anderson might be poised, but as for the rest of it…

He dragged a hand back through his hair. There was no denying, though, that his body reacted to her like a bee to honey. He swallowed. It was probably to be expected, right? He'd been cooped up here away from all human contact for four months. This was just a natural male reaction to the female form.

'I don't know, Russ.'

That snapped him back.

'Yeah…' She flicked a glance in his direction. 'I've seen him.'

Mac winced at her tone.

'You have yourself a deal.' He pitched his words low, so they wouldn't carry down the phone to Russ, but they still came out savage. He couldn't help it. He held up one finger. 'Give me one week.'

'Hmm… Well, he's looking a little peaky—as if he's had the flu or a tummy bug.'

He seized her free hand. Startled sage eyes met his. 'Please,' he whispered.

The softness and warmth of her hand seeped into him and almost made him groan, and then her hand tightened about his and his mouth went dry in a millisecond.

When she shook herself free of him a moment later he let out a breath he hadn't even realised he'd been holding.

'I expect it's nothing that a bit of rest, gentle exercise, home-cooked food and sun won't put to rights in a week or two.'

He closed his eyes and gave thanks.

'Nah, I promise. I won't take any risks. I'll call a doctor in if he hasn't picked up in a few days. Here—you want to talk to him?'

And before Mac could shake his head and back away he found the phone thrust out to him.

He swallowed the bile that rose in his throat and took it. 'Hey, Russ, how you doing?'

'Better than you, by the sounds of it. Though it explains why you haven't answered my last two calls.'

He winced. 'It's all I've been able to do to keep up with my email.' *I'm sorry, bro.* He hadn't been good for anyone. Least of all his brother.

'Well, you listen to Jo, okay? She's got a good head on her shoulders.'

He glanced at said head and noticed how the wavy dark hair gleamed in the sun, and how cute little freckles sprinkled a path across the bridge of her nose. She had a rather cute nose. She cocked an eyebrow and he cleared his throat.

'Will do,' he forced himself to say.

'Good. I want you in the best of health when I come to visit.'

He choked back a cough. Russ was coming to visit?

'Give my love to Jo.'

With that, Russ hung up. Mac stared at Jo. 'When is he coming to visit?'

She shrugged and plucked her phone from his fingers.

'Why is he coming?'

'Oh, that one's easy. Because he loves you. He wants to see you before he goes under the knife.' She met his gaze. 'In case he doesn't wake up after the operation.'

'That's crazy.'

'Is it?'

'Russ is going to be just fine!' His brother didn't need to exert himself in any fashion until he was a hundred per cent fit again.

She stared at him for a long moment. 'Are you familiar with the Banjo Paterson poem "The Man From Snowy River"?'

Her question threw him. 'Sure.'

'Can you remember what comes after the first couple of lines? "There was movement at the station, for the word had passed around that the colt from old Regret had got away…"?'

'"And had joined the wild bush horses—he was worth a thousand pound, So all the cracks had gathered to the fray",' he recited. His class had memorised that in the third grade.

'Wild… Worth… Fray…' she murmured in that honeyed liquid sunshine voice of hers.

'Why?'

She shook herself. 'No reason. Just an earworm.'

She seized her suitcases and strode back towards the house with them, and he couldn't help feeling his fate had just been sealed by a poem.

And then it hit him.

Honey! The ingredient he'd been searching for was honey.

CHAPTER TWO

Jo TOOK A couple of deep breaths before spooning spaghetti and meatballs onto two plates. If Mac said something cutting about her efforts in the kitchen she'd—

She'd dump the contents of his plate in his lap?

She let out a slow breath. It was a nice fantasy, but she wouldn't. She'd just act calm and unconcerned, as she always did, and pretend the slings and arrows didn't touch her.

Seizing the plates, she strode into the dining room. She set one in front of Mac and the other at her place opposite. He didn't so much as glance at the food, but he did glare at her. Was he going to spend the entire week sulking?

What fun.

She stared back, refusing to let him cow her. She'd expected the shouting and the outrage. After all, he wasn't known as 'Mad Mac'—television's most notorious and demanding celebrity chef—for nothing. The tabloids had gone to town on him after the accident, claiming it would never have happened if 'Mad Mac' hadn't been so intimidating.

She bit back a sigh. It was all nonsense, of course. She'd had the inside scoop on Mac from Russ. She knew all of that onscreen TV shouting had been a front—a ploy to send the ratings skyrocketing. It had worked too. So it hadn't surprised her that he'd donned that persona when she'd stormed in on him earlier. But the sulking threw her.

'What?' he bit out when she continued to stare.

She shook herself. 'For what we are about to receive, may the Lord make us truly thankful. Amen.' She picked up her cutlery and sliced into a meatball.

'You're religious?'

'No.' The prayer had just seemed a convenient way to handle an awkward silence. 'I mean, I do believe in something bigger than us—whatever that may be.'

Mac didn't say anything. He didn't even move to pick up his cutlery.

She forged on. 'One of the guys on the mineral exploration camps was a Christian and we all got into the habit of saying Grace. It's nice. It doesn't hurt to remember the things we should be grateful for.'

His frown deepened to a scowl. 'You really think that's going to work? You really think you can make my life seem okay just by—?'

She slammed her knife and fork down. 'Not everything is about you, Mac.' She forced her eyes wide. 'Some of it might even be about me.' Couldn't he at least look at his food? He needn't think it would taste any better cold. 'Your attitude sucks. You know that? Frankly, I don't care if you've decided to self-destruct or not, but you can darn well wait until after Russ has recovered from his bypass surgery to do it.'

'You're not exactly polite company, are you?'

'Neither are you. Besides, I refuse to put any effort into being good company for as long as you sulk. I'm not your mother. It's not my job to cajole you into a better temper.'

His jaw dropped.

And he still hadn't touched his food.

'Eat something, Mac. If we're busy eating we can abandon any pretence at small talk.'

A laugh choked out of him and just for a moment it transformed him. Oh, the burn scars on the left side of his face and neck were still as angry and livid as ever, but his mouth hooked up and his eyes momentarily brightened and he held his head at an angle she remembered from his television show.

It was why she was still here. Earlier this afternoon he'd fired up—not with humour, but with intensity and passion. He'd become the man she'd recognised from the TV, but also from Russ's descriptions. *That* was a man she could work with.

Finally he did as she bade and forked a small mouthful of meatball and sauce into his mouth. When he didn't gag, a knot of tension eased out of her.

'This isn't bad.' He ate some more and frowned. 'In fact, it's pretty good.'

Yeah, right. He was just trying to butter her up, frightened of what she might tell Russ.

'Actually, it's very good—considering the state of the pantry.'

She almost believed him. Almost. 'I'll need to shop for groceries tomorrow. I understand we're halfway between Forster and Taree here. Any suggestions for where I should go?'

'No.'

When he didn't add anything she shook her head and set to eating. It had been a long day and she was tired and hungry. She halted with half a meatball practically in her mouth when she realised he'd stopped eating and was staring at her.

'What?'

'I wasn't being rude. It's just that I haven't been to either town. I was getting groceries delivered from a supermarket in Forster.'

'Was?'

He scowled. 'The delivery man couldn't follow instructions.'

Ah. Said delivery man had probably encroached on

Mac's precious privacy. 'Right. Well, I'll try my luck in Forster, then.' She'd seen signposts for the town before turning off to Mac's property.

He got back to work on the plate in front of him with… She blinked. With *gusto*? Heat spread through her stomach. *Oh, don't be ridiculous!* He'd had his own TV show. He was a consummate actor. But the heat didn't dissipate.

She pulled in a breath. 'I'm hoping Russ warned you that I'm not much of a cook.'

He froze. Very slowly he lowered his cutlery. 'Russ said you were a good plain cook. On this evening's evidence I'd agree with him.' His face turned opaque. 'You're feeling intimidated cooking for a…?'

'World-renowned chef?' she finished for him. 'Yes, a little. I just want you to keep your expectations within that realm of plain, please.'

She bit back a sigh. Plain—what a boring word. *Beauty is as beauty does.* The old adage sounded through her mind. *Yeah, yeah, whatever.*

'I promise not to criticise your cooking. I will simply be…' he grimaced '…grateful for whatever you serve up. You don't need to worry that I'll be secretly judging your technique.'

'I expect there'd be nothing secret about it. I think you'd be more than happy to share your opinions on the matter.'

His lips twitched.

'Is there anything you don't eat?' she rushed on, not wanting to dwell on those lips for too long.

He shook his head.

'Is there anything in particular you'd like me to serve?'

He shook his head again.

There was something else she'd meant to ask him… *Oh, that's right.* 'You have a garage…'

They both reached for the plate of garlic bread at the same time. He waited for her to take a slice first. He had nice hands. She remembered admiring them when she'd watched him on TV. Lean, long-fingered hands that looked strong and—

'The garage?'

She shook herself. 'Would there be room for me to park my car in there? I expect this sea air is pretty tough on a car's bodywork.'

'Feel free.'

'Thank you.'

They both crunched garlic bread. He watched her from the corner of his eye. She chewed and swallowed, wondering what he made of her. She sure as heck wasn't like the women he was forever being photographed with in the papers. For starters she was as tall as a lot of men, and more athletic than most.

Not Mac, though. Even in his current out-of-form condition he was still taller and broader than her—though she might give him a run for his money in an arm wrestle at the moment.

Her stomach tightened. He was probably wondering what god he'd cheesed off to have a woman like *her* landing on his doorstep. Mac was a golden boy. Beautiful. And she was the opposite. Not that *that* had anything to do with anything. What he thought of her physically made no difference whatsoever.

Except, of course, it did. It always mattered.

'You've shown a lot of concern for Russ.'

Her head came up. 'Yes?'

He scowled at her. 'Are you in love with him? He's too old for you, you know.'

It surprised her so much she laughed. 'You're kidding, right?' She swept her garlic bread through the leftover sauce on her plate.

His frown deepened. 'No.'

'I love your brother as a friend, but I'm not in love with

him. Lord, what a nightmare *that* would be.' She sat back and wiped her fingers on a serviette.

'Why?'

'I'm not a masochist. You and your brother have similar tastes in women. You both date petite, perfectly made-up blondes who wear killer heels and flirty dresses.' She hadn't packed a dress. She didn't even own a pair of heels.

He pushed his plate away, his face darkening. 'How the hell do *you* know what type I like?' He turned sideways in his chair to cross his legs. It hid his scarring from her view.

'It's true I'm basing my assumption on who you've been snapped with in the tabloids and what Russ has told me.'

'You make us sound shallow.'

If the shoe fits...

'But I can assure you that the women you just described wouldn't look twice at me now.'

'Only if they were superficial.'

His head jerked up.

'And beauty and superficiality don't necessarily go hand in hand.'

No more than plain and stupid, or plain and thick-skinned.

He opened his mouth, but she continued on over the top of him. 'Anyway, you're not going to get any sympathy from me on that. I've never been what people consider beautiful. I've learned to value other things. You think people will no longer find you beautiful—

'I *know* they won't!'

He was wrong, but... 'So welcome to the club.'

His jaw dropped.

'It's not the end of the world, you know?'

He stared at her for a long moment and then leaned across the table. 'What the hell are you *really* doing here, Jo Anderson?'

She stared back at him, and inside she started to weep—

because she wanted to ask this man to teach her to cook and he was so damaged and angry that she knew he would toss her request on the rubbish heap and not give it so much as the time of day.

Something in his eyes gentled. 'Jo?'

Now wasn't the time to raise the subject. It was becoming abundantly clear that there might never be a good time.

She waved a hand in the air. 'The answer is twofold.' It wasn't a lie. 'I'm here to make sure you don't undo all the hard work I've put into Russ.'

He sat back. 'Hard work?'

She should rise and clear away their plates, clean the kitchen, but he deserved some answers. 'Do you know how hard, how physically demanding, it is to perform CPR for five straight minutes?' Which was what she'd done for Russ.

He shook his head, his eyes darkening.

'It's really hard. And all the while your mind is screaming in panic and making deals with the universe.'

'Deals?'

'Please let Russ live and I'll never say another mean word about anyone ever again. Please let Russ live and I promise to be a better granddaughter and great-niece. Please let Russ live and I'll do whatever you ask, will face my worst fears… Blah, blah, blah.' She pushed her hair back off her face. 'You know—the usual promises that are nearly impossible to keep.' She stared down at her glass of water. 'It was the longest five minutes of my life.'

'But Russ did live. You did save his life. It's an extraordinary thing.'

'Yes.'

'And now you want to make sure that I don't harm his recovery?'

'Something like that.'

'Which is why you're here—to check up on me so you can ease Russ's mind?'

'He was going to come himself, and that didn't seem wise.'

Mac turned grey.

'But you don't have it quite right. Russ is doing me a favour, organising this job for me.'

He remained silent, not pressing her, and she was grateful for that.

'You see, Russ's heart attack and my fear that he was going to die brought me face to face with my own mortality.'

He flinched and she bit back a curse. What did she know about mortality compared to this man? She reached across to clasp his hand in a sign of automatic sympathy, but he froze. A bad taste rose in her mouth and she pulled her hand back into her lap. Her heart pounded. He wouldn't welcome her touch. Of course he wouldn't.

'I expect you know what I'm talking about.'

Mac's accident had left him with serious burns, but it had left a young apprentice fighting for his life. She remembered Russ's relief when the young man had finally been taken off the critical list.

'What I'm trying to say is that it's made me reassess my life. It's forced me to admit I wasn't very happy, that I didn't really like my job. I don't want to spend the next twenty years feeling like that.'

She blew out a breath.

'So when Russ found out you needed a housekeeper and mentioned it to me I jumped at the chance. It'll give me two or three months to come up with a game plan.'

Mac stared at her. 'You're changing careers?'

'Uh-huh.' She looked a bit green.

'To do what?'

She turned greener. 'I have absolutely no idea.'

He knew that feeling.

Mac didn't want to be touched by her story—he didn't

want to be touched by anything—but he was. Maybe it was the sheer simplicity of the telling, the lack of fanfare. Or maybe it was because he understood that sense of dissatisfaction she described. He'd stalled out here in his isolation and his self-pity while she was determined to surge forward.

Maybe if he watched her he'd learn—

He cut that thought off. He didn't deserve the chance to move forward. He'd ruined a man's life. He deserved to spend the rest of his life making amends.

But not at the expense of other people. Like Russ. Or Jo.

'You're wrong, you know?'

She glanced up. 'About…?'

'You seem to think you're plain—invisible, even.' *Not beautiful.*

'Invisible?' She snorted. 'I'm six feet tall with a build some charitably call generous. Invisible is the one thing I'm not.'

'Generous' was the perfect word to describe her. She had glorious curves in all the right places. A fact that his male hormones acknowledged and appreciated even while his brain told him to leave that well enough alone.

He leaned back, careful to keep the good side of his face to her. 'You're a very striking woman.' *Don't drool.* 'So what if you're tall? You're in proportion.' She looked strong, athletic and full of life. 'You have lovely eyes, your hair is shiny, and you have skin that most women would kill for. You may not fit in with conventional magazine cover ideals of beauty, but it doesn't mean you aren't beautiful. Stop selling yourself short. I can assure you that you're not plain.'

She gaped at him. It made him scowl and shuffle back in his seat. 'Well, you're not.'

She snapped her mouth shut. She wiped her hands down the front of her shirt, which only proved to him how truly womanly she happened to be. The colour in her cheeks deepened as if she'd read that thought in his face.

'There's another reason I'm here,' she blurted out.

The hurried confession and the way her words tripped over themselves, the fact that she looked cute when flustered, all conspired to make him want to grin. He couldn't remember the last time he'd smiled, let alone grinned. He resisted the urge now too. In the end, grinning... Well, it would just make things harder, in the same way the sunlight and the sea breeze did.

But he did take pity on her. 'Another reason?' he prompted.

She moistened her lips. Like the rest of her they were generous, and full of promise.

'Mac, one of the reasons I came out here was to ask if you would teach me to cook.' She grimaced. 'Well, if we're being completely accurate, if you'd teach me to make a *macaron* tower.'

His every muscle froze. His nerve-endings started to scream. For a moment all he could see in his mind was fire—all red and heat. A lump the size of a saucepan wedged in his throat. It took three goes to swallow it.

'No.' The word croaked out of him.

He closed his eyes to force air into protesting lungs and then opened them again, his skin growing slick with perspiration.

'No.' The single word came out cold and clear. 'That's out of the question. I don't cook any more.'

'But—'

'Ever.' He pinned her with his gaze and knew it must be pitiless when she shivered. 'It's absolutely out of the question.'

He rose.

'Now if you don't mind. I'm going to do a bit of work

before I retire for the night. I'll move my sleeping quarters to the end bedroom tomorrow.'

She seemed to gather herself. 'I'll clean it first thing.'

That reminded him that she meant to do a grocery shop tomorrow too. 'There's housekeeping money in the tin on the mantel in the kitchen.'

'Right.'

He hated the way she surveyed him. Turning his back, he left, forcing knees that trembled to carry him up the stairs and into his room. He lowered himself to the chair at his desk and dropped his head to his hands, did what he could to quieten the scream stretching through his brain.

Teach Jo to cook?

Impossible.

His chest pounded in time with his temples. Blood surged in his ears, deafening him. He didn't know how long it took for the pounding to slow, for his chest to unclench, and for his breathing to regain a more natural rhythm. It felt like a lifetime.

Eventually he lifted his head. He couldn't teach her to cook. She'd saved his brother's life and he owed her, but he couldn't teach her to cook.

He rose and went to the double glass doors. With the curtains pushed back they stood open to the moonlight. Below, starlight dappled navy water. He couldn't teach her to cook, but he could do everything else she'd asked of him. He could ensure that Russ didn't have one thing to worry about on Mac's account.

One week of halfway human behaviour? He could manage that.

He thought back to the way he'd just left the dining room and dragged a hand through his hair. She must think him a madman. Hauling in a breath, he rested his forehead against cool glass. He might not be able to help her on the cooking front, but could he help her in her search for a new vocation?

The sooner she found a new direction the sooner she'd go, leaving him in peace again. A low, savage laugh scraped from his throat. He would never find peace. He didn't deserve it. But he could have her gone. He'd settle for that.

Mac had been awake for over an hour before he heard Jo's firm tread on the stairs. She moved past his door and on to the bedroom at the end. No doubt to clean it, as she'd promised. The need for caffeine pounded through him. So far he'd resisted it—not ready to face Jo yet.

He blamed the light pouring in at the windows. It had disorientated him.

Liar. It wasn't the light but a particular woman he found disorientating.

He could bolt down to the kitchen now, while she was busy up here.

Yeah, like *that* would convince her to tell Russ all was fine and dandy. He flung the covers back, pulled on a clean pair of jeans and a sweater, and stomped into the en-suite bathroom to splash water on his face. He stood by his bedroom door, counted to three, dragging in a breath on each count before opening it.

'Morning, Jo,' he called out. Amazingly his voice didn't emerge all hoarse and croaky as he'd expected.

She appeared at the end of the hallway. 'Good morning. Sleep well?'

Surprisingly, he had. 'Yeah, thanks.' He remembered his manners. 'And you?'

'No.'

She didn't add any further explanation. He took a step towards her, careful to keep the right side of his face to her. With all the curtains on this level now open there was a lot of light to contend with.

'Is there something wrong with your room? The bed? The mattress?'

She laughed and something inside him unhitched. 'I never sleep well in a new place the first night. Plus, I did a lot of driving yesterday and that always makes me feel unsettled. I'll sleep like a dream tonight.'

He rolled his shoulders. 'How long did you drive for?'

'Five hours.'

Five hours? And she'd arrived to… His stomach churned. She'd arrived to his bitterness, resentment and utter rudeness.

'Mac, we need to talk about my duties.'

That snapped him to.

'I mean, do you want me to make you a full cooked breakfast each morning? What about lunch?'

He noticed she didn't give him any quarter as far as dinner went. 'I'll help myself for breakfast and lunch.'

'Not a breakfast person, huh?'

He wasn't. He opened his mouth. He closed it again and waited for a lecture.

'Me neither,' she confessed. 'Most important meal of the day, blah, blah, blah.' She rolled her eyes. 'Just give me a coffee before I kill you.'

He laughed, but he was still careful to keep his good side to her. She hadn't flinched at his scars last night or so far this morning. But he knew what they looked like. He could at least spare her when he could.

One thing was for sure—she didn't treat him like an invalid, and he was grateful for it.

'There's a pot of freshly brewed coffee on the hob.'

He didn't need any further encouragement, and turned in the direction of the kitchen.

He swung back before he reached the stairs. 'Jo?'

Her head appeared in the bedroom doorway again.

'Don't bust a gut trying to get the house shipshape all at once, will you?' He'd long since dismissed his army of hired help. 'I've…uh…let it get away from me a bit.' At her raised eyebrow he amended that to 'A lot.'

She merely saluted him and went back to work. He made his way down to the kitchen, wondering if he'd passed the *don't worry Russ* test so far this morning. He poured himself a coffee, took a sip and closed his eyes. Man, the woman could make a fine brew.

Mac clocked the exact moment Jo returned from her shopping expedition.

His first instinct was to continue hiding out in his room. He stared at the half-written recipe on his computer screen and pushed to his feet. If he walked away and did something else for half an hour he might remember if he reduced the recipe's required infusion by a third or a quarter.

If he could just see it in the saucepan and smell it he'd have the answer in an instant and—

He cut the thought off with a curse and went to help Jo unpack the car. She'd only given him a week. He'd better make the most of it.

She glanced up when he strode out onto the veranda, and in the light of her grace and vigour he suddenly felt awkward and ungainly.

He scowled, unable to dredge up a single piece of small talk. 'I thought I'd help unpack the car.'

She pursed her lips and he realised he was still scowling. He did what he could to smooth his face out—the parts of his face he *could* smooth out.

'You have any trouble finding the shops?'

Heck. Scintillating conversation.

'None at all. You feeling okay, Mac?'

'I'm fine.' Striding to the car, he seized as many bags as he could and stalked back into the house with them.

It took them two trips.

He wasn't quite sure what to do after that, so he leant

against the sink and pretended to drink a glass of water as he watched her unpack the groceries. There were the expected trays of meat—hamburger mince, sausages, steak and diced beef. And then there was the unexpected and to be deplored—frozen pies and frozen pizza. Fish fingers, for heaven's sake!

He flicked a disparaging finger at the boxes. What are those?'

'I'm assuming you're not asking the question literally?'

She'd donned one of those mock patient voices used on troublesome children and it set his teeth on edge. 'Is this to punish me for refusing to teach you to cook?'

She turned from stowing stuff in the freezer, hands on hips. 'You told me you weren't a fussy eater.'

'This isn't *food*. It's processed pap!'

'You're free to refuse to eat anything I serve up.'

'But if I do you'll go running to Russ to tell tales?'

She grinned, and her relish both irked and amused him. She lifted one hand. 'Rock.' She lifted the other. 'Hard place.'

Which described his situation perfectly.

She grinned again and his mouth watered. She seized a packet of frozen pies and waved them at him. 'Pies, mash, peas and gravy is one of my all-time favourite, walk-over-hot-coals-to-get-it meals, and I'm not giving it up—not even for your high-falutin' standards. And before you ask—no, I haven't mastered the trick to pastry.' She shook her head. 'Life's too short to fuss with pastry. Or to stuff a mushroom.'

She was wrong. A perfect buttery pastry, light and delicate, was one of life's adventures. And mushroom-stuffing shouldn't be sneezed at. But why on earth would she ask him to teach her to cook if that was the way she felt?

'And I'll have you know that fish fingers on a fresh bun with a dollop of tartare sauce makes the best lunch.'

'I will *never* eat fish fingers.'

'All the more for me, then.'

He scowled at the pizza boxes.

'Also,' her lips twitched, 'as far as I'm concerned, there's no such thing as a bad slice of pizza.'

'That's ludicrous!'

'Don't be such a snob. Besides, all of this food is better than whatever it is you've been living on for the last heaven only knows how long. Which, as far as I can tell, has been tinned baked beans, crackers and breakfast cereal.'

She had a point. It didn't matter what he ate. In fact the more cardboard-like and tasteless the better. It had been his search for excellence and his ambition that had caused the fire that had almost claimed a young man's life and—

His chest cramped. He reached out an unsteady hand and lowered himself into a chair at the table. He had to remember what was important. He wanted to do all he could to set Russ's mind at rest, but he couldn't lose sight of what was important—and that was paying off his debts.

A warm hand on his shoulder brought him back to himself. 'Mac, are you okay?'

He nodded.

'Don't lie to me. Do you need a doctor?'

'No.'

'Russell told me you were physically recovered.'

'I am.' He pulled in a breath. 'It's just that I don't like talking about food or cooking.'

Realisation dawned in those sage-green eyes of hers. 'Because it reminds you of the accident?'

It reminded him of all he'd had. And all he'd lost.

CHAPTER THREE

MAC TENSED BENEATH her touch and Jo snatched her hand back, suddenly and searingly aware that while Mac wasn't in peak physical condition he was still a man. He still had broader shoulders than most men she knew, and beneath the thin cotton of his sweater his body pulsed hot and vibrant.

But at this moment he looked so bowed and defeated she wanted to wrap her arms around him and tell him it would all be okay, that it would work itself out.

She grimaced. She could just imagine the way he'd flinch from her if she did. Besides, she didn't know if it *would* be all right. She didn't know if it would work itself out or not.

She moved away to the other side of the kitchen. 'I can make you one promise, Mac.'

He glanced up.

'I promise to never feed you fish fingers.'

He didn't laugh. He didn't even smile. But something inside him unhitched a fraction and his colour started to return. 'I suppose I should give thanks for small mercies.'

'Absolutely. Have you had lunch yet?'

He shook his head.

She seized an apple from the newly replenished fruit bowl and tossed it to him.

This time she'd have sworn he'd laugh, but he didn't.

'I can see I'm going to get nothing but the very best care while you're here.'

'Top-notch,' she agreed. She grabbed her car keys from the bench. 'I'm going to put The Beast in the garage.'

Mac didn't say anything. He just bit into his apple.

The moment she was out of sight Jo's shoulders sagged. If Mac looked like that—so sick and grey and full of despair—just at the thought of the accident, at the thought of cooking…

She had no hope of getting him to give her cooking lessons. None at all. She twisted her fingers together. It was obvious now that it had been insensitive and unkind to have asked.

Why do you never think, Jo?

With a sigh, she started up her car and drove it around to the garage. It didn't solve her problem. She needed to make a *macaron* tower and she had just over two months to learn how to do it.

She pushed her shoulders back. Fine. She had a whole two months. She'd just teach herself. There'd be recipes online, and videos. What else was she going to do out here? Keeping house and cooking dinner would take—what?— three or four hours a day tops? Probably less once she had the house in order.

A *macaron* tower? How hard could it be?

'Don't say that,' she murmured, leaping out of her car to lift the roller door to one of the garage's two bays. The bay she'd chosen stood empty. Out of curiosity she lifted the second door too.

She had a French cookbook Great-Aunt Edith had given her. Maybe there was something in there—

Her thoughts slammed to a halt. She stood there, hands still attached to the roller door, and gaped at the vision of loveliness that had appeared in front of her.

Eventually she lowered her hands, wiped them down the sides of her jeans. Oh. My. Word.

Oh.

Dear.

Lord.

The sky-blue classic eighties sports car was her very own fantasy car brought to life and it was all she could do to not drop to her knees and kiss it.

'Oh, my God, you are the most beautiful car ever,' she whispered, daring to trail a finger across the bodywork as she completed a full circle around it, admiring the front curves, the fat spoiler, its gloss, its clean lines and its shape. What wouldn't she do to test drive this car?

What wouldn't she do just to sit in one!

She tried the driver's door. Locked.

With a jump, she spun around and closed the garage door. One needed to protect a piece of perfection like this from damaging elements. She parked The Beast in the bay beside the sleek machine.

Beauty and The Beast.

She cast one more longing look at Mac's beautiful car before closing the second roller door and racing into the house. Mac was still in the kitchen—eating a sandwich now, rather than the apple.

He glanced up when she clattered in. 'I take it I'm allowed to help myself to the provisions?'

'You have my dream car in your garage!'

'Is that a yes?'

How could he be so cool? She gaped at him and then mentally kicked herself. She spread her arms wide. 'Of course! You can help yourself to anything.'

He stared at her and his eyes darkened. He licked his lips and she had a sudden feeling he wasn't thinking about food, but an altogether different primal need. She pulled her arms back to her sides, heat flooding her veins. *Don't be ridiculous.* Men like Mac didn't find women like her attractive.

Mac turned away from her on his chair as if he'd just

come to the same conclusion. She dragged a hand back through her hair to rub her nape.

'You said something about my car?'

She swallowed back the request that he let her drive it— just once. She swallowed back asking him if he'd just let her sit in it. For all she knew that might be as insensitive as asking him to teach her to cook.

'I… It's beautiful.'

He glanced at her, raised an eyebrow, and she shrugged, unsure what to say, unsure what constituted a safe topic— because she never wanted to witness that look of defeat and despair on his face again. So she shrugged again and filled the jug. She measured out tea leaves.

'Feel free to take it for a spin any time you want.'

The jug wobbled precariously as she poured boiling water into the teapot.

Mac leapt up. 'Don't burn yourself!'

She concentrated on setting the jug back in its place. 'I didn't spill a drop.' Her heart thump-thumped. 'I'm fine.' She set the teapot and two mugs onto the table. 'But I gotta tell you, Mac, you shouldn't offer a girl her heart's desire while she's pouring out boiling water—and for future reference probably not while she's wielding sharp implements either.'

She smiled as she said it. Mac didn't smile back. He just stared at the jug with haunted eyes, the pulse in his throat pounding.

She sat down as if nothing in the world was amiss. 'Would you truly let me take your car out for a drive?'

He sat too. He wiped a hand down his face before lifting one negligent shoulder. 'Sure.' But he reached out to pour the tea before she could. 'It could use a run. I turn it over a couple of times a week, but I don't take it out.'

She gaped at him. 'You'd let me drive it? Just like that?'

That same slow lift of his shoulder. 'Why not?'

It took an effort of will to drag her gaze from that broad sweep of corded muscle. 'I…uh… What if I pranged it?'

'The insurance would cover it. Jo, it's just a car.'

'No, it's not. It's…' She reached out to try and pluck the appropriate description from the air. 'It's a gem, a jewel—a thing of beauty. It's—'

'Just a car.'

'A piece of precision German engineering.'

She almost asked how he could not want to drive it, but choked the question back at the last moment. That *would* be tactless. He'd been in the most dreadful accident, had suffered a long and painful recovery, and would bear the scars for the rest of his life. He'd been hounded by the media. She could see how fast cars might have lost their appeal.

So why hadn't he sold it?

She stared at him and pursed her lips. Maybe Mac hadn't given up on life as completely as he thought.

He glared. 'What?'

'You wouldn't consider selling it, would you?'

He blinked. 'Could you afford it?'

'I've been working in the Outback for the last eight years, making decent money but having very little to spend it on.'

He scratched a hand through his hair. 'But you're not earning a decent wage now.'

She was earning enough to cover her needs.

He jabbed a finger at her. 'And you may, in fact, be training for a new job shortly.'

'I suppose it wouldn't be the most practical of moves.'

He glared. 'You can say that again.'

He didn't want to sell it! She bit back a grin. There was still some life in Mac after all.

He settled back in his seat with a *harrumph*. 'But the offer stands. You can take it for a spin any time you want.'

'Lord, don't say that,' she groaned, 'or your house will never get cleaned.'

He laughed. It made his eyes dance, it softened his lips, and Jo couldn't drag her gaze away. 'You...uh...' She moistened her lips. 'You wouldn't want to come along for a spin?'

His face was immediately shuttered, closed, and she could have kicked herself. 'Well, no, I guess not. You're busy writing up your recipes and stuff.'

'Speaking of which...' He rose, evidently intent on getting back to work.

She surveyed his retreating back with a sinking heart. *Well done, Jo.*

In the next moment he returned. He poured himself a second cup of tea before unhitching a set of keys from the wall and setting them in front of her. 'Ms Anderson, you brew a mighty fine pot of coffee and not a bad cup of tea. Reward yourself and take the car for a spin.'

She shook her head. 'Not until I have your house looking spotless.' It would be a nice treat to spur her on. 'Maybe the day after tomorrow.'

He merely shrugged and left the keys on the table.

After lunch, two days later, Jo made a pot of tea and poured a mug for both her and Mac. Mac reached across to rattle the keys to his car. For the last two days those keys had sat on the table, where they'd tempted, teased and cajoled Jo mercilessly. Neither she nor Mac had put them back on the hook

'Does the house pass muster?' he asked.

Yes, it did. And so did the driveway since she'd found a pile of blue metal gravel out behind the garage. She'd used it to fill in the worst of the potholes along the driveway.

'You can retract your offer any time,' she told him.

'I'm not going to retract the offer, Jo. Go take the car for a spin and enjoy yourself.'

He tossed her the keys. She stared down at them, and then at him. 'I won't be gone long—maybe twenty or thirty minutes tops.'

He shrugged as if he didn't care how long she'd be gone. 'Just don't get a speeding ticket,' he tossed over his shoulder, before taking his mug and heading back upstairs to his mysterious work.

She wondered how on earth he could write recipes if he didn't cook them first.

She wondered how he could bear not to take his beautiful car out for a drive.

She drained her tea and then headed straight out to the garage. Would she even fit into the low-slung sports car? She planted her hands on her hips. If Mac did then she would too. She folded herself into it and sat for a long time, revelling in the moment and familiarising herself with the dashboard, the gears, the fact the indicator was on the left of the steering wheel rather than the right.

She started it up and gave a purr of delight at the throaty sound of the turbo engine. Would the reality of driving this car live up to the fantasy?

She negotiated the driveway with ludicrous care. She had no intention of bringing this car back in anything but perfect condition. When she finally reached the open road she let out a yell of pure delight, relishing the perfect handling, the smooth ride and the responsive power of the car. A body could get addicted to the sheer exhilaration!

After her first initial experimentation with the accelerator she made sure to stick to the speed limit. Instead of speed she savoured the way the car handled the twists and turns of these old country roads.

Oh, how could Mac stand to leave this amazing car in his garage and not use it?

She explored the roads that branched off from Mac's property, along with a couple of others that it seemed justifiable to explore, and discovered two tiny hamlets—Diamond Beach and Hallidays Point—both of which had tiny general stores if she needed to pop out for bread or milk. She also discovered more glorious coastal scenery.

Mac had certainly chosen a beautiful part of the world for his exile. Odd, then, that he didn't seem to spend much time appreciating it, that he'd taken such pains to shut it out from his sight.

It was grief, she supposed. Grief at having lost the life he'd had. There was no denying that until six months ago it had been a charmed life. Maybe when his grief had had time to abate he'd see a way forward again. Perhaps he'd realise his old life wasn't irrevocably lost to him forever.

Not if he refuses to cook.

She sighed, but a signpost pointing down another winding road had her slowing. *'Dog Shelter'.* A grin built through her and on impulse she turned down the road.

Mac will freak!

So what?

It's his house.

Nothing had been said about not being allowed a pet.

She turned into the signposted driveway. She wasn't the only person at the dog shelter. An elderly man emerged from the back of a small sedan as she pulled up beside it. A border collie leapt out behind him.

A woman dressed in overalls strode up from a nearby dog run. 'Mr Cole? And I expect this is Bandit?' She nodded to tell Jo she'd be with her shortly.

Mr Cole's hand dropped to Bandit's head and tears filled his eyes. 'It breaks my heart to leave him.'

Jo's throat thickened.

The woman glanced at the younger couple who had remained in the car. 'Your family can't take him?'

He shook his head and Jo had a feeling that *won't* rather than 'can't' was the operative word on that.

'Please find a good home for him. He's such a good boy

and has been such a good pal. If I wasn't going into a nursing home I'd…'

Jo couldn't stand it any more. She leapt forward. 'Oh, please let me take him. He's beautiful and I promise to love him.'

And then she was on her knees in front of Bandit, who obligingly licked her face. As she ran her hands through his fur she realised what a spectacle she must look. She rose, aware of how much she towered over Mr Cole and Bandit—not to mention the dog shelter lady.

'I was driving past and saw the sign and…well, it suddenly occurred to me that I'm at a point in my life where I can offer a dog a good home.'

Did that make her sound like a stark raving lunatic? Or a responsible, prospective dog owner?

'Maybe…' She swallowed. 'Maybe, Mr Cole, I could bring Bandit to visit you in your new home?'

Mac paced back and forth along the veranda. Jo had been gone for over an hour.

An hour!

Anything could have happened to her. His stomach churned. She could be lying in a ditch somewhere. Or wrapped around a tree. What had he been thinking to let her go driving off like that on her own? Had she even driven a performance car before? Why hadn't he gone with her?

He closed his eyes. He'd have enjoyed it too much. His hands fisted. If he didn't keep fighting the distractions this cookbook would never get written.

And he had to finish it.

He gripped the railing and stared out to sea. Jo was capable. She'd be fine. He drew air into his lungs. Of course she'd be fine. She'd just be caught up in the experience.

He knew exactly what that felt like.

He started pacing again. He hadn't done any real maintenance on the car since he'd buried himself out here. What if it had broken down? What if she was stuck on the side of the road somewhere? Did she have her phone with her?

He dug out his own phone to check for messages.

Nothing.

At that exact moment he heard the low rumble of the car's engine and he had to lower himself to the top step as relief punched through him. He closed his eyes and gave thanks. Jo was his responsibility, and—

Since when?

She was an employee, and that made her his responsibility.

Responsibility *and* a thorn in his side.

Nonetheless, when she parked the car in front of the house it took all his strength to remain where he was rather than leap down the stairs, haul her from the car and hug her. Those would be the actions of a crazy man. And, despite her first impressions of him, Mac wasn't crazy.

She bounced out of the car with a grin that held a hint of trepidation and, thorn in his side or not, he silently acknowledged how glad he was to see her.

'Have fun?' he managed.

'I didn't mean to be gone so long. I hope I didn't worry you?' She sent him a wary glance. 'The car is amazing.'

He tried to tamp down on the rising wave of enthusiasm he felt for the car too. 'I'm glad it lived up to expectations.'

'Oh, it exceeded them.'

He closed his eyes and refused to ask her how she'd felt as she'd swept around a wide bend in the road, or what she thought of the vehicle's magnificent acceleration.

'But I got a bit distracted.'

He snapped his eyes open and leapt to his feet. Had she scratched his car?

'What do you mean—?'

And he found a dog sitting at her feet. His jaw dropped.

'You put a *dog* in my car?'

'I… We made sure to use a blanket so Bandit, here, wouldn't damage the upholstery.'

He stared at her. 'You put a flea-ridden mutt in my car?'

She grimaced, shifting from one foot to the other.

Get over it, pal, he told himself.

Get over it? That car was his most treasured possession! It—

He suddenly flashed to Ethan, in the burns unit at the hospital, and had to lower himself back to the step. He'd give the car up in a heartbeat if it would turn the clock back, if it would change things. But it wouldn't.

Nothing he could do would achieve that. What did a bit of dog hair matter in the grand scheme of things?

She moved to sit on the step below him. The dog remained where he was. 'I know it's scandalous, Mac—a dog in your precious car. But…'

'What are we doing with a dog, Jo?'

Her gaze drifted to his scar. He turned that side of his face away from her and pretended to stare out to sea.

'Is this some underhand attempt to provide me with pet therapy?'

She huffed out a breath. 'No.' She patted her knee. 'Come on, Bandit.' The dog remained sitting by the car. 'I… He's for me, not you, but I don't think he likes me very much.'

He glanced at her to find her frowning at the dog.

'Bandit's is a sad story…' She told it to him, and then said, 'So, you see, when Mr Cole's face lit up so much at my promise to bring Bandit to visit him *and* he started crying I had to take Bandit then and there. Mr Cole would've fretted and thought me no fit carer for Bandit if I'd insisted on getting The Beast rather than letting him ride in Beauty.'

She'd dubbed his car *Beauty*?

It certainly suited the car. And it suited the woman who'd just driven it.

'You do see that, don't you?'

He let out a breath and nodded.

She reached forward and clasped his hand briefly. 'Thank you.' She turned to survey the dog again.

He stared at the hand she'd clasped. He closed it to a fist and tried to stave off the warmth threatening to flood him.

'Do you think he doesn't like me because I'm so big?'

'You're not big!'

Astonished sage eyes stared into his.

He clicked his fingers. 'Bandit.'

The dog immediately rose and leapt up the steps to sit at Mac's feet. 'See—I'm bigger than you and he's fine with it.'

'But you're a man, and I'm big for a woman. I expect animals sense those kinds of things.'

'Nonsense.'

'He likes you.'

Her crestfallen face told him that she had indeed bought the dog for herself, and not some attempt to lure him out of whatever dark pit of depression she imagined him in.

'His previous owner was a man, so it only stands to reason that he's used to men.'

'I guess…'

'Besides, he'll be missing this Mr Cole of his and not understanding what's happening.'

'Oh, yes, the poor thing.' She reached out and gave the dog a gentle hug and a kiss to the top of his head.

Mac's heart started to thump when he imagined—

Don't imagine!

He cleared his throat and tried to clear his mind. 'Once he works out that you're the person who feeds him you'll win both his undying love and his loyalty.'

'Are dogs really that simple?' She gave a funny little grimace. 'I've never had one before.'

'Feed them and treat them with kindness and they'll love you. End of story. You just need to give him some adjustment time. I'd suggest you set him up a bed in the kitchen or the laundry, so he doesn't try and wander off at night to find his old home.' He shrugged at her questioning glance. 'Russ and I had dogs when we were growing up.'

'Thank you.'

She suddenly leaned away from him and it made him realise he'd been talking to her, facing her, with his scar in full view.

'What are you doing outside anyway? Were you waiting for me to get back? Oh, I didn't worry you, did I? I didn't mean to be longer than twenty or thirty minutes but then—'

'Not at all.' His heart pounded. Hard. 'I was just going for a walk.' People went to hell for lying as well as he did.

She pressed a hand to her chest. Her lovely, generous chest.

'That's a relief. I was worried you'd think I'd made off with your fabulous car.' She bit her lip. 'I don't suppose Bandit and I could come on that walk too?'

What could he say to that? He glanced out at the beckoning sea, the field of winter grass and wild native flowers, noted the way the breeze rippled through it all and how the sun shone with winter mildness and tried not to let it filter into him, relax him…gladden him.

'Sure.'

'I suspect, though, that you should wear a sunhat to protect you…' She touched the left side of her face to indicate that she meant his burn scar. 'From sunburn.'

He should.

'You go get a hat and I'll put Beauty in the garage.'

They both rose. Bandit looked at Mac expectantly. Her face fell almost comically.

'You're not taking that fleabag in my car again,' he said to mediate her disappointment at the dog's reaction.

'So much for "It's just a car, Jo",' she muttered, but her

lips twitched as she said it. She patted Bandit on the head. 'You be a good boy. I'll be back soon.'

She folded herself into the car and her face broke into the biggest grin when she started it up again. She touched the accelerator just for fun and the car roared in instant response.

He turned on his heel and strode through the house to hide his sudden laughter. 'Bandit, I hope one day your new mistress gets herself her dream car. She'll know exactly how to enjoy it.'

Bandit wagged his tail, following Mac all the way through the house and up to his bedroom.

Mac rifled through drawers, looking for a hat. 'Don't look at me like that, dog. I'm not your master. *She* is.'

Bandit just wagged his tail harder. Mac shook his head and slathered sunscreen across his face. What on earth did Jo think she was going to do with a dog?

She was waiting on the veranda when he finally returned. She wore a basketball cap. 'I always have one in The Beast,' she explained when he glanced at it. 'Sunstroke is no laughing matter on a survey camp.'

'It's not a laughing matter anywhere, is it?'

She shrugged and pulled her hand from behind her back to reveal a tennis ball. Bandit started to bark.

'He came amply provided for.'

With that, she threw the ball and Bandit hurtled after it. She set off after him, turning back after four or five strides.

'Well? Aren't you coming?'

The previous two days he'd walked the property line behind the house and away from the sea. With an internal curse he kicked himself into action, trying not to let the holiday spirit infect him. But when Bandit came back and dropped the ball at Mac's feet and Jo gave a snort of disgust all he could do was laugh.

'Shut up and throw the ball for the ungrateful bag of bones.'

So he did.

They walked down a steeply inclined field, and then across level ground, and the whole time Mac tried to ignore the scent of the sea and the tug of the breeze caressing his face and the feeling of ease that tried to invade him. He hadn't realised it but he'd grown cramped in the house these last few weeks, and moving now was like releasing a pent-up sigh.

He didn't deserve to enjoy any of it.

He slammed to a halt. But it was going to prove necessary if he was to remain healthy. Jo was right about that. And he had to remain healthy. He had a debt to pay off.

'Are you okay?'

That warm honey voice flowed over him, somehow intensifying the sun's warmth and the silk of the breeze.

'Not tired out already, are you?'

He kicked forward again. 'Of course not.' That wasn't to say that the hill on the way back wasn't going to give him a run for his money. 'I'm just…'

'Yes?'

'I'm just trying to figure out the best way to apologise for my behaviour on Monday, when you arrived.'

'Ah.' She marched up a low sand dune.

He didn't want to go onto the beach. He hadn't guarded his privacy so fiercely to blow his cover now. As if sensing his reluctance, she found a flat patch of sand amongst a riot of purple pigface and sat to watch as Bandit raced down to the water's edge to chase waves. After a moment's hesitation he sat beside her. He kept his right side towards her.

'You *were* expecting me on Monday, weren't you?'

'Yes.'

'Then why the foul temper? You didn't seriously expect to live under the same roof as someone and manage to avoid them completely, did you?'

Had he? He wasn't sure, but he could see now what a ludicrous notion that was. 'I've obviously fallen into bad habits. It wasn't deliberate, and it certainly wasn't the object of the exercise.'

'By *exercise* I suppose you're referring to holing up out here in royal isolation? What's the object?'

'The object is to write this darn cookbook, and I was having a particularly rough day with it on Monday.'

She let out a breath. 'And I waltzed in like a…'

'Like a cyclone.'

'Wreaking havoc and destruction.'

'And letting in the fresh air.'

She turned to stare at him. His mouth went dry but he forced himself to continue. 'You were right. I've been shutting myself up for days on end, hardly setting foot outside, and some days barely eating. If you hadn't shown up and shaken me up I'd have been in grave danger of falling ill. And I can assure you that's *not* what I want.'

He wasn't on a suicide mission.

He readied himself for a grilling—did he mean what he said or was he trying to manipulate her for Russ's benefit, et cetera, et cetera?

Instead she turned to him, her gaze steady. 'Why is the cookbook so important?'

CHAPTER FOUR

WAS THE COOKBOOK a way for Mac to take his mind off the fact he no longer had a television show? No longer had a job? His fisted hands and clenched jaw told her it consumed him, and not necessarily in a good way.

When he didn't answer she tried again. 'What's the big deal with the cookbook, Mac?'

He finally turned to look at her. 'Money.'

'You have a deal with a publisher?'

He gave a single nod before he turned back to stare at the sea.

'If you hate it that much—' and she was pretty certain he did '—can't you just…?' She shrugged. She didn't know how these things worked. 'Change your mind? Apologise and pay back the advance?'

'You don't understand.'

Obviously not.

'I *need* the money.'

She had no hope of hiding her surprise, but she did what she could to haul her jaw back into place in super-quick time. 'But you must've made a truckload of money from your TV show.'

Not to mention all those guest appearances and endorsements. Still, if he'd gone around buying expensive cars willy-nilly she supposed he might have burned through it pretty quickly. Not that it was any of her business. And it wasn't any of Russ's business either.

'I… Sorry, I just thought you were rolling in it.'

'I was.'

So what on earth had he done with it all?

She had no intention of asking, but possibilities circled through her mind—bad investments, gambling, living the high life with no thought for the future.

'It's all gone on medical bills.'

That had her swinging back. 'Yours was a workplace accident.' It had occurred during the filming of one of his TV episodes. 'Insurance should've taken care of the medical expenses.'

'Not *my* medical bills, Jo. The money hasn't gone on *my* medical bills.'

A world of weariness stretched through his voice. And then it hit her. That young apprentice who'd also been involved in the fire. 'Ethan?' she whispered.

He didn't respond with either a yea or a nay.

She rubbed a hand across her forehead, readjusted her cap. 'But the insurance should've covered his medical expenses too. I—'

He swung to her, his eyes blazing. 'He's still in hospital! He still has to wear a bodysuit. His family wanted to move him to a private facility, where he'd get the best of care, but they couldn't afford the fees.'

Living the high life with no thought for tomorrow? Oh, how wrong she'd been!

She reached out to clasp his arm. 'Oh, Mac…' He'd taken on so much.

He shook her off and leapt to his feet. She pulled her hands into her lap, stung. A man like Mac would resent the sympathy of a woman like her.

Striking, huh? *Yeah, right.*

He spun to her, lips twisting. 'Who should pay but me? *I'm* the reason he's lying in a hospital bed with second- and third-degree burns to sixty per cent of his body. I've ruined that young man's life. I'm the guilty party. So the least I can do is—'

'What a load of codswallop!' She shot to her feet too. 'If we want to take this right down to brass tacks it's the producers and directors of your television show who should be paying in blood.'

Kitchen Encounters, as Mac's television show had been called, had followed the day-to-day dramas of Mac's catering team as they'd gone from event to event—a charity dinner with minor royalty one week, a wedding the next, then perhaps a gala awards night for some prestigious sporting event. Throughout it all Mac had been portrayed as loud, sweary and exacting—an over-the-top, demanding perfectionist. So over the top that even if Jo hadn't had the inside line from Russ she'd have known it was all for show—for the ratings, for the spectacle it created.

That wasn't how the press had portrayed it after the accident, though. They'd condemned Mac's behaviour and claimed the *Kitchen Encounters* set had been an accident waiting to happen. All nonsense. But such nonsense sold newspapers in the same way that conflict and drama sold TV shows.

Mac remained silent. He fell back to the sand, his shoulders slumping in a way that made her heart twist. Standing above him like this made her conscious of her height. She sat again, but a little further away this time, in the hope she wouldn't do something stupid like reach out and touch him again.

She moistened her lips. 'Russ told me that the persona you adopted for the show was fake—that it was what the producers demanded. He also said everyone on the show was schooled in their reactions too.'

Conflicts carefully orchestrated, as in any fictional show or movie, to create drama, to create good guys and bad guys.

Some weeks Mac had played the darling and others the villain. It had led to compulsive viewing.

'The accident wasn't your fault. You were playing the role you were assigned. You weren't the person who dropped a tray of oysters and ice into a pot of hot oil.' That had been Ethan. 'It was an accident.' A terrible, tragic accident.

'For God's sake, Jo, I was yelling at him—bellowing at him to hurry up. He was nineteen years old, it was only his second time on the show, and he was petrified.'

He didn't yell or bellow now. He spoke quietly, but there was a savage edge to his words that she suspected veiled a wealth of pain.

'He was acting. Just like you were.'

'No.'

He turned and those eyes lasered through her. Blond hair the colour of sand, blue eyes the colour of the sea, and olive skin that was still too pale. His beauty hit her squarely in the chest, making it hard to breathe.

'He was truly petrified. I just didn't realise until it was too late.'

She gripped her hands tightly in her lap to stop them from straying. 'From all accounts if you hadn't acted so quickly to smother the fire Ethan would be dead.' The other actors on the set had labelled Mac a hero.

'He hasn't thanked me for that, Jo.'

It took a moment for her to realise what he meant. She stared out to sea and blinked hard, swallowing the lump that was doing its best to lodge in her throat.

'Do you know how painful his treatment is? It's like torture.'

'He's young,' she managed to whisper. 'One day this will all be behind him.'

'And he'll be disfigured for life. All because I played the game the TV producers wanted—all because I was hungry for ratings and success and acclaim. At any time I could've

said no. I could've demanded that we remain true to the "reality" part of our so-called reality show. I could've demanded
that everyone on set be treated with courtesy and respect.'

If he had, she suspected the show wouldn't have lasted
beyond a single season.

'I didn't. I chose not to.'

There was nothing wrong with wanting to be successful, with wanting praise and applause for a job well done.
If anyone took a poll she'd bet ninety-nine per cent of the
population wanted those things too.

'My pursuit of ratings has ruined a boy's life.'

And now he was doing all he could to make amends, to
make Ethan's life as comfortable as he could. She shuddered
to think how expensive those medical bills must be. She
didn't believe for a moment that Mac should hold himself
responsible, but neither did she believe she had any hope
of changing his mind on that.

What a mess!

One thing seemed certain, though. If he didn't ease up
he'd become ill. At least he seemed to recognise that fact
now.

Or was that just a clever manipulation on his behalf so
she wouldn't go telling tales to Russ?

She glanced at Mac from the corner of her eye as Bandit came racing up from the beach, tongue lolling out and
fur wet from the surf. He collapsed at Mac's feet, looking
the epitome of happy, satisfied dog. If only she could get a
similarly contented expression on Mac's face her job here
would be done.

Unbidden, an image punched through her, so raunchy
that she started to choke. That *wasn't* what she'd meant! She
leapt to her feet and strode a few steps away. Mac would
laugh his head off if he could read her mind at the moment.

Laughter is good for the soul.

Yeah, well, in this instance it would shrivel hers.

She put the image out of her mind, pulled in a breath and turned to face him. His gaze was fixed on her hips. He stared for another two beats before he started. Colour slashed high across his cheekbones.

Had he been checking out her butt?

She wiped her hands down her jeans. Ridiculous notion.

But he couldn't meet her gaze, and then she couldn't meet his. She stared up at the sky. 'So what's the problem you've been having with your recipes?'

'They're complicated.'

'Naturally. It's one of the reasons your show was so gripping. There seemed to be so many things that could go wrong with each individual dish.'

'I promised the publisher a troubleshooting section for each recipe.'

That sounded challenging.

'I'm not a writer!' He dragged both hands back through his hair. 'This stuff—the explanations—doesn't come naturally to me. I don't know if they're coherent, let alone if a lay person could follow them.'

And if he refused to actually cook the dishes then how much harder was he making this on himself? He'd always proclaimed himself an instinctive chef. Just getting the order right of when to do what must be a nightmare.

It hit her then. How she could help him. And how he could help her.

She moistened her lips. 'Why don't you give me the drafts of your recipes and we'll see if I can make them? See if they make sense to me?'

She shifted her gaze to Bandit—it was easier than looking at Mac—but she couldn't help but notice how Mac's feet stilled where they'd been rubbing against Bandit's back.

'You'd do that?'

Forcing in a breath, she met his gaze. His eyes held hope,

and something else she couldn't decipher. 'I'll try, but you have to understand that I'm no cook.'

'You're the perfect demographic.'

She was?

'A plain cook who wants to branch out and try her hand at something new—something more complicated and exotic.'

That wasn't her at all. She just wanted to learn how to make a *macaron* tower.

'This would help me out. A lot.'

And her too, she hoped. He might refuse to stand side by side with her in a kitchen and show her how to make fiddly little *macarons*, but he might be worked on to create a sensible, within the realms of possible, *macaron* recipe for her.

'If you're sure?' he added.

So much for the demanding, overbearing kitchen tyrant. Russ had always chortled at Mac's on-air tantrums. She was starting to see why.

'As long as you're prepared to eat the odd disaster for dinner if things don't always work out.'

'What the heck? We've always got fish fingers to fall back on.'

She laughed.

'What if I give you the first recipe tomorrow?'

She nodded. And then glanced around at the lengthening shadows and shivered a little. The warmth quickly leached from the air as the afternoon closed in.

'Speaking of dinner, I'll need to get back and start it soon.' The beef stew she'd planned needed to simmer for at least an hour and a half.

'And I should get a bit more work done.'

He moved to get up and she started to offer him her hand, and then snatched it back, remembering the way he'd shaken off her touch earlier.

Mac's gaze narrowed and he leant back on his hands,

peering up at her from beneath the brim of his hat. 'Did my lascivious gaze earlier embarrass you?'

She almost swallowed her tongue. His *what*? So he *had* been…? Was he saying…? Surely not!

'Of course not,' she lied.

He rose to his feet in one smooth motion. Bandit immediately leapt to his feet too. 'I did tell you that you were a striking woman.'

She snorted and turned towards the house. 'You've been stuck out here on your own for too long.'

Without warning, cool, firm fingers gripped the suddenly overheated flesh of her forearm, pulling her to a halt. 'And you're selling yourself short.'

No, she wasn't. She just knew what she was. And she wasn't the kind of woman who turned men's heads. Mac was just trying to charm her, manipulate her.

'I should put your mind at rest, though.' He stroked her skin with his index finger before releasing her. 'I want to assure you that you're perfectly safe from unwanted attention. I have no intention of thrusting myself on you. I do mean to act like a perfect gentleman towards you, Jo.'

She wished he hadn't used the term *thrusting*.

She drew herself up to her full height but he still towered over her. 'No other scenario occurred to me, I assure you.'

'Good.' His eyes twinkled for a moment. 'It doesn't mean I can't enjoy looking at you, though.'

Jo stumbled. Mac laughed. Bandit barked and raced off towards the house.

Mac paced back and forth outside the kitchen door.

Jo peered around the doorway. 'You *can* come in and watch, you know. You could sit at the table.'

If he did that he'd bark instructions at her the moment she started. He'd make her nervous and she'd have an accident and burn herself. His stomach churned at the thought. If he sat in the kitchen he wouldn't be able to resist the temptation to take over.

He didn't deserve to indulge his passion when a boy lay in a hospital bed, suffering because of that passion.

'So, all I'm doing at the moment is infusing these few ingredients for the béarnaise sauce I'm to make tonight, right?

'That's right.'

'And—'

'No questions,' he ordered. 'I need to know if you can follow the recipe.'

'Okay—gotcha.'

He couldn't have said why, but her earnest expression made him want to kiss her.

He could just imagine how she'd recoil from *that*. He grimaced, and tried to push the thought from his mind, but it didn't stop the itch and burn that coursed through his body.

'If you're not going to watch then you best go somewhere else to pace. You're making me nervous.'

Go where? Do what? He didn't have a hope of settling to work at the moment. What if she didn't understand an instruction? What if—?

'Go toss a ball for Bandit.'

With a nod, he barrelled outside. The dog had a seemingly boundless reserve of energy.

Mac threw the ball three times. When Bandit brought it back the third time he gave the border collie an absent-minded scratch behind the ears. 'How do you think she's getting on in there, boy?'

He glanced back towards the house. It wasn't as if she had to do anything difficult—just measure out a few ingredients, chop up a tablespoon of onion. Simple, right?

He sprang up the steps and moved soundlessly across to the door. He breathed in deeply but couldn't smell anything. He straightened, ran a hand back through his hair. He should at least smell the vinegar being brought to the boil by now, surely? She should be reducing the mixture and…

Maybe she hadn't started the reduction yet.

He reached for the door handle.

Bandit barked.

With a curse, Mac wheeled away and clattered back down the steps. He threw the ball until his arm grew tired and then he switched arms. Bandit didn't show any signs of tiring. All the while Mac kept his attention cocked for any sign of sound and movement behind him.

Finally Jo emerged from the front door, bearing a plate of sandwiches, a jug of water and two glasses. 'Hungry?' she called out.

Not a bit—but he moved to where she'd set the things on the wooden table that stood at one end of the veranda and poured them both glasses of water. He drank his in an effort to appear nonchalant.

'Run into any problems?'

She settled on the bench that sat between the living room windows, bit into a sandwich and lifted one shoulder.

He peered at her sandwich and blinked. 'Is that peanut butter and honey?'

'Yup.'

He stared.

'What?' She glared. 'I *like* peanut butter and honey. You don't have to eat one. I made you roast beef and pickles.'

He obeyed the unspoken demand in her voice and selected a sandwich. 'What did the shrug mean?' He promptly bit into the sandwich to stop himself pressing her further.

She licked a drizzle of honey from her fingers. It was unconsciously sensuous and very seductive. The fact that she didn't mean it to be didn't make a scrap of difference. He forced his gaze away and concentrated on chewing and swallowing.

'I think I should probably tell you that I'm not up on a lot of cooking terminology. The very first time a recipe told me to *"cream the butter and sugar"* I thought it was directing me to add cream to the butter and sugar.'

He'd been leaning with a hip against the railing but he surged upright at her words. 'This recipe didn't ask you to cream anything.'

She waved a hand through the air. 'That's just an example. But…you know…*"reduce the mixture by a third"* isn't the kind of thing I read every day.'

'Do you think I need to add an explanation to describe what reducing means?'

She pursed her lips. 'No, I figured it out, but…'

He leaned towards her. 'Yes?'

'Why go to all the trouble of reducing at all? Why not just add less vinegar, water and onion to begin with?'

'Simmering the ingredients together infuses the flavours to provide a base for the sauce.'

She sat back and stared. 'Now *that's* interesting.' She pointed a finger at him. 'That should go in the cookbook.'

Really?

'But, you know, I want you to realise that I might be more clueless than your real demographic, so—'

'No, you're perfect.'

She glanced up, obviously startled at this statement. Their gazes locked for a moment. They both glanced away at the same time.

Mac's heart surged against his ribs. Why did this woman have to affect him like this? He'd known beautiful women in the past who had left him cold. Why couldn't Jo leave him cold?

Oh, no, not her. She threatened to ignite him. And for the first time in months the thought of heat and fire didn't fill his soul with dread. He glanced back at her. The pulse at the base of her throat fluttered madly. Unlike him, though, it wouldn't be desire but fear that had sent the blood surging through her veins. Fear that he would touch her.

It left a bad taste in his mouth.

'So…' She cleared her throat. 'My reduction is cooling and infusing, and I'll strain it later when I'm ready to make the sauce. Feel free to go and check it out.'

He started for the door.

'But…'

He turned back.

'I didn't know what tarragon vinegar was.'

He strode back to where she sat, one eyebrow raised.

'So I just used plain old white vinegar.'

He let out a breath.

'I briefly flirted with the idea of adding a herb to the mixture—like rosemary.'

He grimaced. It wouldn't be the end of the world, but—

'Though in the end I decided not to risk it.'

'It sounds as if you've done a great job.'

She didn't look convinced. 'I have another request to make. I've no idea what a double saucepan is.'

She needed to use one when adding butter—bit by tiny bit—to the reduction later, to create the sauce.

'I'm not asking you to tell me what it is, but can I bring my laptop into the kitchen with me? I would if I were cooking at home.'

'Of course you can.'

'And the final thing,' she said before he could walk away again. 'This recipe is Steak with Béarnaise Sauce, but you haven't said what you want served with it.'

'New potatoes and green beans.'

'Then you might want to include that at the end of the recipe too.'

Good point.

She suddenly laughed. 'I can see you're itching to check

it out, so go. But wash your hands first. I don't want dog hair in my reduction.'

He raced into the kitchen. He washed and dried his hands and then moved to the small saucepan sitting on the stovetop. He could tell at a glance that she'd used too much onion. He lifted the saucepan to his nose and sniffed. It was a pity about the tarragon vinegar—if she was happy to continue this experiment of theirs then they'd need to stock up on some of the more exotic ingredients—but all in all she'd done okay. The tension bled out of his shoulders.

She glanced up when he stepped back out onto the veranda. 'Well?'

'You've done a fine job. It's not exactly how I'd want it, which tells me what parts of my instructions I need to fine-tune.'

Elation suddenly coursed through him. He could make this work. He *could*! Then there'd be enough money for Ethan's hospital bills for the foreseeable future.

And after that?

He pushed that thought away. He had every intention of making sure Ethan was looked after for the rest of his life. Maybe he could do a whole series of cookbooks if this one sold well?

'This was a brilliant idea of yours, Jo. I can't thank you enough.'

She waved that away.

'If there's anything I can do in return…?'

She glanced up. The sage in her eyes deepened for a moment. 'I believe you mean that.'

'I *do* mean it.' He'd have sat on the bench beside her, but that would mean sitting with the left side of his face towards her. He leant against the railing again instead.

'Hold that thought.'

She disappeared into the house. She returned a moment later with a picture. His heart sank when she handed it to him. It was that damned *macaron* tower she'd already mentioned.

'*Macarons* are tricky.'

'Yes, but could you write me a recipe telling me how to make them—how to make that?'

He blew out a breath. 'This is an advanced recipe.'

'But practice makes perfect, right? I have plenty of time on my hands. I'll just keep practising.'

'Why do you want to make a *macaron* tower?' He could name a hundred tastier desserts.

He handed her back the picture. She took it, but a bad taste stretched through him when he realised how careful she was not to touch him.

She stared down at the picture before folding it in half. 'My grandmother turns eighty-five in two months, one week, four days and—what?—eleven hours twenty minutes? I've promised to make her one of these.'

Wow.

'I want to do something nice for her.'

'Nice' would be taking her flowers, or treating her to lunch at a decent restaurant. *Or making her a* macaron *tower.*

'Please, Mac, don't look like that! This *has* to be possible. I'm not that much of a klutz in the kitchen. This is something I can build up to.'

'Of course you can.'

'He says with fake jollity,' she said, so drily he had to laugh.

'I didn't mean that you can't do it. I'm just blown away by the fact you *want* to.'

'I love my grandmother. I want to do something that will make her happy. She's as fit as a horse, and as sharp as a tack, but she's still coming up to eighty-five.'

She rose and seized the other half of her peanut butter and honey sandwich and came to lean beside him on the railing, on his left side. He turned to stare out to sea, giving her his right side instead.

'My grandmother and my great-aunt raised me. Their relationship has always been tempestuous. My grandmother always praised me and indulged me. My great-aunt always thought it in my best interests to…um…not to do that.'

He stilled and glanced at her, but he couldn't read her face.

'There's an ongoing dispute over the rightful ownership of my great-grandmother's pearl necklace. My great-aunt scoffed at the idea of my making that *macaron* tower and I'm afraid my grandmother has staked the pearl necklace on the fact that I can.'

His jaw dropped.

'I believe my so-called *womanly* qualities have always been in dispute, and I'm afraid my great-aunt is now convinced that the necklace is hers.'

He straightened. 'What exactly does she mean by *womanly* qualities?' As far as he could see Jo's 'womanly qualities' were exemplary. 'You mean the domestic arts?'

She pointed what was left of her sandwich at him. 'Exactly.'

He reached around her for another sandwich. It brought him in close. She smelled faintly of onions, vinegar and honey. His mouth watered. He ached to reach across, touch his lips to her cheek to see what she tasted like.

Jo polished off the rest of her sandwich and pushed away from the railing to amble down the veranda a little way before turning. 'I don't mean to give up without a fight.'

He turned to face the house again, presenting her with his good side. 'I can understand that.' But didn't she resent being piggy in the middle between the two older women?

'Why do you keep doing that?'

A chill fluttered through him. 'Doing what?'

'Keeping the right side of your face towards me? Isn't it tiring?'

CHAPTER FIVE

IT WAS REALLY starting to bug her, the way Mac tried to hide his scar. Jo understood physical self-consciousness all too well, but Mac couldn't spend the rest of his life trying to hide one side of his face. It just wouldn't work.

'The way you're going, you'll give yourself whiplash.'

'I have no idea what you're talking about.'

How cold he could sound when he wanted—but she knew better. Mac wasn't cold. He was… Well, he was hot. But that wasn't what she meant.

He was devoting his life to making Ethan Devlin's life better. Those weren't the actions of a cold man.

'Really?' she said, walking around to his left side and deliberately surveying his scars. She'd noticed them before, of course, but scars didn't make the man, and she'd had other issues with Mac that had nothing to do with what he looked like.

The scars were red and angry. She sucked in a breath. Heck, they must hurt!

The pulse at the base of his jaw pounded. He held his body taut, as if it were taking all his strength to remain where he stood, and let her look at him.

He finally turned to glare at her, eyes flashing and lips pressed into a thin line. 'Satisfied?'

She stared back at him and had to swallow. Mac, when he was riled like this, was pretty virile. She had a feeling that the glare, the set of those shoulders and the angle of his jaw were all supposed to have her shaking in her boots. *Uh, no.* Though it certainly had her pulse racing. She moistened her lips. What it really made her want to do was run *to* him—not away from him.

Lord, wouldn't he laugh if he knew?

'I don't precisely know what you mean by *satisfied*, Mac.'

He swung away to stare out to sea, presenting her with his 'good' side again. 'Satisfied,' he growled, 'as in have you had your fill of looking at it?'

Oh.

He kept his gaze firmly fixed in front of him, but she had a feeling he didn't see the glorious view—the cobalt sky, the indigo and aquamarine of the sea, the white foam of the surf and the golden beach, all at their most vivid at this time of the year before the sun bleached everything pale with summer intensity.

'Doesn't it sicken you to look at it?'

Her head rocked back. 'Of course not.'

He turned to glare, a blast of arctic chill from frigid eyes. 'When you first arrived you said these scars shocked you to the core. Those were your exact words.'

She drew herself upright. 'I wasn't referring to your scars, you stupid—' She bit back something rude and vulgar. 'I was referring to how much you'd let yourself go!'

His jaw dropped.

She reached out and poked him in the shoulder. 'Don't you *dare* accuse me of being so shallow.'

His shoulders unbent.

She frowned and adjusted her stance. 'Does it sicken *you* whenever you look in a mirror?'

One of those lovely shoulders lifted. 'I'm used to it.'

'But what? You don't think anyone else can get used to it? You don't think anyone else can see past it?'

He didn't say anything.

'I've met beautiful people who've proved to be spiteful or

selfish or snobs, and suddenly I find their allure loses most of its gloss. I have friends who may not fit society's rigid ideal of beautiful, but they have such good hearts I think them the most beautiful people in the world.'

'Jo, I—'

'No! You listen to what I have to say! If you value yourself and others only through physical beauty then you deserve to suffer every torment imaginable at the thought of losing your so-called pretty face. But, as far as your face is concerned, I think it's as pretty as it ever was.'

He stilled. He stared at her for a long moment. 'You really mean that?'

She did.

He dragged in a breath and then turned to lean against the railing, his left side towards her. 'I'm sorry I insinuated…' He glanced at her. 'That you were shallow. I didn't mean to.' He paused. 'I agree that a person's attractiveness is more than how they look, but…'

She tried not to focus on the languid line of his body. 'But…?'

'There's no denying looks have an impact on how a person is perceived.'

'If a person is repelled by your scars they're not worth the time of day.' She folded her arms. 'You know, it could prove a useful filtering device.'

He gave a bark of laughter. 'You can't say that.'

'Don't let anyone know you feel self-conscious about it, Mac. That's my best advice. They'll see it as a weakness, and there are people in the world who pounce on others' weaknesses in an effort to build themselves up.'

He turned to her more fully. 'That sounds like the voice of experience.'

She shrugged and tried to walk the walk she'd just talked. 'Look at me.' She gestured down at herself.

'I've been doing my very best not to do that, Jo. I promised you gentlemanly behaviour, but when I look at you…'

She rolled her eyes. '*Do* be serious.'

Mac moved to trap her against the veranda post and the side of the house. He planted one hand on the weatherboards by her head, the other on the railing near her waist. Her mouth dried. Her heart thudded so hard she found it impossible to catch her breath.

'What on earth do you think you're—?'

'Shut up or I'll kiss you.'

She almost swallowed her tongue.

'You have the nerve to give me a lecture about shallowness, beauty and an individual's true worth, and then you want to carry on with *you're not attractive*?'

She opened her mouth. His eyes suddenly gleamed, fixing on her mouth with a hunger that had to be feigned! But she remembered his threat and snapped her mouth shut.

'What a shame,' he murmured, and in his eyes was a mixture of laughter and regret.

She wanted to call him a liar, but she didn't dare.

'When I said you were a striking woman I meant that in every positive way there is. I meant that I find you attractive. I meant that it takes a Herculean effort on my part whenever I look at you to conceal my desire.'

She choked.

'And it's not because I've been isolated for the last four months.'

Again, she was tempted to call him a liar. She was tempted to say anything that would make him kiss her. Warmth threaded through her stomach at the thought, her thighs softened and her breasts grew heavy.

But if he kissed her she wouldn't be able to help it. She'd kiss him back and then he'd know how much she wanted him, how attractive she found him, and it would make her vulnerable. She swallowed. She didn't want to be vulnerable around this man.

'You seem to think you're too tall for a woman...'

He moved in closer, his heat swamping her, though he still didn't touch her. He smelled of soap and freshly ironed cotton...and very faintly of dog. She really wished that last would put her off, but it didn't.

'I don't think you're too tall. I think you and I would fit perfectly.'

They might not be touching, but this close to him she felt dwarfed.

'I could stare into your eyes all day. They're so clear, and the colour changes depending on your emotion. I find myself wanting to learn what each shade means.'

That voice of his, its low intimate tone and the words he uttered, could weave a spell around a woman.

He eased back a fraction and she managed to draw air into her lungs again. Until she realised what he was doing and the breath jammed in her throat again.

'You have the most intriguingly womanly shape—all dips and curves.'

He was staring at her body the same way she'd stared at his face a short while ago. Had *he* felt this exposed? For heaven's sake, she was fully clothed, but Mac's eyes were practically undressing her—as if he was imagining what she'd look like without said clothes—and his eyes started to gleam and he actually licked his lips. She swallowed a moan and sagged against the wall, her pulse racing, bustling, jumping.

'Your body is lush and strong, and I'd be a liar if I said I wasn't aching to explore it. Thoroughly and intensely.'

The words scraped out of him, a hoarse whisper, and Jo's head fell back against the house as she struggled to draw air into her lungs.

'But that's just the outside packaging. The woman I'm

getting to know is passionate, she gives no quarter, but she is remarkably generous.'

His gaze burned fiercely down into hers. She couldn't have uttered a word if her life had depended on it.

'And all of that makes me ache that much more to make love with you.'

How on earth had the morning descended to this? For years she'd worked among teams of men in remote locations in the Outback and she'd always managed to keep things on a professional footing.

This was only her fifth day with Mac, and the air was charged with so much blatant sensuality it would melt any-one foolish enough to stumble into its path.

'But I promised to be gentlemanly, so I won't, but I'm sick to death of this ridiculous belief of yours that you're not attractive. You're a beautiful and very desirable woman.'

It frightened her. *He* frightened her. Because she wanted to believe him. Yet in her heart she knew it was all lies.

Mac eased away and she tossed her head. 'I know my worth, Mac, make no mistake. I'm smart and strong and I'm a good friend. But let's make one thing very clear. Boys like you do *not* kiss girls like me.' Not unless it was for a bet or a dare, or they were trying to manipulate them in some way. 'It's a fact of life.' A fact she had no intention of forgetting.

He'd started to turn away, but now he turned back, a flare of anger darkening his face. And then a slow, satisfied gleam lit his eyes, his mouth, even his shoulders—though she couldn't have explained how.

'Perfect…' he crooned.

And then he moved in.

She raised her hands. 'Don't you—'

He claimed her lips swiftly, pushing her back against the house, taking his time exploring every inch of her mouth. She tried to turn her head to the side, but he followed her, his hands cupping her face. He crowded her completely, pressing every inch of his rock-hard self against her. His chest flattened her breasts—breasts that strained to get closer. He thrust a leg between her thighs, pressing against her most sensitive spot in the most irresistible way. It made her gasp. With a purr of satisfaction his tongue plundered her mouth.

Stop! Stop! Stop!

But he didn't stop kissing her, savouring her, pressing against her, making her feel desired, making her feel beautiful, and with a moan scraping from the back of her throat she curled her hands into the soft cotton of his sweater and kissed him back. She wanted to know him, taste him. She wanted to savour him in the same way he savoured her. Her hands explored his shoulders and dived into the thickness of his hair. But she wanted more—so much more.

One of his arms went around her waist—he spanned it effortlessly—and hauled her closer as if she weighed nothing. It sent shivers of delight spiralling through her. Their kisses went from tasting and savouring to a deepening hunger. Held in his arms like this, dwarfed by his height and breadth, Jo felt almost dainty, utterly feminine and beautiful.

When his hand slid beneath her shirt to cup her breast his moan made her shake. He was moaning for *her*. He wanted *her*!

His thumb flicked across her nipple through the nylon of her bra. Desire spiked from her nipple to the core deep at the centre of her. She shifted against him, restless for more, seeking relief…seeking release and—

If they kept this up there was only one way it would end. She stilled. So did he. He didn't remove his hand from her breast and his heat branded her, tormented her. She didn't remove her arms from around his neck.

They both breathed hard, as if they'd run a race.

'I beg to differ.'

She blinked up at him blankly.

'Guys like me most certainly *do* kiss women like you. And what's more, Jo, they enjoy every moment of it.'

One kiss couldn't erase a lifetime of taunts, a lifetime of feeling she'd never measured up. A lifetime of never feeling beautiful.

She swallowed. Mac had kissed her as if he found her beautiful, but she still wasn't convinced he wasn't playing some deeper game. She removed her arms from around his neck. With the wall of his house behind her, she had nowhere to move to.

'Let me go, Mac.'

He did immediately.

Regardless of any of his reasons for kissing her, regardless of how much her body clamoured otherwise, this couldn't go any further.

'I've known you for five days.' Not even five full days. 'I don't jump into bed with men I've known for such a short time.' Was that his style?

He moved down to the next veranda post, leaving a whole span of veranda railing between them. 'I'm forty years old, Jo. The days when I thought one-night stands and flings were fun are long behind me.'

She'd never thought one-night stands or flings fun. Sharing her body with a man had always been a fraught experience and not one she'd ever raced into.

And yet today she'd almost…

She bent at the waist to lean her forearms along the railing, unconsciously mimicking Mac's posture.

'That kiss became a whole lot more a whole lot quicker than I meant it to,' he said.

She winced at the apology, glanced at him from the corner of her eye and found him staring stolidly out to sea. She grimaced, shuffled, and finally gave in, huffing out a breath. 'Yeah, well, it takes two to tango. It was just as much my fault as yours.'

He straightened and surveyed her. She tried not to picture what he must see—a clumsy giant of a woman. She remained in what she desperately hoped was a nonchalant, casual pose—a pose that proclaimed a kiss like that *hadn't* rocked her world. That kisses like that happened to her all the time and she was used to them.

Ha! If kisses like that happened to her all the time she'd be…

A very satisfied woman.

You mean a nervous wreck.

'I don't want to give you the wrong signals, Jo.'

She turned her head to stare at him. *Oh, right. Here it comes.* Inside, she started to shrivel.

'I'm not in the market for a fling. At twenty I thought such things could be uncomplicated, but I don't believe that any more. And I'm not in the market for a relationship. My life is already too complicated. A relationship would be one complication too many.' He swallowed and shuffled his feet. 'I…uh…hope you're okay with that.'

Men really were the most arrogant creatures. She straightened. 'Well, it might surprise you to hear that I'm not in the market for a relationship either—and I can't possibly imagine what gave you the idea that I was.'

He glared. 'You decided you had room in your life for a dog. It seems only logical a boyfriend would be next.'

Her jaw dropped. She hauled it back into place. She opened her mouth, then with a shake of her head snapped it shut. She moved to the door instead. 'I'm sure there's cleaning I should be doing.'

'So, we're okay?' Mac asked as she reached the door.

She folded her arms and turned. 'I don't know what *we* you're referring to, but I can tell you one thing—if I *were* in the market for a boyfriend, Mac, it wouldn't be with a man like you.'

His eyes practically bugged from his head. All his life

he'd probably had women falling over themselves for him. She had no intention of being one of them.

'This—' she gestured to the view and their surroundings '—is beyond beautiful. It's glorious. But you don't even seem to notice it, let alone appreciate it. You hide from life.' She'd had enough of hiding. 'Life's too short. I mean to live my life to the full and I'm not giving that up for any man.'

Not even for one as pretty as Mac.

'Then what the hell are you doing out here?'

'I'm having a breather—but I'm not hiding.' She flung out an arm. 'I relish that view every single moment I can. I'm learning to cook fancy French food. I'm adopting homeless dogs and driving fast cars. I suspect I've lived more in the last three days than you have in the last three months.'

He gaped at her.

There didn't seem to be much more to say so she whirled into the house and didn't stop until she came to the kitchen. And then she didn't know what to do. She'd already cleaned it after making that reduction.

She put the jars of honey and peanut butter that still stood on the table back into the pantry. She slammed her hands to her hips. She'd left the plate of sandwiches on the veranda, along with their glasses. She didn't feel like going back out there and facing him yet.

She could spout off all she liked about how she didn't want a relationship and she didn't do flings, but one look at the broad span of his shoulders and her blood surged, her thighs weakened and her resolve threatened to dissolve.

Almost against her will she tiptoed back down the hallway to the front door. She peered out through the screen door, but Mac was nowhere to be seen. With a sigh of relief she retrieved the dishes, spying Mac and Bandit halfway across the field leading down to the sand dunes and beach.

He moved with an unconscious grace and—

Argh! She stomped back into the house and then jumped when the hall phone—an ancient contraption—rang.

Russ, no doubt. She set the dishes on the floor and picked up the receiver. 'Hello?'

A quick intake of breath greeted her. 'Who are *you*?'

Jo blinked. Not Russ, then, but an angry female. It hadn't occurred to her but, despite Mac's protestations, was there some woman waiting for him in the wings? Some woman he was dangling until—?

She shook her head. She might only have known him for a few days but that seemed seriously unlikely.

She cleared her throat. 'May I ask who's speaking, please?'

'This is Mrs Devlin.'

Jo rested back against the wall, her stomach twisting.

'You may have heard of my son, Ethan Devlin?'

The apprentice burned in the accident.

Jo closed her eyes. 'Yes, of course. I'm terribly sorry about what happened to your son, Mrs Devlin.'

'Put that low-life swine Mac on the phone.'

Mrs Devlin's bitterness threatened to burn a hole right through the receiver. Jo managed to swallow. 'I'm sorry, but he's not available at the moment. Can I take a message?'

'What do you mean, he's not there? He should be *working*! And who the hell are *you*, my girl? His fancy woman?'

Wow. Just...*wow!* 'My name is Jo Anderson and I'm Mac's housekeeper—*not* his girlfriend. I don't appreciate the insinuation and nor do I deserve your rudeness.'

The sudden silence almost deafened her. 'He doesn't deserve the luxury of a housekeeper,' Mrs Devlin said, though her voice had lost the worst of its edge. 'He doesn't deserve a moment of peace.'

Jo dragged a hand through her hair. If Mac had been bearing the brunt of this woman's bitterness then no wonder he'd been driving himself so hard. She saw it then, in that moment—Mac was punishing himself. He refused to notice the glorious views, he refused to engage in physical activity he found pleasurable, he shut himself off from the things he loved, like his car, his brother…his cooking.

Oh, Mac.

'He needs to send more money. Tell him that. Where is he anyway?'

'He's out walking the dog.' Not that it was any of her business.

'He has a *dog*?' Outrage laced her words.

'It's my dog. And, Mrs Devlin?' she said, before the other woman hung up. 'I… Look, Mac is working so hard he's in danger of becoming ill.'

'He *should* suffer!' the other woman yelled down the line. 'He should suffer the way he's made other people suffer!'

Such venom. She understood Mrs Devlin's fear and concern for her son. She understood her fighting for the very best care he could get. But to blame Mac like this? It was wrong. So wrong.

To say as much would be pointless. Mrs Devlin didn't want to listen to reason. Not yet. But what if she was to become afraid that the cash cow might dry up?

Jo hauled in a breath, wishing her stomach would stop churning. 'If Mac does become ill, Mrs Devlin, the money for Ethan's care will dry up.'

'How dare you—?'

'All I'm doing is stating facts. You want Mac to suffer—that much is clear—but if he does get sick he won't be able to earn money.' Certainly not the kind of money they were talking about here. 'My job is to make sure he eats three square meals a day and gets out into the fresh air for some exercise. Basically, I just nag him. I doubt he enjoys it.'

But even after only a few days of this routine Mac was starting to look better.

'What are you trying to say to me?' the other woman asked stiffly.

'What I'm saying is that, for the moment at least, you need to choose between your desire for revenge and your son's care. If you choose the latter then I suggest you ease up on the venom for a bit.'

The phone was slammed down.

'Well…' She grimaced at the receiver before setting it back in place. 'That went well.'

Mac stomped across the fields. What on earth had possessed him to kiss Jo? From the first moment he'd clapped eyes on her he'd sensed that she'd be dynamite, that given half a chance she'd blow his life apart.

He clenched his hands to fists. That couldn't happen from a single kiss.

Except it hadn't been a single kiss but a full-on necking session that had hurtled him back to his teenage years, when he'd first discovered girls and sex. Kissing Jo had shaken him to his absolute foundations.

Bandit barked and spun in a circle—first one way and then the other. 'Okay, okay,' he grumbled, moving towards the sand dunes. 'Go for a swim, then.'

Bandit didn't need any further encouragement. Mac settled at the same spot where he and Jo had sat yesterday and raked both hands back through his hair. Okay, so those kisses had rocked his foundations, but they hadn't toppled them. As long as he didn't kiss her again he'd be fine.

He gave a low laugh. Kiss her again? The look she'd flung at him before she'd flounced into the house had told him she'd squash him like a bug if he so much as tried. Man, how he'd like to take up that challenge—to make her sheath her claws, to stroke her until she purred and—

He swore. She made him want all the things he'd turned his back on—all the things he couldn't have.

Bandit, damp and sandy, raced up the beach to fling himself at Mac, leaping onto his lap and covering his face in sloppy dog kisses. The show of affection took Mac off guard, but he put his arms around the dog and held him close. It was a warm body, and at that moment Mac found he needed a warm body.

Eventually the dog settled beside him.

'So you've decided to love someone else, huh?' Mac scratched Bandit's back and the dog groaned his pleasure. 'You should've chosen Jo, you know? She's a much better proposition.'

How would she take it when she realised the dog had chosen *him* as his new owner? He suspected some part of her had already realised, but…

He folded his arms across his knees and rested his chin on them. She'd take it as more proof that she wasn't good enough, that she'd been overlooked once again.

He lifted his head and glared at the glorious breakers rolling in. Why on earth couldn't she see how gorgeous she was? She'd mentioned something about her grandmother and great-aunt having a challenging relationship. Did that extend to her as well? Did they make her feel she hadn't measured up? A scowl lowered through him. Or had some jerk made her doubt her own loveliness?

So what if she wasn't one of those little stick figures who paraded around in tiny dresses and squealed that a carrot stick would make them gain weight? It was no fun cooking for those women. It would be fun to cook for Jo, though.

If he still cooked.

He blew out a breath. If he'd met Jo before all this had happened…

But he hadn't.

He clenched a handful of sand in his fist before releasing it. He couldn't imagine going through his entire life believing he was completely unattractive to the opposite sex.

He'd been lucky. Until the accident. Now he could definitely relate. No woman would look twice at him—

He froze.

Jo had. In fact Jo had kissed him with so much unbridled hunger and joy that... Well, it meant he'd been mistaken. There was at least one beautiful woman who found him desirable enough to kiss. He scowled. Even if she had discounted the possibility of something deeper and more permanent with him.

You discounted it first.

He swallowed. He'd kissed her and she'd given him an unexpected gift. She'd made him realise that other people might see beyond his scars too.

Which was a moot point if he never left this place. But if he ever did manage to pay off his debts? Well, it would matter then. Either way, it had lightened something inside him.

Could he make her realise she was beautiful too?

How? Not by kissing her, that was for sure. That would lead to too much trouble and too much heartbreak. Until he could guarantee Ethan would be looked after for the rest of his life Mac wasn't free to offer any woman his heart.

But it didn't stop him from liking the way she looked. He loved her height, her stature, and the way she held herself. She was strong and powerful—a force to be reckoned with. And she'd fitted into his arms as if she'd been designed to be there.

He turned to Bandit. 'How can I prove to her that she's gorgeous?'

Bandit merely rolled onto his back, presenting his belly for a rub. Mac stared. 'Bandit! You're not a boy dog!' He ran his hand over the fur of Bandit's tummy. 'You're a girl dog.'

He ran both hands gently over Bandit's tummy and started to laugh.

'You're a girl dog who I *think* is expecting puppies.'

CHAPTER SIX

MAC FOUND JO in the kitchen and opened his mouth to give her the news about Bandit, eager to get things on an easy footing between them again and hoping this latest news would push the memory of their kiss—kisses—to the nether regions of their minds, where it would never see the light of day again.

Jo beat him to the punch, though. 'You had a phone call,' she said, without preamble.

She didn't smile, and his nape and his top lip both prickled with sudden perspiration. There was only one person who called the house phone. Russ and his friends had his mobile number, though they usually resorted to email.

'Mrs Devlin,' she said—unnecessarily, though she couldn't know that.

'How…?' He swallowed. 'How's Ethan doing?'

'She didn't say.'

A weight settled across his shoulders. He pulled out the nearest chair and fell into it. 'Did she want me to ring her back?' Which was a ridiculous question. Of course she'd want him to return her call.

'She didn't say.'

He stared at her and she finally turned from where she was rinsing a few dishes and shrugged.

'She hung up on me.'

He closed his eyes. He could imagine the conclusion Diana Devlin had come to upon hearing a woman's voice at the end of his phone—especially a voice as rich and honeyed as Jo's.

When he opened his eyes he found a glass of water sitting in front of him. He drained it.

'She's a cheery soul, isn't she?'

'Jo, she's spent the last few months in fear for her son's life and now she fears for his future. There isn't much in her life to feel cheerful about.'

'Garbage.' She dried a plate. 'Her son's alive, isn't he? That's something to be grateful for. His recovery is coming along nicely, isn't it? Another thing to be grateful for.'

'He'll bear the scars from this accident for the rest of his life.'

'Oh, for heaven's sake—we're not going to have this argument again. Ethan's mother will love him no matter what he looks like.'

She bent down to place the plate in a cupboard and Mac got an eyeful of the curve of her hips. His heart started to pound. Jo had the kind of hips that could make a man salivate. He dragged his gaze to the glass he twirled between his fingers. He lifted it to his lips and managed to find another drop or two, but they did nothing to ease the thirst coursing through him.

Jo turned around. He kept his gaze on the glass.

'All I can say,' she said, 'is that I wouldn't want her in *my* sick room.'

Slowly he lifted his head to stare at her. She squeezed out the dishcloth and wiped down the table, not meeting his eyes. As far as he could tell the table was perfectly clean as it was, but he lifted both the glass and his arms out of her way and did his best not to draw the scent of her into his lungs.

'She's his mum. She'll be his best source of support…' He trailed off. He hadn't thought about it before. Not in that context. Ethan *was* doing okay, wasn't he?

For the first time he wished he hadn't so comprehensively cut himself off from his colleagues on the show.

He rose. 'I'll…um…' For heaven's sake—he didn't have to justify his every movement to her.

Turning on his heel, he strode out of the kitchen and headed upstairs. Seizing his mobile from the desk he punched in Mrs Devlin's number. As he waited for her to answer he glanced at the curtains. He moved to close them, to shut out the day, and then stopped. He didn't have the heart for it. What difference would a bit of sunlight make? Even if Mrs Devlin cared, she'd never have to know.

'Malcolm,' she said, obviously having checked her caller ID before answering. She never called him Mac. She never said hello. She just said Malcolm.

'How are you, Mrs Devlin?'

She didn't answer him. She usually made some sarcastic comment—*How did he think she was, sitting at her son's sick bed day in day out?*

While he welcomed the silence he forced himself to push on. 'I understand you rang earlier?'

He waited for her to demand to know who Jo was and what she was doing in his house. He could imagine her sarcasm when he told her Jo was his temporary house-keeper. It would be something along the lines of *It's nice for some.*

'I wanted to tell you that this quarter's bills have come in.'

He closed his eyes. This lot would just about clean him out. To receive a much-needed portion of his advance he had to get something substantial to his publisher. *Soon.* That would cover the next quarter's costs. After that… He swallowed. If necessary he'd sell the car, his Sydney apartment. And then this house.

And if Ethan's treatment needed to continue after that… He rested his forehead against the glass sliding door, welcoming its coolness against his skin. They'd better hope this cookbook did well. *Really* well.

'Malcolm?'

It hit him that her voice lacked its usual stridence, though it could by no means be considered friendly.

'Please send the bills to my lawyer. I'll take care of them.' His heart pounded. 'How's Ethan?'

'He's doing as well as can be expected.'

It was her standard line whenever he asked. And he always asked. He didn't ask her to send his best to the younger man. She'd made it clear that Ethan wanted nothing to do with him.

'How...?' She cleared her throat. 'How are *you*?'

He nearly dropped the phone. He coughed and swallowed back his automatic reply—*fine*. That would seem a mockery, considering Ethan's condition. 'I...I'm working hard at wrestling this cookbook into shape.' She knew he meant all its profits to go to Ethan.

'Right. Goodbye, Malcolm.'

'Uh...goodbye.'

He stared at the phone. Normally she hung up without so much as a by-your-leave. What on earth was going on?

He threw the phone back to the desk and dragged a hand through his hair. Was everything really okay with Ethan? Had he suffered some setback? He paced across the room. Could Diana have said something to Jo? Who knew? Maybe they'd had a moment of woman-to-woman bonding. Maybe—

'She's a cheery soul, isn't she?'

Hell.

He clattered back down the stairs. Jo wasn't in the kitchen. She wasn't in the living or dining rooms either, but as he walked through the house he couldn't help noticing how light and airy it all seemed. The curtains were pulled back and sunlight poured in at freshly cleaned windows. The heavy wooden furniture gleamed, the rugs were plush underfoot, and plump scatter cushions invited him to recline on the sofa. Not that he spent any time in this part of the house any more.

Why not?

He ground his teeth together. His life consisted of eat, sleep and work. It didn't leave room for loafing on the sofa in front of the television.

He pushed out to the veranda and strode halfway down the steps to survey the view in front of him. But there was no sign of a tall, lush woman striding down that field of native grass, or along the beach with Bandit. Maybe she was pegging laundry on the line. He turned back.

'Are you looking for me?'

He started at the voice to his left and found Jo on her knees, pulling weeds from a garden bed. He was pretty sure that wasn't part of her job description.

He nodded towards the few spindly rose bushes. 'I'm not sure you need to worry about those.'

'I want to.'

Whatever... He planted his legs. 'What did you say to Mrs Devlin?'

'Ah.' She went back to digging. 'I told her to wake up to herself.'

He choked. 'You *what*?' He dropped to the bottom step, head in hands. 'Hell, Jo, the poor woman has been worried half out of her wits and—'

'I said it in a nice way.'

He lifted his head.

'I didn't say the actual words, *Wake up to yourself.*'

That had been her message, though.

'She had a big go at me for being here. I didn't like her insinuation, so I set her straight.'

He opened his mouth. After a moment he shut it again. He deserved everything Diana threw at him, but Jo didn't. She'd had every right to defend herself, to demand respect.

'When she started mouthing off that you didn't deserve the luxury of a housekeeper I…' She shrugged.

'You what?'

'I told her you were working so hard you were in danger of falling ill. And I made it clear that if that happened you wouldn't be able to earn. And that, therefore, her cash cow would dry up.'

'Tell me you put it nicer than that?'

'I expect I did.' She dusted off her hands and rested back on her heels. 'Like you, she's been focussing on all the wrong things.'

His mouth dried. What else had Jo said to the poor woman?

'I told her she needed to choose between her desire for revenge on you and what was best for her son.'

He clenched his jaw so hard he thought he might crack a tooth. 'I wish you'd kept your mouth shut.'

She rose and planted her hands on her hips, towering over him. Her chest rose and fell, her eyes flashed, but even when she was angry her voice washed over him like a balm.

'She's turned you into her whipping boy. What's worse is that you've let her.'

He shot to his feet. 'I owe that family!'

'Codswallop!' She glared. 'Next you're going to tell me you're responsible for the national debt and world hunger.'

'Don't be ridiculous.'

'What did you do that was so bad, huh? You yelled at an apprentice. Even if it hadn't been scripted, we've all been hauled over the coals by our bosses before. In the view of things that you're taking one could equally accuse Ethan of being a spineless little ninny. I mean *he's* the clumsy clod who dropped a tray of cold food into hot oil.'

He couldn't believe what he was hearing.

'I'm yelling at you now, but if you trip up the stairs in a huff and sprain an ankle is that going to be *my* fault? I don't think so, buster.'

'That's different. We're equals!' he hollered back. 'On set I had seniority, and that boy—'

'Oh, and that's another thing that's getting up my nose. You keep referring to Ethan as a boy—but he's nineteen years old. He's a man. He has the right to vote and he has the right to choose what kind of work he wants to do. He *chose* to work with you. He *wanted* to be a part of your team. You wanted your show to be a success, and you've been blaming your ambition for the accident. You forget that Ethan wanted the show to be a success too—why else was he there?—but you don't take *his* ambition into account.'

His mind whirled at her words, but he lifted his chin and set his shoulders. None of that made a scrap of difference.

'No,' she carried on, 'you won't take *any* of that into account, will you? It's much easier to carry on the way you have been.'

Something inside him snapped. 'Easier!' He started to shake with the force of his anger. 'Tell me how any of this is easy?' he yelled. 'Every day—*every single day*—I have to fight the urge to go driving in my glorious car, resist the impulse to go down to the beach and relish the feel of salt water against my skin, turn my back on the desire to race into the kitchen and try out a new recipe that's exploded into my mind!'

With each named temptation he flung his arm out as he paced up and down in front of the garden bed.

'I chain myself to my computer all day to write a book I should be qualified and competent to write. But instead I find myself battling with it as if it's an enemy that's determined to bring me down. So will you kindly tell me how any of that is *easy*?'

She moved to stand in front of him. She stood on a slightly higher piece of ground than he did so she was almost eye to eye with him.

'It's easier than facing the consequences of the accident.'

Ice crept across his scalp.

'It's easier than attempting to rebuild your life.'

He didn't have a life, and for as long as Ethan remained in hospital he didn't deserve a life.

She gave a mirthless laugh, as if she'd read that thought in his face. 'You really feel *that* responsible for Ethan?'

That wasn't worth dignifying with an answer.

'Then this—' she gestured all around '—is easier than meeting with Ethan face to face, easier than witnessing his struggles, and easier then offering him the true moral support of a friend.'

He had to swallow before he could speak, and he felt every last drop of anger draining away. 'I have it on good authority that the last thing Ethan wants is to clap eyes on me.'

'Ethan's mother is *not* a good authority—and if you think she is then you're an idiot.'

He couldn't speak past the lump that had stretched his throat into a painful ache.

'Have you even spoken to Ethan yourself?'

He hadn't. Diana had demanded that he not plague her son, that Mac leave Ethan in peace. Call him a coward, but he hadn't *wanted* to speak to Ethan—hadn't wanted to hear the boy's recriminations.

'A real man would show up and say sorry.'

It was Russ's voice that sounded in his head now. He shied away from the thought, from what it demanded of him. What good would facing Ethan do for either one of them? He would do whatever he could not to upset the younger man. But he *could* check up on him—see how he was doing. He could ring Terry, the creative director, or one of the producers of the show. He'd bet someone from the old team would know.

He could at least ring. Not Ethan, but one of the others. How hard could that be?

'I do have one final burning question.'

He blinked himself back into the here and now to find Jo halfway up the steps to the house.

'Precisely what calamity do you think will befall us—' she shot the words over her shoulder '—if you *did* go for a drive in your car, or went for a swim, or if you *did* go and cook some delicious meal?'

She didn't wait for an answer but continued straight into the house on those long, strong legs of hers.

'So that was a hypothetical question, then?' he muttered. Good. Because he didn't have an answer for it.

Jo sensed the exact moment when Mac loomed in the dining room's doorway. She didn't turn from where she'd set down dishes of new potatoes and buttered green beans.

'You're just in time. Take a seat.'

'On one condition.'

She turned at that. 'What?'

'That we call a truce and promise not to holler at each other for the next hour.'

The tension in her shoulders melted away. 'Make it two and you have yourself a deal.'

His lips lifted. Not quite a smile, but almost. Maybe they'd achieve one by the end of the meal.

He took a seat. 'Did you have any trouble with my instructions?'

'I don't think so. Proof is in the pudding, though, so to speak.'

She went to retrieve their steaks, oddly nervous as she set his plate in front of him.

He helped himself to potatoes and beans. Jo dug straight

into her steak, slathered in béarnaise sauce. She closed her eyes. *Oh, dear Lord, the sauce was to die for.* She'd be lining up for his cookbook the moment it came out.

'You've overcooked your steak.'

She opened her eyes. 'Try yours.'

He did.

'And?' she prompted.

'It's perfect.'

'For you, maybe.' She wrinkled her nose. 'I prefer my steak properly cooked—not underdone, the way you seem to like it.'

'This is *not* underdone. It's how steak should be cooked.'

'And the sauce?'

He frowned. 'You've cooked it a little too long and it's started to separate.'

Truly? She stared at it.

'It's a pity about the tarragon vinegar, and you used too much onion to flavour the reduction, but only an experienced foodie would know.'

He frowned at her steak again, but she ignored the silent censure. 'Relax, Mac.' She reached for the beans. 'I'm actually pretty chuffed with my efforts—and that's the point, isn't it?'

He blinked.

'I mean the people who try out your recipes—they're going to adjust them to their own tastes, right? Like I did with my steak?'

'I guess.'

'But as long as they feel they've created a nice meal they're going to be happy, aren't they? Mission accomplished.'

He straightened as if she'd zapped him. 'You're right. Nobody's going to be assessing their creations with a mark out of ten.'

'Uh, no.'

She tried not to focus on the shape of his lips, or the scent of coconut that came from his still-damp hair. Hair that was a touch too long. Hair that had felt glorious when she'd run her fingers through it and—

She reached for her glass of water and drained it.

'I think I've been getting too hooked up on every detail.'

He really did need to let up a bit.

'But as long as my targeted audience is satisfied then that's the best I can hope for.'

Yup.

He suddenly grinned. Her heart skidded, and then settled to pound too hard too fast. She took back her earlier wish that he'd smile. She wished he wouldn't. Why couldn't her heart just behave normally around him?

'So, have you come any closer to discovering your new career path today?'

This had become a habit—at dinnertime he'd throw suggestions at her about a new vocation.

'Go on—thrill me,' she said. *Not literally.*

'Chef?'

She wrinkled her nose. 'I expect I'd need to like cooking for that.'

'You don't like to cook?'

'I never became interested in it until I started watching your show. Russ made all of us watch it.' She blew out a breath. 'But I'm afraid you're not going to make a convert of me. It's all far too fiddly for my liking.'

'Gardener, then?'

'It's a pleasant enough way to while away an hour or two, but a whole day of it? A whole week of it? Month after month? No, thanks.'

Bandit pattered into the dining room. 'Then maybe you'd like a stint as a dog breeder?' Mac's grin suddenly widened. 'It could be the perfect fit. I discovered today that Bandit is, in fact, Bandita.'

'What?'

'He is a she. Bandit is a girl dog.'

Her jaw dropped. 'You're joking?'

'I take it you didn't check before you agreed to adopt him…uh…her?'

She stared at the dog. 'It never occurred to me to check. I mean he's…she's…fluffy, and has lots of fur, and it's not like it's…um…obvious. I just—'

She folded her arms and glared. 'That nice old man told me Bandit was a boy.'

'I suspect "that nice old man" has taken you for a ride.'

'Why, though? What's the big deal if Bandit is a boy or a girl? It certainly makes no difference to me, and—'

She broke off at his laughter. He looked so different when he laughed.

She moistened her lips. 'What?'

'Bandit is a girl dog who I suspect is going to be a mother in the not too distant future.'

'Noooo…'

'Yes.'

'So that nice old man was just trying to fob Bandit off onto some poor sucker?'

'Bingo.'

And she was the sucker.

She stared at Bandit. She stared at Mac. 'We're going to have puppies?'

'Looks that way.'

Puppies? She grinned. She ate some more steak. 'Well, that'll be fun.' In the next instant she stiffened. 'What else did that rotten old man lie about? Is she microchipped? Has she had her vaccinations?' She set her knife and fork down. 'Well, that's that, then.'

Mac frowned. 'That's what?'

'It means I'll have to take her to the vet's tomorrow for a thorough check-up.'

'It wouldn't hurt,' he agreed.

She found herself grinning again. 'Puppies, huh? Do you think there's any money in dog breeding?'

'Not really.'

Oh, well. She'd think of something on the job front soon enough.

She gestured to the food. 'I don't think this effort has disgraced me.'

'Absolutely not.'

But he didn't meet her eye as he said it. Her heart started to thump. There was loads of time yet to learn all she needed to know about *macaron* towers.

She swallowed. Béarnaise sauce one day. *Macarons* the next.

'What on earth are you trying to do?'

Jo turned at Mac's voice. Bandit twisted out of her grasp and ran a few paces away, where she turned to glare at Jo. Jo let a growl loose from her throat. 'I'm trying to get Bandit into The Beast.' She gestured to her car. 'But Bandit doesn't seem too enamoured with the idea of going for a ride. Either that or it's the V-word—V. E. T.—that has her spooked.'

She pushed her hair off her face, thinking she must look a sight before telling herself that it didn't matter one iota what she looked like.

'For heaven's sake, how hard can it be? I'm bigger than her. I'm stronger than her. And if you make one derogatory comment about my intelligence in comparison to hers you'll be getting fish fingers for dinner.'

He raised his hands. 'No comments, derogatory or otherwise. I'm hoping for a cheese soufflé. I just put the recipe on the kitchen counter.'

She hoped it would taste as good as the words sounded

coming from his lips. 'Do I need to pick up any exotic ingredients?'

'Not for today—but you'll need these for later in the week.'

He handed her a shopping list. Wrapped inside it was some housekeeping money.

'Here, Bandit.' He clicked his fingers and Bandit was at his side in an instant.

Jo scowled. Typical female. She rolled her shoulders. Actually, when she thought about it, she couldn't fault Bandit's taste.

'Up.' He patted the front passenger seat and Bandit leapt up and settled there. Mac turned back to Jo. 'There you go. I'll see you when you get back.'

He started to walk away and Bandit immediately leapt down to follow him.

'Ahem…'

Mac turned at Jo's cleared throat. He shook his head. 'C'mon, Bandit, let's try that again.'

This time when Bandit was seated in the car Mac shut the door. But when he started to walk away Bandit set up a long, mournful howl.

'Don't cry, lovely girl.' Jo reached into the window to pat her. 'It's okay.'

None of which made the slightest difference. Bandit continued to howl.

Jo swung back to Mac. 'She's pregnant. I'm pretty sure that means she's not supposed to get upset.'

He lifted both arms. 'What do you want me to do about it?'

'It's more than obvious what needs to happen.'

'What's that?'

'You're going to have to come with us.'

Mac's face shuttered. 'That's out of the question.'

Jo took one look at him and had to rest her hands on her

knees for several long moments. Pulling in a breath that helped haul her upright, she opened the car door to release Bandit—who leapt down in an instant.'

'I'm sorry, beautiful girl.' She went to fondle Bandit's ears, but the dog dodged away from her and for some reason it cut her to the quick. It was all she could do not to cry.

'What are you doing?'

Disbelief was etched across every line of Mac's face. A face, it occurred to her now, that had become a little too familiar to her.

She tried to swallow the lump in her throat, but only partially succeeded. 'I'm not going to put her through that kind of distress. Not while she's in such a delicate condition.' Her voice came out high and tight, due to the lump. 'She'll hurt herself, or spontaneously abort. Or...' She shook her head, her stomach churning. 'I'm not going to be responsible for that.'

She walked past Mac and tried to hold her head up high. 'But... But...' he spluttered.

She stopped and waited, but he didn't say any more. She turned. 'Are you waiting for me to bully you? If you are you'll be waiting a long time. You're an adult. You know what's right and wrong.'

His jaw went tight and a tic started up beneath his right eye.

'I'm going to conserve my energy for when I have to contend with Bandit *and* her puppies when I eventually leave.' That was going to be awfully traumatic for poor Bandit. The thought made her stomach churn even harder.

'You can't take her when you leave.'

Jo started to stalk away, but he strode after her.

'She loves it here. Jo, I... Look, I know it's unfair, but she's adopted *me*—bonded with *me*. I didn't mean for it to happen.'

From the corner of her eye she saw the weak excuse for a smile that he shot her.

'I'll make a deal with you. You keep the puppies and Bandit stays here with me. I'll look after her—I promise.'

'Look after her?' She whirled to face him. 'You can't even take her to the vet! I can't in any conscience leave her here—even though she loves you and merely tolerates me. Even though I know she'll be way happier here than she will be with me.'

He took a step back from her, his mouth pressed so tight it turned his lips white.

'I don't know why I expected something better from you. You wouldn't even visit your brother when he was in hospital, though you had to know it was the thing he most wanted.'

He'd frozen to stone.

There was no room in his life for compassion or love or responsibility to his family…just a manufactured guilt that took over his every breathing moment.

She turned away, not knowing why her heart hurt so hard.

CHAPTER SEVEN

JO COUNTED OUT the eggs she'd need for the soufflé and had started to read the 'Hints on soufflés' section of a cooking website she'd found when voices floated in through the open front door.

Voices? She lifted her head and frowned. Surely not? She hadn't heard *voices*—as in more than one person speaking, having a conversation—since she'd arrived. She didn't count the way either she or Mac spoke to Bandit. Or her and Mac's often fraught and adversarial conversations.

He doesn't kiss like an adversary.

He kissed like a dream.

Stop it!

She cocked her head and listened harder. There was definitely more than one voice.

The voices grew stronger as she marched through the house. She pulled up short of the front door when she found Mac talking to an unknown man by the front steps—a man carrying what looked like a doctor's bag.

Mac didn't appear the least bit self-conscious. Could the man be an old friend?

She looked at the bag again and then it hit her. A *vet*! Mac had called out a vet.

She had to fight the urge to race outside and throw her arms around him. Oh, he'd love that, wouldn't he? *Not.* She straightened her shirt and then pushed outside as if it what was happening in front of her was the most normal thing in the world.

Could Mac conquer his fear of what the world thought of him one person at a time? She crossed her fingers behind her back.

She strode across the veranda. 'I thought I heard voices.'

'Jo, this is Daniel Michener. He's the local mobile vet.'

She hadn't considered for a moment that this area would warrant a mobile vet.

'There are a lot of hobby farms—not to mention dairy farms—in the area,' Daniel explained when she said as much. 'It's a bit hard to bring a cow, horse or an alpaca into the surgery.'

Which made perfect sense when she thought about it. 'Well, I'm really glad you can give Bandit a once-over.'

'I understand you adopted her and know nothing of her history?'

Jo grimaced. 'I was told she was a purebred seven-year-old male border collie, microchipped, neutered, and fully vaccinated.'

He laughed. 'Let's take a look at her, then.'

Mac played veterinary nurse, soothing Bandit and convincing her to co-operate with Daniel. He made a rather nice veterinary nurse, with those big hands gentle on the dog's neck. She shivered at the way he'd run a hand down Bandit's back while talking to her in low, reassuring tones. The sight of the broad man with the small, fine-boned, not to mention *pregnant* dog made her heart pitter-patter.

He glanced up and caught her staring, raised an eyebrow. She shrugged and forced her gaze back to Bandit, tried to ignore the way her breath hitched in her chest.

The vet gave Bandit a clean bill of health. 'You should expect the puppies in about a month.' He clicked his bag shut. 'My best guess, looking at her teeth, is that she's three years old—and this is not her first litter, so she'll probably be a good mother.'

Not her first?

She moved in a little closer and Mac's scent—all warm cotton, coconut and dog—hit her. It was all she could do not to swoon. She had to step back again.

'Can you tell how many puppies she's going to have?'

He shook his head. 'With a border collie, though, you can expect somewhere between four and eight.'

Eight!

The vet handed her his bill. Mac stood beside her as they waved him goodbye.

'Can Bandit stay here with me?' Mac said without preamble. 'I promise I'll look after her.'

'Yes.'

He plucked the bill from her fingers. 'She's my dog now, so I'll take care of her bills.' He strode back towards the house. 'But those puppies, Jo…' he called over his shoulder. 'They're all yours.'

Puppies? She smiled. *Eight* puppies? She groaned. What on earth would she do with eight puppies?

Maybe Russ would like one after he'd recovered from his surgery. Weren't pets supposed to be good for people— a form of therapy?

She bit back a sigh. What Russ really needed was a visit from his brother.

Mac ostensibly studied the cheese soufflé that Jo had set on the table, but all the time his mind whirled. Tomorrow Jo would have been here for a week. *What did she mean to tell Russ?*

He glanced at her. She wiped her hands down the sides of her jeans. 'Does it pass muster?'

He pulled his attention back to the soufflé. 'On first glance, yes. It's a nice colour.'

She folded her arms, narrowing her eyes.

'Okay, okay.' He raised his hands. 'I'd want it higher and fluffier if you were one of my apprentices—but you're not. This is the very first time you've made a soufflé, right?'

'Right.'

'Then in that case it definitely passes muster.'

She sat and motioned for him to serve it.

He drew the warm scent of the soufflé into his lungs. 'It smells good.'

She leaned in closer to smell it too, her lips pursed in luscious plumpness. A beat started up inside him, making his hand clench around the serving spoon.

'So this whole food-assessing thing…it's a bit like wine-tasting? You check the colour of the thing, smell it and finally taste it?'

'Though in this instance one hopes it doesn't get spat back out.'

She sort of smiled. There hadn't been too many smiles from her in the last day and a half.

What was she going to tell Russ?

'I'm trying to get away from the demanding level of perfection that's necessary in a top-notch restaurant. The people who buy my book aren't cooking for royalty.' Not like he had. They'd be cooking for their eighty-five-year-old grandmothers. 'I'm correct in thinking, aren't I, that they just want to have some fun?'

'Fun.' She nodded, but he could tell she held back a sigh.

He shook his head. How was he going to teach her the intricacies of a *macaron* when she didn't even like cooking?

He pushed the thought from his mind and sampled a forkful of soufflé.

'Well?'

He'd give it to her straight. Somehow she sensed it whenever he fudged. And she didn't seem to mind the criticism. *Because she wants to get better.* Yes, but he wasn't sure her reasons for wanting to get better were going to help her conquer the laborious process of making a *macaron* tower. He shook that thought away. If she left tomorrow there'd be no need to figure that out.

The thought of her leaving filled him with sudden darkness. He moistened his lips. He didn't want her leaving because he wanted her to tell Russ that there was nothing to worry about. That was all.

He dragged his mind back to the soufflé. 'An accomplished soufflé should be lighter. You probably needed to whip the egg whites a bit longer. But it's very good for a first effort.'

'You mean it's passable?'

He needed to work on that whole giving-it-to-her-straight thing.

She sampled it too, and shrugged. 'I don't understand the difference between beating, whipping, creaming, mixing and all that nonsense.'

It wasn't nonsense.

'What's all that about anyway?'

He stared at her. 'Would it help if I put a glossary defining those terms in the book?'

'Yes!' She pushed her hair off her face. 'I mean *I'd* welcome one.'

Done.

'And could you also add a definite length of time for how long egg whites should be whipped?'

'That depends on the size of the eggs, the temperature of the room in which you're whipping them, the humidity in the air and any number of other factors.'

She stared at him. He wished he could ignore the intriguing shape of her mouth. He wished he could forget their softness and the spark they'd fired to life inside him.

'Mac?'

He jumped. 'What?'

'I just asked if you could include a photo, then, of what properly beaten egg whites should look like?'

He wrote that down on the pad he'd started to keep at his elbow when they had dinner. With the addition of Jo's suggestions, the cookbook finally felt as if it were taking shape. He just had to remember he wasn't writing a text-book for apprentices.

In the kitchen, the oven timer dinged. He frowned. 'What else are you cooking?'

She didn't answer. She was already halfway to the kitchen.

She returned with a pizza. One of those frozen jobs she'd shoved in the freezer after her first shopping trip. *What on earth...?*

She took one look at his face and laughed. 'I'm a carni-vore, Mac. I'm sure cheese soufflé with a vegetable medley is all well and good, in its place, but give me a meat lovers' pizza every time.'

She seized a slice and proceeded to eat it with gusto. His stomach tightened, his groin expanded, and it was all he could do not to groan out loud.

She tilted her chin at the pizza. 'Help yourself.'

'I haven't eaten that pap since I was a teenager. It's full of chemicals and MSG and—'

'You don't know what you're missing.' She suddenly grinned, and it made him realise how remote and subdued she'd been. 'Have a slice and I'll put you out of your misery.'

His chin came up. 'What misery?'

'What I'm going to tell Russ tomorrow.'

He didn't try pretending that it didn't matter. It mat-tered a lot.

Without another word he took a slice of pizza and bit into it. 'Yuck, Jo!' He grimaced and she laughed. 'This is truly appalling.'

If she liked pizza that much he'd make her a pizza that would send her soul soaring—

He would if he still cooked, that was.

She reached for a second slice. 'On one level I know that. Whenever I eat pizza from a restaurant I can tell how much better it is. But this…? I don't know—I still like it.'

He finished his slice and gazed at what was left.

'It's strangely satisfying. Addictive.'

She was right. He reached for a second slice and polished it off. 'What *are* you going to tell Russ?'

He watched as she delicately licked her fingers—eight of them. He adjusted his jeans. He drained his glass of water. *Don't look. Don't think. Don't kiss her again.*

She rose and opened the bottle of red wine sitting on the sideboard. He hadn't noticed it before. He didn't know if she was making him wait to punish him, or whether she was trying to gather her thoughts.

She handed him a glass of wine and sat. 'I'm going to tell Russ that you're one of the most pig-headed, stubborn men I've ever met. I'm going to tell him you argue every point, and that whenever your work is interrupted you have creative type-A tantrums that would do a toddler proud. I'm going to tell him that you sulk and scowl and swear under your breath. And I'm going to tell him you've stolen my dog.'

He stared at her and the backs of his eyes prickled and burned. 'I could kiss you.'

Everything she'd just said was designed to allay each and every one of Russ's fears. He couldn't have done better himself.

'I'm not going to tell him that.'

The air between them suddenly shimmered with a swirl of unspoken desires and emotions as the memory of the kiss they'd shared rose up between them. He knew she recalled it too, because her eyes dilated in exactly the same way as they had before he'd kissed her the last time.

And it had to be the last time. *Don't kiss her again!*

But the way her lips parted and her breathing became shallow…it could slay a man.

She dragged her gaze away and took a sip of wine, but even in the dim light he could see how colour slashed high on her cheekbones. He searched his mind for something to say.

'Do you really mind about Bandit?'

Her lips twisted. 'More than I should, I suspect. But not so much now I know there are puppies on the way.'

Her chin came up and her gaze lasered him to the spot.

'Can I ask you a question?'

He set his glass down. 'If I get to ask one of you in return.'

She twirled her glass in her fingers. Eventually she set her glass down too.

'Deal.'

He stiffened his shoulders, because he didn't expect her question would be an easy one. That was okay. Neither was his.

'Shoot.'

'Why won't you visit Russ?'

He tried to not let her words bow him. He should have known this was what she'd ask.

'It's funny…you don't seem a particularly vain man.'

He wasn't.

'But actions speak louder than words.'

What was she talking about?

'Are you really *that* afraid of showing your ugly mug to the outside world?'

At any other time he'd have laughed at the 'ugly mug'. He happened to know for a fact that she was rather partial to his particular 'ugly mug' no matter how much she tried to hide it. Except…

Was that what she really thought of him?

His shoulders slumped. 'I'm not vain, Jo.'

She gnawed at her bottom lip, but didn't say anything.

He dragged a hand down his face. 'I made a promise to Mrs Devlin that I would lie low and stay out of the limelight until Ethan was out of hospital. Tabloid journalists would hound me like a dog if they knew I was in Sydney.'

She opened her mouth, but he continued before she could voice her protests.

'They'd find out—no matter how quiet I tried to keep it.'

'Why did you make such a promise?'

'Because the media brouhaha surrounding me and the accident was seriously upsetting for Ethan.'

'And you wanted to do what you could to make things easier for him.'

'At the time I'd have done anything either he or his mother asked of me.' He still would. He leaned towards her. 'Why don't you think what I'm doing for Ethan is good enough?'

She reached out and twirled the stem of her wine glass in her fingers. 'Is that your question?'

Dammit! 'No.'

She didn't say a word. Just sat there like the rotten sphinx, sipping her wine. She picked a piece of pepperoni from the pizza and popped it into her mouth.

He watched the action, suddenly ravenously hungry. Their gazes clashed and she stilled mid-chew. For a moment she was all that filled his vision, and then she looked away.

'What's your question?'

Her voice came out high and thready. He knew why. The same frustration coursed through his veins and made his skin itch. Would a brief physical relationship really be such a bad idea?

He forced himself back in his seat, closed his eyes and drew a deliberate breath into his lungs. He opened his eyes, but the question on his tongue about the relationship between her, her grandmother and her great-aunt dissolved, to be replaced by an altogether different one.

He leaned towards her and her eyes widened at whatever she saw in his face. 'What I want to know, Jo, is why you're so convinced that you're not beautiful? Who or what made you feel that way?'

She glanced away, traced the edge of her placemat. She opened her mouth, but he cut her off.

'I want the truth.' Not the lie he could see forming on her lips. 'If you won't give me the truth then don't give me anything.'

She swallowed and met his gaze. He stared back. He knew how forbidding he must look, but he wanted her to know he was serious about this.

'We might not be able to explore the physical relationship I'm aching to explore with you, but out here in the boondocks we can at least be honest with each other.'

Eventually she nodded. 'Okay.'

She pushed her hair behind her ears and then drained what was left of her wine—which was a not inconsiderable half-glass.

'When I was in school I was always teased for being a giant. I might have been picked first for basketball games, but I was always picked last at school dances. Boys obviously didn't like to date girls who were taller than them.'

He grimaced. Kids could be cruel.

'But when I was nineteen and at university I fell madly in love with a chemistry student. I thought…I thought he had feelings for me.' Her knuckles turned white around her glass. 'It turned out, though, that I was a bet—a dare. It was some kind of Chemistry Club challenge—the guy with the ugliest date for the Christmas party won.'

Mac couldn't believe what he was hearing. 'He... You—'
He broke off, shaking all over.

'Me and some of the other girls caught wind of it and
dumped them all before the event, but...'

But it had made her doubt her beauty. And she'd been
doubting it ever since.

She refilled their glasses and handed him one, glancing up at him from beneath her fringe, her eyes bruised
and wounded.

'I don't want to talk about this, Mac. I answered your
question and the conversation is now over.'

'No!' He exploded out of his chair. 'I can't believe you've
let a bunch of immature jerks let you feel like this—made
you feel ugly and worthless. You're beautiful and you're
worth a million of them.'

'Go and see Russ, Mac, and then we can talk about this
as much as you like. But until then—zip it.'

She rose, collected their plates and strode into the
kitchen. He wanted to go after her, shake her and tell her
those boys had been wrong. He curled a hand around the
doorframe of the dining room before he could storm through
it. If he went after her he'd kiss her. And this time neither
one of them would stop.

He strode out to the front veranda, Bandit at his heels,
into the chill night. If only he could get his hands on those
cruel twerps. If only he could prove to her that she was
beautiful.

You can. Go see Russ. For her.

He sat on the top step and held his head in his hands.
That would mean something to her. But...

Go see Russ? Though he wanted to, with everything that
was inside him, he couldn't break his promise.

Jo searched for signs of pity in Mac's face the next day,
when he gave her a brand-new recipe to try out—coq au
vin—but couldn't see any.

What did disconcert her was the way his gaze rested on her lips and the answering hunger that rose through her. She didn't want to want this man. She wished she hadn't told him that nasty sordid tale last night. She wished she'd been able to resist his appeal for honesty. He made her feel far too vulnerable.

She gazed at the recipe and gave her brain a metaphorical kick. *Think of something halfway intelligent to say.*

'So, this needs to simmer for a long time?'

'That's right.'

'Simmer, boil, poach, stew—all that nonsense should probably go in your glossary of terms.'

He wrote that down on his notepad. 'A genuine simmer is just below boiling point, but where there's still the occasional bubble surfacing.'

Right. She filed the information away.

'C'mon—sit down,' he ordered, gesturing to the kitchen table. 'There's hours before you need to get the stew on to simmer.'

'There's a lot of chopping to do,' she said, referring to the recipe.

He switched on the laptop he'd brought downstairs with him. 'Jo, not even *you* need five hours to chop some chicken and vegetables.'

He had a point. If only she hadn't done the grocery shopping yesterday afternoon she could have used that as an excuse to avoid him now. She sat, but she'd have much sooner grabbed the broom and started sweeping the laundry, or headed outside for a spot of weeding.

Anything except being in the same room as him, sitting so close to him. And if he thought they were going to continue last night's conversation then he was going to be sadly disappointed.

'What do you want?'

He raised an eyebrow and she knew she wasn't being

particularly gracious—but then she didn't *feel* particularly gracious. She felt grumpy, out of sorts, frustrated…

She stuck her nose in the air. 'I'll have you know I'm very busy with important housemaidy things.'

His lips twitched. 'Do you think you can fit the making of tea into all that important housemaid business?'

With an exaggerated sigh, she rose and made tea while he fiddled around with his computer.

When she set the pot and two mugs on the table and took her seat again he said, 'We're going to take a vocational test.'

Something inside her started to shrivel. The sooner she worked out the next stage of her life the sooner she'd leave him in peace, right?

He fixed her with the clear blue of his eyes. 'You've helped me and now I want to help you.'

The shrivelling promptly stopped. He *wasn't* trying to get rid of her?

'Ready?'

She shrugged. 'I guess.'

He turned to the laptop. '"Are you more motivated by achievement or appreciation?"' he read.

She blinked. 'Um…' She liked to *see* the results of her hard work—as in the way Mac's house now currently shone after all her dusting and sweeping. 'Achievement.'

He leaned back in his chair with a frown. 'Are you sure?'

She glared back at him. 'Of course I'm sure.'

'Why do you want to make that *macaron* tower for your grandmother, then? Aren't you hoping to gain her appreciation and help her win a bet?'

What she really wanted to do was bring her grandmother and great-aunt's differences to an end. She knew they loved each other, so why couldn't they show it?

Because of her? She'd always been a bone of contention between them.

'Jo?'

She shook herself. 'Fine—whatever. Appreciation, then.'

His glare deepened. 'You have to take this seriously.'

She lifted her hands. 'I am.'

He glared at her for a few more seconds before returning to his computer. '"Do you tend to rely on your past experiences or on hunches?"'

She was tempted to fish a coin from her purse and toss it. 'Hunches...'

He checked the appropriate box just as she was about to change her answer. *Oh, well.*

'"Are you more interested in what is real or what is meaningful?"'

He stared at her. She stared back.

'Meaningful,' they said at the same time.

He asked her over sixty questions!

At the end he gave her a score. 'And that means... Hey!' he said when she took the computer from him.

She shook her head. 'Now it's your turn.' Let's see how he liked being put under the microscope. '"Do you tend to be easily distracted or able to concentrate well?"'

He glared. 'I can concentrate just fine when I want to.'

She checked the box for 'easily distracted'. As far as she could tell Mac actively *searched* for distraction.

'"In most situations do you rely more on careful planning or improvisation?"'

He dragged a hand down his face. 'Improvisation— more's the pity. Or these recipes I'm trying to drag out of my head would be a lot easier to commit to paper.'

'"Do you prefer step-by-step instructions or to figure things out for yourself?"'

He scowled. 'If only I *did* prefer step-by-step instructions!'

She was going to have to get him cooking again. Somehow.

When they'd finished she gave him a score and then read

out the associated job suggestions. '"Artist",' she said. Chef fitted into that category perfectly. '"Teacher. Entertainer."'

'Very funny.' He retrieved the computer.

She wasn't trying to be funny, but she kept her mouth shut.

'According to your score, you'd make a good girl scout. What *is* this garbage?'

'You tell me.'

'No, no—here we go. It says you'd be a good scientist.'

'Except I'm tired of being a scientist, remember?'

'You're tired of being a *geologist*,' he corrected. 'You could go back to university and major in a different science.'

'Yay,' she said, with a deplorable lack of enthusiasm. 'Also, I want to live in a city. Find me a job in one of those.'

'Why?'

'I want to go to the cinema, and the library, and to big shopping centres and all those lovely things.' All the places she'd missed when working in the Outback.

'Here we go. As you're apparently service-orientated you'd also make a good nurse.'

The sight of blood didn't worry her. But... 'I hate hospitals.'

He took on a sick pallor. 'Me too.'

And just like that she wanted to reach out and take his hand, offer silent support and comfort. He wouldn't welcome it. He'd probably kiss her in retaliation.

Ooh!

She pulled her hands into her lap. 'Well, that's certainly provided me with food for thought.'

'It was complete and utter nonsense!'

She smiled at him. 'I appreciate the effort.'

Finally—*finally*—he smiled back.

CHAPTER EIGHT

JO PULLED THE *macarons* from the oven and set the tray on a trivet. Hands on hips, she surveyed them. These weren't pretty, like the picture on the internet. They were crooked, misshapen and kind of flat. For the love of everything green and good! How hard could it be to make these fussy little confections?

She hunched over her laptop and reread the recipe, but she couldn't find where she'd gone wrong.

She'd made a halfway decent cheese soufflé. As far as she could tell her coq au vin had been good, even if Mac hadn't eaten very much of it. And, okay, so her béarnaise sauce hadn't held together the way it was apparently supposed to, but it had tasted just fine to her.

Her hands clenched. For a week now she'd been religiously following Mac's instructions and cooking recipes with names she couldn't even pronounce. She'd figured she was ready to try her hand at *macarons*.

She cast a glance at the tray and her lip curled. Apparently not.

Baring her teeth, she made a pot of tea and then pulled another egg carton towards her. She would master this if it was the last thing she ever did.

She separated eggs. She'd need to buy more. Luckily a nearby hobby farm sold farm-fresh eggs. The way she was going through the rotten things she'd be on a first-name basis with the owners of said hobby farm by the end of the week.

Mac strode into the kitchen, staring down at a sheet of paper in his hands. Tonight's recipe, she supposed. Yay, more cooking. She forgot all about cooking, though, when she noticed how amply he filled out his beaten-up jeans. The material stretched across strong thighs and she could almost see the muscles rippling beneath the denim.

He glanced up and froze when he saw what she was doing.

Her chin shot up. Well, bad luck, buddy! She'd been making his recipes for seven days now. *Seven days of cooking.*

He turned to leave. 'Don't even think about it.' Her voice came out on a snarl. He turned back and raised an eyebrow. 'Sit!' She pointed to a chair. She could see he was about to refuse. 'I will tie you to it if I have to.'

He blinked. His eyes turned dark and lazy. Deliberately his gaze lowered to her lips, all but caressing them. 'I'm almost tempted to put that to the test.'

She had to swallow. Wrestling with him would be so very intriguing.

And foolhardy.

She backed up one step and then another. She seized the tray of *macarons*. 'Look at these.'

He did, and then grimaced.

She dropped the tray to the table and swung away to pour him a mug of tea. She pushed it across the table towards him. 'Would you like a *macaron* to go with that?' she asked drily

His lips twitched, but he didn't sit. 'No, thanks.'

'Of course you don't. No rational person would touch one of those with a twenty-foot pole. Have you seen anything less appetising in your life?'

He took a hasty slug of his tea.

She glared. Why did this cooking gig have to be so

hard? 'If you say one more thing against my béarnaise sauce I'll…'

'Tie me up?'

Images pounded at her. 'Pelt you with my *macarons*.'

He laughed. It seemed like an age since he'd laughed. 'A fate worse than death.'

She tilted her chin at the tray. 'Those suckers would probably knock you out. Please, Mac, I need your help. Can you please, please, *please* tell me what I did wrong?'

He sat and pulled the tray towards him and something inside her chest started to flutter and thrash. *Two birds. One stone.* If she could get him to do something that was halfway related to cooking it would teach her a technique she obviously needed and maybe—just maybe—it would help him overcome his resistance to preparing food again. Maybe he would find his way back to his passion and find some comfort in losing himself in it for a while.

'I suspect you didn't beat the egg whites for long enough.'

There seemed to be a theme emerging there.

'Or perhaps you didn't use enough confectioners' sugar. Or you cooked them at too high a temperature.'

There were too many variables. With a growl she finished separating the eggs—a full dozen—and shoved the bowl and a whisk at him. 'Show me how it's done,' she demanded. 'There must be something wrong with my technique.'

His face closed up and his body drew in on itself, tight and unbending. 'You know I—'

'I'm ready to beg. And it's not real cooking, Mac. It's just whisking.'

And then it hit her—how she could keep him in the kitchen with her. She moistened her lips. 'I haven't really told you why it's so important that I master this stupid *macaron* tower, have I?'

'You mentioned the bet between your grandmother and great-aunt.'

She snorted. 'Ah, the bet. It wasn't our finest hour I'm afraid. My grandmother had been flicking through a magazine and came across a picture of one and made some throwaway comment. I said it was pretty. Great-Aunt Edith then said there was no way on God's green earth—her words—that I could make one for my grandmother's next birthday. Grandma, thinking she was standing up for me, said I could do it standing on my head.'

He winced.

'Naturally, of course, I said it'd be a piece of cake.' *What an idiot.*

'And then the pearls were put up as a stake…?'

'It's like something from a bad comedy.' And she was caught squarely in the middle.

'Why did you let yourself get drawn in?'

'Habit. But lately I've been thinking it's a bad habit all round—this adversarial bent we've developed.'

'It must've been there before you came along.'

'I guess so, but I want to do something to change it. I want to mend it.'

He leaned in towards her and her heart did some more of that fluttering and thrashing.

'You know the whole "Russ having a heart attack and me suddenly re-evaluating my life" stuff. I know they love each other. So…'

'How are you going to change it?'

'I don't know yet.'

'Isn't making a *macaron* tower just falling in with their continued rivalry?'

She shrugged. 'My plan so far is that I make the best damn *macaron* tower that's ever been seen and then I take the pearls and claim them for my own.'

He started to laugh. 'I suspect that'd be something to

see.' He sobered. 'But, Jo, isn't the necklace just the object of something that goes deeper between them?'

She slumped into a chair. 'I guess.'

'Tell me about them.'

So she did. She told him about Great-Aunt Edith first. 'I mean I know she loves me. And she's the one I most physically resemble. So it's odd—I can't understand why she's been on my case since, like, for*ever*. I shouldn't wear this and I shouldn't say that, and I shouldn't act like this and I shouldn't draw attention to myself like that, and I shouldn't wear my hair like this. On and on and on.'

It wore her out just thinking about it.

'It made me rebel in every dreadful way when I was a teenager. I wore tight pants and even tighter tops—things that didn't suit me. I'm afraid she was right on that subject.'

'And your grandmother?'

'My grandmother is the opposite. She's pretty, petite, and oh-so ladylike. She's stuck up for me forever, declaring I should wear, say and do whatever I damn well please—always telling me that I look gorgeous and pretty regardless of my get-up.' She glanced at Mac. 'And I'm afraid that's not always been the best advice to be given.'

It was her grandmother's vision that she'd never really been able to live up to.

He leaned back. 'They love each other, you say?'

'Oh, yes.' There wasn't a single doubt about that. 'But after one particularly vehement argument twelve months ago Great-Aunt Edith moved out.' Which was crazy. Her grandmother and aunt belonged together.

'Is it possible your great-aunt feels like you do—overshadowed by the petite women who surround her and made to feel she's never measured up?'

As far as Jo could tell, her great-aunt was indestructible.

Or was that just the attitude she assumed?

She sat up straighter.

'That attitude—it's wrong. You're a beautiful woman, Jo, which means your great-aunt must've been a great beauty too. But if she didn't believe herself beautiful, can you imagine how she must've felt, growing up with a sister who fitted into society's "classically beautiful" mould?'

Jo's throat tightened.

'If they love each other, as you say…'

'They do.' She might not be certain of much, but she was certain of that.

'Could it be that your grandmother is showing her love and acceptance for your great-aunt through you? If your great-aunt has felt overshadowed all these years then your grandmother treating you—the child who looks so like her much-loved sister—with adoration and such disregard for what the world thinks… Well, that's powerful stuff.'

Wow.

Things started to fall into place.

Holy Cow! 'I don't know what to say.'

His eyes narrowed. 'You're not going to cry, are you?'

She tipped up her chin. 'Most certainly not.'

And that was when she noticed that he was whisking her egg whites. A fist tightened about her heart even as she noticed that his technique was way better than hers. *Keep it casual.*

'Wouldn't it be easier to use an electric beater?'

He glared and she raised her hands. 'Sorry—is that some weird food purist thing?'

Humour lit his eyes although it didn't touch his lips. 'It *would* be easier.'

'But?'

'But this kitchen doesn't happen to be stocked with that kind of equipment.'

Oh, that sealed it. She was going out and buying an electric mixer first thing tomorrow.

'Here—you try.'

She took the bowl and tried to mimic his whisking action.

He didn't grimace, but she suspected he wanted to. 'It just takes a bit of practice,' he assured her.

She wished she felt reassured.

'Oh, for heaven's sake, Jo!' he exploded a moment later. 'That whisk isn't a hammer. You're trying to whisk air into those egg whites.'

She held the bowl out to him. He didn't shrink back, but she could see what was going through his mind.

She snapped, 'This isn't *real* cooking. It's just some stupid egg whites and a rotten whisk.'

He ground his teeth together, snatching the bowl from her. 'You have an attitude problem when it comes to the kitchen.'

Wasn't that the truth?

'Look—*this* is how you're meant to be doing it.'

He demonstrated what he meant. He looked so at home with a whisk—kind of commanding and…right. She could watch him do this all day.

'Why did you grow up with your grandmother and great-aunt?'

She'd answer all the questions he wanted if he'd just keep whisking.

'There was a twenty-year age difference between my father and my mother. When I was five, my mother left. I think she was tired of hanging out with older people. When she left, Grandma and Great-Aunt Edith moved in.'

'Do you still see your mother?'

'Occasionally.' She peered into the bowl. 'She lives in the UK now. Aren't they done?'

'No. Test it.'

He kept hold of the bowl but handed her the whisk. She swirled it through the mixture.

'See?' he said. 'It's not thick enough yet.'

Right… She glanced at the tray on the table. Well, that

was one question answered. She bounced up and measured out confectioners' sugar and set it on the table within Mac's easy reach.

'And your father?'

She wrinkled her nose. 'We're not close. He moved out to a bachelor pad when I was six. He's a geologist. I became a geologist because I thought it might give us something to talk about.'

'But?'

'But I don't like being a geologist—and if he has a problem with that then he can just suck it up.'

Mac stopped whisking to stare at her.

'Relationships are two-way streets. If he wants a proper relationship with me then he needs to put in an effort too.'

'You sound kind of well-adjusted on that?'

She simply shrugged.

'Here—test the mixture now.'

She did.

'Feel how much stiffer it is? That's what you're aiming for.'

Oh, okay. So that explained the cheese soufflé too…

Mac looked ready to leave again. She handed the whisk back to him.

'My father is what he is. Grandma and Great-Aunt Edith have raised me, loved me and stood by me even when we've all been at loggerheads with each other. They're my family and they're important to me. I don't want to think what my childhood would've been like if it wasn't for them.'

'And that's why you want to bring their silly feuding over the pearls to an end? And you think a *macaron* tower will help?'

'It can't hurt.'

'Well, there's a start.' He pushed the bowl over to her. 'Perfectly whisked egg whites.'

He stood.

He couldn't leave yet! She took the sugar she'd measured out earlier and went to tip the lot into the egg whites.

Mac's hand on her wrist stopped her. 'What are you doing?'

He sounded utterly scandalised.

She forced her eyes wide. 'I'm adding the sugar.'

'You're supposed to add it *slowly*.'

He proceeded to show her exactly how to add it, and how to beat it into the mixture. She might have feigned a bit more stupidity than necessary, but it was worth it to see him work. Surreptitiously she measured out the other ingredients and had them ready whenever he needed them.

She moistened her lips. *Keep telling him stories. Don't give him time to think about what he's doing.*

'Grandma and Great-Aunt Edith are the reason I want to move back to the city. They're eighty-five and eighty-three, respectively. I want to spend more time with them.'

He glanced up. 'So the cinemas, libraries, cafés—they're just…?'

'Attractive fringe benefits.'

He continued to stare at her. It took an effort not to fidget.

'They're getting on. They're independent, and in good health at the moment, but it won't last forever. When the time comes I want to care for them. They spent so much of their lives looking after me and…well, we're family and it matters.'

Russ's heart attack had taught her what the important things in life were and it wasn't a lesson she meant to forget.

Those blue eyes flashed and she swore she almost felt heat searing her skin.

'Are you trying to make me feel guilty about Russ?'

She blinked. 'Of course not.'

He pushed the bowl towards her and stood. 'I think you'll find your mix is ready.'

'Don't go, Mac. I'm not trying to make you feel bad about Russ. I tried that the other day and I'm not one to go back over old ground. I just wanted to make sure you knew how he felt—that while he won't say anything he's hurt that you haven't been to see him. Now that you do know the rest of it is up to you.'

'There is no "rest of it", Jo. There's nothing that can be done.'

'You could at least tell him why. You could at least acknowledge that you're letting him down and apologise. I understand you feel responsible for Ethan, but he's not the only person who needs you.'

This wasn't the way to make him stay.

She stuck out a hip. His gaze fixed on it for a heartbeat before returning to her face. She tried to control her breathing.

'Look, I'm doing my best with your rotten recipes, aren't I?'

'They're not supposed to be rotten.'

'Then why do I keep dreaming of fish-finger burgers?'

He adjusted his stance. 'Your point being…?'

'I'm trying to help you out, so the least you can do is sit there and watch as I try to shape this unholy mess into pretty little *macarons*. Give me tips where appropriate and whatnot.'

He folded his arms, lowered his gaze to her hip again. When he raised it his eyes had started to gleam. 'I'll do it for a boon.'

A…*what*?

'A kiss.'

Something inside her softened. He smirked. She hardened it. Did he think she'd run away from the challenge? She hitched up her chin. She wasn't in any mood to be browbeaten.

'Done.'

A kiss on the cheek. She bit her inner cheek to stop from smiling. Simple.

'A kiss on the lips,' he said, as if he'd read her mind.

She could feel her eyes narrow. 'I thought you said kissing was a bad idea?'

'I was wrong. I want to kiss you. A lot. And for a long time. In fact I want to do more than kiss you, Jo.'

Everything inside her thrilled to his words. She should be running for the hills, but she needed steady legs for running and hers were far from steady. The temptation to follow the beat of this particular drum flooded through her. It addled her mind, but it didn't completely scramble it.

'Fine, then. A kiss on the lips. But no hands.' She didn't need even the tiniest bits of their bodies touching. 'And not until the *macarons* are in the oven.'

'Deal.'

He sat. Her heart chugged. This was craziness—absolute craziness. Why on earth did he want a kiss from a great lug like her?

'You're a beautiful woman.'

She didn't believe that for a moment, but she couldn't deny the heat that flared between them. It didn't make sense, but it existed all the same.

She picked up a spoon.

'Your hands are shaking.'

She gritted her teeth and handed the spoon to him. 'Cooking makes me nervous. Show me how you dollop this mess out to make pretty little domes.'

'You don't *dollop* it. You pipe it.'

He flung open a kitchen drawer, seized a freezer bag and snipped off the end. She watched as he masterfully filled the makeshift piping bag and then proceeded to pipe a perfect row on her newly prepared cookie sheet.

'We'll take it in turns. You do the next row.'

His hands were steady. Hers weren't. That had to be the

reason his rows looked so much neater than hers. And even while she lectured herself to pay attention and follow his instructions precisely all she could think about was what beautiful hands he had and what an idiot she'd been to make that no-hands rule for their kiss. It would be divine to have those fingers tracing across her naked flesh.

'They're ready to go in the oven now.'

Her pulse fluttered up into her throat, jamming her breath and making her knees tremble. *Don't show weakness.* She did what she could to force steel to her backbone. With an insouciance she was far from feeling she picked up the tray and moved towards the oven.

'Wait.'

She wanted to scream.

Mac clicked his tongue. 'I'd better check the oven temperature.'

It reminded her of what she'd just achieved in here. Mac had all but made those *macarons* himself.

He opened the oven door and put his hand inside. Apparently satisfied, he took the tray from her and placed it inside. When he turned back he wore the most satisfied smile she'd ever seen a male of the species wear.

'Now you have to kiss me.'

She might doubt her attractiveness to the opposite sex, but there was no denying the relish in Mac's grin. That relish gleamed from his eyes, practically spilling from his every pore. Her throat started to tighten. She couldn't trust it. Mac was a consummate actor.

She slammed her hands to her hips. 'You think it's fair to blackmail a kiss from me?'

'God, but you're beautiful when you flare up like that.'

The shrivelling started. 'And now I *know* you're not being serious. I've never been beautiful and—'

'I've never understood the urge some men have to bend

a woman over their knee and give them six of the best... until now.'

Her eyes started from her head. Her throat thickened and she had to swallow a couple of times. 'You wouldn't dare!'

He leaned in close, his eyes blazing back into hers. 'You'd better think very carefully about what you say from here on. Believe me, Jo, you don't want to test me on this.' His lips hooked up with self-satisfaction. 'After all, you don't know what boon I might demand next time.'

She couldn't look away. 'What makes you so sure there'll be a next time? If those *macarons* turn out perfectly I won't need your help again.'

'You still need to master the filling—not to mention the assembling of the tower.'

Heck.

'And if I hear you make one more disparaging remark about your appearance I promise you, Jo, you *will* be sorry.'

She believed him. He looked utterly and completely forbidding.

Mac wasn't sure if anything had ever satisfied him as much as the gobsmacked expression plastered across Jo's face.

He leaned in closer to her again. 'You are divine, desirable, and all I can think about is kissing you. And more. *So* much more.'

'Stop.' Her voice came out as a hoarse whisper.

'You know how to make me stop, my beautiful, *beautiful* Jo.'

Her eyes widened. He could see the struggle she had not to open her mouth and contradict him. His heart twisted at the uncertainty that flashed in her eyes, at the vulnerability she tried to hide. She was one of the most beautiful women he'd ever met and it hurt something inside him that she doubted her loveliness like this.

'You have a face that poets have only ever dreamed of,'

he continued. 'And, speaking of dreams… I dream constantly of unbuttoning your shirt and freeing your pretty breasts from your bra, feasting my gaze on them until I can't resist, until I lose control and have to touch them, taste them, caress them. I want to give you the same physical pleasure I get from just looking at you. Oh, and, Jo…I dream of you losing control and—'

Her lips slammed to his and Mac was determined to kiss her until she finally believed she was beautiful.

Except her lips touched his and every thought, his very ability to think, dissolved as if rational thought had never existed. All that was left was sensation. Kissing Jo was like standing on a storm-tossed headland, with the wind whipping past and thunder clapping overhead and lightning creating jagged patterns across the sky. It was crazy and elemental and not to be withstood.

He didn't try to withstand it. He'd never felt more alive in all his life.

He curved his hands around her face to deepen the kiss.

'No hands,' she murmured against his lips, before her tongue tangled with his and her hands went to the back of his neck to pull him closer.

Where he was hard she was soft. Where he was famished she spread a banquet at his feet. Where he thirsted, she bathed him in water until he felt quenched. He never wanted to stop. Kissing Jo didn't just make him feel alive. It made him feel free.

He groaned when she eventually reefed herself out of his arms. She stood there staring at him, her chest rising and falling and her fingers pressed to swollen lips. He reached out a hand to her, but she backed up and shook her head.

'Did I hurt you?' he managed to croak out.

She pulled her hand away. 'Of course not. I… It's just—' She tried to glare, but it didn't quite come off. 'I thought you promised me gentlemanly behaviour?'

So had he. 'I lost my head.' He glared too. 'This whole thing we decided…that kissing is a bad idea…that's a load of hogwash. Kissing you is the best idea I've ever had. I *like* kissing you, Jo. I like it a lot. I think there should be more of it.'

'No.'

'Why not?'

The glare she sent him should have withered him. 'Too complicated, remember?' she snapped.

She swung away to grab a couple of sodas from the fridge. She set the one he guessed was meant for him on the far side of the table from her. She opened hers and took a long swig. He couldn't drag his gaze from the long line of her throat. The longer he watched the thirstier he became.

'Mac, please stop looking at me like that!'

'I can't help it.'

And he didn't want to help it. Right or wrong, he wanted to get naked with Jo as soon as humanly possible.

'I want you and I love looking at you.'

She scrubbed a hand down her face. 'You're deliberately trying to make this as difficult as possible.'

'My body is on fire. If you want to call a halt to things, then fine. That's your prerogative. But I want your body burning as badly as mine.'

And he could tell from the tight way she held herself that it was. There was a remarkably simple solution to that. She just had to say the word. He continued to gaze at her with naked hunger, hoping she'd lose control and kiss him again.

If he asked, would she stay? Here at the beach house? With him? He'd just made *macarons* and the world hadn't caved in. Maybe—

'Fine,' she snapped. 'I'll simply remove myself from your presence.'

'You can't. You have *macarons* in the oven.'

'Then *you* go somewhere else. Take Bandit for a walk or do some work.'

He shook his head, his eyes never leaving hers. 'My house. I can go where I want.'

Her chin shot up and those smoky eyes blazed at him. His mouth watered.

'You're determined to remain here with me in the kitchen?'

In answer he merely reached out and took possession of his can of soda.

She slammed herself into a chair. 'Fine, then I'll raise something that's been playing in my mind about Ethan.'

Was she trying to tick him off? Fine. She might find it harder than she thought. 'And what might that be?'

'Just for a moment reverse your and Ethan's situations. Pretend he's the boss and you're the apprentice.'

He dragged a hand down his face. If only that were the truth. If only—

'Imagine you're the apprentice who screwed up—as apprentices do. Wouldn't you want to see your boss? For starters, wouldn't you want to know he was okay? And, secondly, wouldn't you want to know he thought you important enough to visit?'

Bile burned his stomach. Jo turned him on like no other woman ever had, but she was going to give him an ulcer too.

'Or would I just be glad to never have to clap eyes again on the man who ruined my life?'

She folded her arms. 'Would you believe your life was ruined? And if you did would you hold anyone else responsible?'

He had no idea, but according to Diana Devlin he had indeed ruined her son's life.

'Mac.' Jo rested her forearms on the table, her eyes dark and troubled. 'It occurred to me the other day that Ethan might, in fact, be plagued with the same guilt that torments you.'

Every muscle he had froze.

'*He's* the one who accidentally let a platter of seafood slide into that vat of oil. *He's* the direct cause for the start of the fire. You know it was an accident, and I know it was an accident, but does Ethan? Or does he hold *himself* responsible for the whole sorry mess?'

The thought horrified him. 'He can't!'

'Says who?' She stabbed a finger at him. 'How would *you* feel if the positions were reversed?'

His mouth went dry. How *would* he feel if he'd been the one who'd dropped the iced seafood into the hot oil? *Guilty as sin*. His fingers tightened around his can of soda, crushing it. Bubbles fizzed up and over his hand to drip to the floor.

He barely knew Ethan. They'd probably spoken a grand total of twenty words to each other. Like most of the new apprentices he'd been in awe of Mac.

Mac cursed himself anew for not taking more time to put Ethan at ease for his first couple of appearances on the show.

Jo came to stand in front of him. She smelled of sugar and *macaron* and soda. 'You want me to believe I'm beautiful.'

'Because you're gorgeous,' he croaked out.

'And in the same way I want you to realise you're not responsible for the accident.'

His heart thudded. His temples pounded. And an ache started up behind his eyes. 'Ethan's not responsible either.'

'No, he's not. It was just an awful accident. I just hope he's not lying in that godforsaken hospital bed of his beating himself up about it.'

So did he.

'Mac, you just helped me make *macarons*.' She shook her head. 'If we're being honest, *you* made them. And the world didn't come tumbling down around your ears, did it?'

It took all his strength to swallow rather than howl. 'What are you trying to say?'

'I'm saying ring him.'

But Mrs Devlin said…

This mattered too much for him to get it wrong. He *had* to find out if Ethan blamed himself. If he did then Mac had to do everything he could to make the younger man see sense. To put his mind to rest.

'Mac?'

'I don't want to do anything to make matters worse.'

She handed him a tea towel to wipe his hands. Taking his can from him, she set it on the table before wiping the spill at his feet. When the oven timer buzzed it made them both jump.

He stood frozen as she pulled the tray from the oven and set it on the table.

'Your rows are perfect.' She pointed. 'Look.'

He stared at them and something inside him swelled at their perfection, at the knowledge that he'd made them.

'Mine are less so.'

'Practice. All you need, Jo, is practice.' Practice at making perfect rounds. Practice at believing she was beautiful.

I want you to realise you're not responsible for the accident.

Could she be right? He was too afraid to believe it—too afraid that Ethan would take one look at him and turn away in disgust. But what if he didn't?

His heart pounded so hard it hurt.

Jo gestured to the *macarons* and then around the kitchen. 'You love all this.'

It was pointless denying it. She'd put that whisk in his hand and for a moment he'd felt as if he could fly. He'd tried to ignore it by focussing on her story about her family, but no matter how much he'd lied to himself it hadn't worked. In much the same way it appeared that trying to turn his back on his passion hadn't worked. He could blame his talent and his ambition all he liked, but it didn't stop him from loving cooking as much as he ever had.

'I expect Ethan must love all this too.'

Something inside him stilled.

She blew out a breath and fell into a chair. 'I understand you wanting to help him. You've both suffered a dreadful accident that's changed your lives. But…'

Mac sat too, his mind a whirlwind. 'This is a hell of a way to stop me from kissing you again.'

She bit her lip. 'I shouldn't have started this. It's none of my business.'

He didn't know if he was angry with her, or grateful, or something else entirely. 'Don't stop now.'

She stared at him, her eyes dark. 'We've got in each other's faces so much this last fortnight, with me demanding you take better care of yourself and you taking issue with my body image, and me wanting to change your view of the accident and you trying to help me find a new direction career-wise. And then there's Bandit, which has added a whole new dimension. I didn't know any of this was going to happen, Mac, and it's been intense. I've never experienced this kind of intensity with anyone in such a short time before.'

He dragged a hand down his face.

She straightened, her voice suddenly tart. 'And you needn't interpret that as me being in love with you, or something stupid like that, because that's not what I'm talking about. This is… It's not friendship, but there are elements of that. It's not lust, though that's part of it.'

She shook her head. 'Maybe it's the proximity and the isolation and the fact we've both recently been through something big that's created a kind of melting pot here.' Her chin lifted. 'Do you know what I'm talking about or am I just—?'

'No.'

She glanced down at her hands.

'I mean yes,' he growled, wanting to wipe that look from her face. 'I was saying no to your alternative. I'm saying yes, I understand what you're trying to say. I can't explain it but there's a connection.'

And he didn't want there to be one. Even though he liked her.

She grasped at the air, as if searching for the right words. Her gaze returned to his—troubled, puzzled, dazed. 'When I think about some of the things I've said to you I'm appalled at myself. I don't feel like this—the here and now we're in—is the real world.'

He eased back in his seat. His heart thudded in his ears. 'There's something else you want to say that you wouldn't normally say in *the real world*, as you put it—isn't there?'

She slumped back before straightening again. 'What the heck? In for a penny… Helping Ethan realise there's a future—that he has a future to look forward to—wouldn't that be a fine way to help him?'

Yes. Yes, it would.

'You both share a passion for cooking, right? Well, maybe Ethan would like to help you work on the cookbook.'

'He's still in hospital. He's still recovering.'

She ignored that. 'Maybe down the track the two of you could start up your own cooking show on TV—do it the way it should've been done in the first place.'

His heart tried to pound out of his chest. He leapt from his chair. 'We'd be considered freaks.'

'Is that how you see Ethan?'

Of course it wasn't. But the general public wouldn't be so kind.

'Is that how you see yourself?'

A fist tightened about his ribcage

'You tell me I'm beautiful and expect me to believe you, but you refuse to see yourself fairly.'

He was scarred. End of story.

But he didn't repel her. He met her gaze and swallowed. Maybe other people would see past his and Ethan's scars too.

'Call him, Mac. See how he's doing. Give him something to live for.'

She folded her arms when he didn't say anything. He *couldn't* say anything. A lump the size of a frozen pizza throbbed in his throat.

'Promise me you'll at least think about it?'

He gave a curt nod, feeling bruised all over.

'And tomorrow I think we should try something different. Tomorrow *you'll* come down here and cook one of your complicated recipes, barking your instructions as you go, and I'll jot them down.'

Did he dare?

'Mac, it's time to decide what's more important—your self-imposed punishment or getting this cookbook written.'

With that she left.

Mac fell back into his seat. He let out a long, slow breath from cramped lungs. Man, that really had been one hell of a way to stop him kissing her.

CHAPTER NINE

THE NEXT DAY Jo swept, vacuumed and beat rugs. She did three loads of laundry, washed dishes and wiped down shelves. She cleaned windows—inside and out. This close to the coast, the easterly sea breezes laced the windows with salt. They needed cleaning. *A lot.*

She tried to fill her mind with salt, dust and cleaning, but over and over it returned to Mac and yesterday's kiss, to the words Mac had spoken, to the hunger in his eyes. And every single time her heart fluttered up into her throat, her thighs softened and her eyes burned. Did he really think her beautiful?

She collapsed on the top step of the veranda and stared at the glorious scene in front of her, hugging a bottle of window cleaner and a cleaning cloth to her chest. She could look at it any way she wanted, but Mac wasn't feigning his desire for her. She might not be able to explain the attraction between them, but that didn't make it any less real. He found her attractive. *Beautiful.*

He wanted her.

You are divine, desirable and all I can think about is kissing you.

When he'd said that he'd made her believe it. Hearing his voice in her head now made her believe it. When she saw herself reflected in his eyes she liked what she saw. He had no reason to lie. So why couldn't she keep on believing it?

Her heart did a strange little skip.

Bandit came to sit beside her and even tolerated it when Jo fondled her ears. 'Has he shut you out too, girl?'

Jo hadn't clapped eyes on Mac once so far today and... she glanced at her watch...it was nearly three o'clock. He'd been down for coffee while she'd been pegging clothes on the line—and he'd taken the entire pot back upstairs with him. He'd obviously made himself sandwiches and taken them back up to his room too, while she'd vacuumed the front rooms. She knew he was up there. She'd heard his heavy footfalls as he'd paced back and forth, back and forth.

She scowled. It was time for him to come out of this self-imposed exile and live again.

'If he doesn't come down to cook one of those absurd recipes of his, Bandit, then he's getting fish fingers for dinner.'

'Now, *that* would be a fate worse than death.'

Bandit raced across to the door.

Jo took her time turning around.

It still didn't ready her for the shocking bolt of heat that stabbed through her. She found herself repeating over and over: *One-night stands are bad. One-night stands are bad.*

She didn't mean to be judgmental. One-night stands were all well and good between consenting adults. But instinct warned her that a fling with Mac would be a *very* bad idea. He made her feel too much. Which was a real shame, because she'd be prepared to pay a lot for the physical release he could give her, but in this instance she suspected the price would be too high.

'How are you on this fine day, Jo?'

Was it a fine day? She went to rise, but he motioned for her to remain where she was before taking a seat beside her.

'I was hoping you were about to put me to work,' she said. 'That would make it a fine day.' His eyes suddenly gleamed and she choked. She wanted to add, *In the kitchen—writing down your recipes...* but decided it would be wiser to remain silent.

'Soon,' he said, growing sober. 'I think the suggestion you made yesterday has a lot of merit. So I'll cook and you can make notes.'

Yes! And tomorrow she'd hassle him to show her how to assemble the *macaron* tower. 'Smart move. It'll save you from the fish fingers.'

'First I want to clear the air about yesterday's kiss.'

Was that even possible?

'Or at least try to explain myself.'

The shrivelling started—the dying inside. She stared directly out in front of her. Here it came—the let-her-down-gently speech. For a short time she'd believed... She shook her head and swallowed.

'I don't want you to think I want a fling with you, Jo.'

Ditto. But she remained silent. She didn't have the heart to take part in the conversation. If she had the energy she'd cut him off and ask if they couldn't just get on with the cooking.

'I like you, Jo. I like you a lot. And, yes, I want to make love with you. But you deserve more than that.'

Yeah, right. Blah, blah, blah.

'*I* want more than that.'

She frowned. That wasn't part of the usual routine. Where was he going with this?

He bumped her shoulder gently with his. 'I want more than that with *you*, Jo.'

She blinked. She blinked at the beach, at a flock of seagulls, at the field of native grass.

'Are you ever going to look at me?'

She turned to meet his gaze—his deadly earnest and vulnerable gaze. She had to swallow before she could speak. 'You're saying... Are you saying you want to pursue a relationship with me?'

'Yes.'

Something inside her started to sing.

'But…' he added.

The singing stopped. A weight dropped down on her. She swung back to face the front.

'For heaven's sake, Jo, I'm not trying to blow you off. I'm trying to tell you how I mean to go forward from here. I…I understand that I might not figure in your plans for the future, and that just because a relationship with you is what I want, it doesn't mean you're going to fall in line with me.'

She had to look at him. She couldn't help it.

He was glaring down at his clenched fists, the pulse at the side of his jaw was throbbing, and his mouth was pressed into a thin line. This man… Her heart gave a giant kick. This man was tied up in knots. Over *her*!

She swallowed. 'You know I want you, Mac.'

Blue eyes lasered into hers.

'And I suspect you know that I like you too?'

He gave a cautious nod.

'So keep talking—because, believe me, I'm all ears.'

He straightened, and then he smiled, and it pierced through to the centre of her.

He reached out and took her hand, wrapped it between both his own. 'There are some things I need to clear up before I'm free to follow my heart.'

'Ethan?'

'I need to make sure he's okay. I need to help him in any way I can.'

He wouldn't be the man he was if he didn't want that. She wouldn't like him half so much otherwise. *Like?* Oh, yes, she liked him a lot. A whole lot. And in this particular moment that thought didn't scare her.

'I have to go see him.'

Wow. She straightened.

'I mean to leave tomorrow. I'm not sure how long I'll be gone.' His hand tightened about hers. 'I'm not sure…'

'You're not sure…?' she pressed when he hesitated.

'If you're prepared to wait.' He stared at their interlaced hands. 'I don't know if you're prepared to wait until I return from seeing him. I'm not sure you're prepared to wait and see what my life and career may or may not develop into.' He lifted his gaze to hers, his eyes dark. 'Before the accident I could've offered you the world. But now, Jo, I don't have anything solid to offer you.'

She didn't need anything solid. 'I'll wait until you return from seeing Ethan.' A grin broke through her. 'I mean *someone* needs to keep an eye on Bandit. After that we can take it step by step.'

Once Mac and Ethan had settled on a plan of action, then she and Mac could look to the future. *Their* future.

He lifted her hand and pressed a kiss into her palm, his lips firm and warm. 'Thank you.'

Something inside her soared free then. She had a feeling the only thing that kept her anchored to the ground was Mac's touch.

They should go inside and start cooking. Knowing Mac, he'd have chosen something that would take ages to prepare, but she didn't have the heart—or the strength—to break the spell that wove around them. She imagined that in years to come she'd remember sitting here with him like this, holding hands in the mild winter sunlight, with the sound of the surf in her ears and the promise of their future in front of them.

'What are you hoping will happen with Ethan?' she finally asked.

'That he'll work on a couple of projects with me when he's ready to.'

'That sounds nice.'

'I'll move back to the city so we can do that. And so I can see you.'

'That sounds even nicer.' She tightened her hand in his. 'So far it sounds as if we're on the same page.'

He pressed another kiss into her palm. She wished he'd

kiss her properly, but she knew why he didn't. If they kissed they'd lose control.

'I bless the day you came here, Jo. You've made me see possibilities I hadn't considered.'

She leaned against him, relishing his warmth and strength. 'You were grieving. You were mourning the life you'd had that was suddenly snatched away, and you were mourning for Ethan and *his* life too. Grief is a process, and you're finding a way through it.'

'Thanks to you.'

His eyes held so much promise it was all she could do not to throw herself into his arms and seek an answer to the desire coursing through her. She'd wait. Because it was what Mac wanted and perhaps what he needed. But when he finally felt free there'd be nothing to hold either of them back. Her skin tightened at the thought.

'You...uh...?' She swallowed and tried to think of something—anything—other than getting naked with Mac. 'You mean to drive your car?'

'I guess.'

'It's a pretty visible car, Mac. The Sydney paparazzi know it, don't they?'

He grimaced. 'I'll hire something.'

And someone somewhere would leak that too. Mac deserved to embark on his mission free from the worries of the press.

'You can borrow The Beast if you want. Nobody'll look twice at you in that.'

'You'd trust me with your car?'

'As you'll be leaving your gorgeous sports car here, in my care, trusting you with The Beast only seems fair.' She was going to trust him with her heart. In comparison, her car was nothing.

He laughed. 'Deal.'

And then he leant forward and touched his lips to hers.

He tasted of coffee and determination, and his kiss tasted like every promise she'd been too afraid to wish for.

It ended far too soon, but she knew why. The spark between them was already too hot, too twitchy. They had to negotiate it carefully or—

Stop thinking about getting naked with Mac!

'You're beautiful, Jo.'

She didn't contradict him. She didn't want to. 'You make me feel beautiful.'

His smile was her reward. 'You don't know the half of how beautiful I'm going to make you feel.'

She groaned. A sound of need and frustration she had no hope of holding back.

He nodded. 'I'm hoping I won't be gone too long.'

So was she.

He rose, pulling her to her feet. 'Come on—it's time to cook.'

'What are we cooking?'

'*Macarons.* I have a good recipe for them—better than the one you were using yesterday—and you need to keep practising.'

She all but floated into the kitchen with him.

Mac left at the crack of dawn the next day.

Leaving Jo behind when all he wanted to do was make love to her, prove to her over and over again how beautiful she was, was one of the hardest things he'd ever done.

He gritted his teeth, resisting the increasingly urgent craving. He had nothing to offer her. Nothing solid. No kind of future. But a future might be possible, mightn't it? A future could be wrestled from the wreckage the accident had wrought.

He held to the thought tightly, because he ached for that future. With Jo.

He tapped his fingers against the steering wheel and wondered what she'd be doing. She'd planned to make more *macarons.* The thought made him smile, because she didn't even like them. She'd taken a bite from one yesterday and with an 'Ugh!' had tossed it in the bin. She'd planned to take yesterday's batch to the farm where she bought the eggs.

'Maybe someone will find a use for them.'

That was what she'd said. He laughed. The very thought of her warmed him to the soles of his feet in a way he could never have imagined a month ago. Beautiful, breath-of-fresh-air Jo, who'd breezed into his life and turned it upside down like some kind of super-heroine from a comic book.

Imagining Jo in a skimpy superhero outfit kept him pleasantly engaged for half an hour. Especially when he imagined peeling it from her gorgeous body.

He spent another hour wondering what kind of dessert would make her mouth truly water. If she didn't like *macarons* then anything too meringuey was off the list. He selected dessert after dessert, only to dismiss them. Eventually he grinned. Maybe pineapple upside-down cake? *Yes.* Something warm and rich and full of flavour. That would suit her perfectly.

As soon as he returned to the beach house he'd make her one. He'd watch every nuance of her expression as she ate it. He could spend a lifetime making food to indulge all her senses. She'd appreciate his efforts too. He had no doubt about that. And he'd relish her relish.

Before he knew it the five-hour drive to Sydney was almost complete. He could hardly wait to return to Jo, but first things first.

He drove over the Sydney Harbour Bridge, but he didn't head for his swanky inner-city apartment. He turned the car in the opposite direction—towards Ethan's private clinic.

Jo pulled her phone from her pocket to glance at it for the umpteenth time, but there were no new messages, no new texts.

In the last two days she'd sent Mac five texts. She grimaced at Bandit, who lay under the kitchen table with her nose between her front paws, evidently missing Mac too.

'Do you think five texts is too many, Bandit? Too needy?'

Jo collapsed into a chair. She flipped out one finger. 'Are you there yet?' She held out a second finger. 'Thinking of you.' She stared at a third finger. 'Sunny and fine here.' She grimaced at the fourth. 'Missing you. Ugh! Now, *that*, Bandit, was too much.'

She dropped her hand to her lap. Her last message had been a simple goodnight before she'd gone to sleep last night.

She straightened. She wouldn't be needy. Mac had a plan he needed to bring off, and in the meantime he'd asked her to wait. She'd wait—because his eyes had promised that once he'd done what he needed to do he'd devote all the time she wanted—needed—to her…to them.

She hugged herself. She still found it hard to believe that Mac wanted her.

And she wanted him.

Oh, what was the point in denying it? Somewhere along the line she'd fallen in love with him. She couldn't pinpoint the exact moment. Their first kiss? Their second? When they'd argued about fish fingers? When he'd helped her polish off that pizza? The scorn in his eyes for her cruel excuse of an ex-boyfriend?

Thanks to Mac, she saw that for what it was now—the attempt of a sad bunch of losers with no self-esteem to build themselves up at the expense of others.

Pitiful.

It was pitiful that she'd let it affect her for so long too, but it had fed into all the insecurities created by her grandmother and her great-aunt. She let out a long breath. It had been easier to believe that she was unattractive than to risk being vulnerable again. Well, no more. She set her shoulders. She'd never fall into that pattern again. Living with that kind of fear emotionally crippled a person, and life was too short.

'Way too short, Bandit.'

She stood and swiped a bottle of water from the fridge, then headed for the front veranda. She turned in the doorway. 'C'mon, Bandit—the fresh air will do you good.'

Bandit huffed out from beneath the table, head hanging low as she scuffed after Jo. When they reached the veranda Jo bent down to caress Bandit's face.

'Aw, honey, he'll be home soon.'

She sat and glanced out at the view. In the meantime she meant to savour her newfound sense of self. She was done with feeling like a freak. She was done with feeling as if she was too tall, too large, too broad—too anything! By whose standards was she any of those things? Even the tiny, gorgeous women who adorned the covers of magazines were airbrushed to within an inch of their lives— their eyes widened, their necks lengthened, their waists trimmed and their thighs shrunk.

What was *that* about? If the so-called beautiful people weren't beautiful enough, then what hope did real people like her have? None. Because the standard was no longer human—it was in the mind of some designer and that was where the real freakishness lay. She was done with trying to live up to such impossible standards.

From now on she meant to wear whatever she wanted to wear—dresses, heels, chunky jewellery—regardless of whether it drew attention or not. She was healthy, she was strong, and she was a good person. She was kind to animals and to moody men. She was independent and able to make her own way in the world.

Mac desired her, wanted her, but she could see now

that too was secondary. It didn't matter what anyone else thought. It only mattered what she thought of herself.

She threw her arms out wide and lifted her face to the sun. 'I am beautiful!' She yelled the words at the top of her lungs and then with a laugh cracked open her water. 'If anyone hears me, Bandit, they'll think I'm a certified nutcase.'

Bandit, who'd collapsed by the door, flicked an ear in Jo's direction, but nothing more.

Jo pointed a finger at her. 'Now, you have to stop being a pathetic female, Bandit. Seriously—neediness is a bad look.'

Nothing. No response at all.

'It's never wise to pin all your hopes on a man.' She wrinkled her nose and grimaced. Well, on that count both she and Bandit had failed. Spectacularly. 'Except we can trust Mac, Bandit.' She swallowed and nodded. 'He's a man among men.'

Bandit's head lifted. Jo stared at the dog and pushed her shoulders back with a proud little shuffle. Well, well... Perhaps Bandit listened to her after all. Maybe she wasn't as indifferent to Jo as she pretended to be.

'I mean Mac won't let either one of us down, and—'

She broke off when Bandit leapt to her feet with a joyful bark and scampered down the steps at full speed. What on earth...?

'Bandit, you have a tummy full of puppies!' she hollered. 'You need to be careful!'

And then she heard it too. A car coming up the drive.

Her heart started to thud. Mac was home? She bounced upright, spilling water. She wanted to race towards the sound in the same way Bandit had.

Pride, she lectured herself, leaning against a veranda post as if she hadn't a care in the world. She did her best not to bounce. She had no hope whatsoever of keeping the smile from her face, though. *Mac was home!* She couldn't wait to hear a about the plans he and Ethan had made. She wanted Mac to be filled with hopes and dreams and plans for the future. She meant to figure large there.

Mac manoeuvred the car along the rutted driveway. He didn't stop to let Bandit into the cab—which, given Bandit's over-the-top exuberance, was probably wise. Jo remained leaning against her post even when he pulled the car to a halt at the front of the house.

She wanted him to see her standing there, tall and proud in the sunlight, elevated by the veranda, and she wanted to make him hungrier than he'd ever been in his life.

When he pushed out of the car, though, that thought fled. She raced down the steps towards him, appalled at his pallor and at the darkness that seemed to drag his eyes deep into their sockets. She took his arm. She'd have hugged him, but he shook her off.

'Not now, Jo.'

She tried not to take it personally. 'You look ill. Do you need a doctor?'

He shook his head.

'Then how about you put your feet up and I'll get you a sandwich and a beer?'

'I'm going to take a shower.'

He hadn't even taken the time to pet Bandit, but he did let the dog follow at his heels.

Lucky Bandit.

Mac and the dog disappeared inside the house. Jo lowered herself back to the step. Things had evidently not gone well in Sydney.

She closed her eyes. *Patience.* She'd let him shower and rest without pestering him, and later she'd put some good food in his belly. By then he might be ready to talk. Between them they'd find a solution to this setback.

She pushed to her feet. Spaghetti and meatballs. Comfort food. That was what they needed.

* * *

Mac closed his eyes as the stinging spray from the shower rained down on him, but he couldn't get the image of Ethan out of his mind. That image was burned there to torment him for all eternity.

Six months on and the nineteen-year-old still had to wear a bodysuit, was still in pain. Mac closed his eyes and braced his arms against the tiles.

Six months might have passed, but Ethan had taken one look at Mac and growled, 'Go away,' before turning his back.

Six years—sixty years—wouldn't be enough to erase the harm Mac had done.

And then Diana Devlin had walked in and it had all gone to hell in a handbasket from there.

He scrubbed shampoo through his hair, digging his fingers into his scalp, wishing he could trade places with Ethan, if only for a day, to give him some respite.

Ethan's doctor had taken time to talk to Mac. Mac had well and truly wanted out of there by that time—going to visit Ethan had been a grave mistake—but the doctor had at least been able to assure him that the upset wouldn't impede Ethan's recovery.

That was something, at least.

In fact the doctor had said Ethan's recovery was going better than any of them had hoped. He'd even implied that Ethan could have gone home weeks ago.

Ethan hadn't wanted to. The doctor hadn't said as much, but Mac had read between the lines. They were keeping him in for 'psychological assessment'—those had been the actual words. Not unusual in these circumstances, as it happened.

Mac twisted the taps off and seized a towel, scrubbing it over his face and hair. They thought Ethan was in danger of committing suicide. No wonder Diana hated him.

The accident hadn't just damaged Ethan physically. It had damaged him mentally. That was Mac's fault.

An ache stretched his throat. He'd never be free from that. *Never.*

He threw down the towel and dressed in the nearest things to hand—worn jeans and a faded sweater. The days of bespoke suits and designer clothes were behind him. He stood at the window and stared out. Eventually he roused himself and spun back to face the room.

He hung up his towel, put his dirty laundry in the washing basket, unpacked.

You can't put off going downstairs forever.

Weight slammed to his shoulders then, threatening to crush him. Earlier, when he'd pulled the car to a halt at the front of the house and had seen Jo standing in the sunshine, proud and magnificent, his chest had cracked open and split down the middle like a hewn log.

He paced from one side of the room to the other, hands clenched and muscles corded. For as long as he owed such a debt to Ethan he didn't have the right to pursue his own happiness. He pushed both hands back through his hair, fighting for breath. What he had to focus on was making enough money to ensure Ethan was looked after.

The dreams he'd started to dream—they were dust. It was what he deserved.

But Jo? She deserved better.

He pressed his palms to hot eyes and eased himself down to the edge of the bed.

Mac forced himself downstairs for dinner. Food was the last thing on his mind, but he didn't doubt for one moment that if he didn't appear Jo would storm upstairs to demand an explanation.

The concern in her eyes when he strode into the kitchen

cut him to the quick. 'I'm fine,' he bit out before she could ask.

He took the jug of iced water and two glasses she had sitting on the kitchen bench through to the dining room. She followed a few moments later with a fragrant platter of spaghetti and meatballs.

She dished them out generous servings, but she didn't start to eat. She gulped down water, the glass wobbling precariously in her hold.

'I take it your trip didn't go precisely as you'd hoped?'

It hurt him to look at her, but he forced himself to do it all the same. He deserved to throb and burn. 'He's a mess, Jo.'

'He's been through a lot.'

'Seeing me didn't help. Seeing me just made things worse.'

'How…?' Her voice was nothing more than a whisper.

He had to pull in a breath before he could continue. 'He hates the sight of me.'

She didn't say anything. She sliced into a meatball, slathered it in sauce and ate it. Her lips closed about the morsel and need rose up in him so hard that wind rushed in his ears, deafening him. Seizing his knife and fork he attacked a meatball, reducing it to a pile of mush. He started in on a second one and then on the spaghetti.

'I can put that in the blender for you if it's how you'd prefer to eat it.'

He set his cutlery down, afraid he wouldn't be able to push food past the lump in his throat. His stomach churned too hard for food anyway.

Jo continued to eat, as if unaware of his mental turmoil. He wasn't stupid enough to believe that, though. She was eating to stave off heartbreak. A fist reached out and squeezed his chest, all but cutting off his air supply.

'So,' she said eventually, with a toss of her head, not meeting his gaze. 'What's the plan from here?'

His very heartbeat seemed to slow. It was all he could do not to drop his head to the table.

From a long way away he heard himself say, 'I revert back to Plan A.'

Her gaze flew to his and he watched with a sickening thud as realisation dawned in those sage eyes. Her eyebrows drew in and she gripped a fistful of her shirt right above her heart.

He swallowed and forced himself to continue. 'I focus on making enough money to take care of every single one of Ethan's needs for as long as he needs me to.'

'I...' With a physical effort she swallowed, but she didn't loosen the grip on her shirt. 'Where does that leave us?'

Bile burned like acid in his throat, coating his tongue. 'There can't be an "us", Jo. At least not for the foreseeable future.'

She stared at him for long, pain-filled seconds, as if she hadn't heard him properly, and then she flinched as if he'd struck her. The colour leached from her face; the creases about her eyes deepened. Heaviness settled over him. His chin edged down towards his chest. His heart was thudding dully there. How could he have done this to her? Why hadn't he taken more care?

I'm sorry! The words screamed through him, but he couldn't force them out.

She swung back, eyes blazing. 'You fall at the first hurdle and give up? Come running home with your tail between your legs?'

He wanted to open his arms and make his body a target, to tell her to hurl whatever insults she could at him. Anything to make her feel better. Only he knew it wouldn't help. Not one jot.

'Has life always been easy for you? Have you never had to fight for anything?'

She laughed, but it wasn't the kind of laugh he ever wanted to hear again.

'Russ used to brag about you—about how you were this *wunderkind* who went from triumph to triumph.' She shot to her feet. 'But the fact of the matter is all that coming so easily for you has made you a…a *loser*!'

Her words cut at him like whips. He wanted to beg her to forgive him.

'When something really matters, Mac, you keep trying until you succeed—despite the setbacks. If Ethan really mattered to you, you'd try harder.'

What she was really saying, though, was that if *she* mattered to him he'd fight harder for her. It was what she deserved.

As for Ethan… He shook his head. He couldn't force his presence on the young man again. He'd done enough damage as it was.

'But you're not going to do that, are you?'

How could he make her understand the extent of Ethan's misery? What was the point anyway? She'd simply tell him to do something to ease that misery. That was beyond Mac's powers. What he *could* do was make money to hire people who'd bring about a positive difference in Ethan's life.

'You're just going to give in.'

There wasn't an ounce of inflection in her voice and that was worse than her anger. Ten times worse.

She dotted her mouth with her napkin, tossed it down beside her plate, and left.

It felt as if his heart had stopped beating.

CHAPTER TEN

MAC BARELY SLEPT, but he forced himself out of bed as the first rays of sun filtered over the horizon. He made himself dress and go straight into the master bedroom. He opened the curtains to let in the light. Shutting himself up in the dark, not caring about what he ate and not getting any exercise had been stupid things to do.

He had to stay healthy.

With that thought he cracked open the glass sliding door. Air filtered in—cold but fresh.

Only then did he turn to his computer and switch it on. A hard brick settled in his stomach, but he ignored it to examine the lists of recipes he'd selected for the cookbook. At least a dozen of them were either not started or unfinished.

That meant a dozen recipes he'd have to make while barking instructions for Jo to jot down. He pulled in a breath. That was twelve days' work, if he made a recipe a day and wrote it up in the evening. Less if he did two recipes a day. On top of that there was the glossary of terms and techniques to write up, and serving suggestions to add to each recipe.

He created a table and a timeline. He printed off a shopping list for Jo. He would get to work on the first recipe this afternoon. After that he'd talk Jo through the icing she'd need to make for her *macaron* tower. She could tackle that under his supervision tomorrow morning.

He rose, collecting the shopping list from the printer on his way to the door.

'C'mon, Bandit.'

A morning and afternoon walk down to the beach each day, perhaps along it for a bit, would keep both man and dog healthy. He set the shopping list on the kitchen table before letting himself out of the house. Quietly. It was still early.

The sun rose in spectacular munificence over the Pacific Ocean, creating a path of orange and gold. At the edges of the path the water darkened to mercury and lavender. The air stood still, and with the tide on the turn the waves broke on pristine sand in a hushed rhythmic lilt.

Mac halted on a sand dune to stare at it all. It should fill his soul with glory. It should fill him with the majesty of nature. It should…

He'd give it all up for a single night in Jo's arms.

He dragged a hand down his face and tried to banish the thought. A single night wouldn't be enough for her. It wouldn't be enough for him either, but it would at least be something he could hold onto in the bleak, monotonous months to come.

He rested his hands on his knees and pulled in a breath. Except he couldn't do that to her. He laughed, although the sound held little mirth. More to the point, she wouldn't let him do it to her.

Good.

The weight across his shoulders bowed him until he knelt in the sand with Bandit's warm body pressed against him.

I can do this. I can do this. I can do this.

He lifted his head. He *had* to do this.

Forcing his shoulders back, he lumbered to his feet and stumbled along the beach for ten minutes before turning and making his way back to the house.

The scent of frying bacon hit him the moment he opened the front door. He hesitated before heading for the kitchen.

Leaning a shoulder against the doorframe, he drank her in—the unconscious grace of her movements, the dark glossiness of her hair and the strength that radiated from her.

'That smells good,' he managed.

She didn't turn from the stove. 'Bacon always smells good.'

He could tell nothing of her mood or state of mind from either her posture or her tone of voice.

He rubbed his nape. 'I didn't think you were much of a breakfast person.' Mind you, she'd barely eaten any dinner last night.

'I'm not usually, but I make an exception when I'm setting off on a car journey.'

She moved to butter the toast that had popped up in the toaster and that was when Mac saw the suitcases sitting by the doorway leading out to the laundry and the back door.

A chill crept across the flesh of his arms and his face, down his back. 'You're leaving?'

'I am.'

His heart pounded. 'Today?'

'That's right.'

She finally turned. The dark circles under her eyes made him wince. She nodded at his shopping list.

'So I'm afraid you'll have to get your own groceries.'

A knife pierced through the very centre of him. She couldn't leave! Just because they couldn't be together in the way they wanted it didn't mean she had to go.

She set the toast on the table and then two plates laden with bacon, eggs and beans. She'd made enough for him too. Maybe she'd had the same thought—that he hadn't eaten much at dinner last night either. It warmed some of the chill out of him, but not for long.

When she indicated he should do so, he sat. He stared

at his plate. He forced himself to eat, but all the while his mind whirled. Jo couldn't leave. He needed her here. She—

She needs to eat. Wait until after she's eaten.

Two rashers of bacon, a piece of toast and a fried egg later, he pushed his plate away. 'Thank you.'

'You're welcome.'

He waited until she'd finished before speaking again. 'Why are you leaving?'

She took their plates to the sink. She wore a pair of jeans that fitted her like a glove. Had she worn them deliberately to torment him? He gulped down his orange juice but it did nothing to quench the thirst rising through him.

She pushed a mug of coffee towards him, cradling another mug in her hands and leaning against the kitchen bench.

She took a sip before finally meeting his eyes. 'I'm leaving, Mac, because I refuse to watch you sacrifice yourself on the altar of guilt and misplaced responsibility.'

He swallowed back his panic. 'I prefer to call it duty.'

'You can call it what you like. Doesn't change the fact it's messed up.'

His head rocked back.

'And I'm not going to support you in that delusion.'

Jo might not understand what drove him, but it didn't mean she had to *leave*! 'You haven't learned how to make the *macaron* tower yet.'

She shrugged. 'I did that stupid vocational test of yours again last night.'

He closed his eyes and pinched the bridge of his nose, concentrated on breathing.

'I considered each of the questions as honestly as I could and you know what? It came back with the perfect job. So thanks for the tip.'

How would he cope out here without her?

He forced his eyes open. 'What job?' he croaked, a fist tightening about his chest.

'Paramedic.'

Saving lives? Dealing with emergencies?

She'd saved Russ's life, and probably Bandit's. She'd forced Mac to turn his life around. Her practicality, her strength, her ability to respond quickly, it made her... *Perfect*. The single word rang a death knell through hopes he hadn't realised he still harboured. Impossible hopes.

Jo deserved to get on with her life.

Without him.

He just hadn't known that letting her go would tear the heart from his chest.

'The NSW Ambulance Service is recruiting soon, so I figured it's time I got on with things.'

Mac found himself on his feet, moving towards her. He cupped her face. Her skin was warm and soft and alive against his hands.

'Stay,' he croaked. 'Please. Just another week.'

In another week he'd find the strength to let her go, but please God don't ask him to relinquish her today. *Please*.

Her eyes melted to emerald for a moment before she blinked them back to a smoky sage. 'If I stay we'll become lovers,' she whispered.

'Sounds perfect to me.'

He ached to kiss her, but she planted a hand on his chest and forced him back a step.

'To you it probably does, but I'm not going to settle for second best. I will never come first with you, Mac. Ethan always will.' She swallowed, her face pale. 'I deserve to come first with the man I choose to share my life with.'

Her words forced him back another step. His heart burned. Ethan had to come first. He had to look after the other man until he was back on his feet, and there was no telling how long that would take.

If he made a lot of money—millions of dollars—he could set up a trust fund to take care of Ethan, and then he'd be free to follow his heart.

If.

He stared down at his hands. Jo had no intention of waiting around to find out if he could manage that. He couldn't say he blamed her.

She cleaned the kitchen. He'd have told her not to bother except that would only mean she'd leave sooner. He took her bags out to The Beast and stowed them in the back. He rested his head against the doorframe before striding back into the kitchen.

'What about Bandit?'

She lifted a hand to her temple and rubbed it, making him wonder if she had a roaring headache too. 'I thought you wanted to keep her?'

He shook himself. 'I mean what about the puppies?'

She seized a tea towel, shook it out and hung it on its rack. 'When they're ready to be weaned I'll come and collect them. If there are any issues let me know. I've left my mobile number, my email address and my grandmother's contact details beside the phone in the in the hall.'

She didn't meet his eyes. Not once.

His heart started to thump—hard. 'Is that where you'll be staying?'

She slung her handbag across her shoulder. 'It's my childhood home.'

He suddenly found it difficult to swallow. He stared at that handbag. She was really leaving?

'Goodbye, Mac.'

He had to swallow the bellow that rose up inside him. They couldn't end like this! There'd been so much promise and—

She reached out as if to touch him, but her hand dropped short. 'I really do wish you well. I hope…'

What did she hope?

'I hope that you succeed.'

She spun on her heel then, and shot through the laundry and out of the back door. He lumbered after her, his limbs heavy and clumsy, as if they didn't belong to him. She was so calm, so cool and untouchable. As if she didn't care. She was tearing him to pieces.

A black knot of acid burned through the centre of him. 'Is this really so easy for you?' The words left him on a bellow. 'Don't you feel the slightest sting or throb? Don't you—?'

'Easy?' She swung towards him, her face contorting. 'Easy to walk away from dreams you let me believe were possible? Dreams that—?'

Her eyes filled and her pain rose up all around him.

'Easy?' She lifted her hands as if to beat out her pain on his chest.

He wanted to wrap her in his arms and make her pain go away, soothe the desperation in her eyes and the despair that twisted her lips.

'Jo...' He swore.

'Easy?' She thumped her chest. 'When you've broken something inside me that I'm afraid I'll never be able to fix?'

His mouth dried. His stomach knotted. He wanted to hide from the accusation in her eyes, from the anguish there—anguish *he'd* caused.

'I'm sorry, Jo. I—'

She twisted her hands in the collar of his shirt and slammed her lips to his. The world tilted. She explored every last millimetre of his lips with a hunger that had the wind rushing in his ears, firing his every nerve-ending to life. She deepened the kiss as if her very life depended on it, and everything he had reached towards her.

But she pushed him away.

'I tried to play nice, Mac, and keep it civilised, but you made it impossible! I hope that kiss torments you every night for as long as you hole up out here.'

She needn't fear. It would burn him through all eternity. As would the tears in her eyes and the pain that turned her lips white.

'That's it, Mac. That's us done.'

She slammed into her car, started up the motor and roared away.

He stared after her, her words ringing in his ears. *That's us done.*

Behind him Bandit set up a whine that became a howl.

Mac spun around. 'You're too late, you dumb dog. You should've told her you loved her while you had the chance.'

Mac picked up a rock and hurled it with all his might at a fencepost. He kicked a tuft of grass, jarring his ankle when he connected a little too well with it. He yelled out his pain and frustration at the top of his lungs. But it didn't help.

The end. *Finito.* This was as far as he and Jo would ever go. He stood there, arms at his sides, breathing hard. Jo was gone. The earth might as well spin off its axis for all the sense that made.

He waited for the sky to darken and a curtain to descend about him. It didn't. The sun kept shining, the breeze continued to rustle a path through the native grass, and on the beach waves kept rushing up onto the sand.

His heart shrivelled to the size of a pea.

Jo was gone.

It was his fault.

And there was nothing he could do about it.

CHAPTER ELEVEN

MAC FINISHED THE cookbook in a fortnight rather than the projected month.

A morning walk, an afternoon walk and making sure he ate three square meals a day still left him with a lot of time on his hands. So he worked.

He didn't sleep much.

He sent the manuscript off to his editor and then cleaned the house from top to bottom. Having neglected it completely since Jo had left, that took him two full days.

On the third morning after finishing the cookbook, with nothing planned for the day, he stared at the omelette he'd made for breakfast and found he couldn't manage so much as a bite. With a snarl, he grabbed his coffee and stormed out to the veranda.

Twiddling his thumbs like this was driving him crazy. When would he hear back from his editor?

He collapsed to the step and ordered himself to admire the view.

'See? Beautiful!'

His scowl only deepened. The view did nothing to ease the burn in his soul or the darkness threatening to tug him under. He'd kept himself busy for a reason. He'd missed Jo every second of every day and every night, but keeping busy had helped him to deal with it, to cope with it, to push the pain to the boundaries of his mind.

He had to find something to do. He leapt up, intending

to stride down to the beach for the second time in an hour. Bandit stood too. He stared at her and pursed his lips. If he went down there she'd want to come, and with her about to drop her puppies any day she should probably be taking it easy.

He glanced around wildly for something else to do and his gaze landed on a rosebush. He nodded once. The garden needed wrestling into shape. He could wrestle while Bandit dozed in the sun.

He gathered some battered implements—a hoe, a trowel and secateurs—from the garage. He barely glanced at his car, even though he still made sure to turn the engine over twice a week. It reminded him too much of Jo.

Digging up weeds and pruning rosebushes reminded him of Jo too. Everything reminded him of Jo. He wondered how she was getting along with her *macaron* tower.

One thing about being so hung up on Jo—it meant he had less time to brood about Ethan.

Jo's voice sounded in his head. *You're just going to give up...? Fight harder...*

What else could he do? He'd make sure Ethan wanted for nothing.

Except a life.

He started reciting multiplication tables.

When lunchtime rolled around he ate cold omelette and a banana. He sat outside in the sun because the kitchen reminded him too much of Jo. So did the dining room.

'I miss her *more*,' he shot at Bandit, who moped nearby. She didn't flick so much as a whisker.

Has life always been that easy for you?

Yep. Right up until the accident. 'But don't worry, Jo—it's hell now.'

Which was unfair. Jo had only ever wanted his happiness.

Fight harder.

'How?' He shouted out the word at the top of his lungs, making Bandit start.

He apologised with a pat to her head. What did Jo mean? How could he fight any harder? He was fighting as hard as he could!

He paced the length of the garden bed. He was fighting as hard as he could to make money.

That wasn't what Jo had meant, though, was it?

He bent at the waist to rest his hands on his knees. He didn't know how to fight for Ethan when the other man hated the very sight of him. How could he rouse the younger man from his apathy and depression if—?

Mac froze. The trowel fell from his fingers. Ethan hated the sight of him in the same way Mac had loathed the idea of a housekeeper. Blackmail had been the only method that had worked on him. Blackmail and playing on his guilt about Russ.

He'd loathed the very idea of Jo, but her presence here had forced him to reassess how he was living, to question the bad habits he'd formed. He certainly hadn't welcomed her with open arms, but she hadn't gone running for the hills.

As he'd done with Ethan.

No, she'd forced his inward gaze outwards. She'd reminded him that he needed food and exercise for his body, along with sunlight and fresh air. She'd forced him to recognise that he wasn't betraying the task he'd set himself if he took the time to enjoy those things. She'd made him see that he needed those things if he was to accomplish that task.

She'd stormed in here and turned his world upside down. He hadn't enjoyed it. He'd resisted it. But it had been good for him.

It had brought him back to life.

Who did Ethan have to give him that kind of tough love?

His mother? Very slowly Mac shook his head. Diana was too caught up in her fear for her son and her anger at the world.

From the corner of his eye he saw Bandit polish off the rest of his abandoned omelette. He didn't bother scolding her. She'd put up with his growly grumpiness and no Jo for the last fortnight too. If omelette helped, then all power to her.

Mac drummed his fingers against his thighs for a moment, before pushing his shoulders back and reaching into his pocket for his mobile phone. He punched in the number for Ethan's doctor.

Jo carefully sealed the lid on the airtight container holding the most perfect dozen *macarons* she'd ever seen. She set them gently on a shelf at the very back of the pantry with the other six dozen *macarons* she'd spent the last few days baking. She had twice as many as she needed, but she wasn't taking any chances. Each and every one of them was perfect.

All the less than perfect ones had been placed in her grandmother's biscuit tin, and even her grandmother's enthusiasm for them had started to wane. After her grandmother's birthday dinner tonight Jo would be glad if she never set eyes on another *macaron* for as long as she lived.

Puffing out a breath, she moved back to the table and pulled a plastic cone towards her. She had another eight of these cones in the cupboard. This one she was going to ice. Easy-peasy. Which was precisely what it wanted to be after the number of cones she'd already practised on.

She pushed her hair back from her face. What on earth possessed people to spend hours—or in this case days—slaving over a dish that would be demolished in a matter of minutes? Where was the satisfaction in that?

If Mac ever rang her she'd ask him.

Her throat ached, her temples throbbed and her chest cramped—as always happened whenever she thought about Mac. And as she thought about him a lot you'd think she'd be used to it by now.

She gripped her hands together. It had been eight weeks since she'd left his coastal hideaway, but she still hadn't grown used to the gaping sense of loss that yawned through her. Some days it was all she could do to get from minute to minute. Some days it was all she could do not to lie in some dark corner and shut the rest of the world out.

But what good would that do anyone?

Please! Some histrionic part of herself that tore at her hair and sobbed uncontrollably pleaded with her. *Please, can't we just...?*

Jo swallowed hard and shook her head, blinking furiously. *No, they couldn't.*

She wished she'd been able to hold onto her anger for longer. That anger had helped initially, but it had slipped away almost as soon as she'd arrived home. Instead, the hope that Mac would come to his senses had grown—the hope that he'd call her and tell her he loved her and was prepared to create a life that included her.

Which made her a certifiable idiot.

'But a beautiful idiot,' she whispered, reminding herself that her time with Mac hadn't been entirely wasted.

Of course it hadn't been wasted. By the time she'd left he'd been healthier, stronger, and sexier than sin. Whether he knew it or not, she'd been good for him.

Oh, he knew it all right. It just wasn't enough.

She collected icing sugar—the good, pure stuff—butter, milk and food colouring. The fact of the matter was she *had* heard from Mac. Twice. A curt email on the evening she'd left, asking if she'd reached her destination safely. She'd answered with an equally short Yes, thank you. And a week later he'd sent her a recipe for a *macaron* tower.

She'd thanked him again. Very briefly. And that had been the sorry extent of their communication. She expected to hear from him soon, though. Bandit must have had her puppies by now, and those puppies must be getting old enough to be weaned.

Why hadn't he let her know when Bandit had had them and how many there were? Why…?

Because he'd been too caught up in whatever his latest scheme was for making money for Ethan, that was why.

She seized the plastic cone and snapped it in half. She dug her fingernails into it and gouged and shredded until some of the frustration eased out of her. Then she calmly retrieved another one and set it on the table. She pulled in a breath.

Okay, now she was ready to start.

The doorbell rang, but Jo ignored it. It would simply be more flowers for her grandmother. Her grandmother could answer it.

Jo set about measuring icing sugar.

Grandma popped her head into the kitchen a moment later. 'Jo, dear, would you mind coming out for a moment? We have a visitor.'

'Is it Great-Aunt Edith?' Had she dropped in early for some reason?

'No, dear, and I don't believe it's an emissary sent by her to sabotage the making of your *macaron* tower either.'

Your macaron *tower.* But Jo remained silent. Her great-aunt mightn't like losing, but she'd never stoop to foul play. Her grandmother, however, had taken to imagining dastardly plots at every turn.

Wiping her hands down the front of her shirt, Jo walked out into the lounge room—and her hands froze at rib level when she saw who stood there.

Mac!

She stared, mouth agape. It took all her strength to snap

it closed again, and the blood pounded in her ears and she had to plant her feet to counter the sudden giddiness that swirled through her.

She glanced at her grandmother, who smiled serenely.

She glanced at Mac, who smiled serenely.

Serene? Her heart tried to pound a path out of her chest. She wanted to scream. Whether in joy or despair, though, she wasn't sure.

'Hello, Jo.'

She swallowed and released the lip she'd been biting. 'What are you doing here, Mac?'

'Didn't I say, dear?' Grandma patted her arm. 'I've hired Mac to cater my dinner.'

She'd *what*? 'But…how?'

'I rang to tell you about the puppies, but you weren't in.'

Grandma hadn't mentioned that!

'We got talking. Your grandmother asked me if I'd be interested in catering her birthday dinner. And…' He shrugged.

It took every last muscle she had not to dissolve in the warmth of his eyes. The heat between them was as blistering as ever. She gripped her hands together. It would be a bad idea. Becoming lovers with this man would make her miserable.

You're already miserable.

She tossed her head and hardened her heart. 'And…?' she persisted.

'And I found I couldn't refuse.'

She would *not* be his consolation prize.

She opened her mouth, a set-down on her lips, but Mac had turned away to rifle in a basket.

He turned back with a handful of squirming fluffy puppy, wearing a pink and green bow around its neck. 'Happy birthday, Lucinda.'

'Oh, my word. Edith will have a fit!' Her grandmother

clapped her hands in delight. 'Thank you, Malcolm, what a lovely gift.'

Jo tried to prevent her eyes from starting from her head.

'And this one here is for you, Jo. I've called her Beauty.'

He placed the puppy in her arms and she had to close her eyes as his familiar scent hit her and the warmth of his voice threatened to cast a spell about her.

She took a step away from him. Liking each other had never been their problem. It was only logical that he'd still like her as much as he ever had—want her as much as he ever had. What wasn't logical was her instant response to him, given all that had happened—or not happened—between them.

It had been two months. She shouldn't love him as much now as she had then. She wanted to weep, only it filled her with so much joy to see him.

You'll pay for it tomorrow.

Her eyes stung. She moved further away from him, from all the temptation and remembered pain, to perch on an armchair with her sweet, sleepy puppy.

'Believe it or not…'

She couldn't help but glance up.

'Bandit has been pining for you.'

Only Bandit? She shook her head. 'I don't believe you.'

On the other side of the room her grandmother cooed over her puppy. Beauty snuggled down on Jo's lap, taking the base of Jo's thumb into her mouth as if determined to keep a hold of her. Jo covered her body with her free hand to let her know she was loved.

'The moment you left she set up a whine that turned into a howl.'

Truly? She gestured for him to take a seat on the sofa opposite, but he didn't move from where he stood. He all but devoured her with his hot, hungry gaze. She rolled her shoulders and swallowed.

'She hasn't forgiven me yet for letting you leave.'

Jo would. Forgive him, that was. If he said he was sorry and asked her to return with him she would. In an instant

No! That would be a bad thing, remember? She had a life. She'd have a new job soon. She had a puppy.

But she didn't have Mac.

You can't have everything.

She lifted her chin. 'Good for her.' She was *not* going to sacrifice her life to a man intent on sacrificing his own life to guilt and regret.

'How's Ethan?' It was a nasty little dart, but they both needed to remember why they couldn't be together.

'He's doing okay. I left him and Diana out at the beach house.'

He'd what?

Her jaw dropped. The puppy let out a yelp and with a start Jo relaxed her grip and bent to soothe it. She stroked it back to sleep, its fat little tummy and its utter trust weakening something inside her.

'How...?' she whispered when she finally dared to look at him. 'How did that come about?'

He glanced at his watch. 'Well, shoot—look at the time? Lucinda, you'd better point me in the direction of the kitchen if I'm to serve you at seven on the dot.'

He went out to his car, returning with two laden baskets filled with the most intriguing-looking ingredients.

He grinned at Jo. 'I understand you're my kitchen hand?'

She tried to smile back, but couldn't. 'Yay,' she said weakly instead.

'Buck up, Jo. All I want you to do is assemble a *macaron* tower.'

That was the problem. Mac didn't want her for anything more substantial. Her fingers curled against her palms. Why had her grandmother hired him? And, more to the point, why had Mac agreed to it?

They settled the puppies in their baskets in the laundry. Mac unpacked his groceries. Jo washed her hands and set about icing two plastic cones.

Mac glanced at them. 'Why two?'

He'd come up so close behind her his breath raised all the fine hairs at her nape. She wanted him to kiss her. She ached with it. But he hadn't given her so much as a kiss on the cheek, and that spoke volumes.

In her heart she knew it was for the best.

'I don't think I've mentioned yet what a sight for sore eyes you are.'

She was wearing an old pair of tracksuit pants and an oversized T-shirt that had once been blue but was now grey. She was a sight, all right, but not the kind he meant.

She spun around. 'What are you doing here, Mac?'

His gaze lowered to her mouth. Beneath tanned flesh the pulse at the base of his jaw pounded. Hunger roared through her. They swayed towards each other, but at the last moment he snapped away.

'If I kiss you now I'll be lost, and I did promise your grandmother I'd make this meal.' He ground that last from between clenched teeth. He glared at her. 'And you promised her that darn *macaron* tower.' He suddenly seized her shoulders in a strong grip. 'But after this party we're talking.'

'Right.' She swallowed. 'Good.'

Except… He wasn't going to go over old ground, was he? He wouldn't ask her to return to the beach house as his housekeeper, would he?

He had to know that wasn't enough.

His fingers tightened, although she sensed how he tempered his strength.

'What's the plan for this evening? Is there anything you'd like me to do?'

Love me.

She swallowed that back, shrugged. 'Just follow my lead, I guess. I think I have it under control.'

Fingers crossed.

They stared at each other for a long fraught moment. She swung away, her heart surging in her chest. One thing was clear—she and Mac still generated heat. Not that it made a bit of difference. Other than to make working with him in the confines of a suburban kitchen all the more fraught, uncomfortable…and exciting.

Focus on making the tower.

She'd been concentrating on this event for weeks now. She couldn't afford to let Mac derail her.

She made the *macaron* tower—carefully inserting toothpicks into the iced cones and then painstakingly attaching the coloured *macarons*. When that was done she decorated it all with swirls of pink, green and lemon ribbon.

She stood back to admire it and almost stepped on Mac. She glanced back at him. 'What do you think?'

Ugh! Think you could sound any needier?

She tossed her head. 'It's pretty fabulous, isn't it?'

'It's beautiful.'

But he was looking at her when he said it, not at the tower. The air between them shimmered. He took a hasty step away and Jo had to bite back the moan that rose through her.

Mac cleared his throat. 'What flavours did you decide to go with?'

She kept her gaze on the tower. 'Lime with passionfruit cream, and strawberry with a vanilla buttercream.'

'Nice.'

She picked up the tower and very *very* carefully walked it into the pantry.

Then she made a second tower, identical to the first. It was just as perfect. She set it in the pantry beside the first one.

Mac raised an eyebrow. She merely shrugged.

'Jo, dear.' Her grandmother came bustling in. 'Guests will start arriving in forty minutes and you've yet to shower and dress.'

'And take the puppies out for a pee and a romp in the back yard,' Jo added. 'Go ahead and finish getting ready, Grandma. I won't be late. I promise.'

CHAPTER TWELVE

JO ROMPED WITH the puppies for fifteen minutes, but all the while she was aware that Mac was in her childhood home and…and…

And what?

She settled the puppies back in their baskets and went to shower. She'd splurged on a new dress for the occasion. And heels. She'd almost be the same height as Mac in them.

Almost, but not quite.

Her grandmother was shooting last-minute instructions at Mac when Jo returned to the lounge room. During her absence Great-Aunt Edith had arrived. They all broke off to stare.

Jo turned on the spot. '*Now* I'm a sight for sore eyes,' she shot at Mac.

Her dress was a simple shift in a startling geometric pattern of orange, purple and black. It stopped a couple of inches short of her knees. She'd never worn anything so short before, and certainly not with heels. She had legs that… Well, they practically went on forever—even if she did say so herself.

Mac's eyes blazed obligingly. Fire licked along her belly in instant response.

'Nice,' he croaked.

'Good Lord, Jo! What *are* you wearing?' Her great-aunt tut-tutted. 'It's far too short for a girl of your height.'

'The shop assistant assured me it was perfect for a girl of my height,' Jo countered.

'You look very pretty, Jo, dear,' her grandma said.

Great-Aunt Edith glared. 'But is it *seemly*?'

Jo glanced back at Mac, who could barely drag his gaze from her legs, and a female purr of satisfaction rose through her. 'Oh, I expect it's quite the opposite, Aunt Edith, but I believe that's the point.'

Before her aunt could remonstrate further the doorbell rang and Jo went to answer it, putting a sway into her step for Mac's benefit.

Eat your heart out.

When she returned he'd retreated to the kitchen and she could breathe easier again. He needn't think he could come around here and get her all het-up without expecting some kind of payback.

Five additional guests had been invited to dinner, all of them longstanding friends of her grandmother's and great-aunt's—people Jo had known all her life.

Each of them stared at her as if they didn't recognise her when she answered the door. They'd stare a whole lot more before she was through this evening.

She went to serve drinks, but Mac was there before her.

'Who *is* that young man?' her great-aunt demanded of her grandmother.

'Aunt Edith, this is Malcolm MacCallum—the famous chef,' Jo said. 'I was his housekeeper for a short time not that long ago.'

'Humph. I remember. I can't believe you'd waste your education on such a lowly position as housemaid.'

'What does it matter?' her grandmother piped up. 'As long as she was happy.'

Happy? Jo shoulders started to droop.

'And I can't believe you're turning your back on the possibility of promotion, not to mention stability, by switching vocations so late in life.'

Late in life? Jo choked.

Mac's lips twitched, and her great-aunt's eyes narrowed. 'Precisely how well do you know this Malcolm?'

She made her smile bright. 'Very well.'

Great-Aunt Edith drew herself up to her full formidable height. 'I'd like to know—'

'I'm afraid it's none of your business.'

'Jo!' her grandmother remonstrated.

'Or yours either, Grandma.'

The sisters stared at each other, evidently nonplussed.

'How long before we eat?' Jo shot out of the corner of her mouth.

Mac cleared his throat. 'If everyone would like to move into the dining room, I'll serve the entrée.'

Jo silently blessed him, and moved towards the kitchen to help, but with a gentle shove he pushed her towards the dining room.

'I have it covered.'

Right. Was he ever going to tell her what Ethan was doing at his beach house? And did it have any bearing on them—him and her?

There is no you and him.

Her grandmother sat at the head of the table and her great-aunt at the foot. Her grandmother's allies sat on the right side of the table—which was where Jo found herself—and her great-aunt's ranged down the left.

Like a battlefield.

As if this were a war.

And then it started.

'Do you think it's *wise* to wear such high heels when you're such a large girl, Jo?'

'Eadie, don't be such an old-fashioned prig. Our Jo is the height of fashion.'

Everyone else around the table weighed in with an opinion.

'I think that dress and those heels are perfect,' Mac said, serving mussels in garlic sauce.'

Both sisters glared at him, united for a moment in their mutual suspicion. Jo hid a smile.

In the next instant, however, the entire table had lost themselves in the delight of the food, forgetting all about Mac. Across the table he caught her eye. He mouthed 'perfect' before disappearing back into the kitchen. Her pulse skittered. Her heart throbbed.

When everyone had finished the entrée her great-aunt said, 'Jo, I really think you need to reconsider this career change you've been talking about.'

'Oh, Eadie, stop fussing. If this is what Jo wants—and if it'll make her happy—then so be it.'

'Heavens, Lucinda—a *paramedic*? Any Tom, Dick or Harriet can train as one of those. Our Jo is better than that.'

'Your Jo is quite simply the best,' Mac said, having whisked their entrée plates away and now serving lamb so succulent it melted in the mouth.

'She'll become a drudge,' her great-aunt said.

Grandma shook her head. 'Her choice.'

'I'd quite happily become *her* drudge,' Mac said.

Jo nearly swallowed her tongue.

'Who *is* he?' her great-aunt demanded.

'He's Mac.' She had no other explanation.

'He's her admirer,' Grandma said.

'If Jo had what it took to catch a man she'd have done so years ago,' scoffed Great-Aunt Edith.

'Ha!' snapped Grandma. 'Jo has her head screwed on right. Life is far easier when one doesn't have to pander to a man. Not that *you'd* know about that, Eadie.'

Ouch! Jo winced on her aunt's behalf.

'If Jo married me I'd be a very lucky man.'

Jo's fingers tightened about her cutlery and her stomach churned. What game was Mac playing?

'If you married him you could eat like this every night,' one of her grandmother's cronies said.

They ate then, mostly in silence, all relishing the amazing food.

Eventually Great-Aunt Edith pushed her plate away. 'Ladies, don't forget to leave room for dessert.' She shot Jo a smirk. 'I take it there *will* be dessert?'

'But of course.'

'Ah, but will it be the *promised* dessert?' She folded her arms and glared down the table. 'What *I* want to know is if she's managed to pull off what she promised she could. Lucy? Did she or did she not make you a *macaron* tower?'

Her grandmother smiled benignly. 'Where are the stakes?'

Jo rolled her eyes when the contested pearls were placed with ridiculous ceremony in the middle of the table.

Mac cleared the plates. 'I'll pour the dessert wine,' he said, moving to the sideboard. 'Jo, you can bring in the dessert.'

'The dishes?' she asked him.

'All cleared.'

'The puppies?'

'Safely tucked away in the laundry.'

Good. Right. She drew in a breath, rose, and moved to the kitchen.

As carefully as she'd ever done anything in her life, Jo picked up the first tower that she'd made and backed out of the pantry. She paused outside the doorway to the dining room for a moment, to pull in a breath, and balancing carefully on her new heels entered the room.

Gasps rose up all around her.

She set the concoction in front of her grandmother and

with a quiver of relief stepped back again. Mission accomplished.

'Happy birthday, Grandma. I love you.' She kissed her grandmother's cheek.

They sang 'Happy Birthday', but throughout the song she couldn't help but notice, even though Great-Aunt Edith's voice was the loudest, how her aunt's gaze kept returning to the tower in awe. And she recognised something else there too—hunger and yearning.

When the song finished Jo left the room and returned with the second tower. She set it down in front of her great-aunt. 'I made this one for you Aunt Edith, because I love you too.'

'But…' Grandma spluttered. 'It's not Eadie's birthday.'

'Maybe not, but you both deserve pretty, beautiful things. To me, you're both the most beautiful women I know, and you've helped to make me the woman I am today.'

They stared at her, but neither spoke.

'My real gift to you today, Grandma, is to bring this ridiculous feud of yours and Aunt Edith's to an end.' She reached across the table and took the pearls. 'These now belong to me. I have no cousins. It's what Great-Grandmother would've wanted. Besides…' She clasped them around her throat. 'They go perfectly with my outfit.'

The sisters' jaws dropped.

'Those towers consist of your individual favourite *macaron* flavours. The combination is perfect—much better than if they were just one or the other. Just as the two of *you* are perfect together.'

Both women's eyes had grown suspiciously damp.

'I love you. I know you both love me. I also know you love each other—even if you find the words too hard to say. Great-Aunt Edith, it's time for you to come home. This is where you belong and this is where you're wanted.'

Grandma blew her nose loudly. 'She's right, Eadie.'

Great-Aunt Edith cleared her throat—twice. 'Lucy, I can't tell you how glad I am to hear it.'

'Excellent.' Mac broke into the moment. 'Now that *that's* settled, I'm stealing Jo away.' He raised a hand before anyone could argue with him. 'She's not fond of *macarons*, so I've made her a dessert of her own.'

He took her arm.

'Jo?' her grandmother and her great-aunt said in unison.

'It's okay,' Jo said. 'I'll shout if I need rescuing.'

With that, she allowed him to pull her into the kitchen.

He turned with a grin that turned her heart over and over. 'That was masterfully done,' he said.

'Yes.' It had left her feeling powerful. 'What dessert did you make me?'

He handed her a plate. 'Pineapple upside-down cake.'

She took a mouthful and closed her eyes in bliss. When she opened them Mac was staring at her with a naked hunger he didn't try to hide. It only made her feel more powerful and assured…and bold.

She tipped up her chin. 'When are you going to tell me you love me?'

He met her gaze uncertainly. 'I thought I'd been saying it all evening.'

He had.

Her great-aunt and her grandmother came bustling into the kitchen.

'My dear, I do believe it's terribly poor form to just leave the table like that.'

'Yes—listen to your grandmother. We raised you better than that.'

'I agree. But I'm afraid there are puppies to attend to. Unless you'd rather deal with the puppies yourselves?'

'Maybe Malcolm could…?'

'Not in a caterer's job description, I'm afraid,' Mac said, edging Jo towards the back door.

'Puppies?' asked Great-Aunt Edith.

'Come along, dear, and I'll tell you about them. Malcolm brought one for me and...' she glanced at Jo '...one for you, Eadie dear.'

Grandma had just given away her puppy!

'There are more puppies back at the beach house,' Mac whispered in her ear.

Jo let out a breath. Okay.

Before Grandma and Great-Aunt Edith could form another argument, Jo took Mac's hand and led him outside.

'You left the puppies behind,' Mac said.

'But I do still have hold of my dessert.'

She released him to eat another spoonful. She took a step away from him so she could breathe and think.

She lifted her plate. 'This is divine.'

'You're divine.'

Mac stared at the woman he loved and wondered if he'd done enough to win her.

If he hadn't he'd just do more. He'd do more and more and still more if he had to—to convince her that they belonged together, to prove to her that he could make her happy.

She led him down to an old swing set and sat on the swing. He leaned against the frame and feasted his eyes on her. He burned to kiss her, but while it killed him he had no intention of hauling her into his arms until he was one hundred per cent certain it was what she wanted.

She had questions. Rightly. It was only fair that he answered them.

'You somehow managed to manipulate my grandmother into asking you to come here today?'

'Guilty as charged.'

'Because you were worried I might fail with the *macarons*?'

He had no intention of lying to her. 'I came here today to help you in whatever capacity you needed me to.'

She'd outdone herself with those *macaron* towers, though.

She pursed her lips, staring at him. 'So you worked out early on that I was trying to get Grandma and Great-Aunt Edith arguing on the same side? Against me?'

'It was a good plan. But it seemed only fair that someone should argue on your side too.'

If she'd let him, he'd always argue her case.

'Why is Ethan at your beach house?'

She sat in the moonlight, eating pineapple upside-down cake in that sexy little purple and orange number, and for a moment he couldn't speak. The urge to kiss her grew, but he tamped it down. After all this time away from her just being able to look at her thrilled him.

The night was mild for this time of year, but not exactly warm. He slipped his jacket off and settled it around her shoulders.

The flash of vulnerability in her eyes when he moved in close stabbed at him.

He eased back, his heart thumping and his mouth dry. 'Everything you said to me before you left was a hundred per cent on the money.'

He closed his eyes. What if he hadn't done enough? What if his best wasn't good enough? What if she simply wished him well and turned away? How would he cope?

'I don't want to play games, Mac.'

His eyes flew open.

She rose. 'If you don't want to talk then I'd like to go back inside.'

He was being pathetic. Spineless. Waiting for a sign from her first.

A real man wouldn't hesitate.

Earn her!

'Please don't go, Jo. I was just gathering my thoughts. It's been a crazy couple of months and I'm trying to work out where to start.'

She searched his face. Slowly she sat again. 'Tell me what happened after I left.'

He leant back against the swing set's A-frame. 'I threw myself into finishing the cookbook. I finished it in record time.'

'Congratulations.'

'And then, with nothing to keep me occupied, I had a lot of time to think.'

'Ah.'

'And some of the things you said tormented me—like trying harder where Ethan was concerned. So I started wondering what more I could do to help him.'

'And…?'

She stared up at him and her lips glistened as if she'd just moistened them. Hunger roared through him.

'It took me longer to work out than it should've.'

'And what did you work out?'

'That he needed to be shaken up the same way you shook me up.'

Her lovely mouth dropped open.

'I talked to his doctor first. I had no intention of barging in like a bull in a china shop like I did the last time. The doctor and I came up with a plan to bring him to the beach house, and then we got Diana Devlin on-side.'

'I bet that wasn't easy.'

He and Diana might never be the best of friends, but they'd come to an understanding.

'Once the doctor told her he thought it'd be for the best she was behind the plan a hundred per cent.'

Jo leaned towards him. 'How did you convince Ethan to go with you?'

'I used emotional blackmail. Just like you had on me. By the way, Russ sends his love. I'm staying with him tonight.'

'You've *seen* Russ?'

'I've seen quite a bit of Russ.'

'He's not mentioned it to me.'

Because Mac had asked him not to. He hadn't wanted to get her hopes up. He hadn't known how long things with Ethan would take.

She sagged, one hand pressed to her chest. 'I'm so glad.'

'I am too,' he said quietly. 'There are some mistakes I'm never going to make again. But back to Ethan. I told him his mother needed a holiday, but that she refused to go without him. I told him she'd fall ill if she wasn't careful.'

Her mouth hooked up. 'Nice work.'

His chest puffed out.

'And he's improving?'

'It's taken a while, but, yes. The sea air and the fact he can see how good the break has been for his mother have both worked wonders. It's the puppies, though, that have really been working magic.'

She leant back, her eyes wide. 'Wow, that's really something.'

It was. 'Every now and again he starts to talk about the future. We even had an argument last week about what recipes I should put in my next cookbook.'

Her urgings to keep trying, not to give up, to try harder, had made a man of him. Regardless of what happened from here, he was glad—and grateful—to have known her.

'He doesn't blame me for the accident, Jo. He's learning not to blame himself either.'

She set her now empty plate on the ground and rose to stand in front of him. 'That's wonderful news.'

His heart started to race. Hard.

'He still has a way to go. There'll be more skin grafts

down the track. But eventually he'll be able to return to work. When he's ready I mean to help him any way I can.'

She moved another inch closer. Mac swallowed, his hands clenching at his sides.

'I don't know—' His voice cracked. 'I don't know if you can live with that. You might see it as me putting him first.'

She shook her head. 'I see it as you being a good friend—a true friend. I certainly don't see it as a sacrifice or self-immolation or a sign of guilt.'

He stared at her. 'That's good, right?'

'That's very good.'

He couldn't drag his gaze from the smoky depths of her eyes. Was she saying what he thought she was saying?

He seized her face in his hands, unable to resist the need to touch her. 'What are you saying, Jo?'

No, wait!

'No, wait,' he said. 'Let me tell you what *I'm* saying. I'm saying I love you, my beautiful girl.' He brushed her hair back from her face. 'I'm saying I want a life with you. I'm saying that fighting for you—by fighting to work out the right thing to do where Ethan was concerned—has made a man of me. I'm saying that if you give me a chance I will prove to you every single day that you are my first, foremost and most cherished priority.'

His hands moved back to cup her face.

'You are my number one, Jo. Please say you'll let me prove it.'

She pressed a hand to his lips. Her face came in close to his, her eyes shining and her lips trembling. 'I love you, Mac,' she whispered.

He wanted to punch the air. He wanted to whirl her around in his arms. He wanted to kiss her.

'No man has ever made me believe in myself the way you have. No man has made me feel so desired or so beautiful or so right.' She swallowed. 'Yes, please. I really want the chance to build a life with you.'

He stared down into her face as every dream he'd been too afraid to dream lay before him in a smorgasbord of promise.

Jo's eyes started to dance. She leaned in so close her words played across his lips. 'This is the part where you kiss me.'

He didn't wait another second, but swooped down to seize her lips in a kiss that spoke of all he couldn't put into words. He kissed her with his every pent-up hope and fear, with the joy and frustration that had shaken through him these last months since he'd met her. And she kissed him back with such ardent eagerness and generosity it eased the burn in his soul.

He lifted his head with a groan, gathering her in close. 'I love you, Jo. I nearly went crazy when I thought I'd lost you.'

Her arms tightened about him. 'You haven't lost me. I'm in your arms, where I belong, and I'm not planning on going anywhere.'

'You mean that?'

'With all my heart.'

And then she frowned. 'Well, I mean, I *do* start my para-medic training next week, so I'll have to leave your arms literally, but you know what I mean.'

He dropped a kiss to the tip of her nose. Her very cute nose. 'But you'll keep returning here? To me?'

Her fingers stroked his nape. 'There's nowhere I'd rather be,' she whispered.

'I can commute between the coast and Sydney,' he said.

'And I can commute between Sydney and the coast,' she said. 'But, Mac, we need to make sure that wherever we go we always have room for friends and for puppies.'

A grin started up inside him until it bubbled from him

in a laugh. 'I'm glad you feel that way, because Bandit had ten of the little beggars.'

Her mouth dropped open, so he kissed her again. When he lifted his head—much, *much* later—she smiled dreamily up at him.

'Did I mention that I happen to love the way you kiss?'

'No.'

So she proceeded to tell him. Which meant, of course, that he had to kiss her again.

When he lifted his head this time he found himself growling, 'Promise me forever.'

She reached up to press her hand to his cheek. 'I promise you, Mac—' she stared deep into his eyes '—that for as long as you make me pineapple upside-down cake, I'm yours. Forever.'

Her voice washed over him like warm honey and he started to laugh…and it filled his soul.

* * * * *

"If this child is mine then I won't dodge my responsibility."

She looked less than impressed by the idea.

"If you're talking about money, I think I've made it pretty clear I'm not interested."

"You can't raise a child on good intentions, Mary-Jayne. Be sensible."

She looked ready for an argument, but she seemed to change her mind. "I'm heating up lasagna. Are you staying for dinner?"

Daniel raised a brow. "Am I invited?"

She shrugged, like she couldn't care either way.

"Sure," she said. "That would be good."

He watched as she removed several items from the refrigerator and began making a salad. And Daniel couldn't take his eyes off her. Her glorious hair shone like ebony beneath the kitchen light and she chewed her bottom lip as she completed the task. And of course thinking about her lips made him remember their night together. And kissing her. And making love to her. She had a remarkable effect on him, and he wondered if it was because they were so different that he was so achingly attracted to her. She was all challenge. All resistance. And since very little challenged him these days, Daniel knew her very determination to avoid him had a magnetic pull all of its own.

And he had no idea what he was going to do about it.

The Prestons of Crystal Point:
All's fair in family…and love!

THE CEO'S
BABY SURPRISE

BY
HELEN LACEY

All rights reserved including the right of reproduction in whole or in part in any form. This edition is published by arrangement with Harlequin Books S.A.

This is a work of fiction. Names, characters, places, locations and incidents are purely fictional and bear no relationship to any real life individuals, living or dead, or to any actual places, business establishments, locations, events or incidents. Any resemblance is entirely coincidental.

This book is sold subject to the condition that it shall not, by way of trade or otherwise, be lent, resold, hired out or otherwise circulated without the prior consent of the publisher in any form of binding or cover other than that in which it is published and without a similar condition including this condition being imposed on the subsequent purchaser.

® and ™ are trademarks owned and used by the trademark owner and/or its licensee. Trademarks marked with ® are registered with the United Kingdom Patent Office and/or the Office for Harmonization in the Internal Market and in other countries.

Published in Great Britain 2013
By Mills & Boon, an imprint of Harlequin (UK) Limited,
Eton House, 18-24 Paradise Road, Richmond, Surrey, TW9 1SR

© Helen Lacey 2012

MILLS
BOON

Published in Great Britain 2015
by Mills & Boon, an imprint of Harlequin (UK) Limited,
Eton House, 18-24 Paradise Road, Richmond, Surrey, TW9 1SR

© 2015 Helen Lacey

ISBN: 978-0-263-25124-1

23-0415

Harlequin (UK) Limited's policy is to use papers that are natural, renewable and recyclable products and made from wood grown in sustainable forests. The logging and manufacturing processes conform to the legal environmental regulations of the country of origin.

Printed and bound in Spain
by CPI, Barcelona

Helen Lacey grew up reading *Black Beauty* and *Little House on the Prairie*. These childhood classics inspired her to write her first book when she was seven, a story about a girl and her horse. She loves writing for Mills & Boon® Cherish™, where she can create strong heroes with a soft heart and heroines with gumption who get their happily-ever-after. For more about Helen, visit her website, www.helenlacey.com.

For my mother, Evelyn.
Who believes in me no matter what.

Prologue

Mary-Jayne Preston yawned, opened her eyes and blinked a few times. The ceiling spun fractionally, and she drew in a soft breath.

I'm not hungover.

She closed her eyes again. The two glasses of champagne she'd drunk the night before weren't responsible for the way she felt. This was something else. An unusual lethargy crept into her limbs and spread across her skin. Her lids fluttered, and she glimpsed a sliver of light from between heavy drapes.

An unfamiliar room.

Her memory kicked in. The Sandwhisper Resort. Port Douglas.

But this isn't my bedroom.

This was a villa suite. And a top-end one, judging by the plush feel of the giant king-size bed and lavish damask drapes. Extravagance personified. Her eyelids drooped before opening again as she stretched her spine—and then nearly jumped out of her skin when she realized she wasn't alone in the big bed.

A man lay beside her. She twisted her head and saw a long, perfectly proportioned back. Smooth skin, like the sheerest satin stretched over pressed steel, broad shoulders, strong arms and dark hair. He lay on his stomach, one arm flung above his head, the other curved by his side. And he was asleep. The soft rhythm of his breathing was oddly hypnotic, and she stared at him, suddenly mesmerized by his bronzed skin and lean, muscular frame.

And then, in stunning Technicolor, it came rushing back.

The party.
The kiss.
The one-night stand.
Her first. Her *last.*

She needed to get up. To *think*. She shimmied sideways but quickly stopped moving when he stirred. She wasn't quite ready for any kind of face-to-face, morning-after awkwardness. Not with *him*. She took a deep breath and tried again, inching her hips across the cool sheet so slowly it was agonizing. Finally one leg found the edge of the mattress and she pushed the cover back. He moved again and she stilled instantly. He made a sound, half groan, half moan, and flipped around, the sheet draping haphazardly over his hips as he came to face her.

But still asleep.

Mary-Jayne's breath shuddered out as she caught sight of his profile. He was ridiculously handsome. No wonder she'd lost her head. The straight nose, chiseled cheeks and square jaw was a riveting combination. And she quickly recalled those silver-gray eyes of his…just too sexy for words. As her gaze traveled lower her fingertips tingled.

His body was incredibly well cut, and she fought the urge to touch him just one more time. She spotted a faint mark on his shoulder. Like a love bite.

Did I do that?

Heat surged through her blood when she remembered what they'd done the night before, and again in the small hours of the morning. No sweet wonder her muscles ached and her skin seemed ultrasensitive. She'd never had a night like it before, never felt such intense desire or experienced such acute and mindboggling pleasure.

It was like a dream. A fantasy.

And she needed to wake up from this particular dream. Quickly.

She managed to ease off the bed and quickly looked around for clothes. Her underwear was by the bed, and she snatched it up with guilty fingers and then quickly dressed into the thong and bra. The shoes were easily spotted—one was by the window, the other under a chair in the corner of the room. But the black dress was nowhere to be seen. The smooth fabric had clung to her curves, and the man in the bed had told her how beautiful and desirable she'd looked. No one had ever said those words quite that way to her before. She found her purse on the chair and continued looking for the dress, keeping a mindful eye on him.

Please don't wake up...

He didn't, thankfully, and a few moments later she found the dress, scrunched in a ball and hidden beneath the quilt that had fallen to the foot of the bed. She stepped into it and slipped it up and over her hips, settling her arms through the bodice before she twisted herself into a pretzel to do up the zipper. Breathless, she cast another look toward the sleeping man.

I'm such a fool...

For weeks she'd stayed resolute, determined to avoid crashing into bed with him. But the moment he'd touched her, the moment he'd made his move she'd melted like an ice cube in hell.

Mary-Jayne pushed her feet into her patent pumps, grabbed her purse and ran.

Chapter One

Pregnant.

Not a bout of food poisoning as she'd wanted to believe.

Mary-Jayne walked from the doctor's office and headed for her car. Her head hurt. Her feet hurt. Everything hurt. The snap on her jeans felt tight around her waist. Now she knew why.

She was three months and three weeks pregnant.

She opened the door of the borrowed Honda Civic and got inside. Then she placed a hand over her belly and let out a long, heavy breath.

Twenty-seven. Single. Pregnant.

Right.

Not exactly the end of the world…but not what she'd been expecting, either.

One day she'd imagined she'd have a baby. When she was married and settled, not while she was trying to carve out a career as a jewelry designer and wasn't exactly financially stable.

She thought about calling her older sisters, Evie and Grace, but quickly shrugged off the idea. She needed time to think. Plan. Sort out what she was going to do, before she told anyone. Especially her sisters, who'd want to know *everything*.

She'd have to tell them about that night.

She gripped the steering wheel and let out a long, weary sigh. She'd tried to put the memory from her mind countless times. And failed. Every time she walked around the grounds of the Sandwhisper Resort she was reminded. And every time she fielded a telephone call from *him* she was thrust back to that crazy night.

Mary-Jayne drove through the gates of the resort and took a left down the road that led to the employees' residences. Her villa was small but well appointed and opened onto the deck and to the huge heated pool and spa area. The Sandwhisper Resort was one of the largest in Port Douglas, and certainly one of the most luxurious. The town of Port Douglas was about forty miles north of Cairns, and its population of over three thousand often doubled during peak vacation times. Living and working at the luxurious resort for the past four and half months hadn't exactly been a hardship. Running her friend Audrey's boutique was mostly enjoyable and gave her the opportunity to create and showcase her own jewelry. Life was a breeze.

Correction.

Life *had* been a breeze.

Until she'd had an uncharacteristic one-night stand with Daniel Anderson.

CEO of Anderson Holdings and heir apparent to the huge fortune that had been made by his grandfather from ore and copper mining years earlier, he owned the Sandwhisper Resort with his two brothers. There were four other resorts around the globe—one in Phuket, another along the Amalfi coast in Italy, another in the Maldives and the flagship resort in the San Francisco Bay Area.

He was rich, successful, uptight and absurdly arrogant.

Everything she'd always abhorred in a man.

He was also reported to be kind, generous and honest.

Well…according to his grandmother.

Eighty-year-old Solana Anderson adored her grandsons and spent her retirement flying between the east and west coasts of Australia and America, living at the resorts during the spring and summer months in alternating time zones. Mary-Jayne liked the older woman very much. They'd met the first day she'd arrived at the resort after the desperate emergency call from her old school friend Audrey had sent her flying up to Port Douglas with barely a packed suitcase. Audrey had moved into Mary-Jayne's small house in Crystal Point so she could be close to her ill mother while Mary-Jayne moved into Audrey's condo at the resort. Once she was in residence, she read the scribbled note with instructions her friend had left and opened the boutique at an unrespectable eleven o'clock. It was meant to be a temporary gig—but Audrey insisted her mother needed her. So her planned three weeks ended up being for six months.

And Solana, straight backed and still vibrant at nearly eighty years of age, had come into the store looking for an outfit to wear to her upcoming birthday party, and within the hour they were chatting and laughing over herbal tea and several outfit changes. It was then she learned that Solana's American-born husband had died a decade earlier and how she'd borne him a son and daughter. Mary-Jayne had listened while Solana talked about her much-loved grandsons, Daniel, Blake and Caleb and granddaughter Renee. One hour ticked over into two, and by three o'clock the older woman had finally decided upon an outfit and persuaded Mary-Jayne to let her see some of her hand-crafted jewelry pieces. Solana had since bought three items and had recommended Mary-Jayne's work to several of her friends.

Yes, she liked Solana. But wasn't about to tell the other woman she was carrying her great-grandchild. Not until she figured out what she was going to do. She was nearly four months along, and her pregnancy would be showing itself very soon. She couldn't hide her growing stomach behind baggy clothes forever.

He has a right to know...

The notion niggled at her over and over.

She could have the baby alone. Women did it all the time. And it was not as if she and Daniel had any kind of relationship. If she wanted, she could leave the resort and go home and never see him again. He lived mostly in San Francisco. She lived in Crystal Point, a small seaside town that sat at the southernmost point of the Great Barrier Reef. They had different lives. Different worlds.

And she didn't even like him.

She'd met him three times before the night of Solana's birthday. The first time she'd been in the store window, bent over and struggling to remove a garment from the mannequin. When she was done she'd straightened, turned to avoid knocking the mannequin over and came face-to-face with him on the other side of the glass. He'd been watching her, arms crossed.

Of course she'd known immediately who he was. There were several pictures of him and his brothers in Solana's villa, and she'd visited the older woman many times. Plus, he looked enough like his younger brother Caleb for her to recognize the family resemblance. Caleb ran the resorts in Port Douglas and Phuket while his twin Blake looked after Amalfi, Maldives and San Francisco. And according to staff gossip Daniel lorded over the resorts, his brothers and the staff from his private jet.

Still, it was hard not to be impressed by his ridiculous good looks, and despite the fact he was not her type, Mary-Jayne was as susceptible as the next woman. The impeccably cut suit, creaseless white shirt and dark tie were a riveting combination on his broad, tall frame, and for a second she'd been rooted to the spot, unable to move, unable to do anything other than stare back, held captive by the look in his gray eyes. For a moment, at least. Until he'd raised one brow and a tiny smile whispered along the edges of his mouth. He'd then looked her over with a kind of leisurely conceit that had quickly sent alarm bells clanging in her head.

There'd been interest in his expression and if he'd been anyone else she might have made some kind of encouraging gesture. Like a smile. Or nod. But Daniel Anderson was out of her league. A rich and successful corporate shark with a reputation for having no tolerance for fools in business, and no proclivity for commitment in his private life. He was the kind of man she'd always planned to avoid like the plague. The kind of man that had never interested her before.

But something had passed between them in that first moment. A look… Recognition.

Awareness…

Heat…

Attraction…

When her good sense had returned she'd darted from the window and got back to the customer waiting in the changing room. By the time she'd moved back to the front of the store and began ringing up the sale he was gone.

Mary-Jayne saw him a day later, striding across the resort foyer with his brother at his side. She'd been coming from the day spa, arms loaded with jewelry trays, when Caleb had said her name. She'd met the younger Anderson many times over the previous weeks. He was rich, charming and handsome and didn't do a solitary thing to her libido. Not so his older brother. She'd fumbled with the trays and stayed rooted to the spot as they approached and then managed to nod her way through an introduction. He was unsmiling, but his eyes regarded her with blistering intensity. Caleb's attention had quickly been diverted by the day-shift concierge and she'd been left alone with him, silent and nervous beneath his unfaltering gaze.

Then he'd spoken, and his deep voice, a smooth mix of his American upbringing and Australian roots, wound up her spine like liquid silk. "My grandmother tells me you're here for six months rather than the few weeks you'd originally planned on?"

He'd talked about her with Solana? "Ah, that's right," she'd croaked.

"And are you enjoying your time here?"

She'd nodded, feeling stupid and awkward and not in the least bit like her usual self. Normally she was confident and opinionated and more than comfortable in her own skin. But two seconds around Daniel Anderson and she was a speechless fool. Übergood looks had never interested her before. But he stirred her senses big time.

"Yes, very much."

"And I trust your friend's parent's health is improving?"

He knew about Audrey's mother? Solana *had* been busy sharing information.

"A little...yes."

A small smile had crinkled the corner of his mouth and Mary-Jayne's gaze had instantly been drawn to his lips. He had seen her reaction and his smile had increased fractionally. There was something extraordinarily hypnotic about him, something she couldn't quite fathom. Something she'd known she had to extricate herself from…and fast.

She'd hastily excused herself and taken off as fast as she could.

And hadn't seen him again for two days.

She'd left the resort for a run along the beach and had come upon him jogging in the other direction. He'd slowed when he was about twenty feet from her and come to a halt right next to her. And the look between them had been electric. Out of this world and all-consuming. She'd never experienced such blatant and blistering physical attraction for anyone before. And it shocked her to the core. He wasn't her usual type. In fact, Daniel Anderson was the epitome of everything she *didn't* want in a man. Money, power, arrogance… They were attributes her small-town, middle-class self had decided long ago were not for her. She dated musicians and out-of-work artists. Not corporate sharks.

His expression had been unwavering and contained hot sexual appreciation. He wanted her. No doubt about it. And the look in his eyes had made it clear he thought he'd get her.

"You know," he'd said with a kind of arrogant confidence that made her tremble. "My villa is only minutes away."

She knew that. The family's quarters were secluded and luxurious and away from the main part of the resort and had a spectacular view of the beach.

"And?" she'd managed to say, despite the way her heart had thundered behind her ribs and her knees wobbled.

He'd half smiled. "And we both know that's where we're going to end up at some point."

Mortified, she'd quickly taken off like a bullet. But her body was thrumming with a kind of intoxicating awareness that stayed with her for hours. For days. Until she'd seen him again two days later at Solana's birthday party. The older woman had insisted she attend the celebration and Mary-Jayne respected Solana too much to refuse the invitation. She'd ditched her usual multicolored skirts and long tops and rummaged through Audrey's wardrobe for a party dress. And she'd found one—a slip of silky black jersey that clung to her like a second skin. The huge ball-room was easy to get lost in…or so she'd thought. But it had only taken ten minutes until she'd felt him watching her from across the room. He'd approached and asked if she wanted a drink. Within half an hour they had been out on the balcony, talking intimately. Seconds later they'd been kissing madly. Minutes later they'd been in his villa tearing each other's clothes off.

But Mary-Jayne wasn't under any illusions.

She knew enough about Daniel Anderson to realize she was simply another notch on his bedpost. He was hand-some, successful and wealthy and played the field merci-lessly. Something he had done without compunction since the death of his wife and unborn child four years earlier. He certainly wouldn't be interested in her for anything other than a one-night stand. She wasn't his type. Oh, he'd knocked on the door of her villa the day after Solana's party and asked her out. But she'd shut him down. She'd piqued his interest for a moment and that was all. Thank-fully, he'd left the resort the following day and returned to San Francisco, exactly as she'd hoped. But she hadn't expected that he'd call the store two weeks later and an-nounce that he wanted to see her again when he returned from California.

See her?

Yeah…right. The only thing he wanted to see was her naked body between the sheets. And she knew that for a man like Daniel Anderson, the chase was all that mattered. She'd refused him, and that was like pouring oil onto a fire.

When he'd called her again two weeks later she'd been in South Dakota for a friend's wedding. Annoyed that he wouldn't take the hint and all out of patience, she'd lost her temper and told him to go to hell. Then she'd returned to the Sandwhisper Resort and waited. Waited for another call. Waited for him to arrive at the resort and confuse and seduce her with his steely-eyed gaze and uncompromising intensity. But he hadn't called. And hadn't returned. As one week slipped into another, Mary-Jayne had slowly relaxed and convinced herself he'd lost interest.

Which was exactly what she wanted.

Only now, the tables had turned. She was having his baby. Which meant one thing—she'd have to see him and tell him she was having his baby. And soon.

Daniel had struggled with the remnants of a headache for two days. The three other suits in the conference room were grating on his nerves. Some days he wanted nothing more than to throw off the shackles of his name, his legacy and everything else and live a simple, quiet life.

Like today.

Because it was his birthday. He was turning thirty-four years old. He had money and power and a successful business at his command. He had apartments in San Francisco, another in London and then there was the family-owned hilltop chateau in France that he hadn't been near for over four years. He also had any number of women willing to warm his bed with minimal notice and who understood he didn't want commitment or anything resembling a serious relationship. He traveled the world but rarely saw anything other than the walls of boardrooms and offices at the resorts he'd helped build into some of the most successful around the globe. Nothing and no one touched him.

Well…except for Mary-Jayne Preston.

She was a thorn in his side. A stone in his shoe. A pain in his neck.

Months after that one crazy night in Port Douglas and he was still thinking about her. She was incredibly beautiful. Her green eyes were luminous; her lips were full and endlessly kissable. But it was her hair that had first captured his attention that day in the store window. She had masses of dark curls that hung down past her shoulders. And of course there were her lovely curves, which she possessed in all the right places.

He'd checked out her history and discovered she came from a middle-class family in Crystal Point, had studied at a local technical college and had an online business selling her handcrafted jewelry. She rented her home, owned a dog, volunteered at a number of animal shelters, had strong opinions about the environment and politics and liked to dress in colorful skirts or jeans with holes in the knees. She had piercings in her ears and navel and a butterfly tattoo on one shoulder.

She wasn't his type. Not by a long shot.

Which didn't make one ounce of difference to the relentless effect she had on him whenever she was within a twenty-foot radius. And the night of his grandmother's birthday party he'd almost tripped over his own feet when he'd caught a glimpse of her across the room. She'd looked incredible in a dress that highlighted every dip and curve of her body. And with her dark hair cascading down her back in a wave he just about had to cleave his tongue from the roof of his mouth. She looked hot. Gorgeous. Desirable.

And he knew then he wanted to get her in his bed.

It took half an hour to get her alone. Then he'd kissed her. And she'd kissed him back.

And before either of them had a chance to come up for air they were in his villa suite, tearing off clothes with little finesse and more eagerness than he'd felt in years. It had been a hot, wild night, compounded by months of abstinence and the fact he'd had Mary-Jayne Preston very much on his mind since the first time he'd seen her.

"Are you listening?"

Daniel shook off his thoughts and glanced to his left. Blake was staring at him, one brow cocked. "Always."

Blake didn't look convinced and quickly turned his attention to the other suits in the room. After a few more minutes, he dismissed the two other men, and once they were alone his brother moved to the bar and grabbed two imported beers from the fridge.

Daniel frowned. "A little early, don't you think?"

Blake flicked the tops off the bottles and shrugged. "It's after three. And you look as if you need it."

He didn't disagree, and stretched back in his leather chair. "Maybe I do."

Blake passed him a beer and grabbed a seat. "Happy birthday," his brother said, and clinked the bottle necks.

"Thanks," he said but didn't take a drink. The last thing he wanted to do was add alcohol to the remainders of a blinding headache.

His brother, who was probably the most intuitive person he'd ever known, looked at him as if he knew exactly what he was thinking. "You know, you should go home."

"I live *here*, remember?"

Blake shook his head. "I meant *home*…not here. Port Douglas."

Except Port Douglas didn't feel any more like home than San Francisco, Phuket or Amalfi.

Nowhere did. Not since Simone had died. The bay-side condo they'd bought still sat empty, and he lived in a villa at the San Francisco resort when he wasn't at any of the other four locations. He'd been born in Australia and moved to California when he was two years old. The San Francisco resort was the first, which made it home, even though he'd spent most of his adult life shifting between the two countries.

He scowled. "I can't do that right now."

"Why not?" Blake shot back. "Caleb's got the Phuket renovation under control. Things are sweet here in San Francisco." His brother grinned. "You're not really needed. CEOs are kind of superfluous to the running of a company anyhow. We all knew that when Gramps was at the helm."

"Superfluous?"

Blake's grin widened. "Yeah…like the foam on the top of an espresso to go… You know, there but not really necessary."

"You're an ass."

His brother's grin turned into a chuckle. "All I'm saying is that you haven't taken a real break from this gig for years. Not even when…"

Not even when Simone died.

Four years, four months and three weeks ago. Give or take a day. She'd been driving back from a doctor's appointment and had stopped at the mall for some shopping. The brakes on a car traveling in the opposite direction had failed. Simone had suffered terrible injuries and died an hour later in hospital. So had the baby she carried. He'd lost his wife and unborn daughter because of a broken brake line. "I'm fine," he said, and tasted the lie on his tongue.

"I'm pretty sure you're not," Blake said, more serious. "And something's been bugging you the past few months."

Something. Someone. *Green eyes... Black curling hair... Red lips...*

Daniel drank some beer. "You're imagining things. And stop fretting. You're turning into your mother."

His brother laughed loudly. They both knew that Blake was more like their father, Miles, than any of them. Daniel's mother had died of a massive brain hemorrhage barely hours after his birth, and their father had married Bernadette two years later. Within six months the twins, Blake and Caleb, were born. Bernie was a nice woman and had always treated him like her own, and wasn't as vague and hopeless as their father. Business acumen and ambition had skipped a generation, and now Miles spent his time painting and sculpting and living on their small hobby farm an hour west of Port Douglas.

Daniel finished the beer and placed the bottle on the table. "I don't need a vacation."

"Sure you do," Blake replied. "If you don't want to go to Australia, take a break somewhere else. Maybe Fiji? Or what about using that damned mausoleum that sits on that hill just outside Paris? Take some time off, relax, get laid," his brother said, and grinned again. "Recharge like us regular folk have to do every now and then."

"You're as tied to this business as I am."

"Yeah," his brother agreed. "But I know when to quit. I've got my cabin in the woods, remember?"

Blake's *cabin* was a sprawling Western red cedar house nestled on forty hectares he'd bought in small town Colorado a few years back. Daniel had visited once, hated the cold and being snowbound for days on end and decided that a warm climate was more his thing.

"I don't need a—"

"Then, how about you think about what the rest of us need?" Blake said firmly. "Or what Caleb and I need, which isn't you breathing down our necks looking for things we're doing wrong because you're so damned bored and frustrated that you can't get out your own way. Basically, *I* need a break. So go home and get whatever's bugging you out of your system and spend some time with Solana. You know you've always been her favorite."

Daniel looked at his brother. Had he done that? Had he become an overzealous, critical jerk looking for fault in everything and everyone? And bored? Was that what he was? He did miss Solana. He hadn't seen his grandmother since her birthday weekend. And it was excuse enough to see Mary-Jayne again—and get her out of his system once and for all.

He half smiled. "Okay."

Chapter Two

"Everything all right?"

Mary-Jayne nodded and looked up from the plate of food she'd been pretending to give way too much attention. "Fine."

"Are you still feeling unwell?" Solana asked. "You never did tell me what the doctor said."

"Just a twenty-four-hour bug," she replied vaguely. "And I feel fine now."

Solana didn't look convinced. "You're still pale. Is that ex-boyfriend of yours giving you grief?"

The *ex-boyfriend*. The one she'd made up to avoid any nosy questions about what was becoming her rapidly expanding middle. The ex-boyfriend she'd say was the father of her baby until she summoned the nerve to tell Solana she was carrying her grandson's child. Raised to have a solid moral compass, she was torn between believing the father of her baby had a right to know, and the fear that telling him would change everything. She was carrying Solana's great-grandchild. An Anderson heir. Nothing would be the same.

Of course, she had no illusions. Daniel Anderson was not a man looking for commitment or a family. Solana had told her enough about him, from his closed-off heart to his rumored no-strings relationships. He'd lost the love of his life and unborn child and had no interest in replacing, either.

Not that she was interested in him in *that* way. She didn't like him at all. He was arrogant and opinionated and as cold as a Popsicle. Oh, she'd certainly been swept away that one night. But one night of hot and heavy sex didn't make them *anything*.

Still…they'd made a baby together, and as prepared as she was to raise her child alone, common courtesy made it very clear to her that she had to tell him. And soon. Before Solana or anyone else worked out that she was pregnant.

She had another two weeks at the store before Audrey returned, and once that was done, Mary-Jayne intended returning to Crystal Point to regroup and figure out how to tell Daniel he was about to become a father.

"I'm going to miss you when you leave," Solana said and smiled. "I've grown very fond of our talks."

So had Mary-Jayne. She'd become increasingly attached to the other woman over the past few months, and they lunched together at least twice a week. And Solana had been incredibly supportive of her jewelry designing and had even offered to finance her work and help expand the range into several well-known stores around the country. Of course Mary-Jayne had declined the offer. Solana was a generous woman, but she'd never take advantage of their friendship in such a way…good business or not.

"We'll keep in touch," Mary-Jayne assured her and ignored the nausea scratching at her throat. Her appetite had been out of whack for weeks and the sick feeling still hadn't abated even though she was into her second trimester. Her doctor told her not to worry about it and assured her that her appetite would return, and had put her on a series of vitamins. But most days the idea of food before three in the afternoon was unimaginable.

"Yes, we must," Solana said warmly. "Knowing you has made me not miss Renee quite so much," she said of her granddaughter, who resided in London. "Of course, I get to see Caleb while I'm here and Blake when I'm in San Francisco. And Daniel when he's done looking after things and flying in between resorts. But sometimes I wish for those days when they were kids and not spread all over the world." The older woman put down her cutlery and sighed. "Listen to me, babbling on, when you must miss your own family very much."

"I do," she admitted. "I'm really close to my sisters and brother and I miss my parents a lot."

"Naturally." Solana's eyed sparkled. "Family is everything."

Mary-Jayne swallowed the lump of emotion in her throat, like she'd done countless times over the past few months. Her hormones were running riot, and with her body behaving erratically, it was getting harder to keep her feelings under wraps. One thing she did know—she wanted her baby. As unplanned as it was, as challenging as it might be being a single mother, she had developed a strong and soul-reaching love for the child in her womb.

Family is everything...

It was. She knew that. She'd been raised by wonderful parents and loved her siblings dearly. Her baby would be enveloped in that love. She *could* go home, and Daniel need never know about her pregnancy. She'd considered it. Dreamed of it.

Except…

It would be wrong. Dishonest. And wholly unfair.

"I should very much like to visit your little town one day," Solana said cheerfully.

Crystal Point. It was a tiny seaside community of eight hundred people. From the pristine beaches to the rich soil of the surrounding farmlands, it would always be home, no matter where life took her.

"I'd like that, too," she said, and pushed her plate aside.

"Not hungry?" Solana asked, her keen light gray eyes watching everything she did.

Mary-Jayne shrugged. "Not really. But it is delicious," she said of the warm mango salad on her plate. "I'm not much use in the kitchen, so our lunches are always a nice change from the grilled-cheese sandwich I'd usually have."

Solana grinned. "Didn't your mother teach you to cook?"

"She tried, but I was something of a tomboy when I was young and more interested in helping my dad in his workshop," she explained.

"Well, those skills can come in handy, too."

Mary-Jayne nodded. "For sure. I can fix a leaking tap and build a bookcase…but a cheese toastie is about my limit in the kitchen."

"Well, you'll just have to find yourself a husband who can cook," Solana suggested, smiling broadly.

"I'm not really in the market for a husband." *Not since I got knocked up by your grandson…*

Solana smiled. "Nonsense. Everyone is looking for a soul mate…even a girl as independent and free-spirited as you."

Mary-Jayne nodded vaguely. Independent and free-spirited? It was exactly how she appeared to the world. And exactly how she liked it. But for the most part, it was a charade. A facade to fool everyone into thinking she had it all together—that she was strong and self-sufficient and happy-go-lucky. She'd left home at seventeen determined to prove she could make it on her own, and had spent ten years treading water in the hope no one noticed she was just getting by—both financially and emotionally. Her family loved her, no doubt about it. As the youngest child she was indulged and allowed to do whatever she liked, mostly without consequence. Her role as the lovable but unreliable flake in the Preston family had been set from a young age. While her older brother, Noah, took over the family business, perennial earth-mother Evie married young and pursued her art, and übersmart Grace headed for a career in New York before she returned to Australia to marry the man she loved.

But for Mary-Jayne there were no such expectations, and no traditional career. She'd gotten her first piercing at fourteen and had a tattoo by the time she was fifteen. When school was over she'd found a job as a cashier in a supermarket and a month later moved out of her parents' home and into a partly furnished cottage three streets away. She'd packed whatever she could fit into her battered Volkswagen and began her adult life away from the low expectations of her family. She never doubted their love... but sometimes she wished they expected more of her. Then perhaps she would have had more ambition, more focus.

Mary-Jayne pushed back her chair and stood up. "I'll take the dishes to the kitchen."

"Thank you. You're a sweet girl, Mary-Jayne," Solana said, and collected up the cutlery. "You know, I was just telling Caleb that very thing yesterday."

It was another not-so-subtle attempt to play matchmaker.

Solana had somehow got it in her head that her younger grandson would be a good match for her. And the irony wasn't lost on Mary-Jayne. She liked Caleb. He was friendly and charming and came into the store every couple of days and asked how things were going, and always politely inquired after Audrey. The resort staff all respected him, and he clearly ran a tight ship.

But he didn't so much as cause a blip on her radar.

Unlike Daniel. He was the blip of the century.

Mary-Jayne ignored Solana's words, collected the dishes and headed for the kitchen. Once there she took a deep breath and settled her hips against the countertop. Her stomach was still queasy, and she took a few deep breaths before she turned toward the sink and decided to make a start on the dishes. She filled the sink and was about to plunge her hands into the water when she heard a decisive knock on the front door, and then seconds later the low sound of voices. Solana had a visitor. Mary-Jayne finished the washing up, dried her hands and headed for the door.

And then stopped in her tracks.

Even though his back was to her she recognized Daniel Anderson immediately. The dark chinos and white shirt fitted him as though they'd been specifically tailored for his broad, well-cut frame. She knew those shoulders and every other part of him because the memory of the night they'd spent together was etched into her brain, and the result was the child growing inside her.

Perhaps he'd tracked her down to confront her? Maybe he knew?

Impossible.

No one knew she was pregnant. It was a coincidence. He'd forgotten all about her. He hadn't called since she'd told him to go to hell. He'd returned to see his grand-mother. Mary-Jayne's hand moved to her belly, and she puffed out the smock-style shirt she wore. If she kept her arms to her sides and kept her clothing as loose as possible it was unlikely he'd notice her little baby bump. She lingered by the doorway, her mind racing at a trillion miles an hour.

Solana was clearly delighted to see him and hugged him twice in succession. "What a wonderful surprise," his grandmother said. "Why didn't you tell me you were coming?"

"Then it's not a surprise," he replied. "Is it?"

As they chatted Mary-Jayne moved back behind the architrave and considered her options. Come clean? Act nonchalant? Make a run for it? Running for it appealed most. This wasn't the time or place to make any kind of announcement about being pregnant, not with Solana in the room. She needed time to think. Prepare.

I have to get out of here.

The back door was through the kitchen and off the dining room. But if she sneaked out through the back Solana would want to know why. There would be questions. From Solana. And then from Daniel.

"Show some backbone," she muttered to herself.

She'd always had gumption. Now wasn't the time to ditch her usual resolve and act like a frightened little girl. Mary-Jayne was about to push back her shoulders and face the music when an unwelcome and unexpected wave of nausea rose up and made her suddenly forget everything else. She put a hand to her chest, heaved and swallowed hard, fighting the awful feeling with every ounce of will-power she possessed.

And failed.

She rushed forward to the closest exit, racing past Solana and *him* and headed across the room and out to the patio, just making it to the garden in time.

Where she threw up in spectacular and humiliating fashion.

Daniel remained where he was and watched as his grandmother hurried through the doorway and quickly attended to the still-vomiting woman who was bent over in the garden. If he thought he was needed Daniel would have helped, but he was pretty sure she would much prefer his grandmother coming to her aid.

After several minutes both women came back through the door. Mary-Jayne didn't look at him. Didn't even acknowledge he was there as she walked to the front door and let herself out, head bowed, arms rigid at her sides. But he was rattled seeing her. And silently cursed himself for having so little control over the effect she had on him.

"The poor thing," his grandmother said, hovering in the doorway before she finally closed the door. "She's been unwell for weeks. Ex-boyfriend trouble, too, I think. Not that she's said much to me about it…but I think there's been someone in the picture."

Boyfriend?

His gut twinged. "Does she need a doctor?" he asked, matter-of-fact.

"I don't think so," his grandmother replied. "Probably just a twenty-four-hour bug."

Daniel ignored the twitch of concern. Mary-Jayne had a way of making him feel a whole lot of things he didn't want or need. Attraction aside, she invaded his thoughts when he least expected it. She needled his subconscious. Like she had when he'd been on a date a couple of weeks back. He'd gone out with the tall leggy blonde he'd met at a business dinner, thinking she'd be a distraction. And spent the evening wishing he'd been with someone who would at least occasionally disagree and not be totally compliant to his whims. Someone like Mary-Jayne Preston. He'd ended up saying good-night to his date by nine o'clock, barely kissing her hand when he dropped her home. Sure, he didn't want a serious relationship, but he didn't want boring conversation and shallow sex, either.

And since there had been nothing boring or shallow about the night he'd spent with the bewitching brunette, Daniel still wanted her in his bed. Despite his good sense telling him otherwise.

"So," Solana said, and raised her hands. "Why have you come home?"

"To see you. Why else?"

She tutted. "Always a question with a question. Even as a toddler you were inquisitive. Always questioning everything, always asking *why* to your grandfather. Your brothers were never as curious about things as you were. Do you remember when you were eight and persuaded your grandfather to let you ride that mad, one-eyed pony your dad saved from the animal rescue center?" She shook her head and grinned. "Everyone wanted to know why you'd want to get on such a crazy animal. And all you said was, *why not?*"

Daniel shrugged. "As I recall I dislocated my collarbone."

"And scared Bernie and me half to death," Solana said and chuckled. "You were a handful, you know. Always getting into scraps. Always pushing the envelope. Amazing you turned out so sensible."

"Who say's I'm sensible?" he inquired lightly.

Solana's smile widened. "Me. Your brothers. Your grandfather if he was still alive."

"And Miles?"

His grandmother raised a silvery brow. "I think your dad would like you to be a little *less* sensible."

"I think my father would like me to eat tofu and drive a car that runs on doughnut grease."

"My son is who he is," Solana said affectionately. "Your grandfather never understood Miles and his alternative ways. But your dad knows who he is and what he wants from life. *And* he knows how to relax and enjoy the simple things."

Daniel didn't miss the dig. It wasn't the first time he'd been accused of being an uptight killjoy by his family. "I can relax."

His grandmother looked skeptical. "Well, perhaps you can learn to while you're here."

Daniel crossed his arms. Something about her tone made him suspicious. "You knew I was coming?"

Solana nodded, clearly unapologetic. "Blake called me. And of course it was my idea." She sat down at the table. "Did you know your grandfather had his first heart attack at thirty-nine?"

Daniel sighed. He'd heard it before. Mike Anderson died at sixty-nine from a massive coronary. His fourth. After two previous bypass surgeries the final heart attack had been swift and fatal, killing him before he'd had a chance to get up from his desk. "Gran, I—"

"Don't fob me off with some vague assurance that it won't happen to you," she said, cutting him off. "You work too hard. You don't take time off. You've become as defined by Anderson Holdings as your grandfather was… and all it got him was an early grave. There's more to life than business."

He would have dismissed the criticism from anyone else…but not Solana. He loved and respected his grandmother, and her opinion was one of the few that mattered to him.

"I know that. But I'm not ready to—"

"It's been over four years," Solana reminded him gently. "And time you got back to the land of the living. Simone wouldn't want you to—"

"Gran," Daniel said, hanging on to his patience. "I know you're trying to help. And I promise I'll relax and unwind while I'm here. I'm back for a week so I'll—"

"You'll need more than a week to unwind," she said, cutting him off again. "But if that's all you can manage then so be it. And your parents are expecting you to visit, in case you were thinking you'd fly under the radar while you're here."

Guilt spiked between his shoulder blades. Solana had a way of doing that. And he hadn't considered *not* seeing his father and stepmother. Not really. True, he had little in common with Miles and Bernadette…but they *were* his parents, and he knew they'd be genuinely pleased that he'd come home for a visit.

From a young age he'd known where his path lay. He was who his grandfather looked to as his protégé. At eighteen he'd been drafted into Anderson's, studying economics at night school so he could learn the business firsthand from his grandfather. At twenty-three, following Mike Anderson's death, he'd taken the reins and since then he'd lived and breathed Anderson's. Blake and Caleb had followed him a few years later, while Daniel remained at the helm.

He worked and had little time for anything resembling a personal life. Simone had understood that. She was a corporate lawyer and worked seventy-hour weeks. Marrying her had made sense. They were a good match…alike in many ways, and they'd been happy together. And would still be together if fate and a faulty brake line hadn't intervened. She'd still be a lawyer and he would still spend his waking hours living and breathing Anderson Holdings. And they would be parents to their daughter. Just as they'd planned.

Daniel stretched his shoulders and stifled a yawn. He was tired. Jet-lagged. But if he crashed in the afternoon he'd feel worse. The trick to staying on top of the jet lag was keeping normal sleep patterns. Besides, there were two things he wanted to do—take a shower, and see Mary-Jayne Preston.

Mary-Jayne knew that the knock on her door would be Daniel. She'd been waiting for the sound for the past hour. But the sharp rap still startled her and she jumped up from the sofa, where she'd been sitting, hands twisted and stomach churning.

She walked across the living room and down the short hallway, grappling with the emotions running riot throughout her. She ruffled out her baggy shirt and hoped it disguised her belly enough to give her some time to work out how she was going to tell the man at her door he was going to become a father. She took a deep breath, steadied her knees, grabbed the handle and opened the door.

His gray eyes immediately looked her over with unconcealed interest. "How are you feeling?"

His lovely accent wound up her spine. "Fine."

"My grandmother is worried about you."

"I'm fine, like I said."

He tilted his head slightly. "You sure about that?"

Her chin came up. "Positive. Not that I have to explain myself to you."

"No," he mused. "I guess you don't."

"Is there something else you wanted?"

A tiny smile creased one corner of his mouth. "Can I come in?"

"I'd rather you didn't," she said, and stepped back, shielding herself behind the door. "But since you own this resort I guess you can do whatever the hell you want."

There was laughter in his eyes, and she realized the more hostile she got, the more amused he appeared. Mary-Jayne took a deep breath and turned on her heels, quickly finding solace behind the single recliner chair just a few feet away. She watched as he closed the door and took a few easy strides into the room.

"I hear you've been taking my grandmother to see fortune-tellers?"

Solana had told him about that? The older woman had sworn her to secrecy, saying her grandsons would think her crazy for visiting a clairvoyant. "It was *one* fortune-teller," she informed him. "And a reputable one, I might add."

His brows came up. "Really? You believe in all that nonsense?"

She glared at him. "Well, she did say I'd meet a man who was a real jerk...so I'd say she was pretty accurate, wouldn't you agree?"

"Is that a question?" he shot back. "Because I'm probably not the best judge of my own character. Other people's characters, on the other hand, I can usually peg."

"Don't start with—"

"Why did you hang up on me when I called you?"

She was genuinely surprised by his question. And didn't respond.

"You were in South Dakota at your friend's wedding," he reminded her. "I was in San Francisco. I would have flown you to the city."

Into the city. And into his bed. Mary-Jayne knew the score. She might have been a fool the night of Solana's birthday party, but she certainly wasn't about to repeat that monumental mistake.

"I wasn't in the market for another meaningless one-night stand."

His mouth twitched. "Really? More to the point, I guess your boyfriend wouldn't have approved?"

She frowned. "My what?"

"My grandmother can be indiscreet," he said and looked her over. "Unintentionally of course, since she has no idea we had that *meaningless one-night stand*."

Color rose and spotted her cheeks. And for several long seconds she felt a kind of riveting connection to him. It was illogical. It was relentless. It made it impossible to ignore him. Or forget the night they'd spent together. Or the way they'd made love. The silence stretched between them, and Mary-Jayne was drawn deep into his smoky gray eyes.

"I don't have a boyfriend or lover," she said quietly. "I made that up to stop Solana from asking questions about…" Her words trailed off and she moved back, putting distance between them.

"About what?"

She shook her head. "Nothing. I really can't… I can't do this."

"Do what?" he asked.

"I can't do this with you."

"We're not doing anything," he said. "Just talking."

"That's just it," she said, her voice coming out a little strangled. "I'm not ready for this. Not here. Not today. I feel unwell and I—"

"I thought you said you were feeling better?" he asked, cutting her off.

"Well, I'm not, okay? I'm not better. And seeing you here only makes me feel worse."

"Such brutal honesty. I don't know whether to be flattered or offended."

She let out an agonized moan. "That's just it. I am honest. *Always*. And seeing you now makes it impossible for me to be anything else. And I'm not ready for it… I can't do this today. I simply can't—"

"What are you talking about?" he asked impatiently and cut her off again.

"I'm talking about… I mean… I can't…"

"Mary-Jayne," he said, saying her name like he had that night, when he'd said it over and over, against her skin, against her breath. "I'm not sure what's going on with you, but you're not making much sense."

The truth screamed to be told. There was no other way. She couldn't stop being who she was. She was an honest, forthright person who wore her heart on her sleeve. Mary-Jayne stepped out from behind the chair and spread her hands across her stomach, tightening the baggy shirt over her middle. Highlighting the small bump that hadn't been there four months ago.

"I'm talking about *this*."

Daniel quickly refocused his gaze onto her middle and frowned. "You're pregnant?"

She nodded and swallowed hard. "Yes."

"And?"

She shrugged and her hair flipped around her shoulders. Now or never.

"And isn't it obvious? You're the father."

Chapter Three

He hadn't moved. Mary-Jayne looked at him and took a long breath. "This isn't how I wanted you to find out. I was going to call and tell you and—"

"You're not serious?" he asked, cutting through her words with icy precision.

She nodded. "I'm perfectly serious. I'm pregnant."

He raised a dark brow. "We used protection," he said quietly and held up a few fingers. "Three times, three lots of birth control. So your math doesn't quite work out."

"My math?" She stared at him. "What exactly are you accusing me of?"

"Nothing," he replied evenly. "Simply stating an irrefutable fact."

A fact?

Right. There was no possible way of misunderstanding his meaning. "I'm not lying to you. This baby is—"

"Yours," he corrected coldly. "And probably the ex-boyfriend who my grandmother said is giving you grief at the moment."

She fought the urge to rush across the room and slug him. "I don't have a *boyfriend*. Ex or otherwise."

"You do according to my grandmother," he stated. "Who I trust more than anyone else."

No punches pulled. He didn't believe her. *Okay.* She could handle it. She didn't care what he thought. "I only told Solana that to stop her from asking questions about why I've been unwell."

He crossed his arms, accentuating his broad shoulders, and stood as still as a statue. He really was absurdly good-looking, she thought, disliking him with every fiber in her body. His gray eyes had darkened to a deep slate color and his almost black hair was short and shiny, and she remembered how soft it had been between her fingertips. His face was perfectly proportioned and he had a small cleft in his chin that was ridiculously sexy. Yes, Daniel Anderson was as handsome as sin. He was also an arrogant, overbearing, condescending so-and-so, and if it weren't for the fact he was the biological father of her child, she'd happily *never* see him again.

"Do I really appear so gullible, Miss Preston?"

Miss Preston?

"Gullible? I don't know what you—"

"If you think naming me in a paternity claim will fatten your bank balance, think again. My lawyers will be all over you in a microsecond."

His pompous arrogance was unbelievable. "I'm not after your money."

"Then, what?" he asked. "A wedding ring?"

Fury surged through her. "I wouldn't marry you if you were the last man left on the planet."

Her words seemed to amuse him and he looked at her

in such a haughty, condescending way that her palms actually itched with the urge to slap his face. In every way she'd played the scene out in her head, and not once had she imagined he wouldn't believe that her baby was his. Naive perhaps, but Mary-Jayne had been raised to take someone at their word.

"That's quite a relief, since I won't be proposing anytime soon."

"Go to hell," she said quietly as emotion tightened her chest, and she drew in a shuddering breath. He pushed her buttons effortlessly. He really was a hateful jerk.

"Not until we've sorted out this little mix-up."

"Mix-up?" She glared at him. "I'm pregnant and you're the father. This is not a mix-up. This is just how it is."

"Then, I demand a paternity test."

Daniel hadn't meant to sound like such a cold, unfeeling bastard. But he wasn't about to be taken for a ride. He knew the score. A few months back his brother Caleb had been put through the ringer in a paternity suit that had eventually proved the kid he'd believed was his wasn't. And Daniel wasn't about to get pulled into that same kind of circus.

Mary-Jayne Preston's baby couldn't possibly be his... could it? He'd never played roulette with birth control. Besides, now that he could well and truly see her baby bump she looked further along than four months. Simone hadn't started showing so obviously until she was five months' pregnant.

"I'd like you to leave."

Daniel didn't move. "Won't that defeat the purpose of your revelation?"

She scowled, and he couldn't help thinking how she still looked beautiful even with an infuriated expression.

"You know about the baby, so whatever you decide to do with the information is up to you."

"Until I get served with child-support demands, you mean?"

She placed her hands on her hips and Daniel's gaze was immediately drawn to her belly. She was rounder than he remembered, kind of voluptuous, and a swift niggle of attraction wound its way through his blood and across his skin. Her curves had appealed to him from the moment they'd first met, and watching her now only amplified that desire.

Which was damned inconvenient, since she was obviously trying to scam him.

"I don't want your money," she said stiffly. "And I certainly don't want a wedding ring. When I get married it will be to someone I actually like. I intend to raise this baby alone. Believe me, or don't believe me. Frankly, I don't care either way."

There was such blatant contempt in her voice that he was tempted to smile. One thing about the woman in front of him—she wasn't afraid to speak her mind. And even though he knew it was crazy thinking, it was an interesting change from the usual lengths some women went to in order to get his attention. How sincere she was, he couldn't tell.

"We spent the night together a little over four months ago," he reminded her. "You look more than four months pregnant."

Her glare intensified. "So it's clearly a big baby. All I know is that the only possible way I got pregnant was from that night I spent with you. I hadn't been with anyone for a long time before that night. Despite what you think of me, I'm not easy. And I don't lie. I have no reason to want this child to be yours. I don't like you. I'm not interested in you or your money or anything else. But I am telling you the truth."

He still wasn't convinced. "So the ex-boyfriend?"

"A figment of my imagination," she replied. "Like I said, Solana was asking questions and I needed a little camouflage for a while."

He kept his head. "Even if there is no boyfriend and you are indeed carrying a supersize baby…we used contraception. So it doesn't add up."

"And since condoms are only ninety-eight percent effective, we obviously managed to slip into the two percent bracket."

Ninety-eight percent effective?

Since when?

Daniel struggled with the unease clawing up his spine. "You cannot expect me to simply accept this news at face value."

She shrugged, as if she couldn't care either way. "Do, or don't. If you want a paternity test to confirm it, then fine, that's what we'll do."

He relaxed a little. Finally, some good sense. "Thank you."

"But it won't be done until the baby is born," she said evenly and took a long breath. "There are risks associated with tests after the fifteen-week mark, and I won't put my baby in jeopardy. Not for you. Not for anyone."

There was such unequivocal resolve in her voice, and it surprised him. She was a flake. Unreliable. Unpredictable. Nothing like Simone. "Of course," he said, and did his best to ignore the stabbing pain in his temple. His shoulders ached, and he could feel the effects of no sleep and hours flying across the globe begin to creep into his limbs. "I wouldn't expect you to put your child at risk."

Her child.

Her baby.

This wasn't what he'd expected to face when he'd decided to come home. But if she was telling the truth? What then? To share a child with a woman he barely knew. It was a train wreck waiting to happen.

And he hated waiting. In business. In his personal life.

He'd waited at the hospital when Simone was brought in with critical injuries. He waited while the doctors had tried to save her and their unborn daughter. He'd waited, and then received the worst possible news. And afterward he'd experienced a heartbreaking despair. After that night he became hollow inside. He'd loved his wife and daughter. Losing them had been unbearable. And he'd never wanted to feel that kind of soul-destroying anguish again.

But if Mary-Jayne *was* carrying his child, how could he turn his back?

He couldn't. He'd be trapped.

Held ransom by the very feelings he'd sworn he never wanted to feel again.

"So what do you want from me until then?"

"Want? Nothing," she replied quietly. "I'll call you when the baby is born and the paternity test is done. Goodbye."

He sighed. "Is this how you usually handle problems? By ignoring them?"

Her cheeks quickly heated. "I don't consider this baby a problem," she shot back. "And the only thing I plan to ignore is you."

He stared at her for a moment, and then when he laughed Mary-Jayne realized she liked the sound way too much. She didn't want to like *anything* about him. Not ever. He had become enemy number one. For the next five months all she wanted to do was concentrate on growing a healthy baby. Wasting time thinking about Daniel and his sexy laugh and gray eyes was off her agenda.

"You don't really think that's going to happen, do you?" he asked, watching her with such hot intensity she couldn't look away. "You've dropped this bombshell, and you know enough about me to realize I won't simply fade away for the next five months."

"I can live in hope."

"I think you live in a fantasyland, Mary-Jayne."

The way he said her name caused her skin to prickle. No one called her that except her parents and her older brother, Noah. Even her sisters and closest friends mostly called her M.J. To the rest of the world she was M. J. Preston—the youngest and much loved sibling in a close-knit middle-class family. But Daniel had always used her full name.

Mary-Jayne took a deep breath. "A fantasyland?" She repeated his words as a question.

"What else would you call it?" he shot back as he looked her over. "You're what, twenty-seven? Never married or engaged. No real career to speak of. And a barely solvent online business. You've rented the same house for nearly ten years. You drive a car that's good for little else but scrap metal. You have less than a thousand dollars in the bank at any given time and a not-so-stellar credit rating thanks to a certain dubious ex-boyfriend who ran up a debt on your behalf over five years ago. It looks very much like you do—"

"How do you know that?" she demanded hotly, hands on hips. "How do you know all that about me? I've not told Solana any of…" She trailed off as realization hit. And then she seethed. "You had me investigated?"

"Of course," he replied, unmoving and clearly unapologetic.

"You had no right to do that," she spat. "No right at all. You invaded my privacy."

He shrugged his magnificent shoulders. "You are working at this resort and have befriended my grandmother—it was prudent to make sure you weren't a fortune hunter."

"Fortune hunter?" Mary-Jayne's eyes bulged wide and she said a rude word.

He tilted his head a fraction. "Well, the jury's still out on that one."

"Jury?" She echoed the word in disbelief. "And what does that make you? The judge? Can you actually hear yourself? Of all the pompous, arrogant and self-important things I've ever heard in my life, you take the cake. And you really do take yourself and the significance of your opinions way too seriously."

He didn't like that. Not one bit. She watched, fascinated as his eyes darkened and a tiny pulse in his cheek beat rapidly. His hands were clenched and suddenly his body looked as if it had been carved from granite. And as much as she tried to fight it, attraction reared up, and heat swirled around the small room as their gazes clashed.

Memories of that night four months ago banged around in her head. Kissing, touching, stroking. Possession and desire unlike any she had known before. There had been a quiet intensity in him that night, and she'd been swept away into another world, another universe where only pleasure and a deeply intimate connection existed. That night, he hadn't been the rigid, unyielding and disagreeable man who was now in her living room. He'd been tender and passionate. He'd whispered her name against her skin. He'd kissed her and made love to her with such profound eagerness Mary-Jayne's entire mind and body had awakened and responded in kind. She'd never been driven to please and be pleasured like that before.

But right now she had to get back to hating him. "I'm going to get changed and go for a walk to clear my head. You know the way out."

He didn't move. And he looked a little pale, she thought. Perhaps the shock that he was going to be a father was finally hitting home. But then she remembered that he didn't believe he actually was her baby's father, so that probably wasn't it.

"We still have things to discuss."

"Not for another…" Her words trailed off and she tapped off five of her fingers in her palm. "Five months. Until then, how about you treat me with the disdain that you've clearly mastered, and I'll simply pretend that you don't exist. That will work out nicely for us both, don't you think?"

Of course, she knew saying something so provocative was like waving a red cape at a bull. But she couldn't help herself. He deserved it in spades. And it was only the truth. She didn't want to see him or spend any more time in his company.

"I don't treat you with disdain."

And there it was again—his resolute belief in the sound of his own voice.

"No?" She bit down on her lip for a moment. "You've admitted you had me investigated and just accused me of being a fortune hunter. Oh, and what about what you said to me on the phone when I was in South Dakota?" She took a strengthening breath. "That I was a flake who dressed like a hippie."

His eyes flashed. "And before you told me to go to hell you called me an uptight, overachieving, supercilious snob, if I remember correctly." He uncrossed his arms and took a step toward her.

"Well, it's the truth. You are an uptight snob."

"And you dress like a hippie."

"I like to be comfortable," she said, and touched her head self-consciously. "And I can't help the way my hair gets all curly in the humidity."

His gaze flicked to her hair and she saw his mouth twitch fractionally. "I didn't say a word about your hair. In fact it's quite…it's…it's…"

"It's what?" she asked.

"Nothing," he said, and shrugged. "I would like to know your plans."

Mary-Jayne stared at him. "I don't have any plans other than to have a healthy baby in five months' time."

He looked around the room. "When are you leaving here?"

"Audrey's back in two weeks. I'll go home then."

"Have you told your family?"

She shook her head. "Not yet."

"Have you told anyone?"

She met his gaze. "You."

His expression narrowed. "And since she didn't mention it while you were throwing up in her garden, I'm guessing you haven't told my grandmother, either?"

"Just you," she replied, fighting the resentment fueling her blood. "Like I said. Incidentally, Daniel, if you're going to disbelieve everything that comes out of my mouth, it's going to be a long five months."

He grinned unexpectedly. "So you do know my name? I don't think you've ever used it before. Well, except for that night we spent together."

Her skin heated. She remembered exactly how she'd said his name that night. Over and over, whispered and moaned, as though it was the only word she'd known.

"Like I said, you know the way out."

He didn't budge. "We still need to talk."

"We've talked enough," she said tensely. "You don't believe me and you need a paternity test. *And* you think I'm after your money. Believe me, I've got your message loud and clear."

"You're angry because I want proof of paternity?"

He actually sounded surprised. Mary-Jayne almost laughed at his absurd sense of entitlement. "I'm angry because you think I'm lying to you. I don't know what kind of world you live in where you have this compulsion to question someone's integrity without cause, but I don't live in that world, Daniel. And I would never want to."

She spun on her heel and left the room, barely taking a breath until she reached the sanctuary of the main bedroom. She leaned against the closed door and shuddered.

It's done now. He knows. I can get on with things.

She pulled herself together, changed into sweats and sneakers and loitered in the room for more than ten minutes to ensure he'd be gone.

She strode into the living room and then stopped in her tracks. The room was empty. He'd left. As if he'd never been there.

A strange hollowness fluttered behind her ribs. She was glad he was gone—arrogant and disbelieving jerk that he was. She was well rid of him. With any luck she'd never have to see him again. Or speak to him. Or have to stare into those smoky gray eyes of his.

She could go home and have her baby.

Simple.

But in her heart she knew she was dreaming to believe he'd just disappear from her life. She was having his baby—and that made it about as complicated as it got.

When Daniel woke up he had a crick in his neck and his left leg was numb. It was dark out. He checked his watch: six-forty. He sat up and stretched. When he'd left her condo, he'd walked around the grounds for a few minutes before heading back to his own villa. Once he'd sat down, the jet lag had hit him with a thud. Now he needed coffee and a clear head.

He got to his feet and rounded out his shoulders. The condo was quiet, and he walked from the living room and headed for the kitchen. He had to refocus and figure what the hell he was supposed to do for the next five months until the baby came into the world.

The baby.

His baby...

I'm going to be a father.

Maybe?

Daniel still wasn't entirely convinced. Mary-Jayne potentially had a lot to gain by saying he'd fathered her child. He wasn't naive and knew some people were mercenary enough to try to take advantage of others. He remembered how devastated Caleb had been when he'd discovered the boy he'd thought was his son turned out to belong to his *then* girlfriend's ex-husband. And Daniel didn't want to form a bond with a child only to have it snatched away. Not again. Losing Simone and their unborn daughter had been soul destroying. He wasn't going to put himself in a position to get another serving of that kind of loss.

He made coffee and drank it. Damn...he felt as if his head was going to explode. He'd had it all planned out... come back to Port Douglas, reconnect with Mary-Jayne for a week and get her out of his system once and for all.

Not going to happen.

Daniel rounded out his shoulders and sucked in a long breath. He needed a plan. And fast. He swilled the cup in the sink, grabbed his keys and left the villa.

By the time he reached her condo his hands were sweating. No one had ever had such an intense physical effect on him. And he wasn't sure how to feel about it. The crazy thing was, he couldn't ignore it. And now that had amplified a hundredfold.

They needed to talk. There was no way around it. Daniel took another breath and knocked on the door.

When she answered the door she looked almost as though she'd been expecting him to return. He didn't like the idea that he was so transparent to her.

"I'm working," she said, and left him standing in the doorway. "So you'll need to amuse yourself for ten minutes before we get into round two."

The way she dismissed him so effortlessly *should* have made him madder than hell. But it didn't. He liked her spirit, and it was one of the things he found so attractive about her.

He followed her down the hall, and when he reached the dining room she was already standing by a small workbench tucked against the wall in one corner. She was bent over the narrow table, one elbow resting, using a small soldering iron. There was enough light from the lamp positioned to one side for him to see her profile, and despite the protective glasses perched on her nose he couldn't miss the intense concentration she gave her craft. There were several boards fashioned on easels that displayed her jewelry pieces, and although he was no expert, there was certainly style and creativity in her work.

She must have sensed him watching her because she turned and switched off the soldering iron. "So you're back?"

He nodded. "I'm back."

"Did you call your lawyer?"

"What?"

She shrugged a little. "Seems like something you'd do."

Daniel ignored the irritation clawing at his spine. "No, Mary-Jayne, I didn't call my lawyer. Actually, I fell asleep."

She looked surprised and then frowned a little. "Jet lag?"

He nodded again. "Once I sat down it hit me."

"I had the same reaction when I returned from Thailand last year. It took me three days to recover. The trick is to stay awake until bedtime."

There was something husky and incredibly sexy about Mary-Jayne's voice that reached him deep down. After they'd slept together, he'd pursued her and she'd turned him down flat. Even from across an ocean she'd managed to throw a bucket of cold water on his attempts to ask her out. And get her back in his bed. Because he still wanted her. As foolish as it was, as different and unsuitable for one another as they were—he couldn't stop thinking about her.

She knew that. She knew they were from different worlds. She'd accused him of thinking she was an easy mark and that was why he wanted her. But it wasn't that. He wanted her because she stirred him like no other woman ever had. From her crazy beautiful hair to her curvy body and her sassy mouth, Daniel had never known a woman like her. He might not like her...but he wanted her. And it was as inconvenient as hell.

"So what do you want, then?"

Daniel's back straightened. She didn't hold back. She clearly didn't think she had anything to gain by being friendly or even civil. It wasn't a tactic he was used to. She'd called him a spoiled, pampered and arrogant snob, and although he didn't agree with that assumption, it was exactly how she treated him.

"To talk," he replied. "Seems we've got plenty to talk about."

"Do you think?" she shot back. "Since you don't believe

that this baby is yours, I can't see what's so important that you felt compelled to come back so soon."

Daniel took a breath. "I guess I deserve that."

"Yeah," she said and plucked the glasses off her nose. "I guess you do."

He managed a tight smile. "I would like to talk with you. Would coffee be too much trouble?"

She placed the soldering iron on the bench. "I guess not."

As she walked past him and through the door to the kitchen it occurred to Daniel that she swayed when she moved. The kitchen seemed small with both of them in it, and he stayed on the outside of the counter.

"That's quite a collection your friend has up there," he remarked and pointed to the cooking pots hanging from an old window shutter frame that was suspended from the ceiling.

"Audrey likes pans," she said without looking at him. "I don't know why."

"She doesn't need a reason," he said and pulled out a chair. "I collect old books."

She glanced up. "Old books?"

"First editions," he explained. "Poetry and classic literature."

One of her eyebrows rose subtly. "I didn't peg you as a reader. Except perhaps the *Financial Times*."

Daniel grinned a little. "I didn't say I read them."

"Then why collect them?"

He half shrugged. "They're often unique. You know, rare."

"Valuable?" she asked, saying the word almost as an insult. "Does everything in your life have a dollar sign attached to it?"

As digs went between them, it was pretty mild, but it still irked him. "Everything? No."

"Good," she said, and held up a small sugar pot. When he shook his head, she continued speaking. "Because I have no intention of allowing my baby to become caught up in your old family money or your sense of self-entitlement."

Daniel stilled. "What does that mean?"

"It means that people like you have a kind of overconfident belief that money fixes everything."

"People like me?" Daniel walked across the small room and moved around the countertop. "Like me?" he asked again, trying to hold on to the annoyance sneaking across his skin. "Like me, how…exactly?"

She stepped back. "You're rich and successful. You can snap your fingers and have any number of minions willing to do whatever you need done."

He laughed humorlessly. "Really? I must try that next time I want someone to bring me my slippers."

Her green eyes glittered brilliantly. "Did you just make a joke? I didn't realize you had it in you."

Daniel's shoulders twitched. "Perhaps I'm not quite the *uptight, overachieving, supercilious snob* you think I am."

"Oh, I wouldn't go that far," she said and pushed the mug along the countertop. "There's milk in the fridge."

"This is fine." Daniel took the mug and leaned a hip against the counter. "Thank you."

"No problem. And you *are* uptight, Daniel. Everything about you screams order and control."

"Because I don't live in chaos?" he asked, deliberately waving a hand around the untidy room. "That doesn't necessarily equate to being a control freak."

She crossed her arms. "Chaos? So now you think I'm a slob?"

He drank some coffee and placed the mug on the

counter. "What I think is that it's interesting that you express every opinion you have without considering the consequences."

"Oh, have I offended your sensibilities?"

"Have I offended yours?"

She shrugged. "I'd have to care what you thought, wouldn't I?"

In all his life he'd never met anyone who tried so hard to antagonize him. Or anyone with whom he'd been compelled to do the same. Mary-Jayne got under his skin in ways he could barely rationalize. They were all wrong for one another and they both knew it.

And now there was a baby coming…

His baby.

Daniel glanced at her belly and then met her gaze.

"Mary-Jayne." He said her name quietly, and the mood between them changed almost immediately. "Are you… are you sure?"

She nodded slowly. "Am I sure the baby is yours? Yes, I'm certain."

Resistance lingered in his blood. "But we—"

"I may be a lot of things, Daniel…but I'm not a liar." She drew in a long breath. "The contraception we used obviously failed. Despite what you think of me, I've been single for over twelve months and I haven't slept with anyone since…except you."

A stupid, egotistical part of him was glad to hear it. One part wanted to believe her. And the other…the other could only think about what it meant for them both if what she said was true.

"I need to be sure," he said.

"I understand," she replied. "You can have your proof when he or she is born."

Guilt niggled its way through his blood. "I appreciate you agreeing to a paternity test."

She shrugged lightly. "There's little point in being at odds over this. Be assured that I don't want anything from you, and once you have your proof of paternity you can decide how much or how little time you invest in this."

As she spoke she certainly didn't come across as flighty as she appeared. She sounded like a woman who knew exactly what she wanted. Which was her child…and no interference from him.

Which of course wasn't going to happen.

If the baby *was* his, then he would be very involved. He'd have no choice. The child would be an Anderson and have the right to claim the legacy that went with the name. Only, he wasn't sure how he'd get Mary-Jayne to see it that way.

"If this child is mine, then I won't dodge my responsibility."

She looked less than impressed by the idea. "If you're talking about money, I think I've made it pretty clear I'm not interested."

"You can't raise a child on good intentions, Mary-Jayne. Be sensible."

Her mouth thinned and she looked ready for an argument, but she seemed to change her mind. Some battles, he figured, were about defense, not attack…and she knew that as well as he did.

"We'll see what happens," she said casually as she crossed the small kitchen and stood in front of the refrigerator. She waited for him to stand aside and then opened the door. "I'm heating up lasagna. Are you staying for dinner?"

Daniel raised a brow. "Am I invited?"

She shrugged, as if she couldn't care either way. But

he knew she probably wanted to tell him to take a hike in some of her more colorful language.

"Sure," he said, and grabbed the coffee mug as he stepped out of her way. "That would be good."

He caught a tiny smile on her mouth and watched as she removed several items from the refrigerator and began preparing food on the countertop. She placed a casserole dish in the microwave and began making a salad. And Daniel couldn't take his eyes off her. She was fascinating to watch. Her glorious hair shone like ebony beneath the kitchen light, and she chewed her bottom lip as she completed the task. And of course thinking about her lips made him remember their night together. And kissing her. And making love to her. She had a remarkable effect on his libido, and he wondered if it was because they *were* so different that he was so achingly attracted to her. She was all challenge. All resistance. And since very little challenged him these days, Daniel knew her very determination to avoid him had a magnetic pull all of its own.

And he had no idea what he was going to do about it.

Or if he could do actually do anything at all.

Chapter Four

Mary-Jayne finished preparing dinner, uncomfortably conscious of the gorgeous man standing by the kitchen table. There was such blistering intensity in his gaze she could barely concentrate on what she was doing. She hated that he could do that to her. If she had her way she'd never see him again.

But the baby she carried bound them together.

He wouldn't, she was certain, simply disappear from her life.

She had five months until the baby came, and she had to figure out how to get through those months with Daniel in the background. Or worse. He wasn't the kind of man who'd simply go away until the baby came…regardless of how much she might wish for things to go that way.

"How long are you staying at the resort?" she asked, hoping he'd say not too long at all. Best he leave quickly.

"I'd planned to only be here a week to visit with my

grandmother," he replied, and shrugged slightly. "But now I'm not sure."

She frowned. "Don't you have a company to run or something?"

"Yes."

"Isn't it hard to do that from here? You live mostly in San Francisco, right?"

He placed the mug on the dining table and crossed his arms. "Most of the time. Anderson's corporate offices are there. And the Bay Area resort is the largest."

"Well, I'm sure they need you back."

His mouth twitched. "Eager to see me gone, Mary-Jayne?"

"If I said no I'd be lying," she replied, and brought plates and cutlery to the table. "And as I've repeatedly said, I don't lie. So if you're thinking of extending your stay on my account, there's really no need. The birth is five months away and there's nothing you can do until then."

Mary-Jayne brought the food to the table and gestured for him to take a seat. When he was sitting she did the same and took the lids off the salad and lasagna. She didn't bother to ask what he wanted and quickly piled a scoop of pasta on his plate. Once she'd filled her own plate she picked up the utensils and speared some lettuce and cucumber with a fork.

"What…is…that?"

She looked up and smirked when she saw how Daniel was staring at his food. "Lasagna. With mushroom, spinach, shredded zucchini flowers and goat cheese."

He looked as if she'd asked him to chew broken glass. He took a breath and met her gaze. "You're a vegetarian?"

"Of course."

Mary-Jayne knew his parents were strict vegans. She

also knew he and his brothers had made a point from his early teens of *not* following in their footsteps.

"Of course," he repeated with more than a touch of irony. "Looks…delicious."

"I'm not much of a cook," she said frankly. "So don't hold your breath."

"Thanks for the warning."

She smiled to herself as they began to eat. He was being good-humored about her attempts to wind him up and it surprised her. Maybe he wasn't quite as straitlaced and up-tight as she'd believed. Which didn't mean anything. He could be nice. He could be the most charming and agreeable man on the planet and it wouldn't change the one significant fact—they were like oil and water and would never mix. Despite the fact that they'd made a baby together and were now bound by parenthood. They were in different leagues, and she had to remember that every time she was tempted to think about his sexy voice and broad shoulders.

"I have an ultrasound appointment on Tuesday at ten-thirty," she said, and speared some pasta. "My doctor gave me a referral to a medical center in Cairns."

The regional city was forty miles south of Port Douglas.

"And?"

"And you're welcome to come along if you want to," she replied flatly.

He didn't really look as though he wanted to. But he did nod. "I'll pick you up."

"I can drive myself."

He raised a brow. "I'll pick you up."

She was about to argue, but stopped herself. Battling with Daniel over the small stuff was pointless. "Okay," she said, and didn't miss the flash of surprise in his eyes.

For a while the only sound in the room was the clicking of cutlery. He seemed happy not to talk and Mary-Jayne was content to eat her food and not think about how intimate the situation was. Once dinner was done he offered to help wash up, and before she had a chance to refuse his assistance he was out of the chair and in the kitchen, rinsing the plates with one hand while he opened the dishwasher with the other.

"You know your way around a kitchen," she said, surprised.

He shrugged. "Bernie made sure my brothers and I knew how to cook and clean up."

"That's your mother?"

"Stepmother," he replied, and began stacking the dishwasher. "She married my dad when I was two."

Her insides contracted. "Solana told me your mother passed away just after you were born."

"That's right."

Mary-Jayne moved into the kitchen. "You were born in Australia, weren't you?"

"That's right. My dad moved to California when he married Bernie and the twins were born there. They moved back here about ten years ago."

"I like your dad."

He glanced sideways. "I didn't realize you were acquainted."

"He came here to visit your grandmother and Caleb a few weeks ago. I was with Solana at the time and she introduced me to him. He had a very relaxed sense of self, if that makes sense. He was very charismatic and friendly," she said, and smiled a little.

"Not like me, you mean?"

Mary-Jayne grabbed a tea towel. "I'm sure you could be the same if you put your mind to it."

He turned and faced her. "And ruin my image of being an uptight bore?"

She laughed softly. "One thing you're not, Daniel, is boring."

"Just uptight?" he asked.

Mary-Jayne shrugged lightly. "I guess it goes with the territory. Solana told me how you took over the business when you were in your early twenties. That must have been quite a responsibility to shoulder. Duty above all else, right?"

He didn't move. "My grandfather was dead. My father had tried his hand at the business and bailed when he realized he was happier growing organic vegetables and pursuing his art. So yes, being drafted into the business that young had its challenges. But I wasn't about to let my family down. Or the people who rely on Anderson's for their livelihood. I did what I had to do... If that made me an uptight bore in the process, then I guess I'll simply have to live with it."

She took a deep breath. There was something so seductive about his deep voice it was impossible to move. She could have easily moved closer to him. The heat that had been between them from the start was as vibrant and scorching as it had ever been.

It's just sex...

Of course she knew that. Sex and lust and some kind of manic chemical reaction that had her hormones running riot. She had to get them under control. And fast.

"So I'll see you Tuesday. Around nine o'clock."

His gaze darkened. "Are you kicking me out?"

Mary-Jayne took a tentative step backward. "I guess so."

He laughed. "You know, I've never met anyone quite like you. There are no punches pulled with you, Mary-Jayne— you say exactly what you think."

"Blame it on my middle-class upbringing."

"I'm not criticizing you," he said, and folded his arms. "On the contrary, I find it intriguing. And incredibly sexy."

She stepped back again. "If you're flirting with me, stop right now. Your *charm* has got us into enough trouble already."

He laughed again. "Good night, Mary-Jayne."

"Good night," she whispered as she followed him up the hall, and she didn't take a breath until she closed the front door behind him.

After a restless night spent staring mostly at the ceiling, Daniel went for a long run along the beach around ten o'clock on Sunday morning. He stayed out for over an hour, and when he returned to his villa, took a shower and dressed and was about to head for his grandmother's when there was a tap on his door.

It was Caleb.

His brother walked across the threshold and dropped a set of keys onto the narrow hall table. "The keys to my Jeep," Caleb said and grinned. "In case you want to visit the folks."

Caleb never failed to remind him or Blake about the importance of family.

"Thanks," he said, and walked down the hallway.

His brother followed, and they each dropped into one of the two leather sofas in the living room. "Have you heard from Audrey?" Daniel asked the one question he knew his brother wouldn't want to answer.

Caleb shook his head. "I screwed up, and she's not about to forgive me anytime soon."

"You did what you thought was right."

"I moved my ex-girlfriend and her child into my house without thinking about what it would mean to my *current* girlfriend. I mean, I know Audrey and I had only been together a couple of months…but still…" The regretful look on his brother's face spoke volumes. "I should have done things differently. I shouldn't have taken Nikki's word that he was my kid without getting tested. I should have known Audrey was going to end up bailing. Hell, I probably would have done the same thing had the situation been reversed. When her mother got sick she had just the out she needed to get away from the resort for a while…and from me."

Which had been the catalyst for Mary-Jayne coming to the resort. Daniel was certain that his brother was in love with Mary-Jayne's friend Audrey. But when his ex-girlfriend had arrived on his doorstep, holding a baby she'd claimed was his, Caleb had reacted instinctively and moved them into his home.

"She's coming back in two weeks."

"Audrey?" Caleb's gaze narrowed. "How do you know that?"

He shrugged. "Gran must have mentioned it."

"Gran did?" His brother raised both brows. "You sure about that?"

"I don't know what—"

"Less than twenty-four hours, hey?" Caleb laughed. "I take it you've seen her?"

Her.

He'd told Caleb about spending the night with Mary-Jayne. He hadn't been able to avoid it since his brother had spotted her leaving his villa early that morning. "Yes, I've seen her."

"You still hung up on her?"

Daniel shrugged one shoulder. Caleb knew him well enough to sniff out a lie. "Things are a little more complicated."

"Complicated?"

He didn't flinch. "She's pregnant."

His brother's eyes bulged. "Hell! And it's yours?"

"So she says."

Caleb let out a long breath. "Do you believe her?"

"Do I have doubts?" He shrugged again. "Of course. But Mary-Jayne isn't like—"

"Like Nikki?" Caleb suggested, cutting him off. "Yeah, you're right. She seems like a real straight shooter. I know Audrey trusted her to run the store in her absence without hesitation. You gonna marry her?"

Daniel's back straightened. "Don't be stupid. I hardly know her."

Caleb grinned. "Well, you'll have plenty of opportunity to get to know her once you start raising a child together."

Raising a child together...

Daniel knew it wouldn't be that simple. She lived in Crystal Point. He lived in San Francisco. There was a hell of a lot of geography separating them. Which would make him what? A once-a-year father? Summer-vacation time or less? He was looking down the barrel at an impossible situation.

"We'll see what happens."

His brother's expression turned serious. "Tell me you're getting a paternity test?"

"Once the child is born," he said, and explained about the risks of doing the test during the second trimester.

Caleb nodded slowly. "And what do you plan to do until then?"

He shrugged a little. "It's not really up to me."

His brother made a disagreeable sound. "I can see that attitude lasting about two days," he said, and smiled. "Until the shock really hits you."

Caleb knew him well. The idea of doing nothing until the baby came sat like a lead weight in his gut. But what choice did he have? Mary-Jayne wasn't the kind of woman to take easily to being watched or hovered over. She was obviously fiercely independent and made it clear she didn't need him for anything.

Which should have put him it at ease.

Instead his insides churned. He was torn between wanting to believe her child was his and knowing it would be much better for them both if it wasn't true. But he had no real reason to disbelieve her. Sure, he thought she was a bit of a flake. But according to Solana she was honest and forthright and exactly as she seemed—a free, independent spirit who answered to no one but herself. Not the kind of woman to claim paternity when she wanted nothing in return.

"I thought I'd visit Gran," Daniel said, and sprang from the sofa. "Feel like joining me?"

Caleb shook his head and grinned as he stood. "I'm not on vacation like you. I have a business to run. And don't forget to go and see the folks this week."

"I won't," Daniel promised, and walked his brother down the hall.

Once Caleb left he locked up the villa, grabbed the keys on the hall stand and headed out. He walked around the grounds for a few minutes, and instead of going directly to Solana's villa made his way to the western side of the resort where the condos were smaller and home to many of the employees. He tapped on Mary-Jayne's door and ignored the interested looks from a few people in corporate shirts who passed him on the pathway that separated the apartments.

The door swung back and she stood in front of him. "Oh…hi."

She sounded breathless, and he was immediately concerned. "Are you okay?"

"Fine," she replied and took a deep breath. "I've been doing Pilates."

Daniel looked her over. Her hair was tied up in a haphazard ponytail and she wore black leggings and a hot pink racer-back tank top that clung to her curves. Her belly looked like it had popped out a little more overnight and he fought the unexpected urge to place his hand on her stomach. Her cheeks were flushed and her lips looked plump and red. There was something wholly healthy and attractive about her that warmed his blood.

"Pilates?" he echoed, and curled his fingers into his palms to stop himself from reaching out to touch her.

"It's good for the baby," she replied. "And me. So did you want something?"

"Only to see how you are feeling today."

"I'm fine," she said, her hand positioned on the door like she couldn't wait to close it. "How are you?"

"Okay," he said.

"Well, thanks for stopping by."

Daniel shifted on his feet. "I thought… I wondered if you would like to have lunch."

Her brows arched. "Lunch? With you? Where?"

He shrugged a little. "There are four restaurants at this resort…take your pick."

Her brows stayed high. "Beneath the prying eyes of wait staff and various employees? Isn't that a little risky? People might start thinking you've been consorting with the help."

Daniel's jaw clenched. She was an argumentative and provocative pain in the neck. And he wanted her anyway.

"First, I don't care what anyone thinks. And second, you are not *the help*, Mary-Jayne. Are you going to be difficult and refuse every request I make? Or accept that you need to eat and since you're a lousy cook anyway, it would—"

"I'm not a *lousy* cook," she retorted and a tiny smile

curved her mouth. "Just not a good cook. And while I appreciate your invitation, I'm hardly dressed for anything other than a cheese sandwich in front of the TV."

He looked her over again and his libido twitched. "I'll come back in half an hour. Unless you need help getting out of your clothes?"

For a second he thought she might slam the door in his face. But to his surprise she laughed softly. "I'm sure I can manage. Okay, see you in thirty minutes."

Then she did close the door and Daniel turned on his heels. And as he walked back down the path he realized he was grinning foolishly.

Lunch.
Great idea.
Not...

As she slipped into a knee-length white denim sundress, Mary-Jayne cursed herself repeatedly for being so agreeable and for finding Daniel Anderson charming and attractive and so darn sexy he could ask her to jet to the moon and she probably would.

She had to get a handle on the chemistry between them. There was no other option.

He tapped on her door exactly thirty minutes later and Mary-Jayne scowled as she moved down the short hallway. He was the punctual type. It figured. Everything about him screamed order and control.

She opened the door and faced him. "I'm ready."

"So I see," he said, and stood aside to let her pass.

Mary-Jayne closed the door and dropped the key into the tote draped over her left shoulder. "Where are we going?" she asked.

"Your choice," he replied. "Like I said."

Mary-Jayne took a deep breath. There were four restaurants at the resort: two bistros designed for families, a trendy Japanese teppanyaki bar and an exclusive à la carte restaurant named after his grandmother that Mary-Jayne had never been in because the menu was way out of her price range, even though Solana had offered to take her there several times.

She smiled sweetly. "Solana's. Think you'll be able to get a table at such short notice?"

His mouth turned up a little. "I'm sure they will be able to accommodate us."

Mary-Jayne looked up at him. "No one would dare defy you, would they?"

"Oh, I could think of someone who would."

He was smiling now and it made her smile back. *Keep your head.* The warning voice at the back of her mind told her to ignore the way her insides fluttered. She didn't want to *flutter* around him. She didn't want to have any kind of reaction. He was her baby's father—that was all. Besides, he didn't actually believe he had fathered her baby, so she should keep being madder than hell and resentful that he thought her so deceptive.

"Well, there's no point in going through life thinking you can have everything your own way, is there?" she replied, and started walking down the path.

He caught up with her in a few strides. "Or thinking you can say whatever you like."

Mary-Jayne stopped in her tracks. "Is that a nice way of saying I have a big mouth?"

"Actually," he said as he came to a halt beside her, "you have a very…lovely mouth."

There was something so flagrantly suggestive about his words that heat quickly travelled up her legs, belly and chest and then hit her directly in her cheeks. Memories banged around in her head. Memories of his touch.

His kiss. His possession. It was too easy to recall the crazy chemistry they shared and the night they'd spent together.

"I wish you wouldn't…"

Her words trailed off as she met his steely gaze. He had a hypnotic power that was uniquely his and it was something she'd never experienced before. She didn't *like* him. She didn't *want* him in her life. But Daniel had a way of invading her thoughts and plaguing her dreams.

"You wish I wouldn't…what?"

She sucked in a shallow breath and stepped sideways. "Stand so close," she said and crossed her arms.

A grin tugged at his mouth. As if he knew just how profoundly he affected her. And as if it pleased him no end.

"Not everything has to be a battle, Mary-Jayne."

And she wished he'd stop saying her name like that… kind of silky and smooth and sexy and impossible to ignore.

He was wrong. Everything did have to be a battle. It was the only way she'd remain unscathed. "Sure," she said and started walking again.

He stopped to make a phone call and was by the main entrance when he caught up with her. Without saying another word she followed him inside, across the foyer and then toward the elevator. The looks and stares from staff as they passed didn't go unnoticed, and Mary-Jayne suspected she'd quickly be the subject of whispers and conjecture. Since she'd arrived at the resort she'd kept to herself. She hadn't socialized with the staff or other store owners. She managed Audrey's store during the day and worked on her jewelry in the evenings. After Solana's birthday party she'd kept her head down and minded her own business, figuring others would do the same in regard to her. And mostly the staff did. Of course everyone knew about Audrey's disastrous affair with Caleb and speculation was rife that her friend had bailed simply to get away from the resort and him and avoid further humiliation. Only Mary-Jayne knew the truth. Sure, Audrey's mother was unwell…but it *was* exactly the excuse Audrey had needed to salvage her pride and put serious miles between herself and the man who'd hurt her so badly.

Mary-Jayne certainly didn't want to trade one scandal for another.

And she certainly didn't want anyone thinking she was sleeping with the boss!

"Everything all right?"

She glanced sideways and pulled her tote close to her belly. "Peachy."

"Worried what people might think?"

Her mouth tightened. He was too intuitive for her liking. "Couldn't care less."

She stepped into the elevator and he moved in behind her. He stared at her for a second before raising one dark brow. "Perhaps you're not as free-spirited as I thought."

She shrugged. "Maybe not."

The door opened, and Mary-Jayne was about to step out when she realized they weren't on the restaurant level. They were one floor up on the conference suites and boardroom level.

He touched her back and gently urged her forward. "Come on."

"Why are we here? I thought we were—"

"This way," he replied, and kept her moving down the short corridor.

A door opened at the end of the hall and a young man in white chef's gear greeted them. Mary-Jayne had seen him around the resort a few times. Daniel greeted him by name and they were shown directly into a private dining area. It was luxury personified. There were half a dozen tables covered in crisp white linen and the finest dinner-ware and crystal. A long panel of windows overlooked the pool area and also offered an incredible view of the ocean.

A waiter emerged from another door and pulled out a seat at a table by the window.

Mary-Jayne rocked back on her heels and looked at Daniel. "Nice view."

"Shall we sit?"

His words were more request than question, and she fought the urge to turn around and leave. Instead she smiled a little and sat down. The waiter offered her some sparkling water, and she gave a grateful nod and only spoke again when the young man and the chef left the room.

She dropped her tote to her feet, stared out the window for a moment before resting her elbows on the table and turning her gaze toward the man sitting opposite. "Clearly I'm not the only one concerned about what people think."

He stilled. "What?"

She waved a hand vaguely. "Up the back elevator and into a secret room?"

"Private," he clarified. "Not secret. I thought you might prefer it. Personally I couldn't care less what people think."

She wondered if that were true. Daniel possessed a kind of confidence she suspected was born from arrogance. He was used to getting his own way. Used to telling people what to do. He called the shots…and she couldn't imagine him tolerating speculation from anyone in his employ.

"Well, they'll be *thinking* plenty once my belly really pops out."

His mouth curled at the edges. "They can think what they like. I should have realized you were pregnant when I first saw you yesterday," he said quietly. "It suits you."

She smirked a little. "Am I glowing?"

He nodded. "Yes."

It was a nice compliment, and her skin warmed. "I'll probably end up the size of a house, though," she said and laughed. "All the women in my family have looked like they've swallowed an elephant when they were pregnant."

His mouth curled at the sides, and it was incredibly sexy. "Tell me about them."

"My family?" She shrugged. "There's not much to tell. We all live in Crystal Point. My parents are both retired. My older brother, Noah, is married to Callie and they have four kids. He builds boats and she's a horse-riding instructor. Then there's my sister Evie, who's an artist and runs a bed-and-breakfast. She's married to Scott—who's actually Callie's brother. He's a firefighter and they have two kids. Then there's Grace, who is married to Noah's best friend Cameron. He's a cop, she's a finance broker and they had their first baby two months ago. And then there's little-old-knocked-up me."

He smiled at her words. "No…not much to tell at all."

Mary-Jayne laughed again. It occurred to her that despite how much he aggravated her, she smiled a lot around Daniel. "They're good people."

"I don't doubt it. I imagine you had a very happy childhood."

"Mostly," she admitted. "Of course it was fraught with the usual teenage-girl angst and rebellion, I suppose. I'm the youngest and therefore it's expected that I would be the most troublesome."

He grinned a little. "What kind of trouble?"

"Oh…crushes on inappropriate boys, late nights, the wrong company…and I got my tattoo at fourteen."

He grimaced. "Brave girl."

"Getting a tattoo? Brave or foolish, you mean, because basically I'm marked for life."

"I mean the pain thing."

"Pain?"

"They use needles…right?"

Mary-Jayne tilted her head. "Well…yes."

"I don't like needles."

She laughed loudly. "Chicken."

"You're mocking me," he said, his mouth twisting a little. "That's something of a habit of yours."

The waiter returned with their drinks and placed a menu on the table. Once the young man left, she returned her attention to Daniel.

"I imagine your ego is healthy enough to take it."

He grinned again. "You're probably right. So…" he said and pushed the glass around the table. "Is there any chance your father is going to come after me with a shotgun?"

She laughed loudly. "Not one. My brother, Noah, on the other hand, is very protective of his sisters." She took a long breath. "Seriously…my family let me live my own life. I'm fully prepared to raise this baby alone, Daniel. Be involved or don't. It's that simple."

His brows rose fractionally. "With me in San Francisco and you in Crystal Point? That's not simple. That's about as complicated as it gets, Mary-Jayne. Because I'm not about to avoid my legal and moral responsibility…no matter how much it seems you would like me to."

She frowned and touched her belly. "If I wanted that I would never have told you I was pregnant. Frankly, I just don't want you to get hung up on what you think you *have* to do. Sure, I'd like my baby to have a father who's involved in his or her life, but I don't want this to turn into some kind of parenting battleground with you on one side and me on the other and our child stuck in the middle."

"Nice speech. Is it meant to put me in my place?"

She shrugged. "Take it how you want. It's all rather

moot, anyhow…isn't it? Since you don't actually believe this baby is yours."

His eyes darkened and she was quickly drawn into them. Something passed between them, a kind of relentless energy that warmed her blood.

"It's not that…it's…"

"It's what?" Mary-Jayne asked, and met his gaze and asked the question hovering on her lips. "Is it because of your wife?"

Chapter Five

Daniel stilled. It was the first time the subject had been mentioned since Mary-Jayne had told him she was pregnant. Had he spared Simone more than a fleeting thought in the past twelve hours? The past twenty-four? He'd become so consumed by Mary-Jayne and the idea she was carrying his baby that he could barely think of anything else.

"I gather my grandmother told you what happened?"

She shrugged lightly. "Solana told me she was killed in a car wreck a few years ago."

"Four years," he corrected. "Four years, four months and three weeks."

Her eyes shone. "She was pregnant, wasn't she?"

He nodded slowly as his throat tightened. "Yes. Five months."

"I'm so sorry." Her hand moved across the table and connected with his for a moment before she quickly pulled it back. "It must have been devastating."

"It was the single worst day of my life."

She gathered her hands together in her lap and opened her mouth to speak when the waiter returned. Daniel watched as she studied the menu for a few seconds and then ordered one of the three vegetarian options he'd insisted be included. When she was done he ordered the swordfish, and when the waiter left he grabbed his glass and took a drink.

He put the glass down and spoke. "If you want to ask me about it, go ahead."

Her eyes widened. "You don't mind?"

He shrugged one shoulder.

"How did it happen?"

Daniel closed his eyes for a second as memories banged around in his head. He'd gone over that day countless times in his mind and the pain never lessened. "Simone was driving home from a doctor's appointment and stopped off at the mall to get a birthday gift. She pulled out of the parking lot and into the flow of traffic and a vehicle coming in the opposite direction slammed into her car. The brake line had snapped on the other car and the inexperienced driver panicked, hit the accelerator and crossed over the road."

"Was she killed instantly?"

He shook his head, almost admiring Mary-Jayne's blunt questioning. There was no false pity in her expression. Only curiosity and genuine concern.

"She died in hospital. The doctors tried to save her but her injuries were too severe."

"And the baby?"

"Our daughter died within minutes of Simone passing away."

"That's so sad. Did you have a name picked out for her?"

Daniel pushed down the heat clawing up his throat.

"We'd planned on naming her Lana, after my grand-mother."

She was quiet for a moment, her gaze lowered, clearly absorbing what he'd said. When she looked up her eyes were bright, almost glistening. He watched as she bit down on her bottom lip as moisture quickly filled her eyes. He'd observed many emotions cross her face in the time they'd known one another—anger, dislike, humor, passion—but this was something else. Sadness. Acute and heartfelt. He didn't like how it made him feel. Dealing with the com-bative, argumentative Mary-Jayne was easy compared to seeing her in tears.

"I'm sorry," she said, and grabbed the napkin to dab at her eyes. "I didn't mean to..." Her words trailed and she swallowed hard. "It's the baby hormones. They get me at the most unexpected times. Anyway," she said, her voice a little stronger, "thank you for telling me."

"It's not a secret. I'm sure my grandmother or Caleb would have told you the same thing had you asked them. It was an accident...and like all accidents, it was simply a series of events that merged into one terrible outcome."

She looked at him with silent intensity. "You mean, if she'd lingered at the mall a little longer, or if she had taken another exit from the parking lot, or the other driver had gotten out of bed ten minutes later that morning things would have turned out differently?"

"Exactly."

"You said she was buying a birthday gift. Who was it for?"

Daniel hesitated for a moment. "My grandmother."

It took a moment, but her eyes widened as realization dawned. "So...that night...the night of Solana's birthday party...it was the...the..."

"The anniversary of their deaths? Yes, it was."

The waiter returned with their meals before she had a chance to respond, and Daniel watched with keen interest as she took a long breath and stared into her plate. Once the waiter left them she looked up.

"Is that why you…why you…"

"Why I what?" he asked.

"The party, you know…and how we…" Her words trailed and she shrugged lightly.

"We had sex, you mean?"

Sex. He wasn't going to call it anything else. He wasn't going to suggest they'd made love because it would have been a lie. He used to make love to his wife. There was love and heart and passion between them. They'd been friends since college and started dating when Simone had finished law school. What he felt for Mary-Jayne wasn't grounded in that kind of friendship or any measure of deep emotion. It was base and instinctual and fuelled by attraction and sexual desire. And he intended for it to stay that way. She might be under his skin, but he wasn't about to let her get into his heart.

"I thought there might be a connection," she said and arched one brow. "Like you were wanting…to forget about…"

"I could never forget my wife," he said quietly.

She flinched a little. "I didn't mean that. I was thinking perhaps you needed a distraction that night and that's why you were interested in me."

"I was *interested* in you from the moment I saw you in the store window."

He knew she wouldn't be surprised by his admission. There had been heat between them from that first glance. Daniel wasn't conceited, but he knew the attraction he felt for Mary-Jayne was very much reciprocated.

"Oh…okay."

"The fact it was my grandmother's birthday was a coincidence," he said, stretching the truth to avoid her questions or her censure. He wasn't about to admit that the hollow feeling that had haunted him since Simone's death had been amplified that night. Or that for a few incredible hours he'd found solace in the arms of a woman he barely knew. "So have you been well other than the nausea?" he asked, shifting the subject.

"Mostly," she replied. "Both my sisters suffered from gestational diabetes when they were pregnant, so my doctor is keeping watch on my sugar levels. But I feel fine at the moment."

Concern tightened his chest. "Does that mean this pregnancy holds risks for you? Is there something we should talk to your doctor about? Perhaps a second opinion is needed to ensure you get the best possible care. I can arrange an appointment with a specialist if—"

"I'm fine," she said sharply, interrupting him as she picked up the cutlery. "The nausea and appetite issues are a normal part of being pregnant. And I like my current doctor just fine, thank you. Stop interfering."

He bit back a grin at her impatience. "Don't mistake concern for control, Mary-Jayne."

She flashed him an annoyed look. "I don't."

"Oh, I think you do. I think you're so desperate to stay in control here that anything I say will be like waving a red flag at a bull."

She looked as if she wanted to jab him in the forehead with her fork. "You really do love to hear the sound of your own voice."

He laughed. "Hit a nerve, did I?"

"By implying that I value my independence?" she shot back. "Not a nerve...a fact. I'm not about to be lorded over like some spineless minion."

"That's a favorite insult of yours," he said and watched her. "Despite what you've conjured in your colorful imagination, I don't live in a house filled with servants. I cook my own meals, launder my own clothes and even tie my own shoes."

Her green eyes flashed. "Doesn't stop you from being a condescending horse's ass, does it?"

He laughed again. They had a way of pushing each other's buttons, and watching her fiery expression quickly stirred his blood and libido. "We have five months to get through until the baby comes, and I'd prefer it if we could manage that time without constantly goading one another, wouldn't you?"

She shrugged as if she couldn't have cared less. But Daniel wasn't fooled. She was as wound up as he was. "Since you'll be in San Francisco and I'll be in Crystal Point, what difference does it make?"

An ocean. Thousands of miles. A different life. There would be so many things between them. Between him and the child she carried. The child she said was his. Most of the shock had worn off overnight. Sure, he wanted a paternity test, but there were months ahead where he either had to accept the child was his, or not. And, despite everything between them, he realized that he believed Mary-Jayne. His grandmother knew her, trusted her... and although some old cynical instincts banged around in his head, Daniel realized he trusted her, too.

"You could come to San Francisco."

She looked up and made a scoffing sound. "Yeah... right."

Maybe not. "What about here?"

Her gaze sharpened. "Here? At the resort?"

"Yes."

"I can't do that, either," she said, and put down her fork.

"Why not?" he shot back. "Your jewelry business is mostly done online, so you could do that anywhere…San Francisco or here."

"This isn't my home, that's why not. I live in Crystal Point… I've lived there all my life. It's where I was born and it's where my baby will be born."

"Our baby."

Her jaw dropped slightly. "You believe me?"

He took a breath and nodded. "I believe you."

She looked wary. "Why the sudden change of heart?"

"Because *not* believing you essentially means I forfeit any rights to be part of this experience."

Mary-Jayne stilled. Rights? What did he mean by that? He wanted rights? He believed her? It should have put her at ease. Instead her entire body was suddenly on red alert. What had she expected? That once she told him about her pregnancy then he would quietly go away and leave her to raise her child alone?

Naive idiot.

The urge to get up and leave suddenly overwhelmed her, and it took all her strength to remain in her seat. She slowly met his unwavering gaze. "I'll be leaving in less than two weeks," she said. "As soon as Audrey returns I'm going home. My home," she reiterated. "Where I belong."

"Then I'll go with you," he said, so casually that her blood simmered. "We need to tell your folks, anyhow."

"I'll tell *my* family when *I* choose," she said, and pushed back her chair a fraction. "Stop bossing me about."

"Stop acting like a child."

It was the kind of verbal gridlock she expected when she was near him. They didn't like one another. They never would. They had sexual chemistry and nothing more. Fatigue and a sudden surge of queasiness shortened her patience and she pushed the seat back.

"Thanks for lunch," she said, and stood. "I'll see my own way out."

"My case in point," he said as he got up. "Run when you don't like what you hear. That's a child's way out, Mary-Jayne."

Her rage sought release. "Go to hell."

His mouth quirked fractionally. "I'll see you Tuesday morning, at nine, for the ultrasound appointment."

"I'd rather—"

"At nine," he insisted, cutting her off.

She didn't respond. Instead she grabbed her tote, thrust back her shoulders and left the room with a pounding heart, more determined than ever to keep him at arm's length.

Back in her condo she calmed down a little, took a shower and called Audrey. Her friend didn't answer her phone so she left a brief message. She spent the remainder of the day staring at her phone, hoping Audrey would call and watching an old movie on the television. By the time she dropped into bed her head was thumping and her rage was festering.

How dare he call her childish? He was an arrogant, pompous jerk! The sooner she was away from him, the better.

On Monday Mary-Jayne lay low. She opened the store and kept away from the front window as much as possible, in case *he* walked by. Or watched her. Or stalked her. But thankfully he didn't show up at the store and didn't call. And since Caleb didn't do his usual midmorning drop in either, Mary-Jayne knew Daniel had told his brother to steer clear.

Puppet master...

Controlling everything and everyone around him.

It made her mad, and got her blood boiling.

On Tuesday morning she set her alarm an hour early, showered and forced herself to eat breakfast. She dressed in a knee-length button-up blue floral dress and tied her hair up in a ponytail. Then she waited on the sofa for him to arrive, hands clasped together. He tapped on the door at nine o'clock with his usual annoying promptness.

He looked so good in jeans and a collared black T-shirt she could barely croak out a greeting when her level gaze met the broad expanse of his chest. She stupidly wished she were taller, more slender, more elegant...and able to meet his eyes without having to look up.

"Good morning."

Mary-Jayne forced out a smile. "Are you always on time for everything?"

"Always."

"It's an annoying trait of yours."

He grinned and motioned for her to pass. Once he pulled the door shut he placed a hand into the small of her back and ushered her forward. "Well, I guess it's one of those things you'll have to get used to."

Not when there's an ocean between us I won't...

By the time they were in his car she was so worked up her teeth chattered. He asked for the address and she replied quietly, staying silent as he punched the information into his GPS. Once they were on their way she dropped her tote to her feet and stared out the side window. But his nearness still rattled her. He was so close and had a kind of hypnotic power she'd never experienced before. Any man she'd ever known paled beside him. Any attraction she'd had in the past seemed lukewarm compared to the heat that simmered between them. The arguments didn't mask anything. It only amplified the undercurrent of desire and made her remember the passion and pleasure they'd shared that night four months ago.

She turned her head to glance at his profile. "Have you ever done that before?"

"Done what?"

"Sleep with someone you hardly know."

His mouth curved, but he looked straight ahead. "I don't recall either of us getting a whole lot of sleep that night."

Her cheeks heated. "You know what I mean." She swallowed hard. "I… It's just that I… Despite how I *seem*… I'm not like that…usually."

"Usually?"

She let out a heavy breath. "I don't sleep around…okay. I might come across as free-spirited and all that…but when it comes to sex I'm not easy. I've had three serious relationships including my high school boyfriend and I've never had a one-night stand before."

"Are you asking how many relationships I've had? Or one-night stands?" He glanced at her for a moment. "Does it really matter?"

His reticence irritated her and she frowned. "Is the subject off-limits for some reason?"

His jaw tightened. "My wife died over four years ago. Have I remained celibate since then? No. Have I had a committed relationship since then? No. Is that enough of an answer, Mary-Jayne?"

She got the message. She was one in a long line of meaningless one-night stands.

Just as well she didn't like him in the least, or she might have been offended by his admission. "I don't have any kind of ulterior motive for asking," she said and stared directly ahead. "I was curious, that's all."

"Well, if your curiosity has you imagining I have a

different woman in my bed every night, you'll be disappointed."

She didn't want to think about any woman in his bed, different or otherwise. "I'd have to care to feel disappointment, wouldn't I?"

"I guess you would," he said quietly. "But in case you've been having sleepless nights over it—my bed has been empty since you left it so quickly in the small hours of the morning all those months ago."

It was a dig. She'd snuck out of his villa, all right, and he clearly didn't appreciate her efforts to avoid any uncomfortable morning-after postmortems. Obviously he'd been stung by her disappearing act. And it took her a moment to realize what he'd said about his empty bed.

"No one since? Have you already nailed every woman in San Francisco? Is that the problem?"

He laughed humorlessly. "You're the problem."

"Me?" She almost squeaked the word out. "I can't imagine why."

"One night didn't really do us justice, did it? Not with that kind of instant attraction."

She knew what he meant. The store window. The resort foyer. The beach. Solana's party. Every time they'd met the heat had ramped up a notch. Until it had become so explosive the outcome was unavoidable.

"So you want…you still want…"

He chuckled. "You know, you really are a fascinating contradiction. For such a *free-spirited* woman, you can be equally shy and self-conscious."

"Because I think sex should mean something? Because I think one-night stands are empty and pointless and of little importance?"

His profile was unmoving. "Since our night together

resulted in this pregnancy, I'd say it's about as important as it gets, wouldn't you?"

She frowned. "You're twisting my words. I meant the sex wasn't important...not the baby."

There was insult in her words, and she was surprised that he stayed silent.

Silent and seething.

He was mad. Perhaps his ego wasn't as rock solid as she thought?

"That's not a complaint, by the way," she said, and pushed the tote around with her feet. "The sex was very... nice."

"It wasn't *nice*, Mary-Jayne. It was hot and incredibly erotic and about as good as it gets."

He was right. They both knew it.

"That, too," she admitted. "And the reason I left," she said, and figured she may as well tell him the truth, "is I didn't want any morning-after awkwardness. I thought it would be easier to bail and forget the whole thing. I mean, it was never going to be any more than one night. I think we both knew that."

"If I believed that I wouldn't have repeatedly asked you out."

It was true. He *had* pursued her. And she'd refused him every time. Because they were too different. As clichéd as oil and water. He wanted her in his bed and he got what he wanted. Only a fool would imagine he was looking for anything more.

"To get me into bed again, right? Which means we would have been back to square one. The point I'm making is men and women generally think about sex differently. I'm not saying I'm after a picket fence quite yet, but I'm not foolish enough to waste time on something or someone where it wouldn't be on the table ever."

"That's quite a judgment."

"Can you deny it?" she asked. "Let's face it, Daniel, you and I are polar opposites in every way. Sure, we have chemistry, but that's all. Most of the time we barely seem to tolerate one another. That's not a recipe for romance. It's a recipe for disaster."

She turned back to look out the side window with a heavy sigh, and they didn't say another word to one another until they'd reached Cairns. With a population of over one hundred thousand, the bustling regional city was a popular tourist spot and served as a starting point for people wanting to visit the Great Barrier Reef.

Within minutes they were pulling into the car park in front of the medical center. She got out of the Jeep, grabbed her tote and waited for him to come around to the passenger side.

"If you like, we can look around town when we're done," he suggested and locked the vehicle. "Maybe have lunch."

"The way you keep trying to feed me, anyone would think I need fattening up."

His brows narrowed. "Well, I have noticed you don't eat enough."

Mary-Jayne put her hands on her thickening waist. "I eat plenty. Have you seen my ever-expanding middle? I told you how the women in my family look when they're pregnant."

"You hardly touched your food the other day."

Mary-Jayne looked up at him. "I was too mad to eat."

"Too hot headed, you mean."

"You were being a bossy, arrogant jerk. It annoyed me."

"Everything I do appears to annoy you," he said and ushered her toward the steps that led into the building. "Perhaps you should consider why that is."

"I know why," she said, and moved up the steps. "Because you're a bossy, arrogant jerk."

He laughed softly and grasped her hand, stopping her before they reached the door. Mary-Jayne looked up and met his gaze. His gray eyes were dark and intense, and for a second she couldn't do anything but stare at him. The pulse in his cheek throbbed and she fought the urge to touch the spot.

He threaded their fingers and drew her closer. "How about you let me off the hook for a little while, hmm?"

Don't do it...

"I can't..."

"Sure you can," he said, and rubbed his thumb inside her palm. "I'm not your enemy, Mary-Jayne...except perhaps in your lively imagination."

"Daniel..."

"Come on," he said, and gently led her inside. "Let's go and meet this baby."

It took about twenty minutes to find the correct office, see reception and be shown to a small room when she was instructed to lie on the bed and wait for the doctor. A nurse appeared and wheeled the imaging machine close to the bed and told them the doctor would be in soon.

"Are you okay?" he asked from the chair he sat on from across the room.

Mary-Jayne lay back on the table and wiggled. "Fine. Peachy. Never better."

"You look nervous."

She shrugged. "Well, I've never done this before, so of course I'm a little nervous."

As she said the words it occurred to her that Daniel probably *had* done this before. With Simone. With the wife he'd loved and the baby they'd lost. It must have been hard for him to come into the room with her, a woman he hardly knew, and potentially have the same experience he'd shared with his wife.

Shame hit her square between the shoulders.

All morning she'd been thinking of herself and hadn't spared a thought for his feelings. *What's happened to me? When did I become so self-absorbed?*

"I'm sorry."

He looked at her. "For what?"

"For not considering how difficult it must be for you to do this."

His gaze didn't waver. "It's not difficult. Just…different. Simone and I had planned everything, from conception to her due date. She'd had endometriosis for several years and had trouble getting pregnant. Eventually we used IVF and she got pregnant after three attempts. It was all rather clinical and organized and more about the treatments and processes rather than the baby…at least in the beginning. So, yes, this is different."

There was heat in her throat. "Okay," she said, and smiled a little. "You're off the hook."

The doctor came into the room then and Daniel got to his feet. Mary-Jayne lay back and tried to relax. He moved beside her and touched her shoulder.

"So," Doctor Stewart said once she'd introduced herself and perched on a stool at the side of the bed. "Would you like to know your baby's sex?"

Mary-Jayne looked at Daniel.

He shrugged lightly. "It's up to you."

She swallowed hard. "I think… Yes…I'd like to know."

She glanced at him again and thought he looked relieved.

The doctor got her to unbutton her dress, and Mary-Jayne tried not to be self-conscious of Daniel's presence in the chair at her side as her belly was bared. A cool gel was placed on her stomach and she shivered a little. Daniel took hold of her hand and squeezed gently.

Once the ultrasound started she was riveted to the image on the small screen. It didn't look like anything at first, until the doctor pointed out an arm and the baby's head. Emotion welled inside her and she bit back a sob.

Hi there, peanut... I'm your mother...and I love you more than I thought possible.

"And there's your baby," the doctor said, and rolled the device lower. "You have a perfectly lovely boy."

She looked at Daniel and noticed he stared directly at the screen, clearly absorbed by what they saw. He'd never looked more attractive to her, and in that moment an unexpected surge of longing rushed through her entire body.

Longing and desire and something else...something she couldn't quite fathom.

Something she didn't want to think about.

"Oh..."

The doctor's voice quickly cut through her thoughts.

"What is it?"

Daniel's voice now. Deep and smooth and quicker than usual. It gave her comfort. If something was wrong, he was there, holding her hand, giving her strength. He glanced at her and squeezed her fingers.

Doctor Stewart looked at them both. "Well...I see."

"What?" he asked again, firmer this time. "Is something wrong?" It was the question she was too afraid to ask.

"Nothing's wrong," the doctor said, and smiled broadly. "It's just...there are two of them."

Mary-Jayne stared at the screen. "What do you mean?"

The doctor smiled. "Congratulations to you both... you're having twin boys."

Chapter Six

Someone could have told him that he was going to live on the moon for the next fifty years and he wouldn't have been more shocked.

Twin boys...

"You're sure?" he asked the doctor, and noticed how Mary-Jayne hadn't moved. He squeezed her hand reassuringly. "And they're fine?"

The doctor nodded. "Fine. Big, strong and healthy. Would you like to listen to their heartbeats?"

Daniel didn't recall saying yes. But within seconds he had small earphones on and heard the incredible sound of his sons' hearts. Emotion rose up and hit him directly in the solar plexus, polarizing him for a moment. He swallowed hard, fighting the heat in his eyes and throat. Nothing he ever heard again would match the sound of the two tiny heartbeats pounding almost in unison. Longing, absolute and raw, filled his chest with such force he grabbed the side of the chair for support.

The doctor said something about having a picture done for them, but he barely heard. He took off the earphones and gently placed them over Mary-Jayne's head. Watching her expression shift from shock to wonderment was incredible. Her face radiated with a joy so acute it was blinding in its intensity. She'd never looked more beautiful.

The doctor stood. "I'll arrange for a picture and come back in a little while," she said, and quickly left the room.

Daniel tightened his grip on Mary-Jayne's hand. "Are you okay?"

She dropped the earphones onto the bed. "Um…I think so."

"Not what you were expecting, huh?"

She sighed. "Not exactly. But…" Her words trailed off for a moment. "I'm happy." She glanced at the now-blank screen. "I can't quite believe it."

"Are there many twins in your family?" he asked, and rubbed her fingertips. She shrugged. "Not really. I know there are in yours, though."

He nodded and grinned. "Yes. My brothers are twins. My grandfather was a twin, and I have two sets of cousins who are twins. It's like an epidemic in my family."

"This is all your doing, then?" she said and smiled.

"I don't think there's actually a genetic link on the father's side, but I'll happily take the credit if you want," he said softly. "Are you okay with this?"

"I'm happy, like I said. And a little scared. I wasn't expecting two." She looked down at her naked stomach. "I wonder if the nurse will come back to get this goo off my belly."

Daniel released her hand and got up. He found a box of tissues on the counter and came back to her side. "This should do it," he said as he sat down and began wiping the gel off her skin.

It was the most intimate thing they'd done in months, and even though he acted as perfunctory as he could, it didn't stop a surge of desire from climbing up his spine. She lay still, perfectly composed. Until he met her gaze and saw that she was watching him with scorching intensity. When he was done her hand came up and she grabbed his fingertips and then gently laid his palm against her belly. She placed her hand on top of his, connecting them in a way that was mesmerizing. Feeling her, feeling their babies, Daniel had no answer for the sensation banging around in his head.

He'd never wanted to feel this again. Not after Simone.

But it was inevitable. They were his children. His sons. They were part of him. How could he not get drawn into feeling such acute and blinding love for them? He couldn't. And he wanted them. He wanted to be part of their lives. Full-time. A real parent.

A real father.

He looked at Mary-Jayne. Her eyes were bright. Luminous. She chewed on her bottom lip and his gaze immediately went to her mouth. He touched her forehead with his other hand and felt the connection down deep. Soul-deep.

In that moment he could nothing else but kiss her.

And her lips, as new as they were familiar, softened beneath his instantly. Daniel's pulse quickened as the kiss quickly deepened. Her breath was warm, her tongue accepting when he sought it with his own. She sighed deep in her throat, and a powerful surge of desire wound through his blood. He touched her hair, twirling the glorious strands between his fingertips. Her hand came up to his chest and he felt the connection through to his bones. And he kissed her again. And again. With each kiss his need for her grew. As did the knowledge he had one option. One way to make things right.

"Mary-Jayne," he said against her lips, trailing his mouth down her cheek to the sensitive spot by her earlobe. A spot he knew made her quiver. "We should get married."

She stilled instantly. Her mouth drew in a tight line and she pushed his hand off her belly. "What?"

Daniel pulled back and stared into her face. "Married," he said again. "We should get married."

She put a hand on his shoulder and gave him a shove. "Don't be ridiculous."

He straightened and got to his feet. "It's the only solution."

"To what?" she said, and pulled her dress closed over her stomach as she swung her legs off the bed. "Since there's no problem, we don't need a solution." She swiftly buttoned up her dress.

He crossed his arms. "There *is* a problem. We're having two children together and we live on opposite sides of the world."

"I said you can see the baby…I mean, babies, as much as you want. But I'm not interested in a loveless marriage, Daniel. Not with you or anyone else."

The doctor returned before he had an opportunity to say anything more. She gave them the photo of the twins and advised Mary-Jayne to make another appointment with her obstetrician in the next few weeks. Daniel listened while she briefly explained how she was returning home to Crystal Point in the next fortnight and how she would see her family doctor once she was back home.

Home…

He almost envied the way she spoke about the tiny town where she'd lived all her life. Nowhere felt like home to Daniel. Not Port Douglas. Not San Francisco.

They left a few minutes later and Mary-Jayne didn't

say a word as they made their way out of the building toward their vehicle.

"Are you hungry?" he asked as he opened the passenger door. "We could stop somewhere for—"

"I'd prefer to just go back to the resort," she said, cutting him off. "I'm a little tired."

Daniel didn't argue. He nodded and closed the door once she was inside. They were soon back on the road, and he made a quick stop to refuel and grab a couple of bottles of water. She took the water with a nod and tucked it by the seat. Fifteen minutes into their return trip he'd had enough of her unusual silence and spoke.

"Avoiding the subject isn't going to make it go away, Mary-Jayne."

"What subject?"

"My proposal."

She glanced sideways. "I thought you must have been joking."

"I'm perfectly serious. Once you calm down you'll realize it's the only thing we can do."

She huffed. "I'm perfectly calm. And marrying you is the *last* thing I want to do."

"Why not?" he asked, ignoring how much disdain she had in her voice.

"Because I'm not in the market for someone like you."

"Like me?" He smiled at her relentless insults. "Straight, healthy and financially secure?"

"Arrogant, judgmental and a pain in the—"

"Don't you think our children deserve two parents?"

"Our children *will* have two parents," she said, her knuckles white where she clasped her hands together. "Two parents who live in different countries. Two parents who have too much good sense to marry because it's expected they should." She turned her head. "Be honest, Daniel. You don't want to marry me, you just think you *have* to. But you don't. You're off the hook here. So please, don't mention it again."

He pushed down his irritation. She wound him up like no one else ever had. "I take it you're not opposed to marriage entirely…just marriage to me?"

"I'm opposed to marrying someone I don't love," she said bluntly. "And someone who doesn't love me. The thing is, I believe in love…and I want it. I want to be with someone who wants *me* above all others. Who wants only me and sees only me and who carries only me close to his heart."

It was foolish and romantic nonsense. "How can that matter when there are children involved?"

"Because it does," she insisted. "You've had some attack of conscience since you saw them on that screen and think marriage will somehow uncomplicate this…but it won't. We're too different to be tied to one another for life. And I'm not criticizing your motives, I'm simply trying to do what's best for everyone involved…including you."

Daniel wasn't convinced. His father and stepmother had married because Bernie was pregnant, and their marriage had turned out fine. They'd scraped a family together despite their differences. And if he was going to have any chance of being a hands-on father to his sons, Daniel knew he had to do the same.

But he knew Mary-Jayne well enough to recognize she wasn't prepared to discuss it any further. At least for now. "We'll talk about it later."

"No, we won't," she reaffirmed. "And what was with that kiss?"

"It was a kiss. People kiss, Mary-Jayne."

She pointed to him and then herself. "Well, not *these* people. Don't do it again."

Had he lost his mind?

Marriage? As if she'd ever agree to that? Couldn't he see it was madness? He'd married for love once…how could he be prepared to settle for anything less? He could still be a father to their children. Sure, it would be challenging, considering the miles between them. But they could make it work. Plenty of people did the same. He was simply being bullheaded about it. Wanting his own way. Trying to control her.

Well, she wasn't about to be maneuvered into a loveless marriage.

She didn't care how much chemistry they had.

And he better not try to kiss her again, either!

"I'd like to stop and see my parents and tell them the news, if that's okay with you?"

Mary-Jayne turned her head. "Sure. Whatever."

It was a small detour, but she didn't mind. She liked Miles and figured they had to start telling people about the babies at some point. It took about half an hour to reach their small hobby farm, and Mary-Jayne sat up straight as he turned off into a narrow driveway and drove half a mile down the bumpy road until they reached the house. She saw the lovely timber home with wide verandas and noticed a small structure built in replica.

"My dad's studio," Daniel explained.

She turned her head. He watched her with such intensity for a moment her breath stuck in her throat. There was something riveting about his gaze, and she turned hot all over. She foolishly thought about the kiss again. It had been sweet and hot and had stirred her libido.

People kiss…

His words fluttered around in her head. Of course she knew it had been a spur-of-the-moment thing—they were looking at their babies for the first time, he'd helped remove the gel from her belly… No wonder she'd kissed him back so eagerly. She was only human. But he had an agenda. He'd decided what he wanted and would use whatever method he could to achieve that goal—which included seducing her!

She stared at him. "Please, Daniel…don't…"

"Don't what?" A smile creased the corners of his mouth. "What have I done now?"

"You know what," she said, pretty sure she sounded like a petulant child but not caring. "You kissed me."

"You kissed me back."

Color spotted her cheeks. "Well, I'm not going to be swept up in a whole lot of sex stuff…if that's what you're thinking."

He laughed as though he thought her hilarious. "I guess time will tell."

She seethed. "Just because you got me into bed once doesn't mean you will again. That night was out of character for me. I don't even *like* you."

Daniel sat back and turned the engine off. "Is this your usual mode of defense, Mary-Jayne? Attack first?"

She made a scoffing sound. "That's rich, coming from you. You're the corporate shark, not me."

"What is it exactly that you think I do for a living— steamroll over whoever gets in my way? I hate to disappoint you, but I'm not that mercenary. I'm the CEO of a large business that employs several thousand people around the globe. I'm not sure what it is you find so disagreeable about that or me."

"Everything," she replied. "Your arrogance for one…

like right now when you think I'm loopy because I dare to admit that I don't like you."

"I think you're scared," he said quietly. "Not loopy. And I think your emotions are heightened because you're pregnant."

Logically, she knew he was right. But he wound her up in a way that fueled every rebellious streak she possessed. And she was fairly certain he knew it.

"It's not baby brain," she shot back. "This is *me*. Emotional and loopy."

He made an exasperated sound. "Can we put a hold on this conversation? My dad is on his way over."

Sure enough, Miles Anderson was walking toward them from his studio, one strap of his shabby overalls flapping in the breeze. At sixty, he was still handsome and fit, and Mary-Jayne got a snapshot of what Daniel would be like in thirty years. The notion made her insides flutter. *Stupid.* She had to concentrate on now, not some time in the unknown future.

Daniel got out of the vehicle and Mary-Jayne remained where she was for the moment, watching as the two men greeted one another and shook hands. No embrace. No obvious display of affection. It saddened her a little. Would Daniel be like that with his own sons? He spoke to his father for a moment and then turned back toward the Jeep. Mary-Jayne was half out by the time he met her at the door. Miles wasn't far behind, and he watched as his son helped her out of the car.

"Lovely to see you again M.J.," Miles said cheerfully.

"Mary-Jayne," Daniel corrected, as though his father had committed the crime of the century.

She grabbed her tote and looked up at him. "No one really calls me that," she said quietly as he closed the door. "Except my folks…and you."

His mouth twitched. "It's your name."

"It's an old-fashioned mouthful."

"I think it's very pretty," Miles said, and took her arm. "Let's get up to the house. Bernie will be delighted you're here."

She could feel Daniel behind her as they walked toward the house. Mary-Jayne made a comment about how lovely the gardens were and Miles began chatting about the vegetable patch, the chickens and the new milking goat he'd recently bought who kept getting into the yard and eating the zucchini flowers.

Once they reached the veranda Miles spoke again. "My wife has a client in half an hour, but we have time for coffee and some of her pecan cookies."

Mary-Jayne noticed a door to the left of the main door and the shingle that hung to one side—Homeopath, Masseuse and Acupuncturist. Daniel's stepmother came through the open doorway, wearing a blue-and-gold tunic over white trousers, her blond hair flowing. She rushed toward him with a happy squeal and gave him a long hug.

"I'm so glad to see you," she said, all breathless energy, as they pulled apart. "Your brother told us you were back. Four months in between visits is too long."

He is loved.

It was all Mary-Jayne could think of. And then she realized how lucky her babies would be to have two such lovely people as grandparents. Her hand moved instinctively to her belly, and she noticed how Bernie's gaze immediately shifted toward the movement. She looked as though she was about to say something when Daniel stepped back and introduced them.

"It's lovely to meet you," Bernie said, smiling broadly. "Solana has told me all about you, of course. You've made quite an impression on my mother-in-law, and she's the best judge of character I know."

Mary-Jayne returned the smile. "Thank you."

Bernie tapped her husband's shoulder. "Why don't you take Daniel to the studio and show him the piece you're working on for the Phuket renovation, and Mary-Jayne and I will make coffee," she suggested, and then looked back toward Mary-Jayne. "My talented husband is sculpting an incredible bronze for the resort's foyer," she explained animatedly. "It's a dolphin pod diving through a wave." She sighed and smiled. "Just breathtaking."

Mary-Jayne grinned at the other woman's enthusiasm. She liked her immensely. "How lovely," she said, and noticed Miles looked faintly embarrassed by the praise. Daniel stood beside her, unmoving. She tapped his shoulder lightly, trying not to think about how her fingertips tingled at the connection. "You go, I'll be fine."

"Of course she will be," Bernie said, and linked their arms.

They headed inside and into the huge red cedar kitchen in the center of the house. Mary-Jayne noticed the dream catchers in nearly every window and smiled. A large pebbled water feature took up almost an entire wall, and the sound of the water slipping gently over the rocks created a charming ambience and feeling throughout the house.

"You have a lovely home," she said and perched onto a stool behind the wide kitchen counter.

"Thank you. We've been here for nearly ten years. We wanted somewhere where Miles could work without disturbing the neighbors," she said and grinned as she fiddled with the coffee machine. "Sometimes the soldering and battering goes on for hours. But we love it here and we wanted a place where our boys could call home. You know, for when they get married and have families of their own."

The innuendo wasn't missed and she dropped her gaze, took a breath and then met the other woman's inquisitive look head-on. "Yes, I'm pregnant. And yes, Daniel is the father. And we just learned we're having twin boys."

Bernie's beaming smile was infectious, and she came around the counter and hugged her close for a few seconds. "I'm so delighted. He deserves some happiness in his life after what he's been through."

Mary-Jayne was pretty sure Daniel wouldn't consider her a tonic for unhappiness.

"He loved his wife a lot, didn't he?" she asked quietly when the other woman moved back around the bench.

Bernie shrugged a little. "Simone? Well, she was easy to love. She was a nice woman, very kind and good-hearted. She was a lawyer, you know, very successful one, too, from all accounts."

As the other woman made coffee for the men and tea for them, Mary-Jayne fiddled with the silver ring on her right hand. She wasn't sure how she felt knowing Daniel had loved his wife so much. Not jealous—that would be plain stupid. Because it would mean she had feelings invested in him. Which she didn't. But displaced. As though she didn't quite belong. She wasn't someone whom Daniel would *choose* to bring home to meet his parents. Or choose to marry. She was there because she was carrying his babies. If she hadn't gotten pregnant that night they spent together then they probably would never have seen one another again.

"I'm sure she was lovely," she said and smiled.

"Daniel doesn't talk much about her," Bernie remarked, and grabbed four mugs. "He's always been a little closed off from his feelings. When Simone and their unborn baby died he kind of turned inward. The only person he really opens up to is Solana—they're very close. He never knew his real mother," she said and sighed. "I've always treated him like my own, of course. He was just a toddler when the twins were born. But I think losing his mother had a profound impact on him. And Miles grieved for a long time," she said candidly. "Even after we married and had our sons he was still mourning her death. I tried not to take it personally. I still don't on those times when he mentions her."

Mary-Jayne didn't miss the message in the other woman's words. But the situations weren't the same. She was sure Miles Anderson loved Bernadette, even if he had still grieved the wife he lost. Whereas Daniel didn't even *like* her. He might want her in his bed, but that was all it was.

"Thanks for the talk," Mary-Jayne said and smiled. "And the support."

"Anytime," Bernie said just as the men walked in through the back door.

Mary-Jayne swiveled on the stool and looked at Daniel. "How's the sculpture look?"

"Good."

Miles clapped a hand onto his son's shoulder. "Why don't you take her to the studio and show her?" he suggested, then winked at Mary-Jayne. "I should've guessed a brilliantly creative girl like you might want to critique my work. Go easy on this old man, though. My fragile artistic ego can't take too much criticism."

Mary-Jayne laughed. She genuinely liked Miles and understood his self-effacing humor. "Of course," she said and slid off the stool.

Daniel watched the interaction in silence and only moved when she took a few steps toward the door. "Coming?" she asked.

She was through the door and down the back steps quickly and didn't wait for him to catch up as she headed across the yard toward the studio. She was already inside and staring at the huge bronze sculpture when he came up behind her.

"Wow," she said as she stepped around the piece and admired the effort and imagination that had gone into its creation. "This is incredible."

Daniel came beside her. "He'll be delighted you approve."

She looked up and raised a brow. "I suppose you told him, then."

"About the babies?" He nodded. "Yes. He's delighted about that, too. Told me it was about time I settled down and raised a family."

"I hope you set him straight?"

"You mean did I tell him you've turned down my proposal? No, I thought I'd try my luck again before I admitted that."

Mary-Jayne offered a wry smile. "One marriage proposal in a day is enough, thanks very much."

"Even if I get down on my knee this time?" he asked, his eyes glittering. "Or get you a ring?"

"You're too uptight to get your kneecap dirty," she shot back, saccharine sweet. "And I want to design my own ring when I *eventually* get married."

He laughed, and she liked the sound way too much. "So, how'd Bernie take the news?"

"Very well. Tell me something, why do you call her Bernie? She's the only mother you've known, right?"

"I call her Mom sometimes," he said, looking just a little uncomfortable. "And stop cross-examining me."

"Gotta take the chance when I can. They're very nice," she said and moved around the sculpture some more. "And they love you."

"I know that," he said, and came closer again. "We just live different lives."

"But you had a happy childhood?"

He shrugged loosely. "I guess. Although there were times when I wished they'd stop moving the furniture around the house to accommodate their feng shui beliefs or eat a steak and fries instead of tofu burgers. Or have an aspirin for a headache instead of Bernie's acupuncture jabs to the temple."

Mary-Jayne stilled and looked up at him. "Is that why you don't like needles?"

"Well, I—"

She was mortified when she realized what it meant. "They stuck needles into their child?"

"They thought they were doing the right thing," he said and moved around behind her.

She turned to face him and looked up. "But that's why you don't like needles?"

"I guess," he said and shrugged again. "Seems foolish to make that kind of connection, though. It was a long time ago and it wasn't as if it was some kind of deliberate torture. Bernie's well qualified in her field and she thought she was helping. They were good parents."

"I know. And we'll be good, too," she assured him. "We've had good role models."

"Good parents who live in two different countries?" He reached out and touched a lock of her hair, twirling it between his fingertips. "I want to be their father, Mary-Jayne. All I'm asking for is a chance to do that."

Her heart tugged, and she pushed back a sudden swell of emotion "I can't. It wouldn't work," she implored. "Look, I'm not saying it's going to be easy doing this with the situation being what it is. We both know there will be challenges, especially as the children get older. But I can't and won't commit to a loveless marriage. I want what my parents have, and I want to raise my children in the town I've lived in all my life." She moved back fractionally and his hand dropped. "And I know you think that's all a load of overly romantic hogwash, but I can't change who I am and what I believe any more than you can. I've never really been in love. But I want to be."

"Yeah," he said, and shook his head. "And you want some romantic sap to carry you next to his heart... I heard all that the other day."

"But did you listen? Love isn't an illusion, Daniel. You loved your wife, right? Bernie said she was smart and beautiful and how everyone adored her. So if love was good enough for you back then, why do you think I'm so foolish for wanting the same thing?"

"Because it doesn't last."

"It does," she refuted. "Our parents are testament to that."

"So maybe sometimes it does last. But when it doesn't... When it's gone it's about as bad as it gets."

There was real pain in his voice, and she unconsciously reached out and grasped his upper arm. The muscles were tight and bunched with tension, and she met his gaze head on.

"You're still hurting," she whispered, fighting the need to comfort him.

He looked down into her face, his expression unmoving. The pulse in his cheek throbbed, and his gray eyes were as dark as polished slate. Her fingers tingled where she touched him, and when he reached up and cupped her cheek Mary-Jayne's knees wobbled.

"Most days...most days I'm just...numb."

Every compassionate and caring instinct she possessed was quickly on red alert. "It was an accident, Daniel. A terrible accident. And she wouldn't want you to feel this way, would she?"

"No," he said and traced her cheek with his thumb. "She'd want me to marry you and raise our sons together. And that's what we're going to do, Mary-Jayne. We have to get married. For the sake of our sons. All you need to do is say yes."

Chapter Seven

She didn't say yes. She didn't say anything. Instead she pulled away from him and headed back inside. They stayed for another twenty minutes, and when Bernie's client showed up they said their goodbyes and Daniel promised to return to see them in a couple of days. Being around his family made her long for her own, and Mary-Jayne stayed quiet on the trip back to the resort.

All you need to do is say yes...

As if it was so easy.

She almost admired his perseverance. Almost. He was relentless when he wanted something. No wonder he was so successful professionally. Solana had told her that he'd pretty much singlehandedly turned the chain of Sandwhisper Resorts into a flourishing enterprise around the globe. When his grandfather had been at the helm, Anderson's had only recently ventured into the new direction after spending years in copper and ore mining. Most of that was sold off now and the business focused on the resorts. While other empires had failed, Daniel had kept Anderson's afloat by using natural business acumen and innate tenacity. She remembered how he'd told her how so many people relied on the company for their livelihood and that was what made him determined to keep the organization growing.

Once they got back to the resort, he walked her to her door and lingered for a moment. "Can I see you tonight?"

Mary-Jayne shook her head. "I don't think so."

His eyes flashed. "You can't avoid me. I'm not going away, and neither is this situation."

"I'm tired, that's all. It's been a long day. And eventful," she said, and waved the envelope that held the picture of their babies.

He nodded. "All right, Mary-Jayne, I'll back off for tonight. But we have to get this sorted out."

"Yes," she said, and sighed heavily. "And we will. Just not today."

He left her reluctantly, and once he was gone she moved into the living room and slumped into the sofa. She was more confused than ever. *Daniel* confused her. Confounded her. He was relentless about the marriage thing. But she wouldn't change her mind. She couldn't. It would be a complete disaster.

She wanted love…not duty. Maybe he wasn't quite the closed-off corporate shark she'd first thought him to be; maybe there were moments when she enjoyed his company and liked the way they verbally sparred. And maybe there *was* a constant undercurrent of attraction and desire between them that made her head spin. But it still wasn't enough. And it never would be. Attraction alone wasn't enough. And those few unexpected moments where she relaxed around him were unreliable.

She hung around the condo for the remainder of the afternoon and at five o'clock was about to call Audrey again when there was a knock on her door. She groaned, loathing the thought of going another round with Daniel when all she wanted to do was talk to her friend and then curl into bed.

But it wasn't Daniel at her door. It was his grandmother.

"Can I come in?" Solana asked.

Mary-Jayne stepped back and opened the door wider. "Of course."

Once they were both settled in the living room, Solana spoke again.

"My grandson came to see me," she said and smiled. "He told me you were expecting twin boys."

Mary-Jayne wasn't surprised. It was the last thing he'd said to her when he'd walked her to her door earlier that day. He'd announced how he planned telling his grandmother about her pregnancy.

She nodded. "Yes, I am."

"And are you happy about it?"

"Very," she admitted. "I'm sorry I haven't told you earlier. Things were a little complicated and I—"

"You don't need to explain yourself. Daniel told me what happened."

She was relieved Solana understood. "Thank you. I know it must be something of a shock."

The older woman smiled. "Well, I was lining you up for Caleb…but now I think about it, you are definitely much better suited to Daniel. He needs someone who won't let him rule the roost. Caleb is way too easygoing. Whereas Daniel," Solana grinned widely, "is as wound up as a spring. You'll be good for him, I'm sure of it."

Mary-Jayne perched on the edge of the sofa. "Oh, it's not like that. We're not together or anything," she explained, coloring hotly. "I mean, we were *together*...just that once...but not now."

Solana's brows raised. "He said you've refused his marriage proposal."

"I did," she replied. "I had to. Please try to understand."

"I do," Solana said gently. "You want to fall in love and be swept off your feet. You want roses and moonlight and real romance."

"Yes," she admitted. "Exactly."

"And my grandson is too sensible and pragmatic for all that, right?"

Mary-Jayne shrugged. "We're not in love. We never would be. It would be a catastrophe."

Solana got up and moved to sit beside her on the sofa. "My son Miles married his first wife after dating her for two years. They were more in love than I'd ever seen two people in love. When she died so soon after Daniel was born Miles was heartbroken. And then along came Bernie and a few months later she was pregnant. It wasn't a love match at first...but they've made a good marriage together and raised three boys into the finest men I know."

She ignored the heavy thump behind her ribs. It was a nice story. But it's wasn't hers and Daniel's. "I know you want to see your grandson happy, but believe me, I could never be the person to do that. We don't even *like* one another."

Solana's hand came out and she briefly touched her stomach. "Oh, I'd say you liked one another well enough."

"That's not love...that's..."

"It's a place to start, that's all," Solana said. "Don't make a rash decision because you're scared of the future. Work on the present and let the future take care of itself."

It was a nice idea. But Mary-Jayne wasn't convinced.

Once the other woman left, she returned to her pacing.

She wasn't about to marry a man she didn't love. She might want him. She might even like him a little bit. Maybe more than a little bit. Maybe she liked him a lot. But it wasn't enough. It would never be enough. And she wasn't about to be railroaded into something she didn't want.

The phone rang and she snatched it up. It was Audrey.

"Thank God," she said, and quickly explained what was happening to her concerned friend.

Fourteen hours later Mary-Jayne was on a flight home.

She was gone.

Gone...

Again.

Daniel's mood shifted between concern and rage and in varying degrees.

How could she leave without a word?

Damn it, they were his children, too. His flesh. His blood.

He'd knocked on her door on Wednesday afternoon after Caleb had called and told him the store was closed again. He knocked and waited, and when she didn't respond he called her cell. It went to message and he hung up. On Thursday morning Audrey Cooper answered the door. And he knew instantly that she'd bailed. Her friend was of little help and regarded him with barely concealed contempt. The pretty redhead stood in the doorway, arms crossed, defiant and clearly willing to go into battle for her friend.

"Is she back in Crystal Point with her family?" he asked, his rage simmering, his patience frayed.

Audrey pushed back her hair, clearly unimpressed. "I'm not saying. But wherever she is, there's no point in going after her. I think it's fairly clear she doesn't want to see or hear from you."

"She said that?"

Audrey, who evidently had as much contempt for him as she did for Caleb, nodded slowly. "If you go after her she'll spook and disappear."

It sounded a little melodramatic. Mary-Jayne wouldn't do that. She wouldn't put their babies at risk. Not for anything. He knew her well enough to realize that. "That doesn't make sense."

Audrey's brows rose sharply. "I know M.J. way better than you do. She doesn't like to be hemmed in, and if you push her she'll react and run. She's got friends all over the place and they and her family would do anything for her…and that includes helping her avoid you at all costs. Just leave her alone."

Run? Jesus…she wouldn't… Would she?

Audrey grabbed the door and closed it a little. "Since you own this place, I should tell you I'm looking for someone to take over the lease on the store. If I can't find anyone in a week I'm closing up and leaving. So if you want to sue me for breach of contract, go right ahead. And tell that lousy brother of yours to stay out of my way."

Then she closed the door in his face.

Daniel was furious by the time he reached Caleb's office. His brother was sitting at his desk, punching numbers into the computer.

"Your redhead is back," he said when the door was shut.

Caleb almost jumped out of his chair. "Audrey?"

"Yeah."

"Is she still…"

"Angry?" Daniel nodded. "She hates you as much as ever and me by association, which is why she wouldn't confirm that Mary-Jayne has gone home."

His brother grabbed his jacket off the back of the chair. "I'm going to see her. Is she at the—"

Daniel pulled the jacket from his brother's hands and tossed it on the desk. "You'd better not. She's leaving the resort, closing up the store if she can't find someone to take on her lease."

Clearly agitated, Caleb grabbed the jacket again. "She can't do that. She signed a contract. We'll get the lawyers to make sure she—"

"Stop being such a hothead," Daniel said, and took the jacket, throwing it onto the sofa by the door. "And leave the lawyers out of it. She's angry and hurt and has every reason to hate you, so if she wants to leave and break the lease agreement then she can do just that...without any interference from you, understand?"

Caleb glared at him. "When did you get so sentimental?"

"When I realized that Audrey has probably already contacted Mary-Jayne and told her I'm looking for her."

His brother's temper calmed a little. "Okay, I get the point. You're concerned Mary-Jayne might do something rash."

"Actually," he said, calmer now, "I think she'll do whatever is best for the babies. Which in her eyes is going home to be around her family."

"And that's where you're going?"

He shrugged. "I have to make this right."

Caleb raised an eyebrow. "You sure you want to make a commitment to a woman you don't love? Hell, you don't even know for sure if those babies are yours."

"I do know," he said. He wound back the irritation he felt toward his brother and tapped his hand to his chest. "I feel it...in here."

And that, he figured, was all that mattered.

Mary-Jayne had been holed up in her small house for four days. Her family knew she was back, but she'd insisted she had a bad head cold and said she needed some time to recover. Her mother had tutted and pleaded to bring her some soup and parental comfort, but Mary-Jayne wasn't prepared for them quite yet. Her sisters called every day and her friend Lauren did the same. Her dog, Pricilla, and parrot, Elvis, were happy she was home and gave her all the company she needed. While she waited for Daniel to turn up. Which she knew he would.

He wasn't the kind of man to give up when he wanted something.

Mary-Jayne had no illusions… His proposal was only about their children. He didn't want to marry *her*. And she didn't want to marry him. He was single-minded in his intent… He wanted the babies. He'd take her, too, if it meant getting full-time custody of their sons.

She wondered what his next move would be. And made herself sick to the stomach thinking about the possibilities. Since she'd refused his outrageous proposal, would he try another tack? Was he thinking about sole custody? Would he fight her in court to get what he wanted? He had money and power, and that equated to influence. He could afford the finest lawyers in the country and they'd certainly be out to prove she was less capable of giving their children the best possible life. Maybe the courts would see it that way, too.

By Sunday morning she was so wound up she wanted to scream. And cry. And run.

But she wouldn't do any of those things. She needed to stay strong and focus on growing two healthy babies. She'd fight the fight she needed to when she faced it head on. Until then, her sons were all that mattered.

When Evie and Grace arrived at her door late on Sunday afternoon she was almost relieved. She hated lying to her sisters, even if it was only by omission.

One look at her and Evie squealed. "Oh, my God, you're pregnant!"

"Well, don't tell the whole neighborhood," she said, and ushered them both inside.

Grace, who was easily the most beautiful woman Mary-Jayne had ever known, was a little less animated. She'd also had her first child two months earlier. But Evie, ever the nurturer, who had a seventeen-year-old son and a toddler daughter, was still chattering as Mary-Jayne closed the door and ushered them down the hallway.

"Tell us everything," Evie insisted as the trio dropped onto the big chintz sofa. "And first the part about how you've managed to keep from spilling the beans about this."

"Forget that," Grace said and smiled. "First, tell us who the baby's father is?"

"Babies," Mary-Jayne said and waited a microsecond before her sisters realized what she meant.

There were more shrieks and laughter and a load of questions before Mary-Jayne had an opportunity to explain. It took several minutes, and when she was done each of her sisters had a hold of her hands.

"And he wants to marry you?" Grace asked.

She shrugged. "That's what he says."

Evie squeezed her fingers. "But you don't want to marry him, M.J.?"

She screwed up her face. "Definitely not."

"Is he that awful?"

She opened her mouth to respond, but quickly stopped herself. She couldn't, in good conscience, make out as if he was some kind of ogre. Once he'd settled into the idea that he was the father he'd been incredibly supportive. And she couldn't forget his caring behavior when she'd had the ultrasound.

And then there was that kiss.

Don't forget the kiss…

Of course she needed to forget the kiss. It shouldn't have happened. It had only confused her. "He's not awful," she said and sat back in the chair. "Most of the time he's quite…nice."

Grace frowned. "Most?"

"Well, he can also be an arrogant jerk," she replied. "You know, all that old money and entitlement."

"Is he tall, dark and handsome to go along with all that old money?" Evie asked and grinned.

"Oh, yeah. He's all that. And more."

"And you *still* don't want to marry him?"

"I want to marry for love," she said and sighed. "Like you both did. I don't want to settle for a man who looks at me as some kind of incubator. We might have a whole lot of chemistry now, but when that goes what's left? An empty shell disguised as a marriage? No, thanks."

"That's a fairly pessimistic view of things," Grace remarked. "And not like you at all."

"I'm tired of being the eternal optimist," she said, feeling stronger. "Being pregnant has changed my thinking. I want to build a good life for my babies—one that's honest and authentic. And if I married Daniel I would be living a lie. Despite how much I…" She stopped and let her words trail.

"Despite how much you *like* him, you mean?" Evie prompted.

She shrugged again. "Sure, I like him. But I dislike him, too, and that's where it gets complicated."

"Maybe you're making it more complicated than it needs to be," Grace suggested. "I mean, you don't really know him very well. Perhaps over time you will change your mind."

"I doubt it," she said. "I live here and he lives in San Francisco. There's a whole lot of ocean in between. Look, I'm happy for him to see his sons and have a relationship with them. I *want* them to have a father. But when I get married I want it to be with someone who wants *me*...and not just because I'm the mother of his children."

She was about to get to her feet when the doorbell rang.

"That's probably the folks," Evie said and smiled. "They've been worried about you. Which might have something to do with the fake head cold you said you had to keep us all at bay."

"Not that it did any good," Mary-Jayne said and grinned.

"Want me to get it?" Grace asked.

"Nah," she said and pulled herself out of the soft sofa. "I got it."

She walked down the hall and opened the front door, half expecting her mother to be standing there with a big pot of chicken soup. But it wasn't either of her parents.

It was Daniel.

He looked so good. So familiar. In jeans and a blue shirt, everything about him screamed sexy and wholly masculine. She wished she was immune. She wished he didn't set her blood and skin on fire. His steely gaze traveled over her slowly until he finally met her eyes with his own and spoke.

"So you didn't run too far after all?"

"Run?"

Daniel had expected her to slam the door. But she didn't look all that surprised to see him on her doorstep.

"Your friend said you might be tempted to run to get away from me."

"Audrey did?" She laughed loudly. "I'm afraid she's got a vivid imagination and a flair for the dramatic."

"Speaking of which," Daniel said pointedly, "taking off without a word was a little theatrical, don't you think?"

She shrugged and her T-shirt slipped off her shoulder. "I needed some breathing space."

"I wasn't exactly smothering you."

"Maybe not to you," she flipped back.

He grinned a little, even though his insides churned. She had a way of doing that—a way of mixing up his emotions. He was as mad as hell with her for taking off without a word, but he wouldn't show her that. Daniel turned to briefly look at the two cars in her driveway. "You have company?"

She nodded. "My sisters."

His gaze dropped to her belly. "You told them?"

"They told me," she said, and pulled the T-shirt over her middle a fraction. "Hard to hide this from the world now."

"You shouldn't," he said quietly. "You look good."

She shrugged. "So...I guess I'll see you around."

Daniel laughed lightly. "Oh, no, Mary-Jayne, you don't get out of it that easy."

Her gaze narrowed. "You plan on camping on my doorstep?"

"If I have to," he replied. "Or you could invite me in."

His eyes widened. "You want to meet my sisters, is that it?"

"Absolutely."

She exhaled heavily and stepped back. "Okay. Best you come inside."

Daniel crossed the threshold of her small cottage and followed her down the hall. Her house was filled with old furniture and bric-a-brac and was as muddled as he'd expected. The Preston sisters regarded him curiously when he entered the living room and as Mary-Jayne introduced him. They were similar, all with the same dark curling hair and wide green eyes. Evie was down to earth and friendly, while Grace had a kind of ethereal beauty that made her look as though she'd stepped off the set of a Hollywood movie.

The eldest, Evie, asked him if he'd had a good trip and began chatting about flying and vacations, which he figured she was doing to break the ice a little. The other sister was more serious and content to stand back and watch Mary-Jayne and him interact. It didn't bother him. All he cared about was Mary-Jayne.

He cared...

Damn.

He didn't want to think about that. But he couldn't get the vision of her staring up at him in his dad's studio, her hand gently rubbing his arm, all wide-eyed and lovely. In that moment he realized she was kind and considerate, despite the bouts of exuberant bravado.

Her siblings were nice women who were clearly curious about him but were too polite to say too much. They stayed for a few minutes, and he asked about Evie's art and mentioned how his father was an artist, and she said she knew his work. Both women talked about Crystal Point and how much they loved the small town. Daniel hadn't taken much notice as he'd driven along the waterfront. His mind was set on seeing Mary-Jayne, not the beach. Evie suggested he drop by her bed-and-breakfast, and he noticed how Mary-Jayne scowled at her sister. Maybe he had an ally in the Preston sisters? Maybe they agreed that she should marry him? He wasn't averse to using whatever leverage he could if it meant he'd have the chance to be a full-time father to his sons.

Once they left, Mary-Jayne propped her hands on her hips and glared at him.

"I suppose you'd like coffee?"

He smiled. "If it's not too much trouble."

She tossed her incredible hair. "Oh, it is…not that it would make one damn bit of difference to you. And by the way," she said as she walked down the hall, "don't think you can sway me by charming my family. I've already told my sisters what a jerk you are."

He laughed and walked after her. "I don't think they quite believed you, Mary-Jayne."

When he reached the kitchen he stood by the counter for a moment, looking around at the crowded room with its cluttered cabinets, colorful drapes and assortment of pots hanging from hooks above the stove top. But as untidy and overdone as it was, there was something oddly welcoming about the room. With its mismatched table and chairs and the wrought iron stand in the corner jammed with an array of ceramic vases containing a variety of overgrown herbs, it was far removed from the huge ultra-modern kitchen in his San Francisco apartment. He never used it these days. Even when he was married, Simone had worked long hours like he did and they preferred to dine out most evenings. But Mary-Jayne's kitchen suited her. It was easy to imagine her sitting at the round scrubbed table, sipping tea from one of the patterned china cups from the collection on the dresser.

"Yes," she said, still scowling. "I'm a slob, remember?"

"Did I say that?"

"Words to the effect. One of my many flaws."

He chuckled and watched her pull a pair of ceramic mugs from the cupboard. She looked so beautiful with her scowl, all fired up and ready to do battle with him. One thing was for sure, life with Mary-Jayne Preston sure wasn't dull!

Daniel came around the counter and stood beside her.

She turned and rested her hip against the bench, arms crossed.

"Yes?"

"Nothing," he said and reached for her, curling his hand gently around her neck.

"Don't you dare," she said, but didn't move.

"What are you so afraid of?" he asked, urging her closer. "That I'm going to kiss you? Or that you'll like it?"

"Neither," she said on a shallow breath. "Both."

"You never have to be afraid of me, Mary-Jayne," he said quietly, bringing her against him. The feel of her belly and breasts instantly spiked his libido. "I'd never hurt you. Or make you to do something you didn't want to do."

"Then, stop asking me to marry you," she said, still breathless as she looked up into his face.

"I can't. When I want something I'm—"

"Relentless," she said, cutting off his words. "Yeah, I know. I'm not used to someone like you," she admitted, her mouth trembling a little. "My last boyfriend was—"

"An unemployed musician," he finished for her, not in the mood to hear about the man she'd once dated. "Yes, I had you investigated, remember?"

She frowned and wriggled against him. "Jerk."

Daniel moved his other arm around her waist and gently held her. "Me or him?"

"You."

He chuckled. "You know, I don't think you really mean that."

"Sure I do," she said, and wriggled some more. "And kissing me isn't going to get me to change my mind."

"Maybe not," he said and dipped his head. "But it sure beats arguing about it."

Her lips were soft when he claimed them. Soft and sweet and familiar. Her hands crept up his chest and reached his shoulders and she clung on to him. Daniel pressed closer and she moaned softly. The sweet vanilla scent that was uniquely hers assailed his senses, and he tilted her head a fraction. Their tongues met and danced. And he was pretty sure she knew exactly the effect she had on him and his libido. His hand moved down to her hip, and he urged her closer. Heat flared between them, and suddenly kissing wasn't enough. Her fingertips dug into his shoulders and she arched her back, drawing them closer together.

"Mary-Jayne," he whispered against her mouth and trailed his lips down her cheek and throat. "Let me stay with you tonight."

She shivered in his arms. "I can't," she said on a shallow breath. "Tomorrow…"

"Forget tomorrow," he said, and pushed the T-shirt off her shoulder. Her creamy skin was like tonic for the desire that churned through his blood. "Forget everything but right now."

It was what he wanted. What he needed. Her skin, her mouth, her tender touch. He'd shut off from truly feeling anything for so long, but Mary-Jayne made him feel in ways he could barely understand. They fought; they battled with words and with ideals. But underneath the conflict simmered an attraction and a pull that was the most powerful of his life.

And it also had the power to undo him.

Chapter Eight

She didn't let him stay. She couldn't. If he'd stayed and they'd made love she wasn't sure she would have had the strength to refuse his marriage proposal. He'd use sex to confuse and manipulate her, even if that wasn't his intention. She was like putty in his arms. One kiss, one touch and being with him was all she could think about.

Idiot...

Mary-Jayne garnered all her strength and sent him packing. And tried to convince herself she couldn't care less where he went. There were plenty of quality hotels in the nearby town of Bellandale. It was barely a twenty-minute drive from Crystal Point. He had a GPS. He'd be fine. She didn't feel bad at all.

She had a shower, made soup and toast and curled up on the sofa to watch TV with Pricilla and pretended she'd put Daniel out of her mind once and for all.

Her dreams, however, were something else altogether.

He invaded them. She couldn't keep him out. His touch was like a brand against her skin, and she could still feel the heat of his body pressed against her for hours later. And his kiss… It was like no other. She remembered his comment about her ex-boyfriend. *An unemployed musician?* Toby had been exactly that. He wasn't even much of a musician. They'd dated off and on for two years and she often wondered if she'd brought home a tattooed, frequently pierced, dreadlocked boyfriend simply because that was what everyone expected of her. Her teenage willfulness made her rebel against what she'd considered the average or mundane. After she'd left home she'd saved her money and quickly headed overseas. She'd returned feeling even more independent and more determined to live her own life.

And Toby was the end result. A deadbeat, she realized now. Someone who took advantage of her generous nature and swindled her out of her money and her pride. She'd been left with a debt for a car he crashed and a guitar he'd taken with him when he walked out the door. He had no goals, no ambition and no integrity. She'd had one serious relationship since with a man who ended up complaining about her spending too much time worrying about her career. He'd had no ambition, either—except the desire to sit in front of his computer all day playing games. She'd foolishly believed she chose men who were free-spirited and artistic. Now they simply seemed lazy and immature.

She tossed and turned all night and woke up feeling nauseated and unable to stomach the dry crackers and green tea that usually helped most when morning sickness came upon her.

She changed into her favorite overalls and grinned when she discovered she had to leave two of the three side buttons undone to accommodate her rapidly expanding middle. Her workshop needed a cleanup before she got to work on the few back orders she had, so she headed outside and began decluttering the counters. It was midmorning before she took a break and snacked on some apple slices and a cup of tea.

At eleven Daniel rocked up.

In dark jeans and a navy polo shirt he looked effortlessly handsome, and her stomach flipped with familiar awareness. He looked her over and smiled.

"Cute outfit."

Her overalls were paint splattered and had holes in each knee. But they were comfy, and she could care less what he thought about her clothes. "Thanks. Did you want something?" she asked, pushing the memory of his kisses from her mind.

"We're going out."

Bossy, as usual. "Are we? Am I allowed to ask where we're going?"

"To see your parents," he said swiftly. "It's about time they were told they're about to become grandparents again."

"I'd rather tell them myself."

"*We'll* tell them," he said, firmer this time. "Stop being stubborn."

Mary-Jayne turned and sashayed down the hall. "I'd really prefer to do it some other time. Please try to understand."

"Well, I don't. We're in this together," he said, and followed her into the house. "We told my parents together… and now we'll tell yours…together. That's how things are going to be, Mary-Jayne. They have a right to know, don't you think?"

When she reached the living room she turned and

propped her hands on her hips. "Of course. I just don't want you to meet them right now."

His brows shot up. "Why the hell not?"

"Because," she said, and dragged out a long breath, "you don't know them. One look at you and they'll get all…thingy."

He stilled. *"Thingy?"*

Her patience frayed. "Excited, okay? Thrilled. Happy. They'll feel as though they've won the lottery in the potential son-in-law department."

He laughed. "They want you to nab a rich husband?"

"No," she corrected. "That's not it. It's just that you're different from anyone I've ever…you know…dated. You're not an *unemployed musician*," she explained, coloring hotly. "Or a beach bum or a lazy good-for-nothing, as my dad would say. You're…*normal*… You're successful and hardworking and come from a nice family. Once they know that, they'll get all worked up and start pressuring me to…to…"

"Marry me?"

"Well, yeah," she admitted. "Probably."

"I thought you said they let you lead your own life?"

"They do," she replied. "But they're still my parents. They still want what's best for me. Once they clap eyes on you, I'll be done for."

His mouth twitched at the edges. "Best you get changed so we can get going."

Mary-Jayne frowned. "Didn't you hear what I said?"

"Every word," he said, and dropped into the sofa. "Hurry up, *dear*."

Impatience snaked up her spine. "You are the most infuriating and—"

"Want me to kiss you again?" he asked as he grabbed a

magazine from the coffee table and opened it at a random page. "If not, go and get changed."

Irritated, she turned on her heels and stomped to her bedroom. He was an ass. He didn't give a hoot what she wanted. Or care about how she felt. By the time she'd dressed, Mary-Jayne was so mad she could have slugged his smug face.

Once they were out of the house she pointed to her car. "I'll drive," she said and rattled her keys. "I know the way."

Daniel stopped midstride and looked at the battered VW in the driveway. "In that hunk of junk? I don't think so." He gestured to the top-of-the-range Ford sedan parked alongside the curb. "We'll take my rental car."

"Snob."

He laughed and gently grasped her elbow. "Come on."

"Sometimes I really don't like you much at all."

He laughed again. "And other times?"

She quickstepped it to the car and waited by the passenger door. It was hard to stay mad at him when he was being so nice to her. "No comment."

Once they were in the car she gave him the address. The trip took only minutes, and by the time they pulled into the driveway her temper had lost its momentum.

"You're something of a hothead, aren't you?" he asked as he unclipped his seat belt.

"Around you?" She raised a brow and smiled a little. "Yeah."

He seemed to find that idea amusing and was still chuckling by the time he was out of the car and had come around to her side. "It's one of the things I find captivating about you, Mary-Jayne."

Captivating? That was quite an admission. He usually didn't admit to anything, not when it came to feelings. Oh, sure, she knew he wanted her in his bed, but anything else seemed off his agenda. He'd said he felt numb. The very idea pained her deep down. He'd lost the woman he'd loved and didn't want to love again… That was clear enough.

"What are you thinking about?" he asked as he took her hand.

I'm thinking about how it must feel to be loved by you…

Mary-Jayne's fingers tingled at the connection with his. She didn't want to be so vulnerable to his touch, but her attraction for him had a will of its own. She simply couldn't help herself. That was why she'd become so caught up in the heat and passion between them the night of Solana's birthday party. It was heady and powerful and drove her beyond coherent thought. It was more than attraction. More than anything she'd felt before.

And the very idea scared her senseless.

Her parents, as expected, were delighted, if not a little shocked at their news. Once the shock settled, her mother had countless questions for Daniel and he answered every one without faltering. He was as resilient as the devil when under intense scrutiny. Barbara Preston skirted around the question about marriage and Mary-Jayne was relieved that Daniel didn't mention that she'd refused his proposal. There was time for that revelation later. Her father, she realized, looked as pleased as she'd ever seen him. Bill Preston approved. Daniel was a hit. Her parents were clearly delighted, even with her out-of-wedlock pregnancy. Her mother was all hugs and tears when they explained she was expecting twins.

Over a jug of iced tea her father spoke. "What do you think of our little town, son?"

Son?

Her dad was already calling Daniel "son"?

Great.

"I haven't had a chance to see much of it yet," Daniel

replied. "But I'm hoping Mary-Jayne will show me around sometime today."

She smiled sweetly and nodded, and then noticed how her mother seemed to approve wholeheartedly about the way Daniel used her full name. He could clearly do no wrong.

I'm doomed.

They stayed for two hours, and Daniel answered every probing question her parents asked. He talked about his career, his family and even his wife and the baby they had lost. Before they left her father ushered him off to his garage to inspect the Chevrolet Impala that he was restoring, and Mary-Jayne was left to endure her mother's scrutiny.

"Now," Barbara said, hugging her closely once the men had left the room. "What don't I know?"

"Nothing," she replied and began collecting the mugs from the table. "The babies are doing fine and I feel okay other than a little morning sickness."

"I meant with the two of you," Barbara said and raised a brow. "He's awfully handsome, isn't he? And such nice manners."

Mary-Jayne smiled. "I know he isn't what you've imagined I'd bring home to meet you."

"Well, your track record hasn't exactly given us confidence."

"I know. And you're right—he's handsome and nice and has good manners."

"Are you in love with him?"

Love...

She'd not considered the word in regard to him. Falling in love with Daniel was out of the question. He'd never love her back. *He was numb.* There was nothing left in his heart. He'd love their sons and that was all.

"No," she said and heard the hesitation in her own voice. "Definitely not."

Barbara smiled. "It wouldn't be the end of the world, you know… I mean, if you did fall in love with a man like Daniel."

"It would," she corrected, suddenly hurting deep in her chest. "He still loves his wife. And she was very different from me. She was smart and successful and everything I'm not."

There…I said it out loud.

Her mother's expression softened some more. "You're smart, and your dad and I have every faith that your business will be a success one day. And sometimes being *different* is a good thing," Barbara added gently.

"Not in this," she said, her heart suddenly and inexplicably heavy. "I know you only want to see me happy, and I am happy about the babies. Really happy. Even though it's been something of a shock I'm looking forward to being a mother."

Barbara rubbed her arm comfortingly. "You'll be a good one, too, I'm sure of it."

"I hope so," she said. "Although I'm sure some people will think having twin boys is my medicine for being such a difficult child myself."

Her mother smiled. "You were spirited, not difficult."

"That's sweet of you to say so, but I know I caused you and Dad some major headaches over the years. Remember when I ditched school for three days to follow that carnival that had arrived in town?"

Barbara laughed. "Every kid dreams of running away and joining the circus at some point. Especially a strong-willed eleven-year-old."

Mary-Jayne giggled. "I had visions of being a trapeze artist."

They chatted for a few more minutes about her child-hood escapades, and by the time her father and Daniel returned her mood was much improved. Daniel looked his usual self-satisfied self and her dad looked pleased as punch. Whatever had transpired in the garage, she was sure it had something to do her father giving Daniel his blessing and full support.

Typical...

Once they were back in the car, she strapped on the seat belt and pasted on a smile.

"Take a left at the end of the street," she instructed.

"Because?"

"You wanted to see my town, my home, right?"

"Well...yes."

"So we'll go to the beach."

He frowned a little. "We're not exactly dressed for the beach."

Mary-Jayne laughed. "Does everything always have to be done to order with you? Live dangerously, Daniel," she said and laughed again. "You might surprise yourself and enjoy it."

His mouth tightened. "You know, despite what you think, I'm not some overworked killjoy."

"Prove it," she challenged. "Get those extrastarched clothes of yours crumpled for a moment."

"Extrastarched?" he echoed as he started the ignition.

She chuckled. "Oh, come on, even you have to admit that you're a neat freak. You even folded your clothes that night we spent together." It was something of an exaggeration...but she had a point to prove. "My dress got twisted amongst the bedsheets and your suit was per-fectly placed over the chair."

"I don't remember it that way."

"Hah," she scoffed. "You have a selective memory."

"I remember everything about that night," he said and drove down the street. "Left, you said?"

"Left," she repeated. "We'll drive past my sister's bed-and-breakfast."

"I know where that is already."

Her brows came up. "You do?"

He nodded. "Of course. I stayed there last night."

Daniel knew it would make her nuts. But he'd thought it was a good idea at the time and Evie Jones seemed to agree. After Mary-Jayne had kicked him out of her house the evening before, he'd driven around the small town for a while and come across Dunn Inn by chance. The big A-framed house stood silhouetted amongst a nest of Norfolk pines and the shingle out front had told him exactly who the place belonged to. So he'd tapped on the door and was met by Evie's much younger husband, Scott, and within minutes Evie herself was insisting he stay at the bed-and-breakfast while he was in Crystal Point.

"You stayed at my sister's place?"

She was all outraged, and it made him grin a little. "Sure. Something wrong with that?"

"Something? Everything! Of all the manipulative and conniving things I could imagine you—"

"I needed somewhere to stay," he said quickly. "You told me to leave, remember?"

"Ever heard of a thing called a hotel?" she shot back. "There are many of them in Bellandale."

"I wanted to stay in Crystal Point."

"Why?"

He glanced at her belly. "You have to ask?"

She glared at him. "Don't use the twins as a way of getting around this. How long do you intend on staying?"

"As long as I need to."

"You could stay for a lifetime and nothing would change. I will not marry you. Not now and not ever."

"We'll see," he said, with way more confidence than he felt.

The truth was, he was tired of arguing with her about it. She was as stubborn as a mule. Last night he could have stayed with her. He'd wanted to. A part of him had needed to. He'd wanted to spend the night making love to her. And her rejection had stung like a bucket of ice water over his skin.

"What about your job?" she asked. "You can't just pack that in for an indeterminable length of time."

"Sure I can," he said, and flipped a lazy smile and drove toward the beach. "I'm the boss, remember? I can do what I want."

She was clearly fuming. "Solana told me you never take vacations."

"This isn't a vacation," he said, and pulled the car into the parking area.

"No," she said, opening the door. "It's a hunting expedition…and I'm the prey."

Daniel got out of the car, ignoring the niggling pain in his temple. "Such drama. Let's just forget my marriage proposal for the moment, shall we?"

"It's all I can think about," she muttered.

"Well, that's something, at least." He locked the car. "So this beach?"

She crossed her arms and stormed off down the pathway. Daniel had to admit the beach was spectacular. The white sand spanned for several hundred meters until it met the pristine river mouth. No wonder she loved this place so much. It was early winter and a weekday, so there was no one about other than them and a lone dog walker playing chase with his pet. He watched as Mary-Jayne flipped off her sandals and strode across the sand until she reached the water. Daniel looked down at his shoes. They were Italian leather and not designed for the beach. He perched on a rock and took them off, stuffing the socks into the loafers. She'd called him an uptight neat freak on several occasions. Maybe she was right. When he was young he'd been impulsive and adventurous. Now he rarely did anything without considering the consequences. Taking over the helm of Anderson's from his grandfather had changed him. He felt the weight of responsibility press heavily on his shoulders 24/7. The most impulsive thing he'd done recently was go after Mary-Jayne. And even that he did with a tempered spirit. What he really wanted to do was haul her in his arms and kiss her senseless.

By the time he stepped onto the sand she was twenty meters in front of him. He quickened his steps and watched her as she walked, mesmerized by the way her hips swayed. She had a sensuality that affected him in a way that blurred the lines between desire and something else. Something more. He couldn't define it. Couldn't articulate in his mind what it was about Mary-Jayne that caused such an intense reaction in him. It wasn't simply attraction. He'd felt that before and it had always waned quickly. No, this was something he'd never experienced before. Not even with Simone. His wife hadn't driven him crazy. Loving her had been easy. She had never challenged him, insulted him or made him accountable for his beliefs. But Mary-Jayne did at every opportunity. She questioned everything and anything.

She made him think.

Feel...

It was a kind of heady mix of torture and pleasure.

Which was why making love with her had been so intense. They had chemistry and more. A connection that went beyond physical attraction. A mental attraction that defied logic.

Yeah, loving Simone had been easy. But loving Mary-Jayne… There would be nothing easy about that. Which was why he wouldn't. Why he'd keep it clear in his head what he wanted. His sons. A family. But where? It could never be here, he thought as he walked along the sand. Sure, it was a nice town. Peaceful and safe… Exactly the kind of place to raise children. The kind of place a person could call home. But not him. For one, Mary-Jayne would never agree to it. And he had his life in San Francisco.

She was walking at a leisurely pace now and stopped to pick something up, perhaps a shell. Daniel caught up with her and matched her slow strides.

"It's a beautiful spot."

She glanced sideways. "It's the prettiest beach along this part of the coastline."

"You're fortunate to have grown up in a place like this. To have made it your home."

She shrugged and tossed the shell in the shallow water. "What about you?" she asked. "Where's home for you?"

Daniel rubbed the back of his neck to ease the tension creeping up his spine. "San Francisco."

"That's where you live," she said quietly. "Where's home?"

He shrugged loosely. "When my grandfather was alive he and Solana had a place in the Napa Valley, and I used to go there for school vacations. Miles and Bernie moved around a lot, so my brothers and I always welcomed the stability of my grandparents' small vineyard. But when Gramps died things changed. Gran wasn't interested in the business end of things and decided to sell the place. Solana likes the warmer weather and divides her time between Port Douglas and San Francisco."

She stopped walking and faced him, her hair flipping around her face from the breeze. "So...nowhere?"

"I guess so," he replied, and started walking again.

She caught up with him quickly. "I don't want that for my babies. I want them to be settled. I want them to have a place they can always call home."

"So do I," he said, and stopped to look out over the water. "What's that called?" he asked, pointing to a land mass separated from the shore by an expanse of water that fed from the mouth of the river.

"Jays Island," she replied. "Years ago they used to bring sugarcane ferries up the river, so this was quite a busy spot. Now they use trains and trucks to transport the sugar so the river doesn't get dredged anymore. The sand banks built up and the island came about. Birds nest over there and at a really low tide you can wade through the shallows to get over there. When I was young I used to swim over there at high tide and come back when the tide went out." She laughed and the sound flittered across the wind. "Much to my parents' despair. But I loved sitting on that patch of rock," she said, and pointed to a ragged rock outcrop on the island. "I used to sit there for ages and just let the wind hit my face. It was the kind of place where a person could dream big and no one was around to make judgment. Where *I* could sit without worrying about other people's opinion."

"You mean your family?"

She shrugged. "My family are the best."

"But?"

Her green eyes glittered. "But everyone has a role, you know... My brother, my sisters. Noah took over the family business, Evie's the successful artist, Grace is the supersmart financial whiz who once worked on Wall Street."

"And you?"

Her shoulders lifted again. "I'm just the youngest. The one who got away with everything as a kid. I guess I have the role of being the one who hasn't amounted to anything."

Surely she didn't believe that. "A college education and a big bank balance don't equate to a person's value, Mary-Jayne. There's greatness in simply being yourself."

She offered a wry smile. "Is that why you've worked so hard to climb the corporate ladder? Because you believe it's enough to live a simple life?"

"An authentic life," he corrected, doing his best to ignore the growing throb in his head. "But I didn't really have a choice when I was drafted into the company. My dad wasn't interested, and my grandfather had a lot of health issues. I either joined or the company folded. Too many people were invested in Anderson's… I couldn't let it go down without a fight. So I made a few changes to the company's structure, sold off most of the mining interests and concentrated on the part that I enjoyed. Ten years later the resorts are now some of the most successful in the world."

"And if you hadn't joined the family business, what would you have done?"

"I'm not sure. Maybe law."

She laughed. "Oh, yes, I can see you as a lawyer. You do pose a good argument."

He reached out and grabbed her left hand, and then gently rubbed her ring finger with his thumb. "Not good enough, obviously. This is still bare."

She went to pull away but he held on. "You know why I won't."

"Because you hate me."

She shook her head. "I don't hate you, Daniel."

"No?" he queried as he turned her hand over and stroked her palm. "But you don't like me."

"I don't *dislike* you," she said quietly. "The truth is, I'm very confused about how I do feel about you. And it's not something I'm used to. Normally I know exactly how I feel about everything. I have an opinion and I usually express it. But around you..." Her words trailed. "Around you all I seem to do is dig myself into this hole and say things I don't mean. And I'm not like that. It's not a reaction I'm particularly proud of."

"So I wind you up," he said, still holding her, even though the pain in his head gained momentum. "We wind one another up. What's wrong with that? It'll keep things interesting."

"What things? A marriage where we're always fighting, always at each other's throats? That's not something I want our children to witness." She pulled away and crossed her arms tightly around her waist. "Because if you do, that's about as selfish and self-destructive as it gets."

Selfish? Selfish because he wanted to give his sons his name and the legacy that went along with it. She was the one being selfish—thinking only of herself. Like a spoiled brat.

"If you had any consideration for their future, for what they deserve, then you would see that I'm right," he said stiffly. "But right now you're acting like a petulant child, Mary-Jayne. Maybe this isn't what either of us planned. And maybe you're right, maybe we would never have seen one another again after that night if you hadn't gotten pregnant. But you did, and we are and I'll be damned if I'm going to let you dictate the kind of father I'm allowed to be. This might be a shock to you, but you're *not* the center of the universe, and right now the only thing that matters is the welfare of our sons."

She glared at him. "You're calling *me* self-absorbed? When you think you can simply snap your fingers and get what you want?"

Annoyance swept over his skin. He tried to keep his cool. Tried to get her to show some sense. But be damned if she wasn't the most infuriating woman on the planet!

In that moment a flashing light appeared out of the corner of his eye. And another. A dreaded and familiar ache clutched the back of his head. He recognized what was coming.

"We have to get back. I'll take you home."

And he knew, as he turned and walked back up the sand, that he was in for one hell of a headache.

Chapter Nine

Two days later Mary-Jayne got a call from her sister Evie. She'd had a peaceful two days. No Daniel. No marriage proposals. No insults. It gave her time to seethe and think and work.

"I think you should get over here."

She ground her teeth together. She didn't want to see him. She was still mad at him for calling her a petulant child. And she certainly didn't want her sister interfering or trying to play matchmaker. "What for?"

"He's been holed up in his room for forty-eight hours. No food or coffee or anything. I don't want to pry…but I thought you should know."

Mary-Jayne pushed down the concern battering around in her head. "He's a big boy. I'm sure he's fine."

"Well, I'm not so sure. And I have an obligation to my guests to ensure their welfare while they stay here."

"Good… You go and check on him."

"M.J.," Evie said, sterner this time. "Whatever is going on between the two of you, put it aside for a moment. *I* need your help."

Unable to refuse her sister's plea, Mary-Jayne quickly got dressed and headed over to the B and B. Evie looked genuinely concerned when she met her by the side door.

"So what's the big emergency?" she asked as she walked into the house and dropped her tote on the kitchen counter. "Maybe he's gone out."

"He's here," Evie said. "His rental car is outside."

"Maybe he's asleep."

"For two days?" her sister shot back. "Something's not right, and since you're the soon-to-be mother of his babies, it's your responsibility to find out what's wrong."

"I think you're under the illusion that Daniel and I have some kind of real relationship. We don't," Mary-Jayne informed her. "We barely tolerate one another."

Evie placed a key in her palm, touched her shoulders and gave her a little sisterly shove. "Go and find out. He's in the brown room."

There were four guest rooms at the B and B, each one styled in a particular color. Mary-Jayne left the family residence area and headed into the bigger section of the house. She lingered outside the door for a moment and finally tapped. Nothing. She tapped again.

She was about to bail when she heard a faint sound. Like a moan.

Did he have a woman in there?

The very idea made her sick to the stomach. He wouldn't…surely.

She stared at the key in her hand. What if she opened the door and found him doing who knows what with some random woman? She wouldn't be able to bear it.

Suck it up…

She pushed the key in the lock and slowly opened the door. The room was in darkness. The heavy drapes were shut and she couldn't hear a sound. There was someone on the bed, lying facedown.

"Daniel?"

She said his name so softly she wasn't surprised he didn't respond. She closed the door and stepped closer. He was naked from the waist up and had a pillow draped over his head. She said his name again and the pillow moved.

"What?"

His voice was hoarse. Groggy. Nothing like she'd heard before. She squinted to accustom her eyes to the darkness and spotted an empty bottle of aspirin on the bedside table. She took notice of everything, and a thought popped into her head.

"Are you drunk?"

He groaned softly. "Go away."

"You're hungover?"

He rolled slightly and took the pillow with him, facing away from her. "Leave me alone, Mary-Jayne."

She walked around the bed and looked at him. "Daniel, I was only wondering if—"

"I'm not drunk," he said raggedly, clearly exasperated. "I've got a headache. Now go away."

She glanced around the room. Total darkness. He hadn't eaten for two days. Empty painkiller bottle. She got to the edge of the bed and dropped to her haunches.

"Daniel," she said gently, and tried to move the pillow. "Do you have a migraine headache?"

He moaned and his hold on the pillow tightened. "Yes. Get out of here."

She got to her feet and headed into the bathroom, emerging a minute later with a cold, wet washcloth. He hadn't moved. She sat on the edge of the bed.

"Here," she said, and pried the pillow off him. "This will help." She gently rolled him onto his back and placed the cloth across his forehead.

"Stop fussing," he said croakily.

She pressed the cloth around his temples. "Let me help you."

"You can't."

"I can," she said and touched his hair. "My mother gets migraines. I know what I'm doing." She glanced at the empty medicine bottle. "When did you last take a pain-killer?"

He shrugged and then moaned, as though the movement took all his effort. "This morning. Last night. I can't remember."

She stroked his head. "Okay. I'll be back soon. Keep the cloth on your forehead."

Mary-Jayne was back in a matter of minutes. Evie had what she needed, and when she returned to his room she noticed he was still lying on his back and had his hand over his eyes. She fetched a glass of water from the bathroom and sat on the bed again.

"Take these for now," she instructed, and pressed a couple of aspirin into his hand. "And I have some paracetamol you can take in two hours."

"Would you stop—"

"Take the pills, okay?" she said, holding on to her patience. "You'll feel better for it." He grumbled again but finally did as she requested. Mary-Jayne took the glass and placed it on the bedside table. "It's important that you take in plenty of fluids."

"Yes, nurse."

"And drop the attitude for a while."

He didn't respond. Instead he rolled over and buried his face into the pillow. Mary-Jayne got up and pushed the drapes together as close as they would go. She knew many migraine sufferers had sensitivity to light. Countless times she'd watched her mother battle for days on end with the nausea and blinding pain.

She stayed with him for the next few hours. She gave him water and made him take some more medication. When she thought he could handle it, she sat on the bed and gently massaged lavender oil into his temples. There was a strong level of intimacy in what she did, but she couldn't let him suffer.

By late afternoon there was significant improvement in his pain level, and she left for a while to make him a sandwich and peppermint tea.

"How's the patient?" Evie asked when she came into the kitchen.

Mary-Jayne looked up from her task. "A little better. He's hungry, so that's a good sign."

Evie nodded and grinned. "Yeah... You were right— you two don't have a relationship at all. What was I thinking?"

"I'm helping someone who's in pain, that's all."

"That someone is the father of your babies. It's a bond, M.J. A strong bond that will forever keep you and Daniel in each other's life."

"I know it will," she said, heavyhearted. "I just don't know why he keeps insisting that we get married."

Evie raised her brows in dramatic fashion. "He lost a child once... I think it's easy to understand why he doesn't want to lose his sons, too."

"Lose them to what?" she shot back.

"Geography," Evie replied. "An ocean between you is a big incentive. Or the idea you might meet someone else one day and get married."

She wasn't about to admit she'd deliberately avoided considering any of that before.

"Marriage without love could never work."

"Are you sure about that?" Evie queried. "I mean, are you sure there's no love there? Looks to me as if you're behaving exactly like a woman in love would act."

She stilled instantly. Her sister's words rattled around in her head.

No, it wasn't true. She didn't. She couldn't.

"I'm not," she said, defiant.

Evie smiled gently. "I've never known you to be afraid of anything. What is it about loving this man that scares you so much?"

Nothing. Everything. Her sister was way too intuitive.

"He's out of my league."

"Why? Because he has short hair and a job?"

The reference to her ex-boyfriend didn't go unmissed. "We're too different. And he'll want to shuffle me off to San Francisco. I don't want to live there. I want to live here. But he'll do and say whatever he has to in order to get his own way. I know he's handsome and can be charming and ticks all the boxes. But I know him... He's a control freak."

"So are you, in your own way," Evie remarked. "So maybe you're not so different after all."

Was that it? Was it their similarities and not their differences that spooked her? He'd called her a hothead. She'd called him arrogant. Were they both guilty of those traits?

Mary-Jayne ignored the idea for the moment and grabbed the tray. "I have to get back in there."

Evie smiled. "See you a little later."

When she returned to his room the bed was empty. The curtains were still drawn and there was a sliver of light beaming from beneath the closed bathroom door. He came out moments later, naked except for a towel draped around his hips, another towel in his hand that he used to dry his hair.

She pushed down the rush of blood in her veins. But his shoulders were so wide, his chest broad and dusted with a smattering of hair and his stomach as flat as a washboard that the picture was wholly masculine. A deep surge of longing flowed through her.

"You're back."

She swallowed hard and tried to not look at his smooth skin. "I'm back," she said, and placed the tray on the small table by the window. "How are you feeling?"

"Weary," he said, and smiled fractionally as he came toward her. "It takes me a few days to come good after."

Mary-Jayne poured some tea and made a determined effort to stop looking at him as if he was a tasty meal. "Have you always suffered from migraines?" she asked, eyes downcast.

He nodded. "Since I was a kid. They're less frequent now, but when one hits I usually just lock myself in my apartment with some aspirin for a couple of days and try to sleep it off."

"Have you tried stronger medication? Perhaps an injection of—"

"No needles," he said, and moved beside her.

He smelled so good. Like soap and some musky deodorant. She swallowed hard and glanced sideways. The towel hitched around his hips had slipped a little. "I should let you have some privacy and—"

"Shy?" he queried, reading her thoughts effortlessly. "It's nothing you haven't seen before."

Mary-Jayne swallowed hard. He was right. She'd seen every part of him. Touched every part of him. Been with him in the most intimate way possible. And still there was something unknown about him, something inviting and extraordinarily sexy. There was nothing overt about Daniel. He wasn't one of those constantly charming men who flirted and manipulated. He was sexually confident but not obvious. It was one of the reasons why she found him so blindingly attractive. He could have her as putty in his hands if he wanted to, but he didn't try to sway her with sex. For sure, he'd kissed her a couple of times, but even then he'd held back. When they'd been kissing in her kitchen days earlier and she'd told him to go, he hadn't lingered. He hadn't tried to persuade her or coerce. Because he possessed, she realized, bucketloads of integrity.

"You know," she said bluntly as she stirred the tea, "if you kissed me right now you'd probably have me in that bed in less than two seconds."

He chuckled. "I know."

"Except for your migraine, of course."

"I wouldn't let a lousy headache get in the way."

His words made her insides jump. She poured a second mug of tea and sat down. "Shall I open the curtains?" she asked, noticing that the only light in the room was coming from the direction of the open bathroom door. "Or are you still too sensitive?"

"I'm okay now."

She pushed the drapes aside a little. "My mother can't bear light when she has an attack. My dad usually bundles her in the car and takes her to the doctor for a painkiller injection."

He flinched. "Bernie used to try acupuncture rather than meds when I was young to combat the worst of the pain."

"Did it work?"

He shrugged loosely and sat in the chair opposite. "At times. Thank you for the tea and…everything else today."

"No problem. Glad I could help."

He sniffed the air. "I can smell flowers."

She grinned. "It's lavender oil," she explained. "I massaged some of it into your temples. It's something my dad does for my mother."

He rubbed his forehead. "Oh...well, thanks. It helped."

She sipped her tea and pushed the sandwich toward him. "You really should eat something."

He nodded and picked up the bread. "How are *you* feeling? Any nausea today?"

"No," she replied. "I've been okay for the past couple of days." She rubbed her belly and smiled. "And it's a small price to pay for having these two growing inside me."

He regarded her thoughtfully. "You're really happy about being pregnant, aren't you?"

"Ecstatic," she said and smiled. "I mean, it's not what I'd planned...but then again, I don't ever really plan anything. My work, my travels... It's always been a little ad hoc. But now I can feel them, I know I couldn't be happier."

"Except for the fact that I'm their father?" he queried, one brow raised.

Mary-Jayne met his gaze. "I've never wished for it to be any different. I think you'll be a really great dad." She sighed heavily. "And I get it, you know...about why you want to get married. You didn't get a chance, last time, to be a father. That was taken away from you. But I would never do anything to keep you from your sons, Daniel. They're a part of you, just like they're a part of me."

His gray eyes smoldered. "So you think all that, and you still won't marry me."

"No."

He tossed the untouched sandwich back onto the tray. "Okay. I won't ask you again."

It was what she wanted. No more proposals. No more pursuit. But somehow, in the back of her mind, she felt a strange sensation. Like…like disappointment. But she managed a tight smile. "Thank you."

"And custody?"

"We can share it. Of course, I'm going to live here and you'll be in San Francisco…but you can see them whenever you want."

"Don't you think that will confuse them?" he asked quietly. "Me randomly turning up to play daddy."

"At first," she said, and gritted her back teeth. "But it's going to be impossible to share custody when we live in two different countries."

"They could live here for six months and then in San Francisco for six months."

Fear snaked up her spine. "You wouldn't?"

"I wouldn't what?"

Mary-Jayne perched herself on the edge of the chair. "Try to get fifty percent custody. I couldn't bear to be away from them for six months at a time. I know you've got money enough to get the best lawyers, but I really couldn't—"

"You misunderstand, Mary-Jayne," he said, cutting her off. "I meant you and the twins could live in San Francisco for six months. Look, I know you love this town and don't want to be away from it permanently, but perhaps we could meet in the middle, metaphorically speaking. I'll buy you a house near where I live and you could settle there every six months."

"You'll *buy* me a house? Just like that?"

He shrugged. "Sure."

"And fly me and the twins back and forth every six months?"

"Yes."

Meet in the middle? Perhaps that was the only way to settle the tension between them. And as much as she protested, she knew she'd do whatever she had to do if it meant retaining full custody of her babies. "We'll see what happens. Anyhow," she said and got to her feet, "you should rest for a while. You look like you need it."

"Can I see you later?"

"No," she replied. "You need to get some sleep. And I have some work to do. I'm making some pieces for a friend of Solana's and I need to concentrate."

"My grandmother is very fond of you," he said, and got to his feet. The towel slipped a little more and she averted her gaze. It wasn't good for her self-control to keep staring at his bare chest.

"I'm fond of her, too."

"I know," he said, and then added more soberly, "and I apologize if I might have suggested you were not pure in your motives when you got to know her. She told me you turned down her offer to finance your business. I should trust her judgment... She knows people way better than I do."

Heat crawled up her neck. He was paying her a compliment. It shouldn't have embarrassed her, but it did. "I understand you only wanted to protect her. But I genuinely like Solana and would never take advantage of her in any way."

"I know that, Mary-Jayne. But if you need help getting your business off the ground, then I would be more than—"

"No," she said and raised a hand. "My business is mediocre because I'm not all that ambitious... I never have been. I like designing and crafting the pieces, but that's where my interest ends. I started selling them online almost by mistake. My friends Lauren and Cassie persuaded me to start a website showcasing the things I'd made and then all of a sudden I had orders coming in. I do it because

I have to make a living doing something, and why not earn money doing what I enjoy creatively."

He nodded as if he understood. She'd expected him to try to sway her some more, but to his credit he accepted her explanation. "I'll see you soon, then."

"Okay," she said, and shrugged lightly, even though the idea of spending more time with him tied her insides into knots. She liked him. A lot. And that made it increasingly difficult to keep him at arm's length. "I hope you feel better."

It took another two days for Daniel to get back to his normal self. He conference called his brothers to keep up with business and spoke to his grandmother. Solana was keen to know the details of his visit with Mary-Jayne, but he didn't tell her much. He certainly wasn't going to admit she'd turned him down again and again.

On Friday morning he headed to the kitchen and found Evie elbow-deep in some kind of baking.

"Good morning," she greeted, and smiled. "Coffee?"

He nodded and helped himself to a mug and half filled it with coffee. "Cooking for the masses?" he asked as he looked over the large bowls in front of her before he perched himself on a stool by the counter.

"For the fire station," she said cheerfully. "My husband, Scott, is a fireman. He's on night shift at the moment and I usually bake a few dozen cupcakes to keep him and the rest of the crew going."

It was a nice gesture, he thought. A loving gesture. "He's a lucky guy."

She smiled. "I'm the lucky one. He moved here, you know, from California. He'd come here for his sister's wedding to my older brother and we fell in love, but he left a few weeks after he arrived. When I discovered I was pregnant he came back and stayed. He knew I could never leave here… I had a teenage son and my family. So he changed his life for me. It was a very selfless gesture."

Daniel didn't miss the meaning of her words.

But live in Crystal Point permanently? He couldn't. It wasn't the place for him. He had a business to run. He couldn't do that from a tiny town that was barely a spot on the map. Plus, he had a life in San Francisco. Friends. Routine. A past. He'd known Simone there. Loved her there. Grieved her there. To leave would be like abandoning those feelings. And Mary-Jayne had made her thoughts abundantly clear. He was pretty sure she didn't want him anywhere near her precious town. That was why he'd suggested she come to San Francisco for six months of the year. It was a sensible compromise. The only way around the situation.

"I'm glad it worked out for you," he said, and drank some coffee.

One of her eyebrows came up. "Things have a way of doing that, you know."

"Or they don't."

She smiled. "I like to believe that anything is possible… if you want it enough."

It was a nice idea, but he didn't really agree. He'd wanted his wife and daughter to be safe. But fate had other plans. Things happened. Bad things. Good things. Sometimes it was simply a matter of timing.

"She's always been headstrong," Evie said, and smiled again. "Don't let that bravado fool you though. Underneath she's as vulnerable as the next person."

"I know she is. She's also stubborn."

"Perhaps that's because she thinks you shouldn't always get your own way?" Evie suggested.

He laughed a little. "You might be right. But I'm not out to change her. I only want to be a father to my children."

"Maybe that's where you're going wrong," Evie said. "Maybe you need to concentrate on her first and foremost."

"Nice idea," he said ruefully. "Have you met your sister? She's not exactly giving me an opportunity."

"She's scared of you."

Daniel straightened. "Of me? Why? I'd never harm her or—"

"Of course you wouldn't," Evie said quickly. "I mean she's scared of what you represent. You're...normal... You know...not a—"

"Unemployed musician?" he finished for her. "Yeah, we've already had the ex-boyfriend discussion. She's anti-wealth, antisuccess, anti-anything that gives her a reason to keep me out of the little bubble she's wrapped in."

"It's protection, that's all. Her first boyfriend was a deadbeat who stole her money. The one after that was a lazy so-and-so. If she's with you, it's as if she's admitting that she's not who everyone thinks she is. That all the other guys were just a phase...an aberration. That she isn't really a free spirit who does what she wants. It means that she's as vulnerable to a perfectly respectable and nice man as the rest of womankind is."

Daniel laughed. "So you're saying she won't marry me because I'm not a deadbeat?"

"Precisely."

He was still thinking of Evie's words when he was in town later that morning. Bellandale was a big regional town and had sufficient offerings to get what he needed done. By the afternoon he was back in Crystal Point and pulled up outside Mary-Jayne's house around five o'clock. She was in the front garden, crouched down and pulling weeds from an overgrown herb garden. She wore bright pink overalls that showed off her lovely curves and the popped-out belly. He watched her for a moment, marveling at her effortless beauty. His insides were jumping all over the place. No one had ever confounded him as much as Mary-Jayne Preston.

She stood up when she realized there was a car by the curb. She dropped the gloves and small garden fork in her hand and came down the driveway. Her crazily beautiful hair whipped around her face.

Daniel got out of the car and closed the door. "Good afternoon."

"You look better," she said as she approached. "Headache all gone?"

"Yes. How are you feeling?"

"I'm good," she said, and came beside the car. "Nice wheels. It doesn't look like a rental."

Daniel glanced at the white BMW and rattled the keys. "It's not."

Her eyes widened. "You bought a car?"

He nodded. "I did. Do you like it?"

She shrugged. "It's nice, I suppose. Very…highbrow."

A smile tugged at his mouth. "It's a sensible family car."

She looked it over and nodded. "I suppose it is. Since you had the rental, I didn't realize you needed a car."

"I don't," he said and grabbed her hand. "I still have the rental." He opened her fingers and rested the key in her palm. "It's yours."

Her eyes instantly bulged and she stepped back. "Mine?"

He nodded. "That's right."

The moment it registered her expression sharpened. "You bought me a car?"

"I did. I thought you—"

"I have a car," she said stiffly. "And it works just fine."

Daniel glanced at the beat-up, rusted yellow Volkswagen in the driveway. "Your car is old and not roadworthy."

Her hands propped onto her hips. "How do you know that? Have you taken it for a spin around the block?"

"I don't need to," he replied. "Take a look at it."

"I like it." She stepped forward and put the key back in his hand. "And I don't need another."

Daniel let out an exasperated breath. "Does everything have to be a battle between us? So I bought you a car. Sue me."

"I can't be bought."

Annoyance surged through his blood. "I'm not trying to buy you. I bought something *for* you. There's a significant difference."

"Not to me," she shot back. "First it's a car and then what…a house? Maybe one to match the house in San Francisco you want to buy? What then? A boat? What about a racehorse? Don't forget the jewels. I'll probably need a private jet, too."

"You're being ridiculous. It's just a car."

"Stop trying to justify this. Take it back. I don't want it."

He kept a lid on his simmering rage. "I want my sons to be safe, and they won't be in that jalopy," he said, and hooked a thumb in the direction of her old VW. "Be sensible, Mary-Jayne."

"I am sensible. And they'll be perfectly safe," she said hotly. "I would never put them at risk. But I won't let you tell me what to do. Not now, not ever."

He shook his head. "This isn't a multiple-choice exercise, Mary-Jayne. And I won't compromise on this issue. The car is yours." He took a few steps and dropped the key on top of the letterbox. "I want you to have it."

"I don't care what you want!"

Daniel stilled and looked at her. Her cheeks were ablaze,

her hair framing her face, her chest heaving. A thousand conflicting emotions banged around in his head. And he knew there was no reasoning with her. No middle road.

"No," he said wearily. "I guess you don't."

Then he turned around and walked down the street.

Chapter Ten

Bossy. Arrogant. Know-it-all.

Mary-Jayne had a dozen names for him and none of them were flattering.

He'd bought her a car. A car! Without discussing it with her first. Without any kind of consultation. He really did think he could do whatever he liked.

On Saturday afternoon she headed to her parents' place for lunch. The whole family got together once a month for a day of catch-up that included lunch, dinner and plenty of conversation and games with the kids. It was a Preston tradition, and since she'd missed the get-togethers while she'd been away, Mary-Jayne looked forward to spending time with them. Her father was manning the barbecue with her brother, Noah, while her brothers-in-law, Scott and Cameron, played pool in the games room, as Noah's wife, Callie, kept their kids entertained. Evie's toddler and Grace's newborn were the center of attention in the kitchen while her mother fussed around making her famous potato salad. Her best friend Lauren was there, too, with her fiancé and her own parents. Lauren was Cameron's sister and her fiancé, Gabe, was Scott and Callie's cousin. It was a close-knit group. The blood ties alone made it a mammoth exercise to remember who was related to whom. She cared for them all, but as she sat at the kitchen table, one hand draped over her abdomen and the other curled around a glass of diet soda, she experienced an inexplicable empty feeling deep down, almost through to her bones.

She couldn't define it. She should he happy. Elated. She had her babies growing in her belly and her whole family around her. But something was amiss. Something was missing. *Someone was missing.*

She quickly put the idea from her head.

"Where's Daniel today?"

Her mother's cheerful voice interrupted her thoughts. She shrugged. "I have no idea."

Barbara frowned a little. "I thought he might have liked to come and meet everyone."

"I didn't invite him."

The room fell silent, and she looked up to see her mother's frown.

"I did," Evie added quickly. "But he said he wouldn't come unless you asked him to be here."

Shame niggled between her shoulders. "Good. He's finally showing some sense."

Evie sighed. "What's he done now?"

Mary-Jayne couldn't miss the disapproval in her eldest sister's voice. It irritated her down to her teeth. "He bought me a car," she said tartly. "A brand-spanking-new BMW with all the trimmings." She laughed humorlessly. "Imagine me driving around town in that."

The three women stared at her. It was Grace who spoke next.

"That was very thoughtful of him, don't you think? Considering how old and unreliable your current car is."

Mary-Jayne's jaw tightened. "I know it's old. And I know it's unreliable. But it's mine by choice because it's what I can afford. And he wasn't being thoughtful... He was being controlling."

Evie tutted. "Have you considered that perhaps he only wants you and the babies to be safe while you're driving?"

"That's what he said," she replied impatiently. "But I know Daniel and he—"

"Didn't his wife and baby die in a car accident?" Grace again, equally disapproving as Evie and their mother.

"Yes, they did," Evie supplied.

"And wasn't the other car involved an *old and unreliable* vehicle that had a major brake failure?"

"Yes," Evie said, looking directly at Mary-Jayne.

She sat up straight in the chair.

I don't care what you want...

Her careless words banged around in her head. Simone and their baby had died because the car that struck them had a broken brake line. She realized what he must have thought when he saw her old car—that history might repeat itself. That their sons' lives might be at risk.

It wasn't control that had motivated him to buy her a car. It was fear.

She stood up, her hands shaking. "I have to go out for a while." She looked toward Grace. "I'm parked behind you. Can you ask Cameron to move your car?"

Evie pointed to a set of keys on the counter. "Take mine," her sister suggested pointedly. "He's there alone, in case you're wondering, working in the office. My other guests left yesterday."

Mary-Jayne nodded, grabbed the keys and left.

The trip took just minutes, and she pulled the Honda Civic into the driveway. The gardens at Dunn Inn were like something out of a fairy tale, and she walked up the cobbled pathway, past the wishing well and headed up the steps to the porch. A couple of the French-style doors were open, and she slid the insect screen back. Her sister's artwork graced most walls, and the furnishings were well matched and of good quality. Evie had a style all of her own. There was a small office off the living room and when she reached the doorway she came to a halt.

Daniel sat in the chair, earphones on, tapping on the computer keys. She came behind him and touched his shoulder. He flinched and turned, tossing the earphones aside.

"Hi," she said, and dropped her tote.

He wore jeans and a blue shirt that looked as though it had been tailored to fit his gorgeous frame. His gray eyes scanned her face, his expression unreadable.

"I thought you had a family thing to go to?"

"I did," she said. "I do."

"Then, what are you doing here?"

"I left." She shrugged one shoulder. "I wanted to see you."

He swiveled the chair around and sat back. "So you're seeing me. What?"

Mary-Jayne swallowed hard. "You're working. I'm probably interrupting and—"

"What do you want, Mary-Jayne?" he asked impatiently.

She let out a long breath. "To apologize."

He stood up immediately and folded his arms. "Consider it done."

"I was wrong, okay," she said when she noticed his expression was still unmoved. "I shouldn't have reacted the way I did. I shouldn't have *overreacted*. I didn't stop to think about why it was so important to you that I have a new car." She rubbed her belly gently. "But I get it now... I understand that you need to know that our sons are safe because of what happened to your wife and daughter... You know, how the other car was old and had brake failure." Her throat thickened as she said the words. She looked at him and tried to read what he was thinking. But she couldn't. She wished she knew him better. And wished she understood the emotions behind his gray eyes.

The shutters were still up, so she pressed on.

"And I shouldn't have said that I didn't care what you wanted. I didn't mean it," she admitted.

His jaw was achingly tight. "I can't bear the thought of you driving around in that old car."

"I know," she said softly. "And I understand why you feel that way. I should have been more considerate of your feelings. But sometimes, when I'm with you, I react before I think about the consequences. It's not a conscious thing." She waved her hands. "But between you and me there's all this...tension. And getting mad at you is kind of like a release valve for that."

The mood between them suddenly altered. There *was* tension between them. Built on a blinding, blistering physical attraction that had never been truly sated. One night would never be enough for that kind of pull. Daniel had known it all along. She realized that as she stared up at him, breathing hard, chest heaving. That was why he'd pursued her for a month after Solana's birthday party. And that was why she'd refused him. She was scared of those feelings. Terrified of the way he made her feel. Because she still wanted him.

"Daniel..."

She said his name on a wispy breath. His eyes were

dark, burning and filled with desire. It was heady and commanding. It made her shake with longing and fear. Of course she wasn't afraid of him, only the hypnotic power he had over her.

He groaned, as though he knew he was about to do something he probably shouldn't. But Mary-Jayne didn't care. In that moment, with nothing between but barely a foot of space, all she wanted was to be in his arms.

"I'm trying so hard to fight this."

"I know. But it's me you're fighting," he said softly. "Not this."

He was right. She fought him. In her heart she felt she had to. But in that moment all her fight disappeared.

"Make love to me," she whispered and reached out to touch his chest.

He flinched against her touch as though it was poker hot. "Are you sure that's what you want?"

She shrugged lightly. "The only thing I'm sure about is that I'm not sure about anything anymore."

He reached for her shoulders and molded them with his hands. He fisted a handful of her hair and gently tilted her head back. "You drive me crazy, do you know that?"

She nodded a little. "I don't mean to."

"You can trust me, you know," he said and lowered his head toward her face. "I'm not your enemy. Even if it does feel as though most of the time we're at war with each other."

He kissed her then. Not gently. Not softly. But long and deep and fueled with heated possession. Mary-Jayne kissed him back and wrapped her arms around his waist. "Do you have any idea how sexy you are?" he whispered against her lips.

"No," she said, and smiled as she trailed her lips along

his jaw. "We've got the place to ourselves... Let's not waste any time."

He got her to his room in ten seconds flat. He closed the door and locked it.

They stood opposite one another by the bed. Last time there'd been no thinking, nothing but desire and pure instinct. This was different. This was conscious and planned and fueled by more than simple attraction.

"Do you know what I thought the first time I saw you?" he asked quietly.

Mary-Jayne shook her head.

"I thought," he said as he reached for her, "that I had never seen a woman with such beautiful hair in all my life."

He kissed her again, and she shuddered and tossed her head. When he pulled back she was breathing so hard she thought her lungs might explode. He slipped her T-shirt off one shoulder and trailed his mouth along her collarbone. There was such blistering intensity in his touch that it thrilled her to the soles of her feet. He kept kissing her, making her sigh and moan until finally she begged him to take her to the bed.

"What's the hurry?" he muttered against her neck.

Mary-Jayne ran her hands over his chest. His heart beat furiously behind his ribs and her hand hovered there for a moment. Last time they'd made love as if there was no time to waste. But now he seemed in no rush to get her naked and between the sheets. He was taking his time exploring her mouth with his own and gently smoothing his hands across her back and shoulders. They stood kissing like that for minutes. Or was it hours? She couldn't tell. She was too overwhelmed by the narcotic pleasure thrumming through her body at the seductive tone of his skilled touch. By the time they worked their way to the side of the bed she was a wriggling mass of need.

He stripped the T-shirt over her head and Mary-Jayne watched, fascinated as he slowly undressed her. It was intensely erotic and made her long for him with such urgency she could barely breathe. When she was naked, when her shirt was on the floor and her bra dispensed with, he hooked his thumbs under the band of her briefs and slowly skimmed them down over her bottom and legs. Then he was on his knees in front of her, touching her belly, pressing kisses across the curved, tightened skin. She'd never experienced anything more intimate or soul reaching in her entire life. He reached up to cup her breasts, and they felt heavy in his hands. As he gently toyed with her nipples, every part of her body felt more alive, more sensitive to his touch than ever before.

She whispered his name, and he looked up to meet her gaze. He was still fully dressed and she wanted nothing more than to feel his skin against her, to wrap herself in his embrace and feel his body deep within hers. Mary-Jayne curled her fingers around his shirt collar and found the top button. She flicked it open with eager hands.

"Take this off," she instructed with way more bravado than she felt.

He smiled, urged her to sit, and once she was settled on the bed he shrugged out of his shirt. Shoes and socks and jeans followed, and once he was naked he sat beside her.

"Better?" he asked, reaching for her again, kissing her neck and shoulders.

Mary-Jayne sighed heavily. "Much."

He palmed her rounded belly. "Pregnancy has made you even more beautiful, if that were possible."

It was a lovely thought. She'd never considered herself all that beautiful. Not like her sister Grace. Or Evie, with her dancing eyes and seductive curves. She was pretty at best. Not even particularly sexy. But beneath Daniel's glittering gaze she felt more beautiful than she ever had in her life.

She placed a hand on her belly. "Are we going to be able to do this?" she asked, smiling a little. "My middle is expanding at an alarming rate."

Daniel grasped her hand and spanned his own across her stomach. "I'm sure we'll manage just fine, darling."

Darling...

It was the first endearment he'd said to her. And it sounded so lovely coming from his lips that emotion unexpectedly gathered at the back of her eyes. She wanted that and more. Despite every argument and every rational part of her brain telling her it was madness—she wanted to be the woman he called darling every day of his life.

Because...

Because she loved him.

She'd fallen in love with the father of her babies. Wholly and completely. Even knowing that he didn't love her back and that he was all wrong for her and she for him. None of that mattered. Her heart had decided.

"What are you thinking?" he asked.

Mary-Jayne shook her head. "Nothing… Just…kiss me."

He smiled and found her mouth again. His kiss was long and slow and everything she wanted. She kissed him back with every ounce of feeling in her heart. He lowered her onto the bed and began to make love to her with such excruciating sweetness she could barely stop herself from calling out his name. He touched her, stroked her and worshipped her breasts with his mouth and hands until she was quivering in his arms. By the time he moved his hand between her legs to caress her she was so fueled with passion she rose up and over and found release almost immediately. It was wondrously intense, and when she came back to earth and the stars had stopped exploding behind her eyes she saw that he was staring down into her face.

"What's wrong?" she asked tremulously, pushing air into her lungs.

"Not a thing," he replied, and kissed her again. "So I guess we don't have to be too concerned about birth control?"

She grinned and stretched. "The horse has already bolted on that one."

Daniel laughed and rolled over, positioning himself between her legs. She relaxed her thighs and waited, so consumed with love for him in that moment that if he'd asked her for the moon she would had flown into the sky to catch it for him.

When they were together, when she couldn't tell when she began and he ended, Mary-Jayne let out a contented moan. He moved against her with such acute tenderness her heart literally ached. Nothing had ever felt so good. And she'd never been more connected to anyone than she was with him as he hovered above her, taking most of his weight on his strong arms, ensuring she was comfortable and relaxed. Release came to her again, slow and languorous and fulfilling, and when he shuddered above her she held on, gripping him tighter, longer and with more feeling than she ever had before in her life.

When he moved and rolled over onto his back, they were both breathing madly. Mary-Jayne closed her eyes and sighed. When her breathing returned with some normalcy she shifted onto her side and looked at him. His chest rose and fell, and he had his eyes closed. He reached for her hand and linked their fingers.

"You know," he said, and sighed, "we should do it down on the beach."

"Do what?" she asked, and kissed his shoulder. "This?"

"Get married. What else?"

Mary-Jayne stilled. A little voice at the back of her mind chanted that she should grab his idea with both hands and say a resounding *yes*. But she couldn't. He didn't love her. He never would. Sure, the sex was incredible and she had his babies growing inside her, but not even that was enough to sustain a lifetime relationship. He had to know that. Only a fool would believe otherwise. She loved him. But she wasn't about to become strapped to a one-side marriage.

"You said you wouldn't ask again," she reminded him.

He shrugged. "I can't help it. I want what I want."

"I can't."

"Or won't?" he asked.

"Both," she admitted, and rolled onto her back. "Can't we just get to know one another a little, Daniel? I mean, I hardly know anything about you and—"

"Because you've never asked," he said a little more harshly. "Okay—I'm thirty-four and recently had a birthday. My favorite color is yellow and I loathe brussels sprouts. When I was fifteen I chipped my two front teeth and now I have veneers. I was seventeen the first time I had sex and since my wife died I've slept with just over half a dozen women. I like imported beer but rarely drink. I haven't had a meaningful conversation with my dad in years and I still think it sucks that I never knew my real mom." He pulled himself up and draped the sheet across his hips. "Satisfied?"

Mary-Jayne sat up and covered her bare breasts with her arms. "That's not what I meant. I'm talking about time. We need time to get to know one another."

"We don't have it," he said flatly. "You live here. I live in San Francisco. I need an answer, Mary-Jayne."

She pulled herself across the bed and got to her feet. "Then, it's no."

* * *

No. Again.

Was there a bigger sucker than him?

Daniel sprang out of the bed and watched her as she snatched up her clothes. "You're being rash…as usual."

"I'm being honest," she said, and pulled on her underwear. "And sure, I'm impulsive and over the years it has gotten me into trouble every now and then. But in this I'm not being rash. I'm using my head," she said, and looked him over with deliberate emphasis. "And not the part of my anatomy that you are if you think having great sex is enough of a reason to get married."

"They're the reason," he said, and pulled on his jeans as he motioned to her belly. "Our children. The great sex is a bonus."

She tossed a shoe at him. And then another.

The first one hit him in the shoulder and the second sandal he caught midair. There was so much fire and spirit in her, so much passion. Daniel was inexplicably drawn to her like a moth to a flame. He liked that she wasn't a pushover, even though it drove him to distraction. "Stop throwing things at me."

"Well, you stop doing what you're doing and I will."

Daniel dropped the shoe and shrugged, holding out his hands. "What have I done now?"

"You know exactly what," she said on a rush of breath. "You know how I feel, Daniel. I don't want to get married and live somewhere else. I want to live here, in Crystal Point. I want our children to grow up in a home, not a house. And I want my family around me while I raise them."

"While *you* raise them?" he said flatly. "Which is exactly my point. *We* need to raise them, Mary-Jayne, together. And I think today proved that we can. We have a connection that's—"

"We had sex," she corrected. "But it's not enough. The truth is, you confuse me when you kiss me and touch me, and then I can't get any of this straight in my mind. I won't let you use sex as a way of—"

"*You* came here today, remember?" he reminded her, cutting her off. "*You* asked me to make love to *you*, remember? Not the other way around. I've left you alone these past few days…just as you asked."

She stilled. "But…"

Her words trailed and she glared at him, her eyes glittering with a kind of fiery rage. She was brash and argumentative and generally on the attack…but caught out, and she was as meek as a lamb. She was a fascinating contradiction. And he craved her more than he'd ever wanted any woman in his life.

"You came here today looking for me. For this," he said and gestured to the bed. "Because we have an insane attraction for one another that neither of us expected."

She sucked in a long breath. "I came here today because I felt bad for what I said the other day. I felt guilty, okay?"

"So today was about sympathy? Throw a crumb to the lonely widower whose wife and baby died?"

"No," she said quickly. "Of course not. I just thought we could…talk, that's all."

"Talk about what?" he asked. "You and me? There is no you and me, right? Or do you want to know about Simone? Or our daughter? What do you want to know? How long I sat in hospital the night my wife died? Eight hours," he said, feeling the memory of those hours through to the marrow in his bones. "Do you also want to know that I never got to say goodbye to her? I never got a chance to tell her what she meant to me—hell, I never even said it enough when she was alive. And yes, I held my daughter's lifeless body for a few moments before they took her away. Do you want to know if I cried? Once, after the wake when everyone had left and I realized for the rest of my life I'd be living with the fact that my daughter's birthday was the same day she and her mom died."

He stopped speaking and looked at Mary-Jayne. Her eyes brimmed with tears, and he immediately felt bad. He didn't want to upset her. He wanted to do the exact opposite, if she'd only let him.

"I'm so sorry..."

"You can't have it both ways," he said as he retrieved her skirt and T-shirt and passed them to her. "Yes, my wife and baby died. And yes, sometimes I feel alone *and* lonely because of that. Who the hell doesn't feel alone at times? But if you want to be here, then really be here, Mary-Jayne. Stop making excuses."

"I'm not," she said, wiping her eyes before she quickly slipped into her clothes.

"You are," he said, suddenly impatient. "And the next time you turn up on my door and ask me to make love to you, it'll only happen if my ring is on your finger."

"Then it will never happen again."

He shrugged, pretty sure she didn't believe that any more than he did. "You should get back to your party."

She shoved her feet into her shoes. "Would you like to come with me?"

He cocked one brow. "Are you sure that's what you want?"

"What I want is for us to get along for the sake of our children." She planted her hands on her hips and spoke in a quiet voice. "I'm trying to be rational and realistic. I don't want to be trapped in a loveless and empty marriage. And if you're honest with yourself, if you can think of only that and not about custody of the babies or how challenging it's going to be to raise them together when we live on opposite sides of the world, you'd realize that you don't want that, either. Especially after the way you loved your wife."

A loveless and empty marriage? Was that what she truly thought it would be? Were her feelings for him that hollow? He did his best to ignore the way that idea made him feel.

"I want," he said with deliberate emphasis, "my family."

"So do I," she said quietly. "But *my* family is here, Daniel. In Crystal Point. I like living a few streets away from my parents and having my sisters and brother close by. I don't come from a family where we greet one another with a handshake and live in different parts of the world. I like knowing that 'I love you' is the last thing I hear from my mother when I hang up the phone after I speak to her, and I like knowing that my dad would be there for me in a heartbeat if I needed him. And maybe that sounds like a silly TV movie to you, but it's what I want for my children."

For a second he envied her. It didn't sound silly at all. It sounded real and authentic and exactly what he'd hoped he'd have for his own children one day. Being around Mary-Jayne and her family had only amplified that need. He wanted to tell her that. But he held back.

I don't want to be trapped in a loveless and empty marriage.

That was what she imagined they'd have. Not a marriage like her siblings' or her parents'. But something less, something that would never measure up to the standards she witnessed in her life. It would never be enough. They would never be enough.

"We should get going," he said, and grabbed his shirt. "I would like to see your parents again."

She nodded and made her way across the room.

They drove separate cars to her parents' home. Him in his rental. She in her sister's Honda. He knew the BMW still sat outside her house. She hadn't driven it once, he was sure. She was stubborn and infuriating. When they arrived at the Preston house, he got out and met her by her car door, not saying a word about the old VW he spotted in the driveway, even though he hated the idea of her driving something so unreliable and potentially dangerous.

"I'm sorry about before," he said, and took her elbow. "I didn't mean to make you cry."

She sniffed. "Okay…sure."

He rubbed her skin. "I don't enjoy seeing you upset."

She nodded, eyes still glistening. "I know that. I don't mean to upset you, either. I just don't seem to be able to help myself sometimes."

Inside, he was welcomed by her family with the warmth he'd come to expect from them. They were good people, and it made him think about the dig she'd made about handshakes and living on opposite sides of the world. She was right. He was close to his brothers but not in the way she was with her siblings. And his relationship with Miles and Bernadette had been taxing most of his life.

He was by the pool talking to her brother and enduring a moderate kind of grilling about his intentions when his phone rang. He excused himself and picked up the call on the fifth ring.

It was Caleb.

Daniel listened to his brother's concerned voice, and once he ended the call went looking for Mary-Jayne. She was inside, in the kitchen with her mother and sister-in-law.

"I need to talk to you," he said, and ignored the thunder behind his ribs.

She must have picked up on his mood, because she

complied immediately and ushered him into the front living room.

"What is it?" she asked once they were alone.

"I have to leave."

"Oh, okay. I'll see you Monday, then. Remember I have an appointment with my OB at ten."

"I'm leaving Crystal Point," he said again, firmer. "Caleb just called me—Bernie's in the hospital in Cairns. She had a massive heart attack a couple of hours ago."

Mary-Jayne gasped and gripped his arm. "Oh, how awful. Is there anything I can do?"

Marry me and stay by my side...

He reached out and touched her belly, felt the movement of his babies beneath his palm and experienced such an acute sensation in his chest he could barely breathe. The connection was mesmerizing. Her green eyes glittered brilliantly, and he got so caught up in her gaze he was rooted to the spot.

"I could... I could..." Her voice trailed off.

"What?" he asked.

She shrugged a little. "I'm not sure... I just thought perhaps I could..."

She could what? Come with him? A part of him wanted that more than anything. But that couldn't be what she meant. She'd have to care one way or another. Daniel swallowed hard. "Take care of yourself, Mary-Jayne."

"You, too," she whispered. "Give your dad and Bernie my love."

But not you...

He got the message loud and clear.

"I'll talk to you soon."

"Please let me know how she is."

Daniel nodded, suddenly numb all over. "Sure." He

shrugged off her touch and walked to the door, but something stopped him. Then he turned and looked at her.

"What?" she asked softly.

"I've just realized that you're a fraud, Mary-Jayne," he said. "You walk and talk like some restless free spirit who can take on the world, but underneath all that talk is someone who's afraid to truly be who she is."

She frowned. "That doesn't make sense."

"Doesn't it? You've wrapped yourself up in this image of being a certain kind of person and it's as though you've locked yourself in a cage. Admit it, if I was some unemployed, tattooed and unsuccessful guitarist things would be very different. You'd have nothing to hide behind. You say you don't want to be trapped in a loveless marriage—but that's not it. You just don't want to marry *me*. Because if you did it would mean that everything you've ever stood for is a great big lie. It would mean that you've settled for the safe road, and then everyone around you would know that your boldness and bluster is just an act and that you're as mainstream and sensible as the rest of us. And that's what scares you—being like everyone else. That's why your last boyfriend was a deadbeat and why your business fails to get off the ground. You think that makes you a free spirit? You're wrong… All that makes you is a coward."

Then he turned on his heel and left.

Chapter Eleven

"Are you still feeling unwell?" Evie's voice cut through her thoughts.

Mary-Jayne battened down the nausea she'd been battling for a week. She'd spent the morning babysitting her niece while Evie and Scott attended an art show in Bellandale. She loved looking after Rebecca and considered it good practice for when her babies arrived.

"On and off. The crackers help a little, but yesterday I spent an hour bent over the toilet bowl. I saw my doctor the other day and we discussed some medication I can take to alleviate the nausea if it gets much worse. I just don't want to do anything that might harm my babies. But after yesterday I think I'm going to have to take his advice. I've got another doctor's appointment tomorrow at three."

Evie grimaced. "That's not much fun. Other than that, is everything going okay?"

"With the pregnancy? Yes, no problems. Except I'm getting as big as a house."

"You look lovely as always," Evie assured her. "Heard from Daniel?"

"Nope."

Evie's brows furrowed. "Everything okay on that front?"

"Nope," she said and sighed. "We sort of had a fight before he left."

"Just a fight? Anything else?"

Her sister was way too intuitive. Mary-Jayne shrugged. She wasn't about to admit he'd called her a coward, or that it was exactly how she felt. "Sex isn't enough to sustain a marriage…no matter how good it is."

Evie came around the kitchen counter and rested her hands on the back of a dining chair. "Why didn't you go with him?"

She shrugged, hurting all over. "He didn't ask me."

"Maybe he thought you'd say no."

She shrugged again, still hurting, and more confused than ever. She wasn't about to admit to her sister that she missed him like crazy. "I'm not part of his life in that way."

"But you're lovers?"

Heat crept over her skin. She could never lie to Evie. "I guess. Does one night and one afternoon together make us lovers? I'm not sure what that makes us. All it makes me is confused."

"But you're in love with him, right?"

"It doesn't matter what I am," she insisted. "I can love him until the cows come home and it won't change the fact that he doesn't love me back."

"Are you sure?"

"Positive," she replied, aching deep down. She pressed her hands to her belly and rubbed her babies as they moved inside her. "He's all one-eyed about what he thinks we should do. Which is get married and raise our children in San Francisco."

"He said that?" she asked. "He said he wants you to move there?"

She nodded. "Well, he offered to buy me a house so I can live there for six months of the year."

Evie tilted her head. "I thought he might have decided he liked it here."

Mary-Jayne's eyes popped wide. "Daniel live here? In Crystal Point?" She laughed shrilly. "Not likely. Too hometown for him. He's all business and logic. He'd be bored out of his mind in a place like this."

Her sister smiled. "Really? He looked pretty comfortable here to me. And since when did you get all stuck on Crystal Point as a be-all and end-all? You spent a good part of the past ten years away from here, traveling from one place to the next." Her brows came back up. "I can remember a certain nineteen-year-old telling me in no uncertain terms that it was the most boring, uneventful spot on the map before you hopped on a plane for Morocco. I think the folks thought you'd closed your eyes and pointed to a spot on an atlas and thought, 'Why not go there?' And then there was Thailand, and Cambodia, and after that it was Mexico. And wasn't it you who spent three months backpacking through Greece and working transient jobs and peddling your jewelry to patrons in sidewalk cafés to make ends meet? And didn't you recently leave here to bail out your old school friend in Port Douglas with only a day's notice?" Evie smiled. "What's happened, M.J.? Have you lost your restless spirit? Have you realized that this little town is not such a bad place after all?"

"I never thought it was bad. I love this town. I've just

always loved traveling and experiencing new places, that's all."

"New places except San Francisco?"

Mary-Jayne stilled. Evie had a point. "You think I should do it? You think I should marry him and move to another country?"

"I think you should do whatever your heart tells you is right."

"That's what I'm doing," she insisted.

"Your heart," Evie said pointedly. "Not your head."

But my heart will get pummeled, for sure...

"I can't." She stood and grabbed her bag. "I have to get going."

Her sister nodded. "Okay. Thank you for babysitting. Rebecca loves spending time with you."

Mary-Jayne smiled broadly. "It's mutual."

Evie reached out and hugged her tight. "By the way, I see you're driving the Beamer."

Mary-Jayne wondered how long it would take for her sister to remark about the car parked along the front curb. She shrugged. "Seemed silly to let it sit there, that's all."

"Smart move. Is it good to drive?"

"Like a dream," she admitted, and grinned. "And two baby seats arrived for it yesterday."

Evie's smiled widened. "He thought of everything, didn't he?"

"Pretty much," she replied, ignoring the jab of pain in her chest. "Anyway, I have to run."

"Let me know how things go at the doctor's."

"Will do," she said as she left.

By the time she got home it was after four. She fed the dog and parrot and took a shower and then changed into baggy sweats and flaked out on the sofa. She flicked channels on the television and stared absently at the screen for an hour. Later, she ate a grilled-cheese sandwich and attempted to do some work on a new bracelet for one of Solana's friends. But she couldn't concentrate. Her mind was filled with thoughts of Daniel and his parting words.

Four days after Daniel left, Mary-Jayne got a text from Audrey informing her that Bernie was finally off the critical list but still in intensive care. There was no word from Daniel. It had been a long, lonely week. Part of her was glad. Part of her never wanted to see him again. Another part missed him so much she ached inside.

Coward...

The word had resonated in her head for days. No one had ever called her that before. No one would ever dare. But not Daniel. He called it how it was. He made her accountable for her convictions. For the first time in her life Mary-Jayne felt as though she had met her match. Her *perfect* match.

If only he loved her...

But he didn't. He thought that physical attraction was enough to sustain a marriage. But in her heart she knew it wasn't. He was kidding himself. Sure, maybe for the first few years everything would be okay. They'd be busy raising their children and there wouldn't be time to think about how loveless their marriage was. But later, once the children were older and there was only them, their differences would be evident and insurmountable. It was an impossible situation. And she wouldn't do it. She couldn't. She owed her babies more than a life where their parents were together for the wrong reasons.

As much as she appreciated her sister's support, Evie didn't really understand. She'd fallen madly in love with Scott and he'd loved her in return. He'd wooed her and fought for her and laid his heart on the line as if nothing else mattered. But Daniel... There was no heart in his proposal. Only logic and his desire to share custody of their sons.

And that would never be enough.

Five days after arriving back in Port Douglas, Daniel and his brothers were still maintaining a rotating vigil outside Bernie's hospital room. Their father hadn't left his wife's side, and at seven o'clock on Thursday evening, Daniel headed for the small hospital cafeteria and returned with two double-shot espressos. Bernie had finally been taken off the critical list, and Blake and Caleb had gone back to the resort to get some much-needed rest while Daniel stayed with his father, ensuring Miles at least ate and drank something.

"Here," he said, and passed his father a take-out cup as he sat in one of the uncomfortable chairs outside the intensive care ward. "And don't let it get cold like the last one I gave you."

Miles managed a grin and then nodded. "Thanks."

His father's pain was palpable. "She's out of danger, Dad. That's good news."

"I know," Miles said, and sighed. "I don't think I could have taken another night of wondering if she was going to make it."

"You heard what the doctor said a few hours ago," he assured his father. "She's going to pull through and be back to her old self in no time."

His dad sighed again. "Who would have thought this might happen? I mean, she's always been so health conscious… I never would have guessed she had a weak heart."

"No one can predict the future, Dad."

His words felt hollow as they left his mouth. How often had he thought that? When his grandfather passed away?

When Simone and their baby died? When Mary-Jayne told him she was pregnant?

"Yeah, I know," his dad said, and tapped him on the shoulder. "Thanks for being here this week. It's meant a lot to me."

"I wouldn't be anywhere else."

Miles shrugged a little. "I know you've got a lot going on."

Daniel drank some coffee and stared at the wall ahead.

"You should go back," Miles said quietly. "You need to sort it out."

"Actually, I think a little time apart might be what we both need."

He wasn't about to admit that he missed Mary-Jayne more than he'd believed possible. But he hadn't called her, even though he craved the sound of her voice. And he was right about thinking they needed some time out.

"Nonsense," his dad said gently. "Time apart serves no purpose. Because one day you might find you have no time left, right?"

Daniel looked at his father. Miles had one of his serious expressions on his face, and as much as Daniel wanted to fob the other man off, he resisted. He'd seen that look once before, right after his grandfather had died and Daniel was preparing to step into the role of CEO. Miles had tried to talk him out of it. At the time, Daniel was convinced his father lacked vision and ambition and simply wanted to sell the company. And it had taken years for that idea to fade. It wasn't until the wake after Simone's death that he'd realized that there was more to life than business. More to life than seventy-hour weeks and meetings and racing to catch flights from one corner of the globe to the other. But still, he hadn't changed. He'd kept on doing the same things. He'd drowned himself in work to avoid thinking about all he'd lost.

"How about we concentrate on Bernie getting better and—"

"I'm very proud of you, you know," Miles said, uncharacteristically cutting him off. "I'm very proud of the man you have become."

Daniel's throat thickened. "Dad, I—"

"And I know I never say it enough." His father shrugged. "I guess I'm not sure if that matters to you."

"It matters," he said quietly. "The talking thing… It goes both ways."

Miles smiled. "Your mom was always telling me I needed to talk more to my own father. When you were born I promised myself I'd be a better father than Mike Anderson…but I'm not sure I have been. When your mom died I fell apart. Thankfully Bernie came along and picked up the pieces, even though she had every reason to run a mile. I was a grieving man with a baby, and I had so much emotional baggage it's a wonder she was able to see through all that and still give me a shot."

"She loved you," Daniel said, and drank some coffee.

"Not at first, she didn't," Miles said. "Some days I think she might have hated me. But we worked it out." His father nodded and grinned a little. "And you will, too."

Daniel didn't share his dad's optimism. Mary-Jayne opposed him at every opportunity. And he couldn't see a way out of it. He wanted her, sure. And sometimes…sometimes it felt as though he needed her like he needed air in his lungs. But it wasn't anything more than that. How could it be? They hardly knew one another. She was dreaming about some silly romantic notion that simply didn't exist. So maybe he did think about her 24/7. And maybe he did long for her in ways he'd never longed for anyone before.

But that was just desire and attraction. Add in the fact that he wanted the chance to be a full-time father to his sons…and of course it might seem like something else. Something more.

"I loved your mom," Miles said quietly. "But I love Bernie, too. It's not more, it's not less… It's simply a different kind of same."

A different kind of same…

He was still thinking about his father's words for hours afterward. And still when he tried to sleep later that night. His dreams were plagued by images of Mary-Jayne. He dreamed of holding her, of making love to her, of waking up with her hair fanned out on the pillow beside him. He awoke restless and missing her more than he'd imagined he could. And in the cold light of morning he realized one irrefutable fact.

He was in love with her.

And their relationship had just become a whole lot more complicated.

On Monday, with the nausea and lack of appetite still lingering, she went back to her doctor to discuss some medication and get her blood pressure checked. She was waiting for the doctor to come into the room when Julie, an old school friend and now the receptionist from the front desk, popped her head around the door.

"M.J.," she said and made a face. "There's someone out here who wants to see you. Who *insists* on seeing you."

She perched herself on the edge of the chair. "Who?"

Julie's eyes widened dramatically. "He says he's your fiancé."

The blood left her face. There could only be one possibility. "Oh…okay," she said, trying not to have a reaction that Julie would see through and then question. "Tall, dark hair, handsome, gray eyes?"

Julie nodded. "Oh, yeah, that's him."

She managed a smile. "You should probably send him through."

"Okay, sure."

She disappeared, and barely seconds later the door opened and Daniel strode into the room. Mary-Jayne looked him over. He seemed so familiar and yet like such a stranger. He wore dark chinos and a creaseless pale blue shirt. Her heart skipped a beat. She'd never found any man as attractive as him. And doubted she ever would. And deep down, in that place she'd come to harbor all her feelings for him, she was happy to see him. More than happy. Right then, in that moment, she didn't feel alone.

She took a breath and met his gaze. "Fiancé?"

He shrugged loosely. "Got me in the room, didn't it?"

She didn't flinch. "What are you doing here? How did you—"

"Your sister told me I'd find you here."

She nodded. "So you're back?"

"I'm back." He moved across the room and sat beside her.

"How's your mother?"

He rested back in the seat a little. "Out of intensive care. She had major bypass surgery for two blocked arteries. She's doing okay now. She'll be in the hospital for another week, though. So why are you here? Checkup?"

Mary-Jayne tried to ignore how her insides fluttered from being so close to him. "I haven't been feeling well and—"

"You're sick?" he asked and jackknifed up straight. "What's wrong? Is it the babies?" he asked and reached out to touch her abdomen.

She flinched a little from his touch, and he noticed immediately because he snatched his hand away. "Just nausea again. And I've lost my appetite."

He frowned. "Why didn't you call me? I would have come back sooner."

She pressed her shoulders back. "You needed to be with your family. It was important for your parents."

"I need to be here for you," he said with emphasis. "That's important, too."

"I'm fine," she insisted, feeling like a fool for thinking his concern must mean he cared. Well, of course he cared. She was carrying his babies. But caring wasn't love. And love was all she'd accept.

He inspected her face with his smoky gaze. "You look pale."

"Stop fussing," she said and frowned. "I'm fine, like I said. Just tired and not all that hungry because of the nausea. But I'm sure it will pass soon."

The doctor entered then, and she was glad for the reprieve. Until Daniel started barking out questions about her fatigue, her blood pressure and the likelihood of risks associated with the antinausea medication the doctor suggested she take if the symptoms didn't abate soon. She gave Daniel a death stare—which he ignored completely.

The doctor, a mild-mannered man in his fifties, just nodded and answered the questions in a patient voice. When he said he was going to draw some blood, Daniel almost rocketed out of his seat.

"Why? What's wrong?" he asked. "If you think there's a risk to her health then I insist we—"

"It's okay," she assured him and grasped his arm. "It's just a blood test. Remember how I told you that my sisters had gestational diabetes? It's only precautionary."

She thought he might pass out when the nurse came

in and took the blood. To his credit he sat in the chair and watched the entire thing, unflinching. When it was over and the doctor passed her a note with some more vitamins he wanted her to take, Daniel got to his feet and wobbled a little. She grabbed his hand and held on. Once they were in the corridor she slowed down and looked up at him, smiling.

"My hero."

He frowned. "It's not funny."

"Sure it is. Big, strong fella like you afraid of a little old needle... Who would have thought it possible?"

"I'm not afraid of them," he said, and grasped her fingers, entwining them with his own until their palms were flat against each other. "I simply don't like them. And just because you aren't afraid of anything, Mary-Jayne, doesn't mean you should make fun of people who are."

She grinned, despite the fact she was shaking inside. Holding his hand, making jokes and simply *being* with him shouldn't have made her so happy. But it did. Even though in her heart she knew it wasn't real. When they were outside he looked around.

"Where's your car?"

She took a second and then pointed to the BMW parked a few spots from the entrance. "Over there."

He glanced at the car and then to her. "Good to see you're coming to your senses."

She shrugged. "I hate waste, that's all. The car seats arrived, too... That was very thoughtful of you."

He gave her a wry smile. "Oh, you know me, an arrogant, entitled jerk and all that."

Mary-Jayne blew out a flustered breath. "Okay...so you're not all bad."

"Not all bad?" he echoed. "That's quite a compliment."

"All right, I'm an ungrateful coward who has been determined to see the worst in you from the moment we met. Satisfied?"

He smiled. "I shouldn't have called you that. I was frustrated and annoyed and worried about my mom and took it out on you. I missed you, by the way, in case you were wondering."

She nodded as emotion tightened her throat. "I might have missed you a little, too."

"I should have taken you with me."

She ached to tell him that was what she'd hoped for. But she didn't say it. "Well, I'm glad she's going to get well."

"Me, too," he said, and grinned. "So, truce?"

She smiled back at him. "I guess. Where are you staying this time? The B and B?"

He shrugged. "I'm not sure. I didn't get the chance to talk to your sister about it. Once she told me where you were I bailed and headed here."

"Would you like to stay for dinner tonight?" she asked.

He nodded. "I would. But I'll cook."

She gave him a colorful glare. "Are you suggesting that my cooking is below par?"

"I'm saying your cooking is woeful." He grabbed her hand and squeezed her fingers gently. "I'll stop at the supermarket and get what we need, and then I'll see you at home."

Home...

It sounded so nice the way he said it. The fluttering she'd had in her belly since he'd first walked into the doctor's office increased tenfold. "Okay, see you a little later."

And then he kissed her. Softly, sweetly. Like a man kissed a woman he cared about. Mary-Jayne's leaping heart almost came through her chest. And if she'd had any doubts that she'd fallen in love with him, they quickly disappeared.

* * *

Daniel pulled up outside Mary-Jayne's house a little over an hour later. He'd been all wound up in knots earlier in the morning at the thought of seeing her again, but the moment he'd opened the door and spotted her in the chair in her doctor's office, hands clasped together and her beautiful hair framing her face, all the anxiety had disappeared. She hadn't looked unhappy to see him. She'd looked…relieved. As if she welcomed him there. As if she wanted him there. Which was more than he deserved after the insensitive words he'd left her with, right before he'd returned to Port Douglas to be with his family.

He'd had a lot of time to think about their relationship in the past week. Sitting in the hospital waiting room with his father had been incredibly humbling and at times fraught with emotion. Memories of his own wife had bombarded him. Of the night they'd brought Simone into emergency and he'd arrived too late. She was already unconscious. Already too far gone for the doctors to try to save her. And then he'd waited while they'd delivered their baby and hoped that a miracle would happen and their daughter would survive. But she hadn't, and he'd lost them both.

And while he'd waited at the hospital after Bernie's surgery he'd really talked to his dad for the first time since forever. About Bernie, about his own mother, about Simone and their baby. And about Mary-Jayne. Miles had been strong, more resilient than he'd imagined. He'd wanted to comfort his dad, and in the end it happened the other way around. He was ashamed to remember how he'd always considered his father as weak. As a kind man, but one driven by his emotions. Daniel had mistaken Miles's lack of ambition as a failing. But he was wrong. His father's ambitions were simply different from his own. And yet, in some ways, very much the same. Because Miles had endeavored to be a worthy, caring dad to his sons, and Daniel was determined to emulate that ambition. He wanted to be around his sons and watch them grow into children and then teens and finally into adulthood. He wanted to share their lives and be the best man he could be for them. And for Mary-Jayne, too. He cared about her too much to simply let her be only the mother of his sons. He wanted more. He *needed* more.

And since he'd screwed up big time in the courtship department, he had to go back to square one and start all over again. Like he should have done in the beginning, on that first time they'd met. Instead of making that stupid, off-the-cuff comment about how they'd end up in his condo at some point, he should have asked her out. He should have wooed her and courted her like she deserved. He should have gone to see her while she was in South Dakota at her friend's wedding and pursued her properly, and not asked her to meet him on his turf as though all he was interested in was getting her into bed. No wonder she'd turned him down flat. And since then they'd been at war—arguing and insulting one another. She'd called him arrogant and she was right. He'd come out fighting on every occasion and hadn't let her really get to know him at all.

She wants romance and all the trimmings…

Well, he could do that if it meant she would eventually agree to marry him.

He walked up the path and saw that her old car had a for-sale sign propped inside the back window. It pleased him, and by the time he reached her door he was grinning like a fool.

"Oh, hi," she said, breathless and beautiful in a white floaty dress that came to her knees and buttoned down the front. Her belly had popped out more and she looked so beautiful he couldn't do anything other than stare at her. "Come inside."

He crossed the threshold and walked down the hall. Her little dog came yapping around his ankles, and he made a point of patting the animal for a moment before he entered the kitchen.

"So what are you making?" she asked when he put the bags on the counter.

He started unpacking the bags. "Vegetarian tagine… Spiced carrots…amongst other things."

Her green eyes widened. "Moroccan?" She laughed and the sound rushed over his skin and through his blood. "My favorite."

"Want to help?"

She nodded and tossed an apron at him. "Only if you wear this."

He opened up the garment and read the words *Kiss The Cook*. "Really?"

She shrugged. "You never know your luck."

He popped it over his head. "I already feel lucky."

She came around the counter and methodically tied it around the back. "You mean because of your mother? You must be so relieved that she's out of danger."

"We all are," he said, thinking how he was imagining he'd get to kiss her again and that was why he felt lucky. "My dad couldn't bear to lose her."

"I can imagine," she said, and pulled a couple of cutting boards from a drawer. "I mean, he already lost your mother, so to lose Bernie, too… I mean, I know your mother was the love of his life because Solana told me… but he loves Bernie dearly, you can tell by the way he looks at her."

Daniel stopped what he was doing and stared at her. Her green eyes shimmered so brilliantly it was impossible to look anywhere else. The awareness between them amplified tenfold, and he fought the urge to reach for her and take her in his arms. Instead he met her gaze and spoke. "Just because he loved my mom didn't mean he had less of himself to give to someone else."

She inhaled sharply. "I...I suppose so... I mean, if he was willing to open his heart."

"He was," Daniel said quietly. "He did."

The meaning was not lost on either of them. "And they've had a good marriage, Mary-Jayne. They got married quickly and didn't really know one another very well. But it worked. It *can* work."

She started to nod and then stopped. "But they love one another."

"They do now. They got married, had children, made a life together. So perhaps it did start out a little unorthodox...but in the end it's how it plays out that's important."

She didn't look completely convinced and as much as he wanted to keep pushing, he backed off and returned his attention to the grocery bags on the counter. They chatted about mundane things, like her new car and the weather. She asked after his grandmother and was clearly delighted when he told her Solana wanted to come to Crystal Point for a visit.

"She'd like it here," he said when the food was cooking. He stood by the stove, stirring the pot. "Once Bernie is assured of a full recovery, I'm sure my grandmother will come."

"I'd like that," she said as she grabbed plates and cutlery and took them to the table. "Um...how long are you staying for this time?"

He kept stirring. "I'm not sure. I have to get back to

work at some point. I need to go to Phuket for the reopening once the renovation is complete in a couple of weeks."

She nodded, eyed the salad he'd made and sniffed the air appreciatively. "That smells good. You really do know how to cook."

He grinned. "Told you," he said, and then more seriously, "There's a lot you don't know about me, Mary-Jayne. But I'd like to change that. You said we should take some time and you were right. But I don't want to pressure you. So if you want slow, then we'll go slow."

She stopped what she was doing and looked at him. "Honestly, I don't know what I want."

"How about you take some time to figure it out?"

"You said we didn't have time."

He shrugged loosely. "I was mad at you when I said that. We have time."

She nodded a little and took a couple of sodas out of the fridge. "I don't have any of that imported beer you like," she said, and placed the cans on the counter. "But I can get some."

"This is fine," he said, and cranked both lids. "I don't drink much."

They ate a leisurely dinner and she entertained him with stories of her youth, and when she was laughing hard and out of breath he did the same. It was interesting to learn they had both been rebellious as children and teenagers.

"I guess you had to rein in all that when you took over the company from your grandfather? Can't have a respectable CEO wreaking havoc, right?" she asked and laughed.

Daniel grinned. "I guess not. Although I wasn't quite the wayward teen that you were. No tattoos...so I was nowhere near as hardcore as you."

She laughed again. "That's only because you're scared of needles."

"No need to rub it in. I'm well aware of my weakness."

She rested her elbows on the table and sighed. "You don't have a weak bone in your body."

He met her gaze. "I have a weakness for you."

"That's not weakness," she said. "That's desire. Attraction. Lust."

Daniel pushed his plate aside. "Maybe it's more than that."

"More?"

He reached across the table and grasped her hand. "I care about you."

"Because I'm having your babies," she said, and went to move her hand.

Daniel's grip tightened. "That's only part of it."

She looked at him, her eyes suddenly all suspicious as she pulled her hand free. "What are you saying?"

He met her gaze. "Can't you guess?"

"I don't understand. Are you saying that you're... That you have feelings for me...?"

"Yes," he replied. "That's precisely what I'm saying."

Her gaze widened. "Are you saying that...that you're in love with me?"

Daniel nodded. That was exactly what he was saying. He *did* love her. The empty feeling he had inside when he was away from her was love. That was why he couldn't wait to return to Crystal Point. He wanted her. He craved her and ached thinking about it. She was the mother of his babies. And she was vivacious and fun and as sexy as anything.

He'd loved Simone. It had made sense. Loving Mary-Jayne made no sense at all. And yet, in the past few days it had become a clear and undeniable truth.

"Would it be so hard to believe?"

"Yes. Impossible," she said with a scowl and pushed the chair back. "I think you should leave."

Daniel got to his feet the same time she did. "Why are you angry?"

She glared at him. "Because you're lying to me. Because you'll say and do anything to get what you want and all of a sudden you seem to think that making some big statement about love will make me change my mind about getting married."

"I haven't mentioned marriage," he reminded her.

"It's on the agenda, though, right?"

"Eventually," he replied. "That's generally the result of a relationship between two people who fall in love."

"But *two* people haven't fallen in love."

Right. So she didn't love him. Didn't care. That was plain enough. His heart sank. Maybe she would… someday? If he tried hard enough to earn that love.

"We could try to make this work."

"Like your parents did?" she asked. "Maybe it worked for them because they actually liked one another to start with. I'll bet they didn't call one another names and look for the worst in each other."

Daniel expelled an impatient breath. "I apologized for what I said the last time I was here."

"You mean when you called me a fraud who had locked herself in a cage?" she enquired, brows up, temper on alert. "Don't be… You were right. I have been in a cage, Daniel. But as of this moment I'm out of it. And do you know what…I'm not going to trade one cage for another. Because being married to you would put me right back inside."

"I don't want to keep you caged, Mary-Jayne. I love your spirit and your—"

"Can you hear yourself? Three weeks ago you were calling me a flake and a gold digger and now you've miraculously fallen in love with me. I'm not stupid. I know when I'm being played. So you can come here with your sexy smile and make dinner and act all interested in my childhood and this town, but it doesn't change one undeniable fact—you want me to marry you because it suits you and your arrogant assumption that you can simply take whatever you want. Well, you can't take me."

He took a step toward her, but she moved backward. "What do I have to say to convince you that I'm serious about my feelings for you?"

"Say?" she echoed. "Nothing. Words are empty. It's actions that matter."

He waved an arm. "I'm here, aren't I? I came back. I feel as if I've been pursuing you for months."

"You first chased me because you wanted to get me into bed," she said hotly. "And now you're chasing me because you want your sons."

"I'm chasing you because I love you."

There… It was out on the table…for her and her alone.

She laughed, but it sounded hollow. "You're chasing me because you think it's a means to an end. Well, forget it. What I want for my life I can't get from you."

Pain ripped through his chest. "How do you know that? Just tell me what you want."

"I've told you in half a dozen ways. I want a man who carries me here," she said and put her hand against her breast. "In his heart. Over his heart. On his heart. Forever. And it might sound sentimental and foolish to you, but I don't care. I think I really know that for the first time in my life. And I have you to thank for it. You've shown me what I want…and what I don't."

"And what you don't want…that's me?" he asked, aching through to his bones.

"Yes," she said quietly. "Exactly."

He moved closer and grasped her shoulders, gripping her firmly. And then he kissed her. Long and hot and loaded with pain and guilt and resentment. When he was done he lifted his head and stared down into her face. She was breathing hard and her eyes were filled with confusion and rage.

He ran a possessive hand down her shoulder and breast and then down to her belly. "Nothing will change the fact that a part of me is growing inside you. Love me or hate me, we're bound together. And we always will be."

Chapter Twelve

The following Saturday, it was her niece's second birth-day and Mary-Jayne didn't have the strength of mind to go, or to excuse herself. She'd exiled herself in her little house for five days, working on new pieces, revamping her website, thinking of her work, her babies and little else. She didn't spare a thought for Daniel. Not one. Not a single, solitary thought.

Big, fat liar...

He was in her dreams. She couldn't keep him out.

He'd said he loved her. It should have made her day. It should have...but didn't. It only made her angry. And achingly sad.

He hadn't contacted her. She knew from Evie that he wasn't staying at the B and B, and could only assume that he was at a hotel somewhere in Bellandale. It suited her just fine. She didn't want to see him. Not yet. She was still reeling from his declaration of love. Still hating him for it. And still loving him more than she had imagined she could ever love anyone.

Jerk...

Plus, her belly was getting bigger every day and now she waddled rather than walked. She went shopping for baby clothes with her sisters and cried all the way home because she felt as though part of her was missing. She considered buying furniture for the nursery and then put the idea on hold. The spare room needed significant work. In fact, she wondered how she was supposed to raise two babies in such a small house. Once she put two cribs, a change table and a cupboard in the spare room there wouldn't be much space for anything else. What she needed was a bigger house. With a large yard. With a swing set that the twins would be able to play on when they were old enough.

She felt a sense of loneliness so acute it physically pained her. And nothing abated it. Not her parents or her sisters. Not talking to her long-distance friends or cuddling with her dog on the lounge. Only her babies growing peacefully in her belly gave her comfort.

On the afternoon of the party she laid her dress on the bed, flicked off her flip-flops and started getting ready. The dress was a maternity smock in bright colored silk that tied in a knot at her nape, and the outrageously red sandals were low heeled and comfortable. Or at least they would have been, had she been able to get them on. Her body simply wouldn't bend like it used to. She twisted and turned herself inside out and still the darn sandals wouldn't clasp.

Frustration crept over her skin as she kept trying. And failing. Fifteen minutes later and she was ready to toss the shoes at the wall. Until the tears came. Great racking sobs that made her chest hurt. After a few minutes she couldn't actually remember why she was crying. Which only made her more emotional. More fraught. More miserable.

She considered calling Evie and then quickly changed her mind. Her sister had enough to do organizing the party. And Grace had a newborn and would be too busy. She thought about calling her brother, but once he saw she'd been crying he'd be all concerned and want to know why she was upset and then act all macho when she told him how much she hated and loved Daniel. He'd probably want to go and punch him in the nose. It would serve Daniel right, too. Although she was pretty sure he'd throw a punch as good as he got.

Not that she wanted to see him hurt. That was the last thing she wanted.

She sat on the edge of the bed and cried some more. And thought about how ridiculously she was behaving. And then cried again. She gave the shoes another try and gave up when her aching back and swollen feet wouldn't do what she wanted.

She flopped back on the bed and grabbed her phone. The battery signal beeped. She'd forgotten to charge it overnight. Typical. She flicked through the numbers and reached the one she wanted. After a few unanswered rings it went straight to message service.

"It's me," she said, and hiccupped. "Can you come over?"

Then she buried her head in the pillow and sobbed.

Daniel had been in the shower when Mary-Jayne called. He tried to call her back several times but it went to message. Unable to reach her back, he was dressed and out the door of his hotel in about two minutes flat. He drove to Crystal Point as speedily as he could without breaking the law. Pulling up outside her house, he jumped out and raced to the front door. No one answered when he knocked. He heard the little dog barking behind the door and panic set in behind his ribs. What if she was hurt? Perhaps she'd fallen over trying to lift something heavy? Or worse. He rattled the door but it was locked, and then saw that the front window was open. He pushed the screen in and climbed through, not caring if the neighbors thought he was an intruder. They could call the cops for all he cared. He just needed to know she was safe.

Once he was in the living room he called her name. Still nothing.

He got to her bedroom door and stilled in his tracks. She was on the bed, curled up.

He'd never moved so fast in his life. He was beside the bed in seconds. He said her name softly and touched her bare shoulder. Her red-rimmed eyes flicked open.

"Hey," he said and stroked her cheek. "What's wrong?"

She shook her head. "Nothing."

"You left a message on my cell."

"I know," she whispered. "I didn't know who else to call. And then you didn't call back and then my phone went dead and…" Her voice trailed off.

Daniel's stomach churned. He grasped her shoulders. "Mary-Jayne, what's wrong? Are you sick? Is it the babies?"

"I'm not sick," she said. "I'm fine. The babies are fine."

She didn't look fine. She looked as if she'd been crying for a week. But she'd called him. She'd reached out when he'd feared she never would. It was enough to give him hope. To make him believe that she did care. "You've been crying?"

She nodded as tears welled in her eyes. She hiccupped. "I couldn't…"

"You couldn't what?" he prompted.

"I couldn't get my shoes on!"

And then she sobbed. Racking, shuddering sobs that reached him deep down. He folded her in his arms and held her gently. "It's okay, darling," he assured her.

"I'm as fat as a house."

"You're beautiful."

"I'm not," she cried, tears running down her face again. "And my ankles are so swollen that my shoes don't fit. I tried to put them on but my belly got in the way."

Daniel relaxed his grip and reached for her chin. He tilted her head back. "Would you like me to put them on for you?"

She nodded, and he moved off the bed and found her shoes by the wall. He crouched by the bed and reached for her legs. He slipped the shoes on and strapped each sandal at the ankle. "See…they fit just fine," he said, and ran a palm down her smooth calf.

She hiccupped and some fire returned to her eyes. "Why are you being nice to me?"

"That's my job," he said, and sat beside her. "Isn't that why you called me?"

She shrugged helplessly. "I just called a number… Any number…"

He grasped her chin again and made her look at him. "You called *me* because you wanted me here."

She sighed. "I don't know why. Probably because I was dreaming about you and—"

"Good," he said, feeling possessive and frustrated. "I want you to dream about me. I ache to be in your dreams, Mary-Jayne," he rasped, and pulled her close. "I won't be kept out of them."

"I couldn't keep you out if I tried," she admitted, and then relaxed against him, despite her better judgment, he suspected. "I don't know what's wrong with me. I feel so—"

"You're pregnant," he said, and gently spread a hand over her stomach. "Your hormones are running riot. Don't beat yourself up about being emotional. It's perfectly normal."

Her eyes flashed. "Aren't you Mr. Sensitive all of a sudden?"

Daniel's mouth curled at the edges. "With you, absolutely."

"Only to get what you want," she said and sniffed. "Now who's the fraud?"

He tilted her chin again and inched his mouth closer to hers. "I really did screw up, didn't I, for you to have such a low opinion of me? I generally think of myself as a good sort of person, Mary-Jayne... Give me half a chance and you might, too."

She harrumphed. "Manipulative jerk," she whispered, but then moved her lips closer.

He kissed her gently. "I'm not manipulating you. I love you."

She moaned. "Don't say things you don't mean."

Daniel swept her hair back from her face. "I mean it. And I'll tell you every day for the rest of my life."

"I won't listen," she retorted, and tried to evade his mouth. "And one day I'll find someone who really does—"

"Don't do that," he said painfully, cutting through her words. "That would just about break me."

"I'll do what I want," she said and pulled back. "You don't own me."

Daniel held her still. "Oh, darling...I do. And you own me. You've owned me since the first time I saw you in that store window. And I'm not going anywhere, Mary-Jayne."

"You'll have to at some point," she remarked, all eyes

and fiery beauty in her stare. "You don't live here. You live in San Francisco. Then I'll be free of you."

"We'll never be free of one another. That's why you called me today. Admit it," he said, firmer this time. "You could have called any one of half a dozen people and they all would have been here in a matter of minutes. But you didn't," he reminded her. "You called me."

"It was the first number I pressed. It was random, and then my battery died. Don't read anything into it."

He chuckled, delighted and spurred on by her reticence. "Admit it… You're in love with me."

"I am not!" she denied, and pulled herself from his arms. "I don't love you. I never will. I'd have to be stark raving mad to fall in love with you. And you're only saying all this to get what you want."

"I am? Really?" He stood up and propped his hands on his hips. "Have I asked for anything? I've given you space. I've left you alone. I've holed myself up in a damn hotel room for a week, even though all I want to do is be here with you every day and hold you in my arms every night. I haven't sent you flowers or bought anything for the babies even though I want to because I know you'd accuse me of trying to manipulate you. I haven't gone to see your parents and explain to them what you mean to me and assure them I'll do whatever is in my power to do to make you happy even though my instincts tell me I should. I'm *trying*, Mary-Jayne… I'm trying to do this your way. Just… just try to meet me in the middle somewhere, okay?" He placed a hand over his chest. "Because this is killing me."

"So he's still in town?"

Mary-Jayne looked at Evie. Her sisters had come over to cheer her up and bring her some gifts for the babies. The tiny pair of matching baseball caps Grace gave her was so incredibly cute that she cried a little. Which seemed to have become a habit of hers in the past few weeks.

Crying... Ugh!

She had become a sentimental sap.

"I guess so."

"You've seen him?" Grace asked.

"Not for a week. Why?"

Her sisters both shrugged and smiled. It was Evie who spoke next. "It's only that...well... In the past few days he's come to see all of us and told us..."

"Told you all what?" Mary-Jayne asked, pushing up on her seat.

"That he's in love with you," Grace supplied. "That he wants to marry you."

Mary-Jayne saw red. "That no-good, sneaky—"

"It's kinda romantic," Evie said and grinned.

"It's *not* romantic," Mary-Jayne said hotly. "It's deceitful and underhanded. And do you know what else he did? He bought all this baby stuff and had it delivered. The garage is full of boxes and toys and baby furniture and—"

"Oh, how awful for you," Evie said and grinned. "Such a terrible man."

Mary-Jayne scowled. "You're on his side, then?"

"We're on your side," Grace said and smiled gently. "You seem unhappy, that's all."

"I'll be happier when he's gone."

"I don't think he's going anywhere any time soon," Evie said. "He told Scott he's going to buy a house here."

The color bled from her face. "I don't believe it. He wouldn't. He's got a business to run and he can't do that from here."

"Maybe he's found something more important than business," Grace said pointedly.

"Yeah—his heirs. He wants his children. Don't be blinded by the good looks and money."

"We could say the same thing to you."

Mary-Jayne stilled. Her sister's words resonated loud and clear. Was that how she appeared—as a judgmental and narrow-minded snob—and exactly what she'd accused him of being?

She'd resented his money and success without good reason. On one hand, she recognized his honesty and integrity. And yet, when he'd told her the very thing she wanted to hear, she hadn't believed him. She'd accused him of trying to manipulate and confuse her. But what proof did she have that he'd ever done that? None. He hadn't manipulated her to get her into bed. Their attraction had been hot and intense from the start. Not one-sided. She'd craved him and he'd made it abundantly clear that he wanted her. And then she'd convinced herself he was all bad, all arrogance and self-entitlement.

To protect herself.

Because he was nothing like any man she'd previously dated she regarded him as an aberration…someone to avoid…someone to battle. And she had at every opportunity. She'd fought and insulted and pushed him away time and time again. Because loving Daniel meant she would be redefined. He was rich and successful and all that she had professed to loathe. He'd asked her to marry him. He'd said he loved her. And still she let her prejudice blind her.

His parting words a week earlier still echoed in her mind. *This is killing me.* Real pain. Real anguish. And she'd done that to him. She'd hurt him. She'd hurt the one person she loved most in the world. She felt the shame of it through to her bones. He'd asked her to meet him in the middle.

But she could do better than that.

"You look as though the proverbial penny just dropped," Evie said.

Both her sisters were staring at her. "I think it just did. He asked me to marry him. He said he was in love with me."

"That's what he told us, too."

Tears filled her eyes. "I never imagined that I'd fall in love with someone like him. I thought that one day I'd meet someone like myself... Someone who wasn't so... conventional, if you know what I mean."

Evie came and sat beside her and grabbed her hand. "You know, just because he's not a bohemian poet, it doesn't make him wrong for you. If anyone had told me a few years ago that I would fall in love with a man nearly ten years younger than me I wouldn't have believed them."

"Same here," Grace said, and sat on the other side. "I never intended to fall in love with our brother's best friend. But I did. When you love, you simply love. That's the thing that's important, M.J. Not how successful or wealthy he is."

"He's a good man," Evie said quietly. "Give him a chance to prove it."

"What if he's changed his mind?" she asked, thinking of the terrible way they'd parted and how she'd told him she didn't love him and never would. "I said some pretty awful things to him the last time we were together. What if he doesn't want to see me?"

"You need a plan," Grace suggested.

"Leave that to me," Evie said, and she grabbed her phone from her bag.

Three hours later Mary-Jayne was at the B and B, sitting in the garden on a bench by the wishing well. She smoothed down the skirt on her white dress and then fluffed her hair. She'd always loved this spot. Through the vine-covered hedge she saw a car pull up to the curb.

Minutes later he was walking up the path, all purposeful and tight limbed. He wore jeans and a polo shirt and looked so good it stole her breath. When he spotted her he came to a halt midstride.

"Hi," she said, and smiled.

His expression was unreadable. "I didn't expect you to be here."

"I didn't expect me to be here up until a couple of hours ago."

His gaze narrowed. "Are you all right? No problems with the babies?"

She touched her abdomen gently. "No… Everything is fine. I feel good. The nausea is gone for the moment. I haven't seen you for a while… Where have you been?"

"I was under the impression you had no interest in seeing me." He took a step closer. "I had a call from your sister. Is she here?"

"No…just me."

His brows drew together. "Subterfuge?"

"Kind of," she admitted. "I wasn't sure if *you'd* see *me* after the last time."

"If you had called me, I would be here. Always. I've told you that before. What's this about, Mary-Jayne?"

He looked so good. So familiar. And she ached to be in his arms. "I'm sorry about what I said the last time we were together."

"Which part? When you said you didn't love me and never would?" he quizzed.

She nodded. "All of it. You came over to help me and I was thoughtless and ungrateful."

"Yes, you were."

She ignored a hot niggle of impatience that crept up her spine. "I hear you're looking at real estate?"

He shrugged loosely. "Do you disapprove of that, as well?"

God, he was impossible. "Of course not. I understand that you'll want to be close to the babies when they are born."

He nodded. "So anything else?"

Mary-Jayne sighed and grabbed the shopping bag by the bench. She stood up and extracted the two tiny baseballs caps. "I thought you might like these. They're cute, don't you think?"

He took the caps and examined them. "Cute. Yes. Is that it? You got me here to give me a couple of baseball caps?"

"I wanted to see you."

"Why now? Nothing's changed."

"Everything's changed."

His mouth flattened. "What?"

Her cheeks grew hotter by the second. "Me. This. Us. A week ago you told me you loved me."

"I know what I said," he shot back. "I also know what you said."

She took a breath. "Shall we go inside? I'd like to talk to you."

"So when you want to talk, we talk? Is that how this plays out? I don't seem to be able to get it right with you, do I?"

Mary-Jayne let her impatience rise up. "I'm going inside. You can stay out here in the garden and sulk if you want to."

She turned on her heels and walked up to the house as quickly as she could. He was about four steps behind her. Once she was through the French doors and in the living room she spun around.

He was barely a foot away, chest heaving. "Sulk?"

She shrugged. "Sure. Isn't that what you've been doing

this week? So I said something mean and unkind. I'm sorry. But you said yourself that I'm running on hormones because of my pregnancy. I should think it's about time you started making allowances for that."

"Allowances," he echoed incredulously. "Are you serious? I've done nothing *but* make allowances since the moment you told me you were pregnant. Nothing I do is right. Nothing I say makes any difference. You trust me, you don't. You need me, you don't. You want me, you don't. Which is it? I'm so damned confused I can barely think straight. I'm neglecting my business, my family, my friends…everything, because I'm so caught up in this *thing* I have with you."

Mary-Jayne watched him, fascinated by the heat and fire in his words. There was so much passion in him. She'd been so wrong, thinking he was some sort of cold fish who didn't feel deeply. He did. He just didn't show that side of himself to the world.

"I do trust you," she said, and moved toward him. "And I do need you," she said, and touched his chest. When he winced and stepped back she was immediately concerned. "What's wrong? Are you in pain? Have you had another migraine?"

"No. Stop this, Mary-Jayne. Tell me what I'm doing here and—"

"I'm trying," she said frantically. "But I need to know if you meant what you said."

He frowned. "What I said?"

"You…you said you loved me," she said, suddenly breathless. "Did you mean it?"

"Do I strike you as someone who says things I don't mean?"

"No," she replied, and blinked back the tears in her eyes. "It's just that…what you said about me being in a cage and about how things would have been different from the start if you hadn't been...well...*you*. If you'd been a dreadlocked, unemployed musician, I wouldn't have been so determined to keep my distance. Because that's what I thought I wanted. What I knew, if that makes sense. All that stuff you said, you were right." She touched his arm, gripped tightly and felt his muscles hard beneath her palm. "For as long as I can remember I've craved freedom and independence. But now I feel as if I've lived a life that isn't authentic. I left home at seventeen, but only moved three streets away from my parents. Some independence, huh? So you're right, I'm a fraud. I'm tied to this little town. I'm not a free spirit at all." She took a breath, not caring about the tears on her cheeks. "And you...you saw through that and through me. What you said about marriage makes sense. Each one starts out differently, like your dad and Bernie. And if this..." she said, and touched her stomach gently. "If this is what we start with, just these two precious babies bringing us together, then that's okay. Because if you do want me, and if you do love me, even a little bit, that will be enough."

He stared at her, holding her gaze captive. "But it's not enough for me, Mary-Jayne."

She froze. "I don't understand..."

"We both deserve more than some half-baked attempt at a relationship."

"But you said you wanted to get married and be a family," she reminded him, crumbling inside.

"I do," he said, and grabbed her hand. "But I want *all* of you, every beautiful, spirited, intoxicating piece. I had a good marriage once. But I want more than that this time. I don't want to leave at six in the morning and arrive home at eight. I don't want to eat out five nights out of seven because work always comes first. I don't want to miss family gatherings because I'm too busy landing some deal or flying from one country to the next. I've lived that life and I was never truly happy. I want us to raise our children together, like *they* deserve."

Tears wet her cheeks again. "I want that, too. You really... You really do love me?"

He grasped her chin and looked directly into her eyes. "I really do love you, Mary-Jayne. And I know they're only words, but they are what I feel."

"Words are enough," she said, happiness surging through her blood. "I love you, too."

"Words will never be enough," he said, and kissed her gently. "Which is why I did this."

"What?" she muttered against his mouth.

"This," he said, and stepped back a little. He tugged at the collar of his T-shirt and showed her what he meant.

Her name, in small but strikingly dark scrolled script, was now written on the left side of his chest. The ink was new and still healing, but she could see through all that to the beauty of what he had done.

"You got a tattoo?" she asked, crying. "I can't believe you did that. The needles... You hate needles."

He shrugged one shoulder. "I love you more than I hate needles." He grasped her hand and held it against his chest. "In my heart. Over my heart. On my heart. Forever."

They were the most beautiful words she had ever heard.

She reached up and touched his face. "I'm so much in love with you, Daniel. And I'm sorry I kept pushing you away."

He held her in his arms. "You had more sense than me. We needed to get to know one another. You knew that. I just arrogantly thought I knew how to fix things."

"At least you wanted to try," she said, and settled against

his shoulder. "I've been fighting this and you since the very beginning."

"I know," he said, and laughter rumbled in his chest. "You took off as if your feet were on fire after Solana's birthday party."

"I was in shock," she admitted. "I'd never had an experience like that before."

"Me, either," he said. "Making love with you is like nothing on earth." He kissed her nape. "But you never have to run from me again, Mary-Jayne."

"I promise I won't."

Seconds later they were settled on one of the sofas and he wrapped her in his arms. "There's something about you that draws me. You have this incredible energy…a life force all your own. I love that about you. And I love that our sons are going to have that, too."

She sighed, happy and content and so in love her head was spinning. "So where are we going to live? Here or San Francisco?"

He reached for her chin and tilted her face toward his own. "Darling, do you think I would ever ask you to leave here? This is your home."

"But San Francisco is *your* home."

"It's where I live," he said and kissed her gently. "I don't think I've ever considered anywhere as really home. Until now. Even when I was married to Simone and we had our apartment, most times it was simply a place to sleep."

She couldn't believe what he was saying. "Do you mean we can stay here permanently? I was imagining we'd do some time here and some over there."

He shook his head. "Your family is here. Your roots are here. And I like this town and I want to raise our sons here. If they turn out half as good as you then I'll be a happy man."

"But your business? How can you—"

"I need to let go a little," he admitted. "I need to trust Blake and Caleb more. They have just as must invested in Anderson's as I do... I think it's about time I lessened the reins. You see," he said, and grinned, "I'm learning to not be so much of a control freak."

"Don't change too much," she said, and pressed against him. "I like you just as you are."

He kissed her, long and sweet, and when he finally lifted his head he stared into her eyes. "You know something...I think it's time I proposed properly."

"What a great idea," she said, and laughed, so happy she thought she might burst.

Daniel grabbed her hand and brought it to his lips. "Mary-Jayne, I'm lost without you... Marry me?"

"Yes," she said, laughing, crying and loving him more than she had believed possible. "Absolutely, positively, yes!"

Epilogue

Three and a half months later...

At seven o'clock at night on a Monday, Mary-Jayne's water broke. Daniel was walking into the bedroom when she hovered in the bathroom doorway.

"What is it?" he asked immediately.

She grimaced. "It's time."

Panic flittered across his face. "You're in labor?"

"Yep," she said, and grinned.

He strode toward her. "But there's still nearly three weeks to go."

"We were told I'd probably go into labor early," she said and touched his arm. "Stop worrying."

"I'm not worried," he assured her. "How do you feel?"

"Better now I know what the niggling backache I had all day is about."

"You were in pain and you didn't tell—"

"Stop worrying," she said again, and ushered him out the doorway. "I'm fine." She rubbed her huge belly. "We're fine. Is my bag still in the car?"

He'd insisted they have her baby bag ready for when she went into labor. He'd also insisted on a trial run in the car and had organized Evie to be the backup driver just in case he wasn't around when the time came. Of course she knew that was never going to happen.

In the past few months so much had changed. Since their wedding two months earlier, he'd taken some much-needed time off from Anderson's. His brother Blake had taken on more global accountability, and general managers had been put in place in some of the resorts to alleviate the workload. Caleb was still recovering from an unexpected and serious boating accident and had been recuperating from his busted leg with Miles and Bernie for the past eight weeks. It had been a fraught time for the entire family, but since Bernie's heart attack, the family had become closer and they all rallied around to ensure Caleb had all the support he needed.

Despite all that, she knew Daniel had never been happier. She still marveled at how well he'd adjusted to not having such tight control over the company anymore. He'd learned to trust his brothers and share the responsibility. Of course, with Caleb out of action for a while, there were times when he was needed to fly back to San Francisco or one of the other locations, but he was never gone for more than a few days. And Mary-Jayne didn't mind.

He'd bought a house in Crystal Point just four doors down from Dunn Inn, and she loved the big low-set brick-and-tile home with its floating timber floors, racked ceilings, wide doorways and sprawling front deck that offered an incredible view of the ocean. She surprised herself by how much fun she had purchasing new furnishings. He was generous to a fault, and they had a wonderful time working on the nursery and getting the room ready for the babies.

Their relationship was amazing. *He* was amazing, and she'd never been happier.

The drive to the hospital took twenty minutes, and another five to find a vacant car space and get her into the emergency ward. She was quickly transported to maternity, and by the time she was settled in a room her contractions were coming thick and fast.

It was an arduous twelve hours later that her doctor recommended a caesarean birth. Mary-Jayne cried a little, and then agreed to do what best for their babes. William and Flynn Anderson were born a minute apart, both pink and screaming and perfect in every way.

Still groggy from the surgery, it was another few hours before she had a chance to nurse her sons. Daniel remained by her side, strong and resilient and giving her every ounce of support she needed. And when he held their sons for the first time, there were tears in his eyes. And he didn't seem to care one bit. Watching him, seeing the emotion and pure love in his expression made her fall in love with him even more.

"They really are beautiful," she remarked as William settled against her breast to nurse and Daniel sat in the chair by her bed and held Flynn against his chest.

Daniel looked at his son, marveling at the perfect beauty in the little boy's face, and smiled. When he returned his gaze to his wife he saw she was watching him. "You did an amazing job, Mrs. Anderson."

She smiled. "You, too. But then again, you do everything well, and I knew this wouldn't be any different."

Daniel reached for her hand and rubbed her fingers. "You know, we're going to have to start letting the masses in at some point. Your sisters are keen to spend some time with you. And Solana has been circling the waiting area with your parents for the past two hours. She's very excited about meeting her great-grandsons."

"I know," she said, and sighed. "I just selfishly want our babies and you to myself for as long as I can."

Daniel stood and gently placed their sleeping son into his mother's arm, watching, fascinated, as she held them both. It was the most beautiful thing he had ever seen. His wife. His sons. They were a gift more precious than anything he could have ever imagined. Love, the purest and most intense he'd ever experienced, surged through his blood.

"I love you," he said, and bent down to kiss her sweet mouth. "And, my darling, you have me to yourself for the rest of our lives."

Tears welled in her beautiful green eyes. "I never intended to love anyone this much, you know," she said, and batted her lashes. "I never thought it was possible."

"Neither did I."

"It's actually all Audrey and Caleb's doing," she said, beaming. "If they didn't have such a dysfunctional relationship we would never have met."

"Oh, I don't know about that," he said, and chuckled. "Audrey would have returned to Crystal Point eventually and Caleb would have eventually followed her, and since my brother is a hothead without any sense I would have had to come here and sort things out. So I'm pretty sure our paths would have crossed."

Mary-Jayne glanced at the twins. "Maybe you're right. Now they're here I can't imagine a world without these two in it." She looked up and smiled gently. "Speaking of Caleb and Audrey…any news?"

Daniel shrugged. "You know Caleb. He's refusing to get the marriage annulled."

They had all been shocked to learn that Caleb and Audrey were in fact married, and had been just a month after they'd met.

She sighed. "Well, I'm glad we don't have all that drama in our relationship."

Daniel smiled, remembering their own fraught beginnings. "Nah...we were a piece of cake."

She laughed, and the lovely sound echoed around the room.

"Shall I let them in?" he asked, kissing her again.

"You bet."

And he was, he realized as he opened the door, just about the happiest man on the planet. Because he had Mary-Jayne's love and their beautiful sons. He truly did have it all.

* * * * *

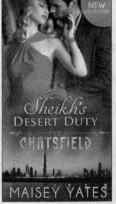

MILLS & BOON®

Cherish ™

EXPERIENCE THE ULTIMATE RUSH OF FALLING IN LOVE

A sneak peek at next month's titles...

In stores from 17th April 2015:

- **The Pregnancy Secret** – Cara Colter
  and **Not Quite Married** – Christine Rimmer

- **A Bride for the Runaway Groom** – Scarlet Wilson
  and **My Fair Fortune** – Nancy Robards Thompson

In stores from 1st May 2015:

- **A Forever Kind of Family** – Brenda Harlen
  and **Bound by a Baby Bump** – Ellie Darkins

- **The Wedding Planner and the CEO** – Alison Roberts
  and **From Best Friend to Bride** – Jules Bennett

0415/23